EXECUTIVE ACTIONS

GARY GROSSMAN

**DIVERSION
BOOKS**

Also by Gary Grossman

The Executive Series
Executive Treason
Executive Command
Executive Force (August 2018)

Old Earth
Red Hotel
Superman: Serial to Cereal
Saturday Morning TV

Diversion Books
A Division of Diversion Publishing Corp.
443 Park Avenue South, Suite 1004
New York, NY 10016
www.diversionbooks.com

For more information, email info@diversionbooks.com

Second Diversion Books edition July 2018.
Paperback ISBN: 978-1-63576-468-0
eBook ISBN: 978-0-9839885-8-8

LSIDB/1807

To Sasha, Zachary, Jake, and my wife, Helene.
Your joy for writing gave me the courage to begin a new book.
Thank you for your wonderful gift.

PART I

CHAPTER 1

WASHINGTON, D.C.
SUNDAY, JUNE 22

"Topic one. Theodore Wilson Lodge. Presidential material?" bellowed the host at the top of his Sunday morning television show. He directed his question to the political pundit to his left. "Victor Monihan, syndicated columnist for *The Philadelphia Inquirer*, is Teddy ready, *yes* or *no?*"

"Yes," Monihan shot back. You had to speak up quickly on the lively program. There was no air between questions and answers. "If the cameras could vote, he'd be a shoo-in."

"But they don't. So again, will it be *Mr. Lodge goes to Washington?*" quizzed the host of *The McLaughlin Group*. The reference to the Frank Capra movie was lost on most of the audience. Even AMC and Turner Classics weren't running very many black and white movies anymore.

"Absolutely." Monihan didn't take a breath between thoughts. The host hated dead air. Pause and you're dead. Someone else will jump in. "He's totally informed, he's had great committee assignments and he can do the job. Congressman Lodge comes off as a highly capable leader. Trustworthy. The all-American boy grown up. And he positively looks like a president should look...presidential."

"So a tan and a good build gets you to the White House?" the host argued.

"It means I don't have to worry about him taking my job." The overweight columnist laughed, which made his belly spread his shirt to a point just shy of popping the buttons. The joke was good, but he lost his platform with it.

"Roger Deutsch, freelance writer for *Vanity Fair*, right now Lodge is trailing Governor Lamden. Can Teddy make it up?"

"No. With only two days before the New York primary, there's no way Lodge can do it. He doesn't have the votes. And there's not enough time to get them. Henry Lamden will be addressing the Democratic Party at the August convention in Denver. But even *when* he gets the nomination, he'll have a hard time against Taylor."

The discussion expanded to include the other members of the panel. They talked about Montana Governor Henry Lamden's qualities. About President Morgan Taylor's rigid persona. About the voters' appetite. And back again to the possibilities. "Is there any way Lodge can do what fellow Vermont favorite son Calvin Coolidge did: go all the way to the White House?" the venerable host rhetorically asked. The panel knew this was not the time to reply. Turning to the camera the host said, "Not according to my watch." This was the throw to the video package from the campaign trail.

Teddy Lodge smiled as he sat on the edge of his hotel bed to get closer to the TV set. He was half-packed. The rest would wait until the videotape report concluded. Lodge pressed the volume louder on his remote.

"It's on," he called to his wife, Jenny.

"Be right out," she answered from the bathroom. Lodge tightened the knot on the hand-painted tie he'd been given the day before. The gift, from a home crafter in Albany, would go into his collection and eventually into his Presidential Library. But first he'd wear it for the cameras. She'd see it and tell everyone she knew. More votes.

Mrs. Lodge leaned over her husband and hugged him as he watched himself on TV. "You look great, sweetheart." He agreed. The footage was perfect: Lodge in the thick of an adoring Manhattan crowd, the wind playing with his wavy brown hair, his Armani suit jacket draped over his arm. He came off relaxed and in charge; less like a politician than an everyday guy. An everyday guy who saw himself as President of the United States. And at 6'2" he stood above most of the crowd.

Lodge knew the unusual statistical edge his height provided. Historically, the taller of the two major presidential candidates almost always wins the election. And he was considerably taller than President Morgan Taylor.

The host obviously wasn't a supporter. But the coverage counted. He hit the bullet points of Lodge's career. "*Teddy's been fast-tracking since college. He graduated Yale Law School and has a graduate degree in Physics at Stanford. The man speaks three languages. He worked on various government contracts until he decided to return to his country home in Burlington, Vermont, and run for State Assembly. Two years later, so long Burlington, hello Washington. Mr. Lodge went to Capitol Hill as a young, energetic first-term congressman. He distinguished himself in international politics and now serves as Chairman of the House Subcommittee on Terrorism and Homeland Security. He's as close to a rocket scientist as they come in Washington. He heads the House Committee on Energy and understands the complexities of the issues. But is he going to the White House?*" the moderator asked in his feature videotape. "*New Yorkers will decide Tuesday.*"

And with that set up came the obligatory sound bite. It couldn't have been better if Teddy Lodge had picked it himself. It was declarative and persuasive. The producer of the video package must have been in his camp.

"*Tomorrow the world will be different. More dangerous. More hateful. Different times need different leaders. Make no mistake, there are no more safe harbors or promised lands. Unless…unless we make better choices today than yesterday. Better friends tomorrow than today.*"

As he watched, Lodge remembered the clincher was yet to come. Things like that just didn't get cut. He was right.

"*So come with me and discover a new America. Come with me and discover a new world.*"

Thunderous applause followed; applause from the audience at a Madison Square Garden rally.

Eighteen seconds total screen time. Unbelievable on *McLaughlin*. But Lodge was not an easy edit. He'd learned to break the sound bite barrier by constantly modulating his voice for impact, issuing phrases in related couplets and triplets, and punching them with an almost religious zeal.

Like everything else in his life, he worked hard at communicating effectively. He punctuated every word with a moderately affected New England accent. Whether or not they agreed with his politics, columnists called him the best orator in years. Increasing numbers of them bestowed almost Kennedy-like reverence. And through the camera lens, baby boomers saw an old friend while younger voters found a new voice.

The video story ended and the host brought the debate back to his panel. "Peter Weisel, Washington Bureau Chief of *The Chicago Tribune*, What sayest thou? Can Teddy un*lodge* Lamden?"

"Unlikely." Weisel, a young, black reporter, was the outspoken liberal of the panel and a realist. "But he'll help the ticket. He's a strong Number Two. A junior pairing with Governor Lamden can work. The flip side of Kennedy-Johnson. Let the Democrats make him VP. Besides, his good looks won't go away in four or eight years. TV will still like him."

Theodore Wilson Lodge, 46 years old and strikingly handsome, definitely could pull in the camera lens. He had the same effect on women and they held far more votes in America than men. The fact was not lost on the show's only female contributor of the week. "Debra Redding of *The Boston Globe*, is Lodge your man?"

Without missing a beat she volunteered, "There are only two problems that I see. One, I'm married. The other—so is he."

What a wonderful way to start the morning, the congressman said to himself.

HUDSON, NEW YORK

Room 301 was on the third floor of the St. Charles Hotel at 16 Park Place. It overlooked 7th Street Park with a clear corner view of the podium constructed at the intersection of Warren Street and Park Place. The hotel, built in the late 1800s, was recently renovated. The charm of the St. Charles lay in the brick work, hand-carved wood appointments and classic wallpaper patterns. The hotel's aura sold on the post cards, if not in the minds of the guests; most of them New Yorkers looking for antiques.

One man was there for another reason.

Sidney McAlister had spent the last three weeks at the St. Charles. He came to town to sell life insurance policies and so far he'd met with some thirty-five people. However, McAlister was careful not to close any deals. If he had, he wouldn't have been able to deliver. This wasn't his real job. What he had to accomplish today was. When that was finished there would be no more Sidney McAlister. There had never been one.

The graying, middle-aged salesman was sitting at the window, thinking. A knock at the door suddenly broke his train of thought. "Excuse me. Room service," called a young woman. McAlister checked his watch. Right on schedule.

He turned to the door slowly. She knocked again with a little more insistence. "Your breakfast, Mr. McAlister."

"Coming, coming," he said as he slowly made his way to the door. Opening it, he barely left enough room for Carolyn Hill to get by without brushing him. She'd remember that and tell the police. He always made her feel uncomfortable, just like he had with his potential clients, which is precisely why no one wanted to sign with him. A long time ago he learned that if people focused on a perception they would ignore who was really there.

"Just put it down on the dresser, dear," he said, emphasizing "dear" much too much for her taste. Carolyn really didn't like him. "There's a twenty for you on the bed. Take it. I'm checking out later today. And don't bother with the sheets now."

Finally good news, she allowed herself.

McAlister wasn't being polite. And he definitely wasn't finished with the room. He had some cleaning to do himself. He would scrub every surface he touched or even might have come in contact with; from the drawers to the toilet. No DNA trail could lead back to him. Seventy-nine percent ethanol working with the 0.1 percent Number 2-Phenylphenol cancelled every personal signature belonging to McAlister. So simple. Off-the-shelf Lysol Fresh disinfectant spray. For good measure he'd take his bed sheets with him. Ejaculate may have dripped during his sleep, or hair or skin could have flaked off. They were all links to him, and he was *that* careful.

McAlister left the money for her, as he always did, without handing it over personally. No fingerprints. He always wore gloves, which made him even more off-putting. And he never, ever signed for anything.

What an eccentric, she assumed. *Almost a month of this. Good riddance.* Nonetheless, Carolyn Hill managed a sincere sounding, "Thank you, Mr. McAlister, will we see you again?"

"Oh, I hope not," he answered curtly, signaling the quality time they'd shared was over.

As she left, he took the blueberry muffin she'd delivered, ignoring the coffee and orange juice. Once the door was closed, he returned to the window knowing that neither Carolyn Hill of Hudson, New York, nor anyone else in the world would ever see Sidney McAlister again.

Activity had picked up outside the hotel. Five students from Hudson High were draping a handmade "Welcome Teddy" banner in front of the bandstand. McAlister could see from his corner window that a few older people were already staking out room for their lawn chairs close to the front. If the reports were accurate in *The Register Star*, the city's daily newspaper, as many as 1,200 people would crowd into the park by one o'clock. That was good. More witnesses to describe different versions of the same thing, McAlister allowed himself. Like *Rashomon*.

He took in the whole park from his window. He knew the dimensions by heart, just as he had committed so many other things to memory.

Columbia Street and Warren were the north-south boundaries. East and west were Park Place and 7th Street. It was a compact space; all in all it was no more than one block by a half a block, hardly bigger than a football field. The St. Charles was only thirty yards away from where the local Democratic Party committee was asked to place the podium. McAlister could hit it with a stone.

In the middle of the park, set among generation-old maple and oak trees, was a modest fountain that had been restored by the local chapter of the Kiwanis. It was dedicated to Hudson's first mayor, Seth Jenkins, and fairly recently surrounded by a small enclosure to keep children out. Not far from the fountain, at the corner of the Park, stood a monument, surrounded by a gate. It bore the inscription, "Erected by the Citizens of Hudson in grateful recognition of her Sons' and Daughters' Services in the Armed Forces of the United States." Two tributes from a community that sought its place in history.

Usually 7th Street Park afforded a comfortable setting for guests at the St. Charles to sit back on one of the benches and take in the quiet Hudson life. McAlister smiled. At 2:04 P.M. today he'd definitely change that.

He peered down. Next door to the hotel, volunteer firemen from J.W. Edmonds Hose Co. were polishing their truck for the day's parade. They took pride in their work, just as he did. They were in full uniform, hardly breaking a sweat. The summer humidity hadn't blanketed the air yet. High cirrus clouds drifted overhead, nudging a comfortable, lazy breeze that flowed across the Catskill Mountains into the Hudson Valley and over to the Berkshires. McAlister noted the wind and its direction. Too light to be a concern.

An old freight train track cut between the park and he saw two young boys balancing on the rails. He remembered doing the same thing as a kid. Hudson was beginning to appeal to him. It reminded McAlister of home. It was like one of those idyllic calendar paintings; the scene frozen in a better, simpler time.

The city was named for explorer Henry Hudson, who sailed up what he called "The River of Mountains" in September, 1609, on his third attempt to discover a Northwest Passage. Though Henry Hudson failed to find the fabled route linking the Atlantic and Pacific, he ultimately established colonies along the river for his Dutch employers, including the town now bearing his name. Hudson was officially founded just after the Revolutionary War.

In the 1800s, Hudson served as a thriving whaling port despite the fact that it was 120 miles up river from New York. Many whalers considered it second only to New Bedford, Massachusetts, in the production of whale oil and by-products. But over the years, as whaling diminished, Hudson turned to textile production and cement manufacturing.

At its peak, the city was home to more than 11,000 citizens. This election year there were considerably fewer voters.

McAlister allowed himself to consider what it would be like to live here, to find a coveted colonial home in Columbia County and blend into the surroundings. But it was too small for his safety and blending in required both more cover and fewer neighbors. The thought totally evaporated when his phone rang. He looked at his watch, not moving to answer the telephone. It rang three times and stopped. Thirty seconds later it rang again twice. Two minutes later it rang four times. All from a Pay-As-You-Go phone and a pre-paid calling card, personally untraceable and bought with cash at a Cincinnati 7-11.

The signal. Time to go to work.

He went into the bathroom, put a towel over his sink, and proceeded to empty the contents of his vanity kit: two bottles containing pale liquids, rubber gloves, and other accessories.

The last time Hudson hosted such a major political candidate in a motorcade was in 1965 when Bobby Kennedy ran for the U.S. Senate. The high school band, in their blue and gold uniforms, marched to Sousa. It was a spring day, much like today. And Bobby was destined to take the Ken Keating seat as a step toward the White House.

Teddy Lodge was due to arrive by motorcade from Albany at 12:45 P.M. He would rendezvous at the corner of Front and Union Street with his police escort, just as Bobby had done years before. The local Boy Scouts troop, three high school bands, five fire trucks, and veterans from World War II, Korea, Vietnam, the Gulf War, Afghanistan, and Iraqi Freedom would accompany him uptown.

Lodge needed a good showing. The city, the county, and the entire state were extremely important to him.

The primary process had recently changed. State officials across the country had scrapped the Super Tuesday primaries, which too often catapulted an untested front runner into national prominence. The new approach grouped convention delegates through regional elections, with the East, South, Midwest and West alternating in order every four years.

Iowa and New Hampshire retained their starting gate positions in the presidential calendar. The new plan contributed to a fairer method, whereby "political heat" would have to develop over time rather than on an arbitrary Tuesday in mid-March.

Seasoned candidates saw it as an improvement. Those sprinters lacking staying power, who previously benefited from a quick start, no longer did.

This year, the East was last to vote. Not all states in a region held their primaries the same Tuesday. Yet, given the fact that there were still many states in any geographic area, bundling still occurred. And so it was in June. New York, Connecticut, Delaware, Maine, New Hampshire, Massachusetts, New Jersey, Pennsylvania, Rhode Island, Vermont, West Virginia, and the District of Columbia would cast their votes at various times during the month.

New York and Rhode Island were last on the calendar. Rhode Island held 32 Democratic Party convention delegates, while New York remained crucial to any candidate's chance of winning the nomination. Its Democratic primary was worth 294 votes.

By all accounts, the only one standing between the congressman and his party's nomination was the respected and seasoned Governor of Montana, who retained the slimmest of leads. Every handshake counted now, and the two candidates were due to face off in a debate tomorrow night. Ultimately, Lodge believed he would pull Republican votes in a national election. But first things first. He had a busy day.

At Promenade Hill, a park rising 500 feet above the Hudson River, band members began tuning up. The Hudson High tuba players drowned out the clarinets and the teenage drummers practiced marching, their snare drums bouncing on their thighs. Many of their parents had seen RFK years ago. This was their chance to reconnect with their own childhood.

A mile up the street, Roger C. Waterman walked out of the St. Charles. He crossed to Sutty's, a vintage candy, peanuts, and soda shop, and ordered a cherry cola. Waterman had checked into the hotel late in the evening two days earlier. He had visited Hudson once a month since February, buying antiques for his store in Soho and perusing galleries like TSL, Ltd., housed in an old bakery on Columbia Street.

Waterman had a self-assured upper-crust manner about him. He looked to be about 40 and spoke in only precise, polite terms. His tweed jacket fit him like he was born to wear it and his thin wire-frame glasses completed his look. Waterman was a walking advertisement for Sotheby's and he was well-liked at all of the Warren Street antique shops where he offered very fair prices.

As Waterman sat and sipped his soda, he casually gazed at the near corner. Workers were putting six bridge chairs in place and testing the microphone.

The honor of introducing the congressman would go to Mayor Tommy Kenton. Waterman understood he was a popular mayor, casual and friendly; the second in his family to hold the job. His full-time job was as a real estate attorney. And since real estate was booming in Columbia County as more and more New Yorkers acquired property, most buyers heard that the Hudson mayor was the man to represent their transactions. Kenton was becoming so successful that he was even thinking of a run for Congress himself.

Waterman imagined the excitement Hudsonians would be feeling. So much history coming to their quiet city. He smiled. After finishing his last sip he stood and reached into his pocket. He decided to leave a tip for twice the amount of the soda. "Thanks so much," he told the old owner. "You've got the best cherry cola from here to Buffalo. And I've tried them all."

"Thanks," was all he got back. The proprietor didn't speak much.

"Probably see you in a few weeks. Leaving in the morning."

"Gonna watch today?" It was the longest sentence Waterman had ever heard out of the man.

"Maybe a little," Waterman answered. With that he waved, walked out and returned to room #315 in the St. Charles where he packed the antique picture frames, art deco jewelry, and crystal fruit bowls he'd bought which meant absolutely nothing to him.

WASHINGTON, D.C.

The president despised polls. They only reminded him of the last election and the wrong way politicians make decisions. As a navy man and a senator he'd seen too many presidents and their advisors stick their fingers in the air to determine which way the wind blew. Now he was beginning to hear the same thing about his stand on Pakistan and India. "We can't do that, we'll lose the vote." "What's this going to mean in November?"

"Fuck getting reelected. I'm probably getting too old for these ungodly hours anyway!" he told his chief of staff.

But, of course, he wanted to win again, and he had to look at the polls.

Right now, five Democrats were left in the running. Only two counted. Lodge, and his old Navy buddy, Governor Lamden. Lodge pulled closer to the governor day by day but would run out of time to move ahead. That was a good thing. The truth of the matter was that in a head-to-head beauty contest with the president, Lodge might beat him where Lamden wouldn't. He was younger, more attractive, and tougher. That's why the president counted on Henry Lamden to take New York and the nomination. That's why he hated the polls. Especially when they were right.

What did President Morgan Taylor have to show for his first term? More stalemates on the Hill. More terrorist scares. More attacks within America's borders. Saber-rattling between India and Pakistan that threatened to escalate every day. More dead ends in the Middle East. Slow economic growth. Try as he might, he had almost nothing to brag about.

For now, most polls had him leading Governor Lamden by a good twelve points and Lodge by 24. But he had been in politics long enough to know that those numbers would change.

Deep down, he was worried. Lodge was a dynamic figure, and masterful in debates. Some saw him as a force of nature, constantly gaining strength in the political storm. To Morgan Taylor, he was more like the storm itself; a Category 5 hurricane, building in warm waters, ready to wreak political havoc at landfall.

Not that the president wasn't capable of calling up a tempest as well. He had graduated from Annapolis in the top ten percent of his class, served as an F/A-18C pilot assigned to the USS *Carl Vinson* aircraft carrier battle group, and did a Persian Gulf tour of duty with her. He used his military record as an edge in the last election, though he couldn't officially talk about his missions much. He wasn't sure his time logged in the single-seat Hornet would hold sway this November.

Following his discharge from the service, Commander Morgan

Taylor, USN (Ret.) signed with Boeing, the parent company of McDonnell Douglas, which manufactured his high performance jet. Other high-tech firms pursued the decorated flier, but Taylor felt allegiance to his hometown Seattle and the company that employed many friends. His experience helped him advance, but business was not his calling. Government was. He used his contacts to wrangle an appointment at the State Department as a military strategist. This was another part of his life he couldn't discuss on the campaign trail. Then a Navy friend-turned-combat-advisor for MSNBC encouraged him to run for the Senate from Washington State. It was a good year to do so. Support came easily, thanks to Navy contractors and colleagues in aerospace. Twelve years later, Senator and Lucy Taylor, the one-time head of the United Fund, moved into the White House.

Morgan Taylor, a fraction under six feet, usually appeared in public wearing a black, pin-striped Brooks Brothers suit. But actually he pre-ferred loose fitting blue turtlenecks, his leather Navy flight jacket and khaki slacks. He maintained a rigorous Navy exercise routine, which pleased his White House doctors. As a result, his weight hadn't drifted north of 195 pounds for twenty years. He still favored regulation length hair, which kept most of the gray from being too obvious.

Though he was Chief Executive, his heart remained in the air. Friends said it wouldn't take much for Taylor, even at age 53, to climb back into the cockpit of his fighter. He always kept the possibility alive by staying current on flight SIMs twice each year at Andrews. More often he played on a *special* game version the Navy department loaded onto his PC, one you wouldn't find in any stores.

Morgan Taylor figured that if his day job didn't pan out, he always could re-up for the reserves. And he wasn't joking.

Reflecting on it all, the president was worried more than he let on. He hadn't felt quite this anxious since he was shot down in Iraq during a classified combat mission gone bad during Desert Storm years ago. The hairs on the back of his neck bristled as he considered the possibilities that lay ahead. Maybe it was the damned *McLaughlin Group* that set him off today, or the morning security briefing pre-pared by the CIA. Either way, he was in a foul mood.

"Okay, worst case, Bernsie. Lodge grabs New York in an upset.

How do we go after him?" the president asked his chief of staff, John Bernstein, whom he always called "Bernsie."

Bernstein had been with Taylor since his years in the Senate. He was ten years older than Morgan Taylor. The president constantly told him he needed to take off some pounds. "Some" meant 35. But Bernsie wasn't the type to go to the gym. Instead, he hid his frame inside pull-over sweaters and loose fitting pants. But his appearance was also part of his deception. He was shrewd, knowledgeable, and daring. He ran the White House and had a direct line to corporate leaders across America. Important ones. That made him an influential fundraiser and a good pulse taker. The joke around Washington was that John Bernstein never slept. Just when people thought they were returning phone calls too late into the night to reach Bernsie, he'd pick up.

John Bernstein was the man Morgan Taylor relied on the most even though they rarely agreed on anything. That was part of the attraction. He would willingly engage the president on policy and philosophy. Their differences made Taylor think twice on every critical governmental decision and three times on political ones.

"Won't happen. Maybe Lamden's VP, but I think even Henry doesn't like him."

"What's his position on India and Pakistan?"

"Hands off. At least for now," Bernsie complained. "He hasn't gotten into it. Personally, I think he's just not ready to run the country."

"You saying we fight him on experience?" the president asked.

"*Inexperience*. Hell, he's from Vermont. Three electoral votes. Not a big springboard to the White House. Just ask Howard Dean."

"Correction. He's transplanted from Massachusetts. And they've got 12." The president knew political history like the cockpit of an F/A-18. "And Massachusetts has some bragging rights to John Adams, John Quincy Adams and, in case you've forgotten, a man named Kennedy." He was ready to continue, "And..."

"All right. All right. Then if he gets the nomination we'll hit his inexperience head on. And his age. And build on it."

"It didn't stop George W., Clinton, or Carter," Taylor replied.

"But he doesn't have much going for him in foreign politics."

Again the president said, "That didn't stop George W., Clinton, or Carter. And it won't fly because he's getting more vocal about the Middle East and Israel's tactics."

"Pretty radical for a Democrat," Bernstein observed. The president folded his arms and considered the argument. He recognized it was a personal issue for Bernstein. "You're right about that. That's why I think he won't take New York. Too many Jewish voters and his rhetoric isn't the typical 'Rah rah Israel'."

"On the other hand, he's fluent in goddamned Arabic and that gives him a leg up with the Muslim leaders," the president asserted. "Hell, he gets more fucking airtime than the weatherman in a blizzard. But I don't know about New York. He could still grab it. If he does we play up his soft support of Israel. America's not ready to ignore Israel."

Bernsie nodded in agreement. Maybe that was the tack to take. He hoped New York voters would make it a moot issue.

11:50 A.M.

Today it would be the Galil SAR, an Israeli-made assault rifle. SAR standing for Short Assault Rifle. McAlister didn't even note that irony in his choice. *Israeli. Developed after the 1967 war when the Israeli Army determined they needed a lighter combat rifle.* He chose the weapon because it was compact, the shortest assault rifle in the world at only 33.07 inches long. Broken down, his 8-pound, 27-ounce Galil could be hidden in suitcases, passing as ordinary travel items, though he'd never be foolish enough to take it on a plane. It had a collapsible sniper stock with a built-in cheekpiece and a detachable 30-round magazine. However, he planned on firing only one silenced 5.56mm NATO bullet.

He attached an Israeli Military Industries mount with an M15 rail and a Colt 6x scope. The M15 rail positioned the optics lower making it easier to sight. He preferred his configuration over the bulkier, heavier Elcan scope. Equipped as the rifle was, McAlister had tracked targets 300 to 500 yards away with deadly accuracy. Early this afternoon his intended victim would be barely 215 feet in front of him. McAlister's single bullet, exiting at 2,953 feet per second, would find flesh and bone before he relaxed his finger.

When he finished his job, he wouldn't escape. He would simply disappear.

CHAPTER 2

The Secret Service had an ironic origin. It was established on April 14, 1865, by President Abraham Lincoln, though it didn't do him any good. Its initial charge was to prevent counterfeiting in the United States, not protect the Chief Executive. So when John Wilkes Booth pulled the trigger on the very same day the United States Secret Service was created, no federal officer was there to protect him.

It took the assassination of two more presidents, James A. Garfield in 1881 and William McKinley in 1901, for Congress to finally add presidential protection to the duties of the Secret Service.

Today, authorized under Title 18, United States Code, Section 3056, the Secret Service is guardian of the Executive Mansion and the neighboring grounds, the Main Treasury Building and Annex, and other presidential offices. They watch over the president and vice president, members of their immediate families, the temporary official residences of the vice president and foreign diplomatic missions in Washington D.C., and around the globe. And following the assassination of Senator Robert Kennedy, the Secret Service has been assigned to protect all official, credible, viable, major presidential candidates and their spouses within 120 days of a general presidential election.

The election was 133 days away.

ALBANY, NEW YORK

Teddy Lodge enjoyed it all. The attention and the power. He rarely got enough sleep, but he trained for campaigning like a soldier preparing for battle.

His routine began every morning at five with 200 pushups, 200 crunches, and a two-mile run in almost any weather. He didn't have an ounce of excess body fat. It had been part of his ritual since he recovered from a near fatal van accident as a teenager.

Following his protein breakfast, Lodge the Athlete turned into Congressman Lodge, answering constituents' e-mail and reviewing research on a bill regarding auto emission standards. By 10 A.M. he closed up his Dell laptop, took his last sip of herbal tea, looked to the eastern sky and the Berkshire Mountains in the distance, and anticipated the knock at the door a moment before it happened.

"Congressman, the governor is ready in the lobby." It was his campaign manager Geoff Newman. Newman, cold and calculating, was said to know Teddy Lodge better than anyone.

Outsiders could never penetrate the inner circle that surrounded Lodge and Newman. Newman had a lock on Lodge's psyche. And Lodge knew that Newman's loyalty was unquestionable. It had been that way for years.

Geoff Newman had transferred to Harvard Essex Academy the same year as Lodge. He was a portly teenager who engaged in a seemingly never-ending battle to keep his weight down. What came easy to him was organizing complex thoughts far beyond his years. They called him "the brain." While classmates at the elite North Shore boarding school struggled through the rigorous course load, he completed the assignments with ease. Though he was extremely smart, he wasn't popular. That hadn't changed in the years since; nor had his weight issues. But Lodge recognized his strengths and relied on him, particularly after his accident.

According to interviews, it was said that the only reason Newman was alive today was because he didn't ski. A number of Teddy's closest friends were killed in a car accident on their way up Mount Washington for a weekend in 1975. Newman wasn't invited. And Teddy narrowly survived.

But according to published biographies, Newman visited Lodge in the hospital, the only real friend left to do so. A few years later they reconnected at Yale. During their college years they developed an unusually strong bond. Few words were needed between them. They spoke an almost non-verbal shorthand that served them well over the years. Lodge made Newman his chief political strategist, his principal advisor and now his presidential campaign director.

Newman was a good deal like Morgan Taylor's chief advisor. Bullish. Controlling. Determined. Argumentative. But unlike John Bernstein, insiders complained that Geoff Newman ran more than the congressman's campaign. He controlled a great deal of his life.

"So? We can count on Poertner?" Lodge asked.

"Finally," Newman replied. "He'll make the announcement at the photo op. But it's going to cost a Cabinet post."

"Fine, if he helps deliver New York."

The endorsement of the Governor of New York was important. The photograph they'd soon pose for would make tomorrow's *Albany Times Union* along with the rest of the breaking news. Newman had staged it like everything else in the campaign. One step, then another. All of them leading right up to the White House.

After the announcement from Governor Poertner, the schedule called for Lodge to drive the 35 miles due south to Hudson. Later in the day he'd have pre-arranged meet-and-greets in Kingston and Poughkeepsie, dinner in Newburgh with $1,000 contributors, and a late evening arrival in Manhattan.

Teddy Lodge was used to the grind and Jenny was his perfect companion. She was nine years younger, a Vassar graduate, and the very picture of a first lady. They had been married for only three years and she had kept her job as a features editor for *Vanity Fair* until the primaries began in earnest. Children would follow. They'd have the first babies in the White House since Jack and Jackie.

Jenny was a statuesque brunette, 5'10", and magnificently proportioned. She could easily carry off everything in a model's closet with elegance and grace. She was particularly partial to Isaac Mizrahi suits and Bobbi Brown makeup, but she looked great in casual clothes, too. Some gossip columnists predictably compared her to Jackie Kennedy in taste, manner and appearance. And, like Jackie, she could stand out in a crowd or look totally at ease on her husband's arm.

Men loved her and women envied her. She always had the right word for everyone and, with her keen editing skills, she helped Teddy craft his speeches.

They met at a Democratic fundraiser she had been invited to

attend. *Whose idea was it?* She tried to remember, but couldn't. A free-lance photographer she met at the magazine? *A guy named Garrison or Harrison?*

"Come on Jenny, you'll have a good time. Who knows, maybe the man of your dreams will come along," she was told.

Somehow she scored a free table right in front of the congressman's. "Hello," said Mister Right.

She was drawn to his deep brown eyes, capped by thick eyebrows. His voice seduced her. His character overwhelmed her.

They saw each other the next night, and the next. Jenny couldn't put her finger on it. It almost seemed preordained. But it was wonderful…and fast.

Her friends couldn't believe the match. Religion: both fairly non-practicing Protestants. Compatible astrological signs: He's a Gemini, she's an Aquarius. Sushi lovers. Both into skiing and sailing. Similar taste in authors: Clancy and Grisham for sheer fun, Halberstam for history. Similar dislikes: olives, SUV's, and bad grammar.

Teddy was good with his words. But Jenny's writing helped him put his ideas into memorable prose. About the only thing they disagreed on was when to have children. And his rumored temper, never seen in public, was always in check with her. The only hint to the pressure he felt was his restless sleep. She explained to herself that he had a great deal on his mind, including the stressful job he was applying for.

Their friends were mostly hers. Teddy had no close buddies from childhood and no living relatives. Their social life was marked by must-attend political dinners and receptions at least three times a week. He rarely made plans with colleagues and preferred to do his exercising alone.

He was outwardly dynamic and inwardly private.

Jenny felt she was lucky to win him—a trophy husband. And yet she was acutely aware of how little she really knew him.

When she thought about it, they shared no leisure time with anyone else. They traveled only to campaign and never for pleasure. Not Europe, not even Israel. Especially Israel, which she maintained would solidify his political future.

"It'll look good if we go there before the election," she said no more than a week ago. She had recommended it before, too. "Then we can visit Egypt, Syria, Iraq, and Jordan. No one could accuse you of not knowing the names of the world leaders." He laughed at the reference Jenny made to the way a reporter ambushed George W. Bush in the 2000 presidential campaign.

"After the election, honey," he always answered. "How about first I win here, then I take on the rest of the world."

There was something about the phrase. Appealing.

She played with it. In time, she rewrote his aside as, "*We can all be part of changing the world.*"

"All be part of changing the world? It has a nice ring to it. I like it," he told her. Jenny recommended he put it to the test on the road. The first time she heard it was at an impromptu press conference in Illinois. It worked. He incorporated it into his stump speeches and it played well with the crowds. It sounded optimistic and youthful. Teddy Lodge would lead a generation forward, helping to change the world. Jenny wanted to be there with him.

As they drove down Route 9, pockets of people came out to wish the candidate and his wife well. Teddy liked rolling down the window and waving. His campaign manager knew it meant more votes and until the Secret Service detail was assigned to him as the official Democratic candidate he'd be free of endless rules and an armed entourage.

Newman scanned a schedule sheet and glanced at his watch.

"How we doing, Geoff?" Lodge asked.

"Five minutes off." The driver flashed his headlights twice. The New York State Police car escort immediately speeded up.

Newman punched a phone number into his Nokia.

He called an advance man in Hudson.

"Newman here," he said, jumping in as soon as he was connected. "TV?" Lodge listened and saw that Newman angrily shook his head at the answer; obviously not what he intended to hear. "Just a stringer? Shit. Then tell him he better be ready to roll. And stay in fucking focus!"

Jenny, who had been enjoying the scenery, now glared at Newman and then her husband. She hated the way her husband's strategist treated people.

Lodge squeezed her hand and whispered, "He's just trying to keep us on schedule." He kissed her cheek, then shot a quick and angry frown at Newman.

Newman had managed all of Lodge's campaigns since he ran for class president in college. Now, like then, he was always in the background; working, manipulating, calculating. Jenny called it something else: scheming. However, her husband had undying confidence in Newman and she had to live with it.

She tried her best to smile at Newman, but nothing genuine came across.

"Geoff. It'll be okay," Teddy calmly said. "Go easier on people."

Jenny was pleased.

Newman relaxed his tone on the phone. "Sorry. The congressman just has an important new position speech today and we need to make the greatest impact possible."

There was peace in the car. And with that, Lodge took five pages out of a file folder sitting on his lap and checked the order. His handwritten notes were on the side. He scanned ahead to page three, studied the words intently, then mouthed them silently to get the precise cadence. This had to play just right.

TRIPOLI, LIBYA
THE SAME TIME

Fadi Kharrazi's desk calendar had three dates circled. Today was one of them. The other two were later in the year.

This was a private calendar, representing a personal schedule, unknown to all but one other man. Fadi put a large "X" through the circle and smiled. He was assured by his associate that the other dates would come and go with equal success.

The Western press reported little about him. In fact, there was virtually nothing to report. They had few inside sources, little real information, and hardly a notion of what made Fadi Kharrazi tick. That's why the CIA wanted to learn more about the son of the latest Libyan leader. But since the violent revolution that ousted

Colonel Mu'ammar Abu Minyar al-Qadhafi, they hadn't been able to effectively penetrate the inner circle of the man who succeeded him—General Jabbar Kharrazi—or the organizations of his two sons Fadi and Abahar. However, they were getting closer.

It should have been easier with regard to Fadi Kharrazi. He kept himself in the public eye as head of the state's principal television channel and newspaper. But Libya's press was no more free under the new regime than it was in Qadhafi's day, even after tensions lessened between Libya and the West. Fadi, known for his closely cropped beard, trademark cigar, and tailored Italian suits, cultivated his public image, while keeping his real persona far from the headlines.

His holdings were estimated in the hundreds of millions of dollars, much of it blood money.

Rumor had it that he participated first-hand in the coup that brought his father to power. Under the influence of too much French brandy, he was said to have boasted how he personally shot five of Qadhafi's senior lieutenants in the back. These pronouncements never made the street. The women he told this to always disappeared after he raped them.

Fadi found other sports interesting as well. However, he often confused "the rules of the game" with one of his favorite pastimes, human target practice.

Shortly after the revolution, he oversaw Libya's national soccer league. He wasn't the most popular executive in the international governing board of FIFA, the Federation International Football Association. On one occasion at a state exhibition game he ordered his bodyguards to shoot at spectators chanting epithets about his father. Dozens were reportedly killed on the spot. FIFA considered removing Fadi from the league, but since no one filed a complaint (for obvious reasons), and the family-run press failed to corroborate the story, the matter was dropped as hearsay.

Later, when Fadi's team lost to Iran, he dismissed the team's manager, had Army officers cane the players on the soles of their feet and threatened them with a jail sentence if they lost again. Since this was not witnessed by FIFA officials and only rumored by other teams, it also failed to warrant anything more than a harsh telephone rebuke.

Two months later, Fadi's team was defeated by Kazakhstan. This was not a good thing. It eliminated Libya from World Cup competition. The team's fate was unclear. However, the following year, Libya fielded an *entirely* new team. After a good deal of debate, FIFA refused to seed them in international competition, citing vague human rights violations.

And through it all, Fadi Kharrazi projected another image. With his inviting, open eyes and a broad smile, the son of the newest gangster dictator was looked upon as a smart and dynamic media mogul. Of course, this was no surprise to anyone. He controlled everything that was reported about him.

His newspaper published only what he or his father deemed printable. His TV station offered only a mix of propaganda, sports and movies. Viewers generally saw pirated American action movies. Saturday nights were the biggest, filled with old Jet Li, Vin Diesel and Schwarzenegger films (with the exception of *True Lies*, banned because of its depiction of Arab terrorists).

By all standards of common decency, Fadi Kharrazi was an evil man. What was troubling to the spooks at Langley, and ultimately the White House, was that General Kharrazi might be seriously ill, perhaps dying, and Fadi was in the line of succession, to which he proclaimed: *al Hamdulillah*—"Thanks be to God."

His only competition was his older brother, Abahar, Arabic for *more brilliant, more magnificent*. Abahar headed Libya's new secret police, and according to American intelligence reports may have already been anointed as first in line to replace his father in the event of his death.

The stage was set for a bloody family power struggle, but Fadi had acquired, through a complex transaction, a plan so secret that neither his father nor brother knew about it. This plan, foremost in his mind, was finally coming to fruition and it would assure his accession as the next strongman of Libya and eventually the entire Muslim world. It had a decades old operational designation, though he failed to recognize the legendary significance of the name. *Ashab al-Kahf.*

HUDSON, NEW YORK
12:52 A.M.

Carolyn Hill fluffed up the pillows while Roger C. Waterman examined his latest purchases. The pair of brass picture frames in his hands looked pretty beaten up. "How much do you think these will fetch in New York?"

The hotel maid was taken by his question. She liked Mr. Waterman, found him attractive, polite and interesting; so much nicer than most of the hotel's guests. And he was single. If he kept coming to Hudson maybe they could have dinner at Kozel's, a three-generation old family-owned restaurant, arguably the area's most popular establishment. *But why would he ever be interested in me?* she wondered. *He lives in New York and he's so successful.*

"I don't know," she answered.

"Come on. Take a guess. What do you think?" he said. "Ten dollars? More?"

Carolyn really had no idea. "Ah, $25 each? What did you pay for them?"

"I picked them up for fifteen. The tarnishing here on the bottom can be polished out. But the patina, the overall aging quality, that's what caught my eye. Displayed with the right pictures, I'll get more than $200 each in New York."

"You think that much?"

"Easy."

"No way, they're just old picture frames."

"Not after I'm through with them. But maybe I won't sell them. Maybe I'll bring them back for you."

Waterman got the smile he intended. He enjoyed flirting with her. She was attractive, probably around 27 or 28 years old and obviously single. No wedding ring. But then again, he already knew that the brown-eyed, brown-haired attendant wasn't married, at least not anymore. He learned that vital piece of information in the hotel bar, the place where things like that can be discussed with little fear of it coming back around. The bartender told him she divorced her husband just after their son was born six years ago. "I bet she's a screamer, that one," the bartender said, wishing he had first-hand knowledge.

True or not, Waterman did sense that Carolyn Hill hid a power-ful sexuality under her hotel uniform. A sexuality that he fantasized exploring one day.

"Now, you better get going," he said good-naturedly. "Everyone's heading out for a good spot to watch."

"Thanks. I've got some more work to do here. But my mom's hold-ing a place up front." She actually wanted to stay longer and talk with Mr. Waterman. Instead, she took her cue. "I'll see you later?"

"I hope so," he threw in for good measure. No doubt she would be a delightful distraction. *Maybe later tonight.* But then he dismissed the thought. He couldn't. Not this trip.

"But aren't you coming out?" she asked. "To see the congressman?"

"No. Not really into politics."

"We don't see many people like him in Hudson. Think he can win?"

"Who knows. Enjoy the show, though. Now, bye. I have to take a shower and get some work done. Go. Shoo," he joked to move her along. It was time for her to leave and time for Waterman to get to the things on his agenda, too.

Today Carolyn was running a little bit late. Of course, he knew that. She was finished with his floor now. After the speech she'd return to do the third. Waterman knew that, too, just as he knew everything about her schedule. Two hours on the 2nd floor followed by a one hour break. One-and-a-half on the 3rd floor. Then another round after lunch for all of the rooms that had a late check out, starting on three and wrapping up on two. He had taken everything into consid-eration when making all the plans.

Police Lt. Joseph Brenner stepped out of his Camaro cruiser and saw the man he needed. He had double-parked next to a makeshift parade float prepared by the Democratic volunteers from the area. In a few minutes the candidate would be arriving and he wanted to make sure everything was ready.

"Morning, Mitch," Brenner said, brushing back his thinning hair with his fingers. Mitch Price was the only man there in a blue blazer and white pants. He looked like he belonged on a yacht. And for the next hour, he was the skipper. Price was in charge of organiz-ing the placement and spacing of everyone in the parade. He was also owner of Mitch Motors and Vice Chairman of the Columbia

County Democratic Party. His jobs overlapped nicely. Price was in the people business.

"Morning, lieutenant."

"Everything on schedule?"

"Like clockwork," Price acknowledged.

"No problems with anyone," Brenner stated more than asked.

Price had a clipboard in his hand, but he didn't have to look at it. "I've got the Boy Scouts lined up at Morrison's Hardware, the VFW up there at First Baptist, the kids in the bands down at Promenade Hill. The official cars are already lined up in front of the train station. And the trucks from Rogers and Hostradt come down in ten minutes. Oh, and the Greenport ambulance is on Second and Warren. Now that you're here, we have a lead-off car."

Mitch Price had been in charge of Hudson parades for years. He supervised every detail. The signal to assemble would be three bursts from Brenner's siren. It was always the same.

"We're just fine here, Joe," Price added. "All we need now is the congressman and we'll get rolling."

"He's about twenty minutes out," the policeman volunteered. "He's got a trooper leading him. Probably needs to hit the head at Washington Hose." That was the nearest downtown fire station. "Then we'll push off. All in all, looks like one, one-fifteen at the latest."

Price tapped his watch. It was five minutes later than he wanted, but since he couldn't control Lodge's schedule, there was nothing he could do.

Brenner heard a crackle over his police band radio and excused himself. He was getting an update, which confirmed the time he just posted with Price.

Over the next few minutes, Price pulled everyone together. The drummers pounded their street beats. The fire trucks rolled into place. Suddenly, a siren cut through the air, followed by cheers. A "gumball" rotated on the New York State trooper's squad car coming down Warren. He pulled a U-turn at the foot of Warren and First Street. A white Lincoln Town Car behind it did the same.

Before the car had come to a complete stop, the door opened and Lodge bounded out. More cheers. And everyone who was ready to march in the parade broke ranks. The high school marching band members. The Women's Auxiliary. The Boy and Girl Scouts. The VFW members. They all raced over to see the presidential candidate for the simple reason that one day they could say they had touched Teddy Lodge. And Lodge let them.

Geoff Newman smiled to Jenny as he helped her out of the car. "Just like Albany, Syracuse, and Rochester. We're going to take this state yet."

She basically ignored him. As much as she loved her husband, she recognized that he still trailed Governor Lamden. The endorsement from Governor Steven Poertner an hour earlier might help. But not enough. Nonetheless, she was proud. This was all a dress rehearsal for her husband's run at the White House.

The congressman jumped on top of the Town Car and waved. The cheers combined with the drum beat, sounding like nonstop thunder. Lodge allowed it to continue unchecked for a good two minutes, jeopardizing Mitch Price's schedule, but not everyone's.

The congressman touched his heart and extended his arm out to the crowd. They loved it. Lodge then eased himself from the roof to the hood and onto the ground. He whispered something to Lt. Brenner, who in turn pointed him to the bathroom. Newman accompanied him, with his arm on his shoulder.

When they returned, Newman got a ride to Park Place and Lt. Brenner called a signal on his walkie-talkie. A moment later, a large, loud, fire department horn sounded from almost a mile up Warren Street. Brenner got in his squad car. Price checked his watch. Five minutes off his timetable. But Geoff Newman smiled as he checked his. Right on time. Schedules were important to him.

Lodge found Jenny, took her hand, and led her to the T-Bird convertible borrowed from Mitch Motors. "Lodge for President" banners adorned both sides.

"Congressman, Mrs. Lodge, my name is Tommy Kenton. I'm Mayor of Hudson. And so pleased to welcome you."

"Mayor, it's a pleasure. This is my wife, Jenny. And you've got a great town."

Kenton didn't correct him. Hudson was actually a chartered city. "Well, are you ready?" he asked.

"Ready as we'll ever be. Let's say hello to Hudson, New York."

The mayor opened the door to the car, pulled the front seat forward, and gestured for the congressman and his wife to take their seats. Teddy hopped up to sit on the trunk, his feet hanging over the back seat. Even in her slim sheath, Jenny did the same.

Mitch Price came over to shake hands. "Pleasure to meet you, sir. Hope everything's all right."

"Just perfect."

"We'll get the vote out for you. That's my job here. Mitch Price, Chairman of the County Democratic Party," he said introducing himself.

"Mitch, it's great to meet you. I've heard great things. I have no doubt that you'll deliver."

"Thank you, sir."

There was another blast from the fire department foghorn. Price stepped aside and waved goodbye. The Mayor was ready to go. He looked in his rear view mirror and asked, "Are you sure you're going to be safe sitting like that?"

"You driving, Mayor?"

"Yes."

"And you're a Democrat?"

"Yes sir."

"Then I'm going to be in good hands."

The exchange guaranteed two things. A smooth ride up the hill and another vote on Tuesday.

Brenner started his lead car, and everyone assembled into the positions that Price had assigned. Then Brenner blasted his siren three times indicating they were rolling. The teenage drum major of the Hudson High School Bluehawks marching band shouted out his commands and the players eventually found their first note to Sousa's 1889 "Washington Post March."

Sidney McAlister thought he heard the cymbals all the way from Front Street through the open window of his St. Charles room.

The Hudson *Register-Star* would report that it appeared as if all of Hudson was out, either lining the street or assembled at the park for the congressman's speech. Grandparents, adults, children. They were all there and the weather couldn't have been more perfect. As the parade advanced, the fire trucks' sirens blared. The Catskill High band segued into their rendition of the theme from *Star Wars* and citizens waved their Lodge for President signs in absolute adoration.

Jenny leaned across the seat and kissed Teddy. The photo op wasn't missed by an AP photographer running alongside. Jenny wore a white linen dress with black piping and sling-back high heels. Hand-crafted silver hoop earrings sparkled as they caught the early afternoon sun. The picture would be a vision of love and support.

Chuck Wheaton got it on tape, too. The freelancer for WRGB-TV in Schenectady shot "run-and-gun" style on his lightweight digital pro-cam. He was the only paid videographer shooting the event. Everyone else had home video cameras. And there were a lot. Wheaton hoped for a few good sound bites from the congressman and another payday from the station. It helped supplement his income as an English teacher at Hudson High.

Wheaton had staked out a head-on position in the park twenty feet back from the podium. He had planted his tripod in place and paid one of his students twenty dollars to watch it. In the meantime, he ran along the parade route getting some good B-roll for the story that he'd uplink directly from his home edit bay in neighboring Claverack.

Nine-tenths of a mile ahead—about twenty-five minutes up the parade route—Newman checked the seats to make sure the line of sight would be perfect. Six folding chairs were slightly arced around a lectern microphone attached to a gooseneck extension. Sitting from left to right: Police Chief Carl Marelli; next to him Mayor Kenton; then Congressman Lodge, who would rise from the center seat and walk forward to speak. Mrs. Lodge would be to his left so he could easily address her, and Mrs. Kenton. Filling in the last chair would be Fire Commissioner Banks.

"Are the seats all right?" Chief Marelli asked Newman.

"The spacing is a little off," he answered as he slipped the last two chairs to the left a bit. "It's all about clean camera angles for the press. The background needs to drop off for the close-ups, the wide shots have to have people in them."

"And where do you want me?"

"Over here, Chief. First chair." He sat Marelli down and shifted his chair a little more to angle into the crowd, with his back to the corner of Warren and Park Place. "This will keep you focused right on the crowd. I always like having an extra set of trained eyes watching," Newman said.

"I understand. We'll have my boys surrounding the park as well."

"Thank you." They could clearly hear the lead band approaching now. They were playing "Camelot" to a 2-4 marching beat. It reminded him of when he was a kid and John Kennedy was president.

CHAPTER 3

HUDSON, NEW YORK
PARK PLACE AND WARREN STREET
1:57 P.M.

"Hello, Hudson!" bellowed Teddy Lodge. His huge smile broadcast his enthusiasm.

WHUC, the local radio station, departed from weekend reruns of Dr. Laura and took the live feed. Another audio split went to Chuck Wheaton's camera. And another to the amplifier.

"Hello!" the crowd screamed back.

It never failed. Even though he did it on all of his stops, this greeting always seemed spontaneous, and the next best thing to "the wave."

"Hello, Columbia County!" he exclaimed stepping back away from the microphone and inviting another response.

"Hello, Teddy!"

More cheers. More votes. Chuck Wheaton's camera rolled on it all.

When the crowd calmed down, Teddy moved closer to the microphone. "I can't tell you how many times I've been on the Taconic Turnpike and passed by at 55 miles per hour. Well maybe a little over 55," he added getting a laugh. "And you know what? I've gotta slow down. You have a great town to call home, a beautiful county. Fifty-five...that's way too fast. From now on, I'll take it just like we did driving up Warren Street. Slow enough so that Jenny and I can see your faces."

Of course, the audience loved it all. And Jenny really liked when he included her. She also knew it was calculated to appeal to the family values constituency.

"Here you are, giving up your Sunday for us, coming out for strangers from Vermont. Heck, this isn't even Veterans Day, and you threw us a parade!"

"We love you," a woman shouted from the crowd.

Teddy threw back a kiss.

"Sorry honey," he said to his wife. Jenny nodded and the hundreds of people laughed.

But Congressman Lodge had to get back to his point. Back to what he had rehearsed.

"Well, here you all are telling me something amazing. You're willing to give me something I don't take lightly at all…a right granted to you in the Constitution of the United States…looks to me like you're willing to give me your vote."

The cheers erupted and the high school band, now assembled behind him, played "Charge."

Lodge let it go on for a minute, then quieted everyone down. "Thank you. You're making it a very special day for me."

The applause started again. Geoff Newman checked his watch. He'd probably never seen Lodge more in his element. And he really wasn't even on the page yet. He hoped his man would deliver his prepared comments with the same intensity. He also hoped he'd pick up some time. The news media had deadlines.

Lodge stepped back to the applause and brought it down with the palms of his hands. "And let me tell you, just believe in me, because I believe in you."

"We do," the audience yelled in one voice. Newman smiled. This was the congressman's cue that he would transition into his prepared remarks.

"You brought Hudson back from despair, from abandonment by industry, from abandonment by your state, and from abandonment by your federal government."

"You discovered that your future lies in the experiences of your past. Just look at Warren Street, reinvested with life…from what? From antiques. From people hungering for something to hold onto that has meaning, that's lasted, that takes them back home." He'd delivered a run at his favorite string, triplets. Now for the first payoff.

"You transformed Hudson. Columbia County. Your home, your community. Now I ask you to join me. Because there's a lot more out there to work on. *We can all be part of changing the world.*"

Years ago, with a line like that, men would have thrown their hats in the air. Today, men, women and children chanted an almost deafening chorus of "Ted-dy...Ted-dy...Ted-dy!"

Lodge felt he was only beginning to hit his stride. "I'll tell you what I'm going to do," he shouted, "Tell ya what I'm gonna do," he said raising his voice even more. "Win or lose, I'm going to make that Hudson turn-off sign bigger. I'm going to make stopping in Hudson the thing to do!

"And," he shouted over the applause. "And if you do hire me... then book me some rooms at the St. Charles Hotel. Cause I'm comin' back!"

He saluted over at the hotel and another minute of cheers redlined the audio meter on Wheaton's camera.

McAlister's sized up the man at the microphone through his Colt scope. There wasn't a bead of sweat on Lodge. The gunman sensed his intensity, his confidence, and through the optics, he could virtually feel Teddy Lodge's breath.

McAlister readied himself, gently squeezed the trigger, and quietly said to himself, *Bang.*

All was ready. The next time he would have the ambidextrous safety off his Galil SAR. He double-checked the seal on the silencer and locked the cartridge loaded with the 5.56 x 45mm NATO ammunition. He put his eye back on the scope and began to take deep, relaxing breaths. Teddy was speaking slowly now.

As he listened, McAlister ran a mental checklist one final time. Fingerprints: His room was clean. He was sure of that. Inside his room he'd worn latex gloves except when any of the hotel help announced themselves at the door. He never used the hotel elevator. When he went to his room he always took the stairs, and never touched the polished hardwood banister. McAlister even took care to wipe the outside of his doorknob after he entered. His suitcases provided no clues to his identity. There were no phone calls to trace. No paperwork left behind. No hairs left in the shower. No fingernail clippings on the floor. His hotel check-in voucher was signed with an unintelligible scribble. And McAlister's MasterCard was issued through a cash-funded Austrian bank account; a dead end.

He was careful not to touch anything outside, as well. Since he wasn't a very effective insurance agent, he hadn't left any materials behind—intentionally. No brochures. No contracts with fingerprints. He didn't even have business cards. He laughed at the notion that anyone would even talk to him about *life* insurance.

The assassin smiled at his patience. While others in his field could take the shot with equal ability, no one else could have set up the assignment in such detail. To him, it was more like a theatrical play, with complex choreography and bravado performances.

"What you've done here, others can do," continued the congressman. "I feel it. I know it. From small towns like Hudson to big cities everywhere, the new spirit of America is in the air. Take it in…fill your lungs with it. It's from your fresh maple trees. Your oaks. Your pines. Tall and strong. Untainted and pure.

"You had factories here, and pollution. And when the factories closed down, Hudson didn't die. It took years to rebuild, and you did it through hard work, not easy handouts.

"What you accomplished here, we can do across the country. We can bring your message of ingenuity, of re-invention, of renewal to all America. Hudson, New York. You hold the key."

Applause spread across the park, overflowing down the streets, over the airwaves and to people listening at home. The Congressman smiled thinking that his triplets really did work wonders.

It was time to move into the real heart of his speech.

"But there's more to the world than just the community you live in: We live in a world where our borders are no longer our barriers… Where danger openly crosses with a passport rather than a missile… Where too often we look over our shoulders nervously rather than straight ahead with confidence…Where we worry about tomorrow, because we've witnessed unspeakable horrors today.

"The world has changed. But, *We can all be part of changing the world.*"

McAlister adjusted his aim ever so slightly and focused directly on his target. He steadied his weapon against his shoulder and a towel on the window sill. He had chosen this hotel, this hotel room, and this window. The St. Charles still had windows that could open. So many hotel windows couldn't anymore. But that was all part of his detailed survey. That was the way he operated. Never quickly. Never foolishly. McAlister had decided a long time ago that this would be the place. It was only a matter of arranging the time with the people he served.

"The United States is a leader among nations," Lodge asserted. "Make no mistake of that. No matter how much you hear that we cannot police the world, there is no one else to fulfill that role. And like the mean streets of America, this is a mean world.

"Suicide bombers target Israeli buses, markets, and streets. In retaliation, Palestinian women and children die as missiles seek out their homes and schools. Wars in Africa create more homeless, more hunger, more anger. Pakistan and India face each other with arsenals too deadly to speak of and too dangerous to ignore. And…America is attacked."

No one coughed. No one moved. Lodge controlled the crowd with the power of his voice and the conviction of his beliefs. "I do know one thing. Somebody has to take charge. Remember the past. Every time we thought we couldn't, we had to. When we said we shouldn't, we ultimately did. Before World War I, Democrats said, 'Stay at home.' We couldn't. Then, before World War II, it was the Republicans who said, 'Stay at home.' Again, we couldn't. We helped before the war with aid to our allies. We helped by fighting and we helped with the European recovery through efforts like the Marshall Plan. And so it was for us through the decades. Earthquakes, storms, or famine. We've been there to help…a world leader…a way of life. Yet wars continued; hatred needs no rest. In the 1990s, we believed terrorism was a world away, someone else's problem. In 2001, we experienced it at home."

Everyone remained quiet, mesmerized by the candidate from Vermont.

"But how do we change this angry world of ours?"

"Oh, do tell, congressman," McAlister whispered. "Do tell."

Teddy Lodge brushed the hair off his forehead.

"We do it together. You and I in a partnership of nations…a partnership of peace.

"We strike partnerships by sharing food and building up economies. We give. We get. We educate the world's uneducated, we make them intellectually stronger against dictators who would take advantage of their lack of knowledge. *We give and we get.*" He articulated the phrase precisely for his audience. They'd catch on fast.

"And yes, we share our knowledge of arms and our technological know-how to fight emerging terror in third world nations. So we won't have to rush in at an unacceptable cost of American lives. We give and we get.

"We build bridges to former adversaries and make them our friends."

By now everyone joined in, "*We give and we get.*"

Even McAlister was now mouthing the words. "*We give and we get.*" And he counted.

The congressman stepped back and smiled.

At his camera, Wheaton realized that Lodge was definitely into new material. He hadn't heard this before. It was a different speech, not the typical stump drivel. He double-checked his camera load to make sure he had enough tape stock left. There really was no need for him to look, although he didn't know it. Everything was scheduled to fit on one 30-minute videotape load. He was ten minutes into it.

Jenny was impressed with the way Teddy handled the words and the crowd. "Yes, we give and we get," she mouthed with him.

And from across the street, McAlister caressed the trigger. *Almost.* The shot was nearly there for him to take. His mind was clear. McAlister didn't really care one way or another about the election. And while everyone would look for the assassin's political motives, he had none.

This was strictly a paid engagement—$2.2 million, wired to a numbered bank account in Liechtenstein. With the signing of the United Nations Convention Against Transnational Organized Crime in December 2000, the country no longer guaranteed anonymity to its bankers. Yet, should investigators ever trace the funds, the trail would lead to the legitimate sale of art, acquired through non-published European estate sales, then sold at vast multiples of the original price. The fact that McAlister was not an art dealer posed no problem. The buying was an elaborate ruse, executed by the only other man who knew about this particular account.

The deal was uncomplicated. One-point-one million upfront; the balance to be wired with the publication of the assassination in *The New York Times*. No bonus for front page; an oversight. McAlister would negotiate for it the next time.

The instructions were explicit. "A clean hit is preferred. And fast. You won't have time to set up your target again," his contact told him on a park bench overlooking San Francisco Bay some six months earlier.

"A single bullet will do it," he assured his employer. "If it won't, I don't take the shot and you get 80 percent of your money back."

If anything, McAlister was ethical; that is if a killer could be ethical. But he would be ready even if his victim was not.

He waited, as if expecting a cue.

"Soon you will have to make a major decision," Lodge continued, building momentum. "But it is not about one man over another. One candidate versus another. We are all responsible individuals, devoted to serving you. No, the decision is not about a person. It's about policy.

"Walk with me to the future. We'll make a partnership for peace, celebrating all people of the world, with the United States of America as a full and valued partner.

"Better we go to *welcomed arms* than with *arms unwelcomed*.

"It will mean we take what we know to the world so the world will know more. And by so doing, we…"

In one voice, everyone recited at the top of their lungs, "*We Give and We Get.*"

He looked over his left shoulder to Jenny. For a long moment he studied her face. She was beautiful. She deserved to have what she wanted. She really was a good woman.

Tears formed in Jenny's eyes as she looked back at her husband, and then to the crowd. They loved him. She loved him. For the first time she truly realized that he could have it all. He could actually win in November. This small Hudson Valley town was voting right now.

They had the power. It was in their eyes. And the feeling would spread across the country. She knew it. It filled the air, over and over.

"*We Give and We Get! We Give and We Get!*" The chorus had taken over from the soloist. "*We Give and We Get! We Give and We Get!*"

McAlister nuzzled the rifle a little to his right. Lodge's head was in the scope again, but the cross hairs were not fully lined up on his target. Another moment.

Lodge turned back to the crowd smiling.

"It's time for a family of nations in a world apart," continued Lodge softly. "Time for a family that will last into all of our tomorrows." His voice was cracking.

Chuck Wheaton eased out his zoom lens to a camera angle that included Mrs. Lodge. He could see her tears welling up.

McAlister smiled. He lived for moments like this. After all, it was the way he earned his living.

"…a family for you…and," the congressman paused with great impact. Everyone held their breath, including the man across the street with the Galil. "And…a family for me."

Theodore Wilson Lodge, candidate for the President of the United States, bowed his head ever so slightly forward for an instant. No more than four inches. He wiped his eyes.

Jennifer Lodge couldn't move a muscle as she listened to his words. *A family? He wasn't talking to the crowd now. Teddy's telling me something…*

CHAPTER 4

There was no sound at street level and hardly anything audible in the hotel room. The silencer on McAlister's SAR suppressed it. No one really knew what happened right away. The bullet just did its job, with deadly, indiscriminate force.

The Fire Commissioner reacted first. Was it the heat? A fainting spell? Then he noticed a small hole two inches above the eyes, squarely in the middle of the forehead. A trickle of blood in front, a red, wet burst in the back.

"Oh my god," he said too softly to be heard. "Oh my god!" he yelled.

Everything began to move in slow motion. People spotted blood oozing down. Police Chief Marelli rose out of his chair and drew his .357 magnum. It was a more than adequate "man-stopper" that he'd never actually used in the line of duty. Maybe today. He also keyed his radio and ran down a litany of orders to his men on the perimeter. They pulled their fully-loaded lightweight Arasaka LEH-451's. The smaller size and comfortable feel delivered lethal force at handgun range. Each officer carried two speedloaders with hyper-penetration rounds. But like Marelli himself, no one on his squad had ever aimed and shot at a human being

"Down. Everybody down!" Marelli shouted. Banks ignored him. But soon he realized it was too late.

The police scanned the crowd for guns. Onlookers ducked down covering their heads. People quickly realized the magnitude of what had happened. Children were the first to cry, then the adults. All of this took a half a minute to unfold. All of it was caught on Chuck Wheaton's tape.

McAlister began to disappear in one smooth motion. He had timed it all, rehearsed his moves, considered each variable and left no margin for error. He didn't believe in mistakes. In his business, the people who made a mistake never had the opportunity to make another one. They were dead.

He quietly rested his weapon on the floor. Better it should be found. There was too much danger in trying to hide it. The serial numbers on the Galil would not give him away. He had milled them off, then, for good measure, burned them. He did the same to the numbers on the scope and the silencer. The latex gloves assured that he'd leave no fingerprints. But the assassin even made certain to wipe down the gun stock. His cheek could give him away. A faint impression, some perspiration. The same was true of the Colt scope atop the rifle. McAlister knew that the FBI labs would drill down to the microscopic degree.

Next, he surveyed the room one last time, which was unnecessary.

He'd already burned all but the clothes he wore in the Berkshires, 30 miles away. By now his car, a used clunker, was rusting in the Hudson River. Two nights ago, McAlister drove it off the side of the road near Stuyvesant, fifteen minutes up the line. So, with nothing left except the Israeli rifle, McAlister quietly walked to the door, unfastened the chain lock, and left.

The commotion hadn't started outside yet. He'd only pulled the trigger 12 seconds ago. Once in the hallway he stopped, listened for any sign of another hotel guest or staff member. None. Everyone was outside. He continued down the hall for 18 fast steps to his destination, room 315, belonging to the antique dealer from New York, Roger C. Waterman.

Outside shock turned into pandemonium. Police fought to control the crowd, searching for gunmen. But they were unprepared.

The mayor took the microphone, "Please be calm. Please stay where you are." No one listened. In the midst of all the chaos was a cute blonde 15-year-old sophomore from Hudson High. Madelyn Schecter. She'd gotten the amazing assignment to cover the speech for the high school newspaper. She was even on the congressman's calendar for a 2:30 interview. But now her cardboard-covered reporter's notepad and pen slipped from her hands. Her heart raced. Tears streamed down her cheeks as she watched the Greenport Rescue Squad ambulance roll up onto the grass and two paramedics go to work. They confirmed what Chief Banks already realized.

Two minutes later they put their equipment away and began the process of transferring the body onto a stretcher, then into the back of their emergency vehicle. Its siren, not really needed, couldn't be distinguished from the wailing of the others as it screamed up Warren toward Columbia Memorial Hospital. Madelyn held her hands to her ears. So much noise. Such incredible noise.

Madelyn slowly turned around. She watched mothers huddle over their children. She saw police stop every man they didn't know and throw them on the ground for a quick search. Directly in front of her, Chuck Wheaton unsnapped his camera from the tripod and went handheld. She was vaguely aware of her civics teacher focusing on her. Madelyn epitomized the anguish. Soon her face would tell the story to millions of people across the country and around the world.

And the noise continued to grow. It was overwhelming, unlike anything Madelyn had ever heard. She continued her slow circle, around and around, until she collapsed. This was her political coming of age.

"Please, please, everybody stay where you are," Mayor Kenton repeated to everybody. No one listened in the chaos. And across the street, Roger C. Waterman was taking a leisurely shower as promised.

Chief Marelli had no experience in public executions, but he was still a cop. The murder occurred on his watch and the killer was at large. The podium was his crime scene. He mentally raced through the procedural questions. *Where did the bullet come from? What angle? What height?*

Okay, the front. Rule out Warren. The fall was backwards. The bullet exited slightly lower than the entrance point. He looked around, blocking out the cries. *The shooter was higher than the crowd.*

He studied the buildings across the street. *On the corner, that old appliance store. No good. Not a high enough vantage point. The barber shop next to it. Still too low and too tight an angle. An art gallery. Not possible. J. W. Edmonds Hose Co. #1. Maybe, from the roof, but unlikely. Too steep an angle. Too high.*

He realized he skipped a building. The St. Charles. Marelli keyed the microphone to his police radio attached to his shirt. "The St. Charles!" he called to his officers. The Chief stared at the front windows on the second and third floors. He looked closer. The third floor corner window. *It's open!*

The 210 pound, 62-year-old chief hadn't run in years. He was grossly out of shape. But today he sprinted like the high school track star he had been in the '60s. Four of his men joined the pursuit. They darted across the street and flew through the heavy oak door, bounding up the twenty-four stairs to the third floor landing. Their Arasakas were drawn. Marelli led the way, pointing to two of his officers, Pomerantz and Hilton, to cover either side of the door to Room 301. Marelli signaled to Pomerantz not to touch the handle.

"Police!" he shouted. "Hands up! Come out, now!"

After a five count he repeated his order. "Now!" Marelli had never faced a real gunman on the other side of a door, not in all his years as an officer and then Chief of Police. Nothing even close. But instincts told him that the shooter could take them all down right through the walls. He motioned for his men to shift to the right of the door, affording more protection from the neighboring hotel room wall. They didn't need further encouragement. Then with his Arasaka in his right hand, steadied with his left, he took a run toward the door, slamming right through. Marelli had also been a tackle for Hudson High and it all came back to him.

He had trouble staying on his feet, but never lost his concentration. In a blink of an eye he saw an assault rifle on the floor but assessed that no one was in the room. *An AK-47? No. Similar, but not the AK.* Three minutes and eighteen seconds had elapsed since it had been fired. The smell lingered in the room.

"Chief?" he heard Hilton call out urgently. "Bedroom is clear." Marelli did not broadcast his intention to check the bathroom. As he continued across the room he heard his men close in behind him, one after another. Pomerantz swept the right side of the room, Hilton covered the left. Marelli stopped at the bathroom door. It was open a crack. He used his left foot to swing it the rest of the way and led with his gun. *Nothing.* Pushing aside the shower curtain he reluctantly and gratefully called out, "Clear!" Another fifteen seconds had elapsed.

"Don't touch anything," Marelli said as he re-entered the bedroom. Hilton had already checked the closets. "Holy shit. This guy's fast," he said to himself more than his men. Then he told Hilton, "Seal the building! He could be anywhere." Marelli realized nervous sweat had soaked his shirt. "We're going room by room."

Hilton nodded and left.

Marelli bent over the assault rifle. *Practical,* he thought, still not recognizing the exact model. Slick. *The shooter's no crazed wacko. We've got a real pro on our hands.*

Marelli clicked his radio again, calling his dispatcher a few blocks down Warren Street. "Pam, get Velz to shut down the Rip Van Winkle." That was the bridge which spanned the Hudson River between Hudson and Catskill. "And I want squad cars to seal the city. Route 9 North at Fairview. 9 South at the old Price farm. 9G at the base of Mount Marino. Route 66 at Greenport School. 23B at the Cement Factory. Copy?"

"Copy, Chief."

"Fast. Then get me the FBI in Albany!"

"What's going on? All hell's breaking loose on the street."

Marelli didn't explain. "Just do it!" Then to Pomerantz he said, "You stay here. No one comes in unless authorized by me. And only me."

With that Marelli was out the door. He took the stairs in a bounding leap. A crowd was growing in the lobby, peering out the windows at the horrifying scene outside. "Listen up, everyone. No one leaves. No one!" he stated to the dozen or more people. Marelli called his officers to guard the doors; two in the front, another along the side entrance.

"Has anyone gone out this door since the shooting?" he yelled.

"No, no, I didn't see anyone." a waitress volunteered through her sobbing.

"Me either," said a father holding his young boy.

"We've all stayed inside."

Next Marelli ran to the check-in desk at the back of the hotel off the main parking lot entrance.

It was unmanned. "Fuck me," he exclaimed. *He's gotten away.*

"Chief, this is Pam, over." The voice came crackling from his radio.

"Marelli. Go."

"I have the FBI for you. I'll patch them through." It had only been four minutes since the shooting.

"Jesus Christ," he whispered. "The shit's gonna hit the fan."

"I want everyone's identification out now," Marelli demanded in the lobby. "If you don't have it with you, officers will accompany you to your room to get it. You cannot leave without permission. And everyone remains in plain view." Marelli's orders came automatically now, but he knew he was too late. Because of the excitement over Congressman Lodge's speech, none of the hotel staff had covered the main desk and entrance. The gunman had ample opportunity for an unobserved exit. Still, he had to question everyone. No doubt the FBI would go through it again when they arrived.

In the meantime, someone might provide worthwhile information. He'd start with the identity of the man in Room 301. "Anne?" he called out through the lobby. Anne Fornado was the hotel manager. She'd have the information in a second.

With six other Hudson police officers now on site, the rooms were searched and all the guests were ushered in the lobby. Marelli divided his men up and began asking a series of pointed questions. "Who are you? What room were you in? Where were you during the shooting? What did you see?"

Marelli got the name he sought—McAlister, an insurance agent who had been trying to sell to people in Hudson since May. Marelli hadn't seen him, but many had. He'd get a picture-perfect description of the man in short time. That description would be on every newscast in America in the next hour. He also learned from the hotel manager what McAlister was driving. A light blue '02 Nissan Sentra. The car was no longer in the parking lot. The make, model, description and plates had been emailed to NYSPIN, the New York State Police Information Network and radioed to the officers at each of the intersections Marelli ordered blocked.

He remembered how quickly Lee Harvey Oswald had been caught in 1963. The same with Sirhan Sirhan in 1968. "We'll get this McAlister," he promised the mayor at the foot of the lobby stairs. "Christ, the whole damned country will be looking for him."

"Excuse me, sir," Roger Waterman said as he squeezed by Marelli. Waterman's hair was still wet from his shower that he'd been taking when police officers entered his room. "I was told to come down here."

The police chief acknowledged the antique dealer with only a nod, directing him into the dining room. As he joined the hotel guests and staff waiting to be interviewed, he spotted Carolyn Hill. She looked dazed. She'd returned to the hotel right after the shooting. Tears still streamed down her eyes. "Carolyn," he said. She turned to his voice and then rushed to him. For some reason Carolyn needed to feel his touch.

"Mr. Waterman, it's so awful," she cried, falling into his uncertain arms, hugging him tightly.

"What? What's going on?" he asked. There was comfort in his voice. "I was in the shower when police came in and told me to get dressed and come downstairs immediately." He gently lifted her head back a few inches, still cradling her face in his hands. He was aware of how nice she smelled and how good she felt.

She looked at him, needing him. "You don't know? You mean you haven't heard?"

Waterman looked baffled. "Know what? What's wrong?"

Carolyn broke down again. "Oh my god. Mrs. Lodge. Someone killed Mrs. Lodge!"

CHAPTER 5

Even before the FBI arrived, they one-upped Marelli and declared the St. Charles and the park a federal crime scene. A team from the Forensic Science Research and Training Center (FSRTC) was already in the air from the laboratories at the FBI Academy in Quantico, Virginia. They would be on ground within two hours.

Everything the FSRTC people needed traveled with them in a black van, flown in the belly of a Lockheed-Martin C-130E transport, on loan from the Marines. The plane's cargo hold, with its rear loading ramp, was perfect for quick response agency use. It rolled on at Quantico Marine Corps Air Base in Virginia and off at Columbia County airport eight minutes north of Hudson on Route 9H. The plane used every inch of the 5,350-foot-long runway before it came to a stop.

Seven FSRTC team members followed their vehicle down the ramp. They each had their expertise and instructions from FBI Director Robert Mulligan.

"Make no mistakes. We want this killer." If anyone could piece the puzzle together, they could. The agents—scientists as much as criminologists—had remarkable tools at their command. They operated on the cutting edge of forensics technology. They developed, tested, and applied the latest breakthroughs in latent fingerprint and footwear identification, DNA analysis, firearms identity, thread examination, and computer imaging.

Case Officer Roy Bessolo was in charge. He looked and sounded like a Marine: tough, all business, with a deep voice and a monotone delivery. He kept his hair closely cropped. His clothes were always pressed and his shoes were never a day away from their last polish.

Bessolo looked military, but he was a career FBI man, one of the most respected forensics investigators in the bureau. He lived by facts and made certain that the people in his command searched everywhere for them.

"I want every square inch documented," he commanded his investigators—four men and two women. "Remember, we've got only one chance to search the scene properly. One chance, people. The local gendarme has done a good job closing the city down, but it may be too late. So we're looking for clues for a man named McAlister."

He was convinced that even his own mother wouldn't recognize him, in a crowd or up close. Sidney McAlister. Roger C. Waterman. These were only two identities he had perfected. They were so completely different from each other. From appearance to age, to stance, body language, facial expressions, and voice. It wasn't only a matter of hair color, glasses, or contact lenses. Of course, they helped. It went beyond that. He created distinct personalities, each with its own idiosyncrasies and speech affectations. Here was the proof he loved. He could stand face to face with a woman who both liked him as one man and despised him as the other.

He was a great performer; classically trained by drama coaches, but a true method actor at heart. Private lessons, of course. He didn't merely play a part, he entered into the psyche of the characters he inhabited. Waterman, the refined and intellectual art dealer. McAlister the smarmy salesman. It was theater on a grand scale. Every day was a performance for the man known only to himself.

In truth, there was no Waterman. There had been no Christianson, Martinez, Collins or Hammacher before them. But they had all played on his stage and then disappeared just as McAlister had, even before he fired the shot that killed Jenny Lodge. Waterman pulled the trigger. And soon the antique dealer would vanish; unless, of course, he decided to come back to fuck Carolyn Hill. He fell asleep early with the thought working its way into his dreams.

11:45 P.M.

Before he went to bed, the president had Louise Swingle place another condolence call to Congressman Lodge. He'd already tried earlier, but he hadn't been able to speak to Lodge in person. The President of the United States usually could reach anyone in the country on the phone. But not tonight. Newman wouldn't put him through.

"I'm sorry, Mr. President, but I'm sure you can understand," Newman said. "He hasn't been able to talk to anyone. It's been too difficult."

"Of course," Taylor said. "It has been a terrible day."

After an awkwardly quiet moment, Taylor continued. "I've assigned Secret Service protection for the congressman. If you haven't seen them already, they're outside of your hotel rooms now." Newman and Lodge were in Manhattan, rushed there by motorcade after the shooting. "The officer in charge of the detail will begin working out the routine with you in the morning."

"Thank you. I saw them briefly. They introduced themselves. I realize it wasn't required by law…yet." Newman intentionally added *yet* as if to say Mrs. Lodge would still be alive if they'd been there earlier.

"It's the least we could do."

"Appreciated."

"Well, again, please convey my deepest sympathies and those of my wife and the entire nation. Oh, and rest assured, we are giving this top priority. We have a good team investigating."

"I spoke with the FBI before we left Hudson. I told them we'd cooperate in every way. But just not right now." Newman had no doubt that the FBI was briefing him at least hourly.

"And Mr. Newman, I *will* find out what happened today."

Newman heard the tone exactly as Taylor intended. It was a message. Taylor was a hunter. He was no longer in the cockpit of a jet fighter on a bombing run, but he was no less lethal.

"I'll convey your sincere condolences and your commitment… to the *candidate*." Newman's use of the word *candidate* was equally intentional. He gave just the right emphasis to it, but concluded it would be useless to continue the dialogue with its political jousting.

"Thank you, Mr. President," he said. "Now goodnight."

"Goodnight, Mr. Newman," the president replied. He really didn't like this man.

CHAPTER 6

The FBI confiscated the camera-original footage that Chuck Wheaton shot at Park Place, but not before he uplinked the entire reel to WRGB and dubbed a copy for himself. It immediately aired in edited form, and then was fed in its entirety to the network in New York. Other news services picked it up and telecast the shocking footage with their own commentary.

NBC: "…Murder in a small town."

ABC: "…An assassin casts a final vote."

Fox: "…Who, what, and why?"

Elliott Strong's edgy all-night radio show, *Strong Nation*, fielded dozens of conspiracy theories from listeners. And the next day, *The New York Times* ran five pictures above the fold. The governor's endorsement, Jenny's kiss during the parade, the fire commissioner desperately applying CPR, the congressman holding his wife, and the photo that would appear on the cover of *Time* and *Newsweek*, the high school girl dazed with the turmoil swirling around her.

A sidebar story ran in the left column, written by Michael O'Connell. The aggressive young writer had been chronicling the New York State primary for months. He had recently interviewed Jennifer Lodge and quickly wrote a 1604-word story Sunday night. He hit "Enter" on his computer and the text worked its way through the editorial system to headline writers, layout artists and, eventually, to the front page. The *Times* syndicate picked it up for national play. By the time the paper hit the stands Monday morning, O'Connell had the go-ahead to clear his other assignments in order to tell the Teddy Lodge story from the beginning.

O'Connell reserved a seat on the noon shuttle to Boston; from there he'd go to Marblehead and begin to put the pieces of Teddy

Lodge's life together. From what he had already learned it had been full of tragedy long before Jenny's death.

He wouldn't be the only one on the trail. After reading the account in his Presidential Morning Briefing package, prepared by the chief of staff, the Director of the Central Intelligence Agency (DCI) and the White House staff, President Morgan Taylor decided to dispatch a man named Roarke to do the same. It wasn't intended as an investigation. The FBI had that authority. As a member of the Secret Service, Roarke was asked to prepare a comprehensive profile of Congressman Lodge in order to provide him with maximum security.

In all, America's phone books listed 5,241 people with the name *S. Roarke* or *Scott Roarke*. None of the numbers would ring through to the president's man. Nor would this particular *Scott Roarke* come up in any Internet search. A computer hacker might find an extract on an Army Special Forces lieutenant by that name. But there'd be no record of any mission.

He wasn't ever *officially* in Beijing, Tehran, Bahrain, or Mazar-i-Sharif. But a number of people at the Pentagon knew he had been there and what he had done.

Roarke maintained Secret Service credentials, but that didn't begin to describe his access to the president or his work. Scott Roarke was definitely the president's man, a friend and confidant ever since Morgan Taylor met him a number of years ago quite by *accident*.

The accident was caused when a Soviet designed SAM-16 surface-to-air missile found one of the General Electric F-110 engines aboard Commander Morgan Taylor's F/A-18C during a less than successful mission over Iraq.

Simply put, the meeting occurred when Roarke rescued him. Roarke, a young lieutenant in the Army's secret Defense Intelligence Agency, was operating well inside the lines of Saddam Hussein's fierce Republican Guard when Taylor dropped in on him.

Taylor paid a surprise, uninvited visit to a pair of suspected biological weapons plants from 25,000 feet. He had one more Rockeye bomb left in his stores and was coming around on his second target when a trio of SAM's locked on to him from a portable launch facility. He evaded two. The last caught Morgan Taylor's left intake.

Taylor was pissed off he couldn't bring back the $24 million machine he'd signed out. But his Air Wing Commander onboard the *USS Carl Vinson* was happy that an Army puke had saved Taylor's sorry butt to fly another day. He'd even take home the Navy Cross, commending his valor in the presence of great danger and at great personal risk.

As a result, Taylor established a special bond with Roarke. The Annapolis pilot and the inner-city kid. They helped each other many times over the past decade. Three years ago, at the request of the first term president, Roarke came to the Secret Service. A personal request with private duties.

A few years following the September 11th attacks on the World Trade Center towers, then-Senator Taylor resolved to personally address the level of *uncertainty* that surrounded the near *certainty* of future attacks.

As Chairman of the Senate Appropriations Committee, he identified the need to centralize much of the internal anti-terrorist intelligence-gathering process. Taylor proposed the creation of a hybrid FBI/Secret Service/Homeland Security unit, piggy-backing on already funded programs.

Behind closed doors he urged the White House to make the paradigm shift from viewing the Secret Service as walking bullet proof vests for the president to strategists and combatants in the terrorist war. Their tools would be political sleight of hand utilizing misinformation, domestic and foreign investigation and, when necessary, outright deception.

He received solid support in the Republican-held Senate, but his measure was undermined when it hit the House. The head of the House Ways and Means Committee was a young congressman named Teddy Lodge. He argued in the Caucus Room of the Old House Office Building, where the House Un-American Activities Committee once held its historic hearings, that "President Taylor was willing to risk too many freedoms; freedoms Americans must not be willing to abandon." The sound bite that led the news and killed the proposal in conference committee sharply stated, "We don't need an enemy within."

The plan was dead, but only for awhile. When Taylor took the Oath of Office as president he finished what he had started, this time without the approval of Congress and the oversight of Congressman Lodge. He simply assigned "unique" Secret Service duties, transferred vast sums, created new budget line items, and brought in an ex-Army special ops commando named Roarke to join the team. Few people beyond the CIA, NSA, and FBI chiefs knew about it. The fewer the better. He designated it PD16, short for Presidential Directive 1600; an homage to his new forwarding address.

No one's the worse for it, thought the president as he signed the papers to reorganize the Secret Service. *Except maybe Lodge.*

CHAPTER 7

HUDSON, NEW YORK
MONDAY, JUNE 23

An assassin fired one round through the silencer of his assault rifle yesterday. It made no sound, yet its impact was heard across the country. The target was a congressman. The victim was the woman he loved. It was time for Theodore "Teddy" Lodge to bury another memory.

Many voters knew that Lodge had cheated death himself before and buried too many people close to him. But Michael O'Connell brought the story forward with facts from the archives and the breaking news of the day. His report in *The New York Times* was written with a passion that left readers more closely connected to the congressman's pain.

Teddy Wilson Lodge cried once more. His tears streamed down his cheeks as he cradled his wife's head in his lap. Another family member was taken from him before he had a chance to say goodbye.

O'Connell took readers through three generations of Lodge family history. Though he represented Vermont voters as a congressman, his roots were in Massachusetts.

Teddy Lodge was born in Marblehead, just north of Boston. He had a famous New England political name, however he wasn't related to the more famous Lodges and their relatives the Cabots. His parents were successful and no less wealthy, but their fortune was owed to his grandfather's North Shore real estate holdings.

During the Depression, when everyone was selling off property to survive, Oliver Lodge leveraged the small bus company that he owned for cash from a prominent Marblehead doctor named Elias R. Crannell.

They had met quite coincidentally during a snowstorm in February, 1930. The good doctor's 1929 $4,500 luxury Duesenberg had spun off Route 129 on the way to a reception at Tedesco Country Club. Lodge, driving one of his three buses, stopped to help the stranded doctor. Despite the fact that it was nearly 10-degrees below zero, Oliver offered to assist the doctor. He dug out the Duesy, then pushed and pulled until the vehicle rolled back on the road. He followed the doctor to his destination just to make sure he made it safely.

One week later Dr. Crannell wrote a thank you letter and expressed his willingness to help the young man. Oliver Lodge was not shy and his wife was out of work. He had come from a hard-working apple-farming family in the Connecticut River Valley near Springfield, Massachusetts. But unlike his father and grandfather, he didn't want to live his life climbing ladders. So one day he told his wife Edna they were leaving for Boston. They packed up their family and what little they owned in their 1924 Model T four-door touring car and set off across the state.

Boston was the first real city they had ever been in and he soon realized it was too big. They followed the roads up the North Shore and settled in Marblehead; a town with a name that he recognized from sea stories he'd read as a kid.

After a number of years and a variety of jobs, Oliver scraped enough money together to put one bus, then two and three, into service. Then the Depression hit everyone's pocketbooks. Even bus fare was a luxury. So his chance meeting gave him an idea. His wife told him he was crazy, but Oliver Lodge decided to propose an outrageous business proposition to the rich doctor with the expensive car.

"Give me $3,500 cash for 80 percent of my bus company. All but $500 of the money will go into real estate. I'll split any of my profits in that business fifty-fifty."

The bus company was a nickel and dime business. Dr. Crannell didn't expect any kind of return. But the doctor saw merit in Lodge's business plan and he admired his entrepreneurial spirit in the worst economic times. His land grab could mean tens of thousands, if not more, when the economy recovered. Crannell agreed to the terms without argument.

Actually, neither Oliver Lodge nor Dr. Crannell could have imagined what this simple deal ultimately would be worth. They acquired, developed and sold their way from rural property to city blocks. There was prime real estate along the ocean for homes and farmland that the state bought up for highways.

By the late 1940s, the $3,500 loan paid dividends of $2.4 million. By the mid 1950s, the Lodge estate was valued at $14 million.

Oliver Lodge died in the mid 1960s, four years after his grandson Theodore Wilson Lodge was born.

Teddy's father, Oliver Jr., continued to manage the business, Lodge Properties. His mother, Katharine, donated her time to proper North Shore charities. They enjoyed their second-generation wealth, but raised Teddy in a supportive, normal, small town environment.

O'Connell wrote extensively about the next years in Teddy's life. He noted how Lodge excelled in school and in sports. He was reading well in First Grade, winning the spelling bees in Second. In Fourth Grade he won a Library Association Achievement Award for submitting the most book reports in a year. In Fifth Grade, he was introduced to music. He loved rock, and felt that James Taylor was writing just for him. But the 20th-century classical composers touched his soul. Copland. Gershwin. They captured the American spirit. The feeling haunted him and stirred his budding political consciousness. When he ran for Middle School president, he promised to advance the music program. And he won.

Outside of school, he threw himself into Boy Scouts. He made it to Eagle, and would have stayed with it longer if he hadn't been distracted. He discovered girls in the Ninth Grade. During this typically uncomfortable period he tried out "Ted" instead of Teddy. He hoped it might give him stature over the amazon women in his class. But it never really suited him well. His first girlfriend told him so.

Debbie Strathmore adored his wavy locks, his sense of humor, and his brilliance. Teddy loved her body and the pleasures it taught him.

They were, by every definition of the words, "going together" freshman year at Marblehead High. According to some friends, "probably doing it" by the spring. Though no biographies really delved into his early sex life.

Young Lodge inherited his grandfather's strength of character and physical ability. Since he was a kid he had always been outside, ruggedly athletic; an avid and able sailor. There was hardly a winter weekend that he wasn't begging to go to the slopes or a summer's day when he wasn't out on a sloop.

A few friends called him Bobby Jr., in honor of his political idol Robert F. Kennedy. In many ways it was a natural association. He looked and somewhat sounded like a Kennedy. The way he rolled his "r's." The way he threw caution to the wind. The way he won school elections. Teddy Lodge had charisma, he cared about people, and he had a beautiful girl on his arm. His friends were right. He was Bobby, Jr. and he probably *was* "doing it" already.

It was about that time that classmates actually envisioned Teddy in the White House. His school paper raised the possibility in an article about his bid for Freshman Class president. One teacher passed the article along to Bob Mehrman, an afternoon talk show host at a nearby radio station in Lynn. Mehrman was intrigued and booked Teddy on his call-in show the next day. This was his first interview; however, he presented himself with poise, humor and dignity. It raised his visibility even more.

A WBZ TV anchorman caught the radio show while driving to work and insisted that the news desk shoot a feature for the 6 P.M. broadcast. Within 24 hours, Teddy Wilson Lodge might as well have been running for President of the United States. He had made great friends with the camera.

His parents saw his potential, too. They decided that private school would give him the edge to get into Yale. And Yale could lead him into politics. So at age fifteen, Teddy applied to Harvard Essex, not far from his home in Amesbury. And that's when his life began to change radically.

His father died the summer before he left for school. It happened during a father-son baseball game at the Elks club—tragically when Oliver was pitching to Teddy.

With two strikes on his son and Teddy determined to get a solid hit off his father, Oliver suddenly clutched his chest. He looked at Teddy through pain and tears, immediately knowing what was happening. Then he collapsed. Paramedics tried to revive him but they couldn't.

Teddy didn't do much for the rest of the summer. He occasionally talked to his girlfriend, but primarily stayed with his mother, who he'd soon be leaving. He told her he should finish school at Marblehead and forget going away, but Katharine Lodge insisted that Teddy get on with his life. And so in September he left for boarding school.

Teddy threw himself into his studies. He became "Mr. Lodge" to most of his teachers and vowed to live up to the Harvard Essex's motto, "*Qui tacet consentit*"—"He who is silent agrees." Except during ski season.

In January of his sophomore year, Teddy and seven friends borrowed a red and gray VW bus for a skiing trip to Mount Washington. They were racing to beat an oncoming Nor'easter.

Teddy later explained how he saw a scruffy hippie on the side of the road, laden with boots, skis and backpack. O'Connell opined in his newspaper article that Teddy, like his grandfather, apparently had a soft spot for helping people in snowstorms. So even though the van was packed, they took on another rider for the trip to the North Conway, New Hampshire slopes.

As they headed up Route 93, the temperature dropped fast. The snow began to fall, then drifted across the road. Visibility diminished rapidly and they were quickly losing the light. According to the police records, a light brown Nova pulled up behind the VW and tailgated for a good 15 minutes, making a dangerous drive even more treacherous.

Teddy knew every twist and turn in the road and kept up the pace. But the driver behind him was on the horn the whole way. He finally drove up alongside Teddy and screamed a string of profanities. The Nova then passed the bus, only to slow down in front of them.

According to what Teddy recalled, at that point the hitchhiker started acting irrationally; signs of a drug high kicking in. He grabbed the steering wheel and swerved toward the rear end of the Nova. Track marks in the snow suggested that another car simultaneously approached from the opposite direction. Its lights may have cut through the oncoming snow, blinding Lodge while he struggled for control of the vehicle. Suddenly, the Nova slammed on the brakes.

First Teddy turned the wheel away from the edge of the road. But that only directed him into the oncoming car. The hitchhiker fought Teddy off and yanked the wheel toward the right again. The sudden maneuver on the slick mountain road put the minibus into an uncontrollable spin.

Teddy couldn't control the 2200-pound VW. It crashed through two baby pines on the side of road and then careened off the edge, headfirst toward a bluff 50 feet below. From there it skidded upside-down onto a mountain access road where it stopped and burst into flames.

A pickup truck with cross-country skiers was the first to find the twisted wreck. Six bodies were recovered from the interior. They could only be identified through their dental records. The driver and a man, later identified as the hitchhiker, had been thrown clear. Only one person survived, though badly hurt. Teddy Lodge.

Eight of his teeth were knocked out. His jaw and nose were broken. His right leg was fractured, four ribs were cracked, his left shoulder was dislocated and he suffered a spinal injury that the paramedics could not fully evaluate. And he was unconscious.

His mother would never see him again. The day after the accident, friends from the Lodges' church came to the house to drive Katharine to the North Conway hospital. They knocked on the door. She didn't answer. After waiting ten minutes they went around the back. The porch door was unlocked. They went inside and discovered that Katharine had collapsed while packing. She'd suffered a fatal heart attack.

Michael O'Connell concluded his article. Lodge's life was the water cooler talk of the morning.

CHAPTER 8

WASHINGTON, D.C.
WASHINGTON CENTER HEALTH CLUB
8:00 A.M.

Scott Roarke's private cell phone hooked to his shorts vibrated while he was spinning at ungodly speeds. "Come on, leave me alone," he said, ignoring the call. After awhile he got his wish and he returned to the front page of *The New York Times* and the various reports on the shooting the day before. He'd already gone through *The Washington Post* but a *Times* writer really seemed to capture the mood.

A minute later the phone vibrated again. Only a handful of people had the number. Given the news, he was actually expecting a call.

"Okay, okay," he said to no one in particular. He stopped pedaling and flung his feet to the side. The pedals would continue to rotate for another minute.

He fumbled for the phone and it fell to the gym floor. The caller was gone by the time he picked it up. The screen read "Caller ID unavailable." He punched in a number from memory. It was a line that was also private and skipped the master switchboard.

A woman's voice answered the phone warmly. "Hi, honey. Thanks for getting back to me."

"Hi sweetheart," Roarke said. "Everything okay?" Roarke topped off at six feet. He was muscular, but with more of a swimmer's physique or the body of someone skilled in the martial arts, which he was. Chest hairs flowed over his t-shirt and his biceps pushed at the threads. Roarke's open smile set him apart from other Secret Service agents with coldness chiseled on their faces. And although he had a slight scar under his chin, he was approachable; more friendly-looking than dangerous. He kept his dark brown head of hair a little longer than required, but clipped his sideburns short. He exuded an air of confidence, though he was quieter than people would at first expect. Roarke also had a flirtatious manner, which came out when he felt comfortable with people. To all others he always remained on guard.

"Fine," she said, "but I miss you."

"Me, too."

"I thought you'd call me this morning and I wouldn't have to call you," she said.

"I'm sorry."

"Well, as long as we're talking now, that's all that matters."

"Yeah," Roarke added. "So…"

"So." Roarke said, wiping the perspiration from his brow.

"So, can you come by this morning?"

"I guess."

"Say ten-thirty?"

"Ten-thirty it is."

"I guarantee you it'll be interesting," she offered.

"I bet. Usual place?"

"You got it. 10:30."

"Uh-huh. See ya," Roarke said and hung up.

The entire exchange lasted only eighteen seconds. Louise Swingle timed it on her stop watch. Roarke had an internal clock that was ticking away as well. They were always careful not to talk long. In fact, he was a second away from hanging up when they finished.

Scott Roarke looked at the newspaper again and shook his head. He wasn't surprised by the phone call. Not one bit. And though it was unlikely anyone was eavesdropping, they kept the exchange sounding like so many others between consenting adults. But in this case they were adults who consented to work for President Morgan Taylor.

Roarke had been Taylor's "go-to guy" for two years. As such, he should have headed over to his boss' office first thing in the morning. Instead, he chose the gym. Deep down inside he liked getting called. Still, he didn't know how much longer he'd be able to keep up the pace.

Officially, he was a salaried government worker earning $114,300 a year. But he didn't have to apply for the job or fill out the damned OF 612 or SF 171 application forms for Federal Employment.

Roarke was hand-picked for PD16. He also drew additional expenses from another account; one that had him banking in Drachmas, Yen, Eurodollars or other national currencies whenever his work took him on the road.

It had been that way ever since Uncle Sam had noted his unique skills in basic.

Early in his training, a mean son of a bitch of a sergeant named Miller took a liking to Roarke. That meant he made his life a living hell, throwing every imaginable obstacle in the recruit's path, all to test his limits.

Nothing stopped Roarke. Not grueling runs. Not lack of sleep. He toughened with heavier backpacks and hardened in extreme elements.

At the end of his basic training, Roarke wasn't shipped off to a cushy assignment in Europe or Asia. On Sgt. Miller's recommendation, Roarke received special papers sending him to a greater hell that the Army made available for future intelligence officers or spies.

His post was in the middle of Utah at a location that didn't officially exist and where commercial jets weren't allowed to fly over. He became a member of the Defense Intelligence Agency (DIA), an outfit that both analyzes data amassed by the CIA and is dispatched to do some "dirty work" around the world.

The DIA turns out "agents no one talks about."

They've deployed clandestine spies in the Persian Gulf, Somalia, Pakistan, Russia and China. They are drawn from Army, Navy and Air Force soldiers who have "volunteered" through the good graces of observers like Miller.

DIA ran their operations under a unit known as Defense Humint Service. In spy language, "Humint" stands for human intelligence—the kind of data that is collected by agents on the ground.

Reporters who dig deep enough to confirm the existence of the DIA's efforts barely scratch the surface. The Pentagon only admits to having retooled some separate intelligence programs run by the numerous services into one. And yet, it is a fully functional, impressively managed operation which outnumbers the CIA analysts by nearly 10 to 1.

Early in their history, Humint teams scored some impressive successes in the field. In the 1990s, DIA officers bought parts of a Russian SA-10 air defense missile system from the former Soviet republic of Belarus. The result of the procurement allowed the U.S. Air Force to better evade Russian radar.

A few years earlier they participated in the capture of an officer in the command structure of Somali warlord Mohammed Farrah Aidid.

In the mid 1980s, Army intelligence officers unearthed a North Korean division that spy satellites had missed. The Army also fractured an agreement that Iraq forged with China to build a nuclear reactor.

These barely supervised, super secret agents of the Pentagon worked in concert with the CIA, which gets most of the attention and all of the credit. And that was just the way Roarke liked it then and now.

Attention was bad. Credit, he didn't need. People who remembered faces could kill you. So he shunned being photographed, always trying very hard to blend into his surroundings.

Now, as the most trusted member of PD16, a unit of the Secret Service not unlike DIA, Roarke knew the faith Morgan Taylor placed in him. Yet, even to most friends, he passed himself off as merely another lowly member of the president's walking bullet-stoppers, when, in truth, he was much more.

Roarke picked up the newspaper from the health club floor. The news was definitely not good. He considered it might be time to think about a radical sabbatical. After all, at age thirty-six, he was becoming an old man in a young man's business.

However, depending upon the election results in November, that decision might be made for him. He could have a considerable amount of time on his hands and a government retirement package waiting at the back door.

Hell, he wondered. *Maybe I should just vote against the boss and help save myself a lot of grief.*

He flung *The New York Times* back onto the health club floor and returned to spinning. He had ninety minutes before he had to be at the White House.

CHAPTER 9

TRIPOLI, LIBYA
THE SAME DAY

Abahar Kharrazi read the *International Herald Tribune*. It carried Michael O'Connell's story from *The Times*. Halfway through he shook his head in disgust. *What an appalling shot.* If this gunman had worked for him, he'd have him thrown into Abu Salim Prison, tortured, and then left to contemplate his failure for the rest of his miserable life. It was the kind of cruel streak that seemed to run in the family.

THE WHITE HOUSE
10:30 A.M.

"This better be important. I was working on my self image," Roarke joked as he entered the Oval Office.

"Most people would open with, 'Hello, Mr. President.'"

"Hi, boss," Roarke managed.

"Here, have some water. Sit down and shut up," the president said, going to his refrigerator.

Morgan Taylor knew he had Roarke's respect. And it went way beyond the presidency. Roarke loved his country. It's just that the accoutrements of the White House didn't affect him. Morgan Taylor's judgement did, however. That was the subject of today's meeting.

The president tossed Roarke a bottle of Evian. "Thanks for coming."

"I work for you."

The president chuckled. "Yes, you do. So let's talk about work for today."

Roarke cracked open the bottle's plastic seal.

"I have a, let's call it, a *project* for you."

"Project? That's different than an assignment or a job. It's certainly different than a mission." Roarke was used to Morgan Taylor choosing his words carefully. All presidents had to. But Taylor was better than most.

"Just call it a *project* for now."

"About Lodge?"

"As a matter of fact, yes."

"You put him under Secret Service protection early?"

Another yes.

Roarke took a seat on the couch opposite one of the two revolutionary-era chairs in the Oval Office. One had been owned by Thomas Jefferson. The other belonged to John Adams. Morgan Taylor sat in the Adams chair, which signaled this was political not philosophical. He never let on that he had the president figured out. It was a great game to play, however.

"By law he wasn't entitled to be under Service watch for another few weeks or until he got the nomination. But considering the circumstance…" The president lowered his eyes.

"Totally understandable. Someone tried to nail him."

"And the killer is still out there. He could try again."

"What does the Bureau have?"

"Nothing."

The president leaned forward and reached for the cup of coffee he'd left on the rectangular table that separated them.

Roarke drank right from the bottle and waited. "So what can I do? It sounds like you already made the right move."

"All that does is put a blanket around him. Since we don't have the shooter and this seems very planned, I have to assume that this is not the work of a wacko. It could be politically based."

"Oh come on. A guy sits waiting to take a pot shot at a presidential candidate. Of course it's *all* politics."

"But whose?"

"Not my area."

The president spoke for him. "He's not all that liberal for a Democrat. He's less supportive of Israel than he probably should be."

"The Mossad?" Roarke asked. "They'd have a reason not to want Lodge in."

"But he wasn't going to get in. Lamden had him beat. And I'd have to fuck it up pretty good not to take Henry in November."

"What's Evans say?"

Jack Evans was the DCI, the Director of the Central Intelligence Agency.

"He's checking his assets inside Israel. It's not out of the question, but I hope to God it's not the Israelis. I can't even begin to fathom…" He didn't need to finish the thought.

"Any right-wing radicals? There are dozens of extremist groups out there."

"The Bureau is running that down."

Roarke repeated his question. "So again, what can I do?"

"I want you to quietly see if Lodge has some old skeletons in the closet, some people who have it in for him."

"Wouldn't you do better with Mulligan? His guys are up in Hudson. They'll find something."

"He's got his number one team there. And so far they're like audience members at a Lance Burton magic show. Clueless."

"But I'm not an investigator."

"Yeah, but you do know how to read signs that no one else sees. You're familiar with Lodge's story?"

"Yeah, I read it this morning."

"And how does it strike you?"

"Sad."

"Is that all?"

"What do you mean?"

"There are two Teddy Lodges. The public one and the private one. The public falls in love with the handsome, dynamic, born-again Kennedy. Those of us who've worked with him in Congress know that he's shrewd and manipulative. But that's no reason for us to permit an assassin to get a good shot at him again. Now that he's under our protection, I'd like to know if there's anyone from his past who might not want him as president."

"I still don't think I'm right for this."

"Just head up to his hometown. See what happens." The president held a finger to his lips. "Quietly."

"With all due respect, you sure this isn't about a certain standing president's job security?"

Morgan Taylor stood at attention then went to his desk. He

returned with the day's editions of *The Washington Post, The New York Times,* and *The Baltimore Sun.* Each of the papers had a picture of Jennifer Lodge in her husband's arms.

"We need to find out who did this, Scott. It's about him. Not me."

CHAPTER 10

MIAMI, FLORIDA
10:59 A.M.

Fisher Island residents cherished their isolation. Although they lived barely a mile from the heart of Miami Beach, it sometimes seemed like an ocean away. In some ways, it was. The only way to reach either the luxurious homes or the magnificent golf course was by boat. The car ferry shuttled back and forth from the mainland every fifteen minutes. Those who could afford it also had the option of coming and going as they pleased on their own yachts.

Ibrahim Haddad was one of them. He bought his palatial estate in the late 1990s. The 8,500-square-foot two-story home contained soaring vaulted ceilings, interior gardens, a stately mahogany library, a computer-run kitchen, and an array of satellite dishes. Haddad rarely entertained or invited neighbors over. He and his staff of four—more bodyguard than domestic help—lived in relative seclusion. He eschewed membership to the Fisher Island Club, an invitation-only facility and golf course. He dined at home, swam in his 50-foot long pool and exercised in his personal gym.

At age 63, Ibrahim Haddad was an enigma to the Fisher Island community. No one really knew him, though they could see him coming. His 6'4" frame made him stand out, and his voice, deep and husky, reinforced an air of self-confidence. He kept his gray hair closely cropped and dyed his pencil thin moustache a deep black. While his face could look open and inviting from a distance, his eyes projected coldness up close. He could actually appear pleasant to anyone who got a brief glimpse of him. But they were few and far between.

For the first two years he lived in Fisher Island, members of the club tried to figure him out. In time, even they grew tired of the sport. Haddad was too hard to read.

His habits wouldn't have suited the club crowd anyway. He didn't smoke or drink. He refused to order off a standard menu and he disdained small talk. He never married or dated in the normal sense. He used women as needed; and even then on his terms, in hotel suites, never at his own home. And only once. Those who did know Haddad, and the list was short, considered him ruthless; ruthless enough never to cross. The people who worked for him followed the same rule, even more cautiously.

Ibrahim Haddad finished his morning tea, checked his watch. He pressed a button and the semi-circular doors of a nine-foot cabinet peeled aside revealing a huge Sony hi-def television set. Another button on his remote turned the television on to the coverage in New York.

NEW YORK CITY
ESSEX HOUSE HOTEL
11:00 A.M.

"You'll have to forgive me," Congressman Lodge said quietly. "I have prepared a statement. I don't think I'll be up for any questions."

Reporters and camera crews from New York's major newspapers and the nation's television networks and news syndicates listened to the man at the far end of the Kensington Conference Room on the second floor of the Central Park South hotel. On another day, these same people would be clawing over one another to shout out their questions. Today they were utterly quiet and respectful.

Lodge began with obvious difficulty. "Yesterday, my wife Jennifer was killed by an assassin. The man is still at large. You have his description. I hope to God that you'll help the FBI find this man.

Please," he strained to say, "I want him brought to justice for what he did yesterday."

The still cameras clicked. Dozens of them...hundreds of pictures would be exposed on film or digital chips before the congressman offered his thanks and left. Yet every photograph would look exactly like the others: painfully sad.

"This man intended to shoot me. In doing so he would have usurped the election process, taken your voice away. He failed at that. He succeeded, however, in taking my wife from me." The congressman broke down. No one dared speak.

THE WHITE HOUSE
THE SAME TIME

President Taylor watched from the White House. Seven television monitors in the Oval Office were tuned to the news. CNBC, MSNBC, CNN, NBC, ABC, CBS, and Fox News.

"He's going to stay in. I can feel it," the president said to his chief of staff.

"I don't know, Mr. President. He could just wait four years or even eight," John Bernstein offered.

"No, Bernsie. He's going for it now. Just look at him. He'll play this out. And triple jump over Lamden right to the convention," the president said dispassionately.

Taylor paced in the back of the room waiting for Lodge to pull himself together. Under his breath he said, "He's good. He's really good."

The president used the remote to turn the sound down. "Okay. Enough of him. We'll figure out what to do with Lodge. What happened overnight in India?"

Morgan Taylor was the 12th American president to deal with unrest between India and Pakistan. He focused on it as much as his predecessors had on Israel and Palestine. And he had about as much success.

Once more, the news was not good and it wasn't getting any better. The tenuous *rapprochement* between the two nations, begun during the Bush administration, was just too fragile to last. Over the past century, there was simply more history of war than there was of peace.

Pakistan's nuclear program was based on a general desire to match India's. At first it was research. Then plutonium production. Actual atomic bomb development eventually followed, then testing. Finally, launch systems came online.

For decades, most of the world ignored what was largely a battle of words between the two nations that had formerly been one. It became easy to forget the thousands of deaths attributable to the 50 years of tension and outright war.

According to the CIA reports that President Taylor now received, India had between 60 to 120 weapons of mass destruction. Pakistan's output of bombs was estimated at more than 65, with another four to six added to the arsenal every year. The overkill was grotesque and, if ever unleashed, the entire world would be embroiled.

In reality, neither country could survive victory, let alone defeat. Yet a war that could obliterate a life-long enemy from the face of the earth was still appealing to some generals. That's what made the danger very real.

Morgan Taylor kept an open channel to the leaders of each country, hoping that calmer minds would prevail. In turn, they privately tried to control their own military and prayed that the United States president could prevent any conflict from intensifying to a full-scale war. But it was getting more difficult. Internal revolts in Pakistan staged by fundamentalists threatened the region. And predictably, India intensified its efforts, building up reserves on the border, which according to CIA Director Jack Evans' written report this morning, only inflamed the situation.

Morgan Taylor looked even further down the line. Should Pakistan, with its splinter regimes and myriad political ideologies, fall into the hands of Muslim fundamentalists, the terrorist possibilities became enormous. But perhaps even more likely was that Pakistan might one day enter into an unholy alliance with another Muslim nation, and provide them with nuclear technology or weapons. The result could destabilize the Middle East or worse. And if President Morgan Taylor knew one thing for certain, it was that Israel would strike quickly and first against any Arab neighbor that acquired the bomb.

"So let's have it, Bernsie."

"According to DCI, his satellites show another 20,000 troops on the way. Convoys and trains. They're taking up positions along a 600 mile front."

"Total numbers?" the president asked.

"Roughly 50,000."

"Damn it. This is turning out to be one fucked up year."

When Teddy Lodge left the podium the room was silent. There were none of the cheers and applause that always accompanied him. Everyone respected his privacy. The press was informed by Newman that the only reason he faced them today was to enlist the public's help in apprehending his wife's killer. Teddy said nothing about the campaign. And as a result, the reporters had their story. They knew what Teddy Lodge was going to do. He'd wait for the New York voters to speak.

Geoff Newman walked beside Lodge down the hall. Secret Service agents were at their front and back. "Just the right tone," Geoff Newman said out of earshot of the agents. "Pushed all the right buttons."

"Shut up, for God's sake. This isn't the time or the place." the congressman shot back.

One Secret Service agent turned. "Is everything all right, sir?"

"Yes. I'm just upset."

Newman held back a half a step and didn't say another word.

Outside, the newly assigned Secret Service made a path for the congressman to the limousine parked in front of the Essex House. Lodge politely acknowledged the well-wishers and their cameras with a simple nod and a hand in the air.

Newman opened his mouth, then thought better of saying anything. A Secret Service agent was driving. Another was in the front seat.

They pulled into traffic along 59th Street and drove to LaGuardia for the flight back to Vermont and Jenny's funeral.

After they merged onto the East Side Highway Ten, Newman said in a low voice not to be overheard, "No more press for the rest of the week. We'll decide on Saturday about the Sunday talk shows. They'll all want you. But there will be ground rules. We've got to manage this very carefully from here on out."

HUDSON, NEW YORK
1:34 P.M.

"I don't like this one bit," the FBI field chief said to his team. Bessolo was pissed. He felt they should have more by now. "Look, people. We're going over everything again. But slower. I want prints. I want hairs. Fibers. Find some of his fucking cum. And I need more than a blind alley on his Galil. This guy's not as good as he thinks. He's slipped up somewhere. Find it!"

Bessolo had confidence in the investigators he brought to Hudson even though he talked to them like a Marine drill sergeant facing a squad of wet recruits. He also believed that the FBI lab could turn the slimmest shred of evidence into something worth pursuing.

The FBI Laboratory had been around since 1932. Bessolo ran his corner of it as if it would lose its funding tomorrow unless his people personally delivered.

Unfortunately for everybody, after the first 22 hours they had nothing.

"We're trying Roy," said Neal Berkowitz, his DNA expert. "It's as if a guy was here for a month and vaporized. I've never seen anything like it."

They had been through 301 thoroughly. First photographing every square inch, then meticulously examining the blankets, pillows, rug, towels, and curtains for hairs, tissues, saliva, skin flakes, and even for the semen that Bessolo demanded. Any residue could prove important. Hair examination could determine race even if disguised through bleaching or dyeing. Fingernails could help plot a biological profile of the assassin. But so far they had nothing for the Forensic Biology section to work with; no samples to send to the new DNA facility in Manhattan.

Latent, or hidden, fingerprints would hold clues. These prints, left by hands or bare feet of a person, are likely to be the most valuable piece of information gathered at a crime scene. But there were no latent prints. Nor were there any visible prints, those transferred to foreign substances such as grease, blood, or dust. There simply were no fingerprints to photograph with the T-Max 400J film they'd brought. None to send to Quantico via satellite for cross-referencing.

Everything had been wiped clean with expert attention, the patience of Job and a combination of ethanol/Phenylphenol, which Berkowitz easily identified as everyday Lysol.

"We're dealing with a real pro, Roy," the agent concluded. "He's not a lunatic. There's purpose to this. This guy knew what he was doing. Except for the fact that he bungled his shot."

MARBLEHEAD, MASSACHUSETTS
2:45 P.M.

Roarke followed Route 1A up the coast to Marblehead. He did a little better than the speed limit in his rented Mustang from Hertz. The car demanded a little pressure on the gas, but Roarke didn't want to get nabbed by any local police. Taylor had been very specific. "*Quiet.*"

His first stop was Marblehead High. O'Connell's article was beside him with key words underlined, each a name or a reference to a possible lead: the high school; Debbie Strathmore, Lodge's first girl-friend; Mehrman, the retired radio interviewer; and the Boy Scouts. Roarke also hoped to get some answers about the disposition of the family estate.

None of this was his strong suit. Roarke liked working the field, staying out of sight. This put him in the public eye. But he had his orders.

He parked near the bank, across the street from the school, and locked his Swiss made Sig Sauer P229 in the glove compartment. He preferred the Sig to the standard Secret Service issue Uzi with its 20 rounds. Just personal taste…touch…and feel. No one took exception. In fact, few people argued with Roarke for any reason. They didn't know much about the president's man, but reputation preceded him.

Roarke crossed the parking lot to the front entrance. He was old enough to be the father of any of the kids. He wondered if that would ever happen.

It had been years since he'd been in a high school. Times had surely changed. Uniformed guards replaced Student Service monitors in the halls. And knives and guns were pulled instead of punches.

Marblehead High was peaceful compared to most other schools in the country, but too many nice schools had been the scene of horrible crimes. No school board could take a chance anymore.

"Hello, I hope you can help me, Ms. Fraser." He read the name Clara Fraser off the nameplate on her desk in the administration office.

"Yes?" the 60-something secretary answered without emotion.

"My name is Roarke. I'm with the Secret Service in Washington."

"Is anything wrong here?"

"No, no, no. This is just routine. We're guarding the congressman now and…"

She interrupted. "A little late, don't you think?"

He ignored the comment. "We were just assigned." This was already getting beyond the "quiet" inquiry the president wanted.

"I suppose you have some identification, Mr.…"

"Roarke. Yes. Here."

He produced his photo ID. Clara Fraser peered at the picture, at Roarke, at the picture again, and once more at Roarke.

"Looks official," she commented.

"I can assure you, it is."

"Then what would you like?"

"Some help finding some people who might remember Congressman Lodge when he was a student. Maybe some of his school records, too."

"Well, Mr. Roarke, we're not allowed to show you any school files," she said gesturing behind her. "Massachusetts State Law prohibits us."

"But perhaps there's a teacher who knew him, someone I can speak with."

She thought for a moment. "No. I think everyone's gone."

"Then someone who's retired and might still be living in the area?"

"Hold on. I'll be right back."

Fraser went into the principal's office and closed the door. About five minutes later, it opened for a moment, then closed again. About fifteen minutes later a vibrant man appearing to be in his early forties came out, followed by Fraser.

"I'm Dr. Huddleston, the principal."

"Dr. Huddleston, thank you. I'm Roarke and…"

"Yes," he interrupted more out of enthusiasm than bad manners. "Ms. Fraser explained. I'm sorry we can't help with Mr. Lodge's academic record."

Roarke noted that Fraser positioned herself directly in front of the 'L's,' as if to block them from view.

"But I do have a telephone number for you," the principal continued. He handed over a green 3x5 card on which he'd written a name and address. "Pat Sullivan. Theodore Lodge's English teacher. He lives about three miles from here. No one else is around. It's hard to keep people in education these days, Mr. Roarke."

"Thank you," Roarke said.

"He was everyone's favorite teacher. I'm sure Pat will have some stories to tell you. He sure could give you an earful about me. We all had him."

Roarke thanked the principal and made a mental note of precisely where the Lodge file was likely to be kept. He considered recovering it at night, but figured the last thing the president needed was a burglary at a Democratic rival's high school. No, a break-in would not be good. He'd have to make friends on the inside for anything he really needed.

Sullivan lived in a weathered two-story New England shaker facing the harbor. Roarke knocked on the retired teacher's door three times before a 75-year-old man opened it.

Sullivan wore a green turtleneck sweater and jeans. Roarke instantly saw why students liked him. He had energy and character, sparkling blue eyes, and a handshake that said he was happy to meet you. Sullivan was easily twenty years more youthful than his age and probably could still be teaching if he wanted to. But a quick assessment of the hand-carved masks that lined his hallway walls told Roarke that Sullivan now spent most of his time traveling.

After the introductions and pleasantries, Sullivan invited Roarke to sit down.

"Teddy was a great student. I remember him well. He was torn about going to Harvard Essex and he asked me what I thought. I wasn't his advisor, but he loved English and he was always in after class to discuss the latest books he'd read. He was a big Cheever and Updike fan. I think he even wrote Cheever once and got an answer back. And Teddy had talent, too. He could have been a brilliant writer. But he let a lot of things drop after his parents died. Who knows, maybe he still will. Presidents always write their autobiographies. And Carter wrote a novel."

"I see you have him elected already."

"Did you see his speech today?"

"No, did he say he was still running?" Roarke asked.

"No, which means yes."

"So you still follow him."

"Well, a bit." Sullivan showed some disappointment in his voice.

"Did you keep in touch after Teddy went to boarding school?"

"For awhile. A few letters. But after the accident I never heard from him again. Not a letter. Not a visit. Never."

Roarke understood why his disposition had changed.

"Why not, Mr. Sullivan?"

"Pat. Please, it's Pat. I was only Mr. Sullivan to my students. Actually 'Sully.' You know I retired nine years back?"

Roarke nodded. "And it looks like you've been keeping busy?"

"Oh?"

"Traveling. You have quite a collection of tribal masks—from the Amazon and South Africa."

"Very good, Mr. Roarke."

"Scott."

"Scott it is. You've traveled some yourself?"

"A bit." Roarke stopped short of saying anymore.

"You asked 'why not.' I can only assume that there was too much pain connected with coming home. He was at school in Amesbury, Harvard Essex Academy, when he had his accident and then his mother died. I'm sure he felt responsible for her heart attack. But I don't know. I'm an English lit teacher, ask a psychologist."

"And you've never talked to him since?"

"Oh, I tried when he got elected to Congress. I sent a letter congratulating him and even proposing that I come to Washington to visit. I didn't hear for a while. Then I called down. They never put me through. But eventually I did get a reply. Very matter of fact, explaining that the congressman was happy to learn that I was well. Blah, blah, blah. But nothing about my interest in seeing him. And no interest on his part to see me. Now, I can read between the lines pretty well. I am an English teacher, after all. And that letter, written by an aide, was a kiss off."

"I'm sorry," Roarke offered.

"I guess people change." He tried to conceal his disappointment. "Of course, I still voted for him in the Massachusetts primary and will again in November if he makes it. Especially now."

Roarke was about to leave not knowing much more than before he came. At the door, just before the good-byes, Sullivan added an aside.

"Funny thing is, no one I know has heard from Teddy since he left the area for good. Isn't that a little odd for someone running for president?"

Roarke had no idea if Lodge would still run, but he had to agree, it was odd.

CHAPTER 11

HUDSON, NEW YORK
4:45 P.M.

Because of the need to question everyone at the hotel, the St. Charles forgave the normal check out times. Roger C. Waterman finally turned in his room key late in the afternoon. He had been extremely cooperative, but he had nothing to offer Bessolo, who wished him well as he settled up his bill.

Carolyn Hill also caught him at the door. "You'll be back soon?" she asked hopefully.

"Might not be until well after the 4th…" There was that thought again. He could almost taste her. She looked that good to him. *As Waterman?* he wondered. Hell, maybe he'd sweep her off her feet as someone else.

"or a few weeks after that," he continued. "Besides, this place will be a little busy for awhile. I think it's going to be hard to get a room at the St. Charles considering all of the reporters and police around."

Waterman was right about that. The St. Charles was sold out for the next three weeks. Television microwave trucks encircled the park; everybody in town would be on camera before they left. But not Roger C. Waterman. It was time for him to disappear, which he did very, very well.

MARBLEHEAD, MASSACHUSETTS
5:10 P.M.

Michael O'Connell asked pretty much the same questions that Roarke had. He talked to Clara Fraser, and then to Pat Sullivan, and learned about a government guy who'd visited earlier.

On a whim he decided to drive to the site of the old Lodge home. It was up closer to the Salem line, a few minutes from town.

Teddy Lodge had sold the property years ago. The structure had since been torn down, the land sub-divided for a 24-unit condominium complex surrounded by a parking lot. The original trees on the estate were gone and the backyard, which had formerly abutted a forest, now bordered a shopping mall.

Across the street was an old Tudor style home, probably a good 150 years old. Maybe someone there would remember the family.

O'Connell waited for traffic to pass, then he ran across the road to see if anyone was home.

An elderly woman answered the door. Yes, she had lived there when the Lodges were neighbors. Yes, she knew young Teddy. Yes, she saw the house come down. All of this would go into the next story he filed.

"Oh, one more thing, Mr. O'Connell," she said at the door. "My daughter Deborah used to be his girlfriend."

"You're Mrs. Strathmore?"

"Yes."

"May I come in?" he politely asked. "I'd like to find out how I can reach her."

The 76-year-old widow lowered her head, then bravely looked at the reporter. "That's not going to be possible. She died three years ago."

"Like I told that *New York Times* writer, it happened six years ago. A hit and run," she repeated to Scott Roarke an hour later. "They never found the driver."

Roarke learned that O'Connell was also on the trail. He had to assume O'Connell knew about him.

"Where did this happen, Mrs. Strathmore?"

"Cambridge. Debbie was teaching at Boston Latin. Six months before her wedding. We'd just sent out the invitations. They never found him. I told you that, didn't I? He's still out there. It makes me sick."

"I'm so sorry," he reached over to console her. She was obviously having a hard time telling the story again.

"Do you mind if I ask whether your daughter had invited Congressman Lodge?"

"Yes, she did. They hadn't seen one another since high school. When he moved away they wrote one another constantly. Then he broke everything off."

"After his car accident?" he speculated.

"Yes. How did you know?"

Roarke ignored the question. He looked around the woman's house. It was feeling empty. Her husband had died of cancer; her daughter was gone. There were only fading memories where there should have been pictures of grandchildren. The notion triggered a question.

"And he was coming to the wedding?"

"No. I remember he checked that he couldn't. But there was no note with it, which was terribly disappointing to Debbie. She never said anything, but I knew she thought it."

"Maybe you have some things I can look through."

Mrs. Strathmore began rubbing her hands. *She must have arthritis.*
"Like what?"

"Letters, or pictures of your daughter and Teddy?"

Now she began scrunching her fingers in her palms, as if to fight off cramping. *Poor woman.*

"Oh, there might be something. I don't know. I can't think of anything in particular. If there were they'd be in boxes in the basement. It's been years. And I lost a lot when the pipes broke."

She realized that Roarke was looking at her hands. "Besides, it's hard for me to go through things," she said uncomfortably.

"I understand."

Roarke knew he wouldn't find anything here. It was just another heartbreaking sidebar to Lodge's early life.

By the time Roarke put his feet up on the bed and switched on the TV, he'd had it. Between traveling, driving, and interviewing people, he was exhausted. He opted for room service and TV at the Marriott in Peabody, about six miles from Marblehead.

"Dateline" was just beginning. Of course, their lead story was on the death of Jennifer Lodge, though there was nothing new to report. FBI Director Robert Mulligan would not comment on the investigation. The witnesses all told slightly different versions of the same thing.

The report contained an interview with a few Hudson police officers. Brenner and another whose name Roarke didn't get because his lobster roll and New England clam chowder were at the door. By the time Roarke settled up his check and tipped the bellman, "Dateline" was into its analysis of Teddy Lodge's now historic Hudson speech. He had heard snippets before, but found himself completely caught up in it now.

"We strike partnerships by sharing food and building up economies. We give. We get. We educate the world's uneducated, we make them intellectually stronger against dictators who would take advantage of their lack of knowledge. We give and we get."

Roarke could see why Lodge exerted such power over voters. He came across as a polished and effective communicator, making every word and gesture count. Nothing was out of place.

"Yes, we give and we get," the crowd chimed in. *"We Give and We Get." "We Give and We Get!"*

Over and over. It was infectious and hypnotizing because Roarke, like everyone watching, knew what they'd see next.

"It's time for a family of nations in a world apart. Time for a family that will last into all of our tomorrows…a family for you…and…" Roarke held his breath on the pause. *"And…a family for me."*

He saw Congressman Lodge tilt his head forward for barely a blink of an eye. He wiped a tear with his left hand. Behind him, his wife suddenly straightened up as if in shock. Then she fell backwards.

No more than a half-second elapsed between the congressman's last words and his wife's death.

Roarke allowed himself the cruelest of thoughts. *If only he hadn't bent forward.*

BURLINGTON, VERMONT
MONDAY EVENING

Teddy Lodge had flown into Burlington via a commuter out of LaGuardia. He sat alone on the plane. If anyone had come close to him, he knew that Newman would have run interference. Newman also took care of all the arrangements for Jennifer Lodge's funeral.

No one questioned his withdrawal from the scheduled 8 o'clock debate with the Governor of Montana. Seasoned columnists and commentators predicted he'd lie back in the running in four years. Virtually every AM radio talk show was filled with public opinion to the contrary. "Teddy should stay in it."

A Secret Service driver met them at the baggage claim. After loading up the car, Lodge went straight to his deadly silent house, where he poured himself a glass of Fonseca 20-year Port. He lit a fire in the rustic fireplace of his library and fell asleep in front of the flames. Tomorrow New York would vote and he would say goodbye to Jennifer.

CHAPTER 12

TRIPOLI, LIBYA
TUESDAY, JUNE 24

The unseasonable heat rose off the city's pothole-strewn cement streets, choking the energy out of the people. Without any breeze to circulate the air today, Tripoli swam in summertime perspiration and the stench of rotting garbage. But according to the weather forecasts on General Jabbar Kharrazi's controlled broadcasts, it was another glorious day in the nation's capital.

This was news in the hands of a skilled propagandist. He could control the temperature that was reported to people. It didn't matter that their own thermometers read 38.8° C or 102° F. If General Kharrazi, the latest self-proclaimed "Brother Leader," said it was the normally comfortable 84° F, then it was comfortable.

But weather wasn't on the mind of another Kharrazi just now. The General's son Fadi slammed his fist on his desk. He had summoned the editor of his newspaper, *Al-Fatah*, to his offices on the 8th floor of his downtown media headquarters. The man in front of him knew why he was there and was praying he would live to see another day. He might not. He'd made the error of printing an unflattering photograph showing Fadi frowning.

"Tell me what you were thinking, you imbecile! I should have my father remove you from the face of the earth," Fadi shouted.

The photograph showed him with a group of Tripoli businessmen. Unfortunately, it caught Fadi in an awkward, unfriendly pose.

"I'm sorry, sir. There were no others that were better."

"Then you shouldn't have run it!"

"But my photographer said you absolutely insisted that we print a photograph from the luncheon."

"Not if it's a shitty photograph!"

"But your instructions…"

"If it is no good, you make it better. You have a graphics station. You should have used it. Can't you think? This makes me look angry. Like I'm plotting to kill them." Fadi didn't say what he really felt. "They have to see me as friendly and compassionate. Do you understand that?" he screamed.

"Yes sir."

Fadi stood and walked around the trembling man.

He stopped directly behind him and said in a lowered voice, "Kalim, I'm told your children count on the reliability of your salary and your Mercedes for trips. Your wife loves her dresses. And your mistress," he added laughing, "ah, yes, I'm right aren't I?" The man nodded. "Your mistress loves the jewelry you give her. Yes?"

The editor breathed deeply. "Yes."

Fadi came around the front of his desk and stood no more than two inches from the editor. "Then I implore you, my friend, to edit *my* newspaper better." Then he added, "To your dying day."

Lakhdar al-Nassar, one of Fadi's personal aides, overheard the tirade while filing some papers his boss had left out. He kept his eyes down while Fadi escorted the man out, for al-Nassar, age 35, desperately hoped to make it to 36. He considered himself an obedient servant, but one who knew his place. Meanwhile, Fadi also saw him as one of his "clean-up men." For five years, he had pushed around papers during the day and people at night. He exercised power on a trickle-down basis. Just as Fadi could make life difficult for others, so could al-Nassar.

Of course Fadi knew al-Nassar was listening. He loved holding court as he practiced the fine art of fire and ice, learned at the foot of his father. If torture administered by a white-hot iron brought unbearable pain, the threat of prolonged cold on the festering blister usually resulted in complete submission. It was important, the General instructed his two boys, to demonstrate how to demand loyalty. "Always have an audience when you inflict pain, when you threaten infliction, or even when you reward your victim. Otherwise it's wasted. Your subject may never live to tell the story of his torture, but the witnesses will. And they will fear you and hold onto their precious power in a similar manner. Foremost in their minds will be their loyalty to you."

Fadi dismissed the editor and peered over at al-Nassar. His aide gave him an approving smile.

"Well, Lakhdar, what do you think he will do now?"

"Surely he will make examples of his own assistants for allowing the photograph to even reach his desk." Al-Nassar offered.

"As well he should, my *trusted* friend," he said, emphasizing the one word he wanted al-Nassar to retain. The aide got the meaning. "I wonder if we'll see the name of any of his principal staff in the obituaries tomorrow," bellowed Fadi.

Al-Nassar nodded but nothing more. Fadi did not invite laughter from his staff just as his ailing father had taught him. However, Fadi laughed himself, then got back to more personal business. He dialed a phone number and spoke softly. Al-Nassar gathered it was one of his boss' many women. He continued to pull the files together, but stopped when he caught Fadi's insistent finger snapping. Looking over he saw that Fadi was shooing him out with a wave of his hands.

The aide held up the stack of files and motioned to the cabinets and his incomplete work as if to ask, *"What about these?"* Fadi had an almost incomprehensible desire to archive any newspaper clip in the Arab or Western press that mentioned him or showed a picture. Lakhdar's principal duty was to supervise the work and make sure that everything was properly clipped and filed. But Fadi shot an insistent scowl back at him that really meant, in no uncertain terms, *"Out now and close the door!"*

He left with everything in his hands as Fadi swiveled in his $3,500 Eames chair and whispered something incredibly filthy to the woman on the other end.

Al-Nassar returned to his desk in the outer office. It had been hours since he peed, even longer since he had a Winston. He stopped long enough to put down his unfinished bundle of work and make for the door.

Omar Za'eem, another glorified paper pusher, rounded the doorway from the hall, nearly bumping into his superior.

"Sorry, sir." Za'eem offered.

"Don't be in so much of a rush you fool. Slow down."

"Sorry," he offered again. "It's just that I have contracts for Mr. Kharrazi. The RTL Television programs he wanted to buy. You know. But of course," he said for the sake of job security, "you need to see them first."

"Not now you idiot," Nassar proclaimed, establishing his position in the food chain. "He's busy. Anyway, I need a smoke. Leave it on my desk. I'll get to it."

Za'eem hated al-Nassar, just as al-Nassar really hated Fadi. It was the order of things.

"Now come have a smoke with me," Al-Nassar stated.

"Okay, okay. But in a few moments," Za'eem said as he passed the impatient Nassar. "Just as soon as I put these down and pick up the outgoing pile."

"I'll be downstairs. Don't take forever."

Omar Za'eem actually had two jobs, which kept the pencil thin assistant extremely busy, not to mention vigilant. He took special care, very special care that al-Nassar did not discover his primary line of work. Neither al-Nassar nor his boss would look kindly on him if they found out.

Part of what Omar did for his *other* work was best done with his supervisor out of the office. So he seized every opportunity for a few moments alone. He entered the offices and put the contracts down on his industrial metal desk. That's when he noticed a pile of documents strewn about. One caught his eye, probably because of the yellow tab sticking out of one dog-eared folder. He focused on it for a moment. He hadn't seen it before.

Ashab al-Kahf.

The name seemed vaguely familiar to him, but be couldn't quite place it.

Omar listened for footsteps in the hall. There were none. Fadi's door was closed, but he caught a few choice words from Fadi and the squeaking of his Eames chair.

Carefully, he sidestepped to better view the open paperwork. He kept his back half-turned to block the outside doorway. The 26-year-old assistant to Lakhdar al-Nassar, who might have looked too poor to eat better, had ample money. His salary from Fadi was a pittance. But his other money, his real life's savings, came from Fadi's brother Abahar. That's why he took extreme chances to read and learn everything he could.

He opened the yellow-tabbed file and read about *Ashab al-Kahf.* His almond eyes scanned the top sheet quickly. Omar Za'eem had a photographic memory; a natural ability, honed further through special training. He turned the page and read on. In less than two minutes he retained much of the text, though he didn't understand it. A good deal more remained, but time suddenly ran out. Fadi's chair had stopped squeaking.

He'd have that cigarette with Lakhdar al-Nassar now.

CHAPTER 13

HUDSON, NEW YORK
NEW YORK STATE PRIMARY ELECTION DAY
7:37 A.M.

"I think we have one," Beth Thomas calmly radioed Bessolo. The FBI agent in charge bounded up the stairs to the second floor to room 301.

"Let's have it," he said just shy of the doorway. He didn't want to disturb the scene.

Beth Thomas held a Ph.D. in criminology. Essentially she was an academician, but her knowledge of firearms was second to no man. She usually kept her gun in her leg holster, which she covered nicely with loose-fitting pants suits. She'd removed her jacket, revealing a simple white cotton blouse. Silk was no good for the job she was doing now. This was where Thomas couldn't afford to sweat. Nothing could be disturbed.

"Looks like McAlister rested his foot on the wall to steady his aim. Like this." She sat in a bridge chair with her arms raised in a standard rifle firing position. Thomas leaned into the seat back and put her left foot flat out but not touching the outer wall. "See, he put it flat against the wall. He probably didn't even realize what he was doing."

A latent footprint impression is usually transferred onto items like windowsills, doors, countertops and furniture. Shoes, as they wear, develop distinct characteristics through grooves, scrapes, and rougher areas or smoother sections. These signatures, when lifted properly and compared to an alleged perpetrator's shoes, can be an important link to a crime. The FBI doesn't have extensive files of footprints or an automated footprint identification system like AFIS for fingerprints. But criminologists have considered it very valuable information.

Naturally, they had to find the wearer and before the characteristics changed too much. But now they had a starting point.

Bessolo walked all the way into the room now and leaned into the spot that Beth pointed out. "Damned if I can find it. How'd you see it?"

"Hit it with my flashlight from an angle and I saw a little texture.

Enough to let me know he made a mistake. I'm sure we'll get the size, the manufacturer and the style. Maybe even more."

"Get the pictures. A 3-D impression would go a long way. And then see if you can lift the damned print."

The process would be time consuming. First the photographer on the team documented what she was doing from general to specific; from wide angle to tight shots. It would be very important to have a frame by frame account of the evidence gathering. The photographs could also be used as a backup if the print didn't lift off the wall properly.

After the FBI photographer was satisfied with his close-ups, it was Beth's turn at the print. She applied fingerprint powder to the surface with a small brush, sweeping it in a slow and careful back and forth motion, as if she were applying blush to her cheeks. She was perfect at it, placing very little pressure against the wall. Too much would remove the ridge detail of the latent impression. Two or three sweeps across were all she needed.

Next, she lightly blew the excess powder away with a small can of compressed air. That eliminated any air pockets over the print. Now it was time to lay a piece of adhesive tape directly over the print and very carefully try to lift the impression.

She carefully applied the four-inch strips of adhesive across the surface. Starting at one edge, she firmly ran her index finger along the center of the tape. The pressure transferred the latent print, outlined by the powder, onto the tape. It took five strips to cover the entire area of the impression.

She removed a pencil from her kit and now rolled it along the seam of the overlapped sections to fill in the breaks. In order to prevent static from building up in the tape and causing it to cling, she pulled the entire piece in one continuous motion. All of this was done precisely at a 45-degree angle. The textbook approach.

Finally, Beth placed the lifted impression onto a piece of poster board she had in her kit. She had chosen one that would be big enough. Experience told her it was a size 12 shoe, maybe 12½. Then she wrote her name, the date, the case number, and location on the upper right corner of the board. The photographer snapped another roll of pictures to document the procedure.

Bessolo watched intently as Beth placed the lift in an oversized plastic bag. As she sealed it she said, "Not much, but it's a start."

She handed it to her boss, blew a streak of her dark brown hair out of the way, then added as an afterthought, "Maybe we should close off the parking lot. There might be another print down there."

STAMFORD, CONNECTICUT
8:02 A.M.

He was Frank Dolan now. And his next stop wouldn't take long. Like his last effort, he had laid it all out well in advance. The time, the location, and the means. He had been waiting for instructions to proceed. He got them this day.

Dolan looked like he was ready for a day of work. Another harried executive clawing up the corporate ladder. He wore a practical summer outfit—tan pants, a smart blue shirt, and a double-breasted blue blazer. Today he parted his blond hair in the middle, had an artificial tan, and spoke with a slight New York accent. He couldn't hide the coldness in his eyes, but he could change the color. They were deep blue. When all was said and done, Dolan had the manner of a fast-paced Madison Avenue ad man. He fit in perfectly on the 8:10 A.M. Metro North commuter train to New York.

He'd made the trip a dozen times in a dozen different disguises. Each time he took a mental picture where his target stood, where he sat on the train, who he talked to, and how he spent his time on the forty-nine minute ride to Grand Central.

Today Steven Hoag didn't break his pattern. He kept to himself, bought the morning edition of the *Times* from the blind vender at the Stamford station, and queued up with the other passengers four minutes before the 8:10 was scheduled to pull in. He opened the paper to the front page and scanned the news.

No one took notice of the commuter except Dolan, who sized him up one more time, thinking to himself: *Once was in shape. Getting slow and flabby. Hair beginning to thin. Squinting at the paper. Could use reading glasses.*

Dolan moved through the crowd and brushed past an Asian man as he jockeyed to get closer to Hoag. He checked his watch just as any impatient ad exec would, shifted his balance on his feet numerous times, and stepped closer to Hoag.

"Pretty interesting," Dolan said over his shoulder.

"Hmm?" Hoag replied. He turned slightly to see who addressed him. A stranger.

"The news. Pretty interesting turn of events. What do you make of it?"

Hoag responded in an off-handed matter. "Yeah." He noted the picture of Lodge at his Manhattan press conference running next to O'Connell's latest article. "Makes you wonder."

"You can't feel safe anywhere," added Dolan over the rumble of the oncoming train.

"I haven't seen you before," Hoag remarked somewhat suspiciously. "New here?"

"Very. Wife's not even up from Atlanta yet," Dolan answered.

"Quiet town. Good place to get lost in. I'm Steven Hoag, and you are?"

Dolan noted definite suspicion in his voice.

"Frank Dolan." Damn, he wished he hadn't used that name. He wasn't certain if anyone had overheard him. Everyone was crowding as the train came to a complete halt. "Nice to meet you."

Dolan had already said too much. He didn't mind killing. He simply didn't want to talk too much to the poor souls.

Dolan climbed onboard ahead of Hoag. He quickly scoped a seat; one right next to Hoag's regular place. "This looks good," he noted to Hoag. "Here, enjoy the view." Hoag happily took the seat at the window.

After some innocuous small talk, Hoag unfolded his newspaper and returned to Michael O'Connell's report and the rest of the news. Dolan settled in and felt inside his suit jacket. His fingers touched his gun. The SIG-Sauer 9mm P-288, his weapon of choice for the day, is widely used by Special Ops forces and police departments around the world. *It might raise some eyebrows,* he thought. *All the better.*

The 8:10 stopped at Greenwich, Port Chester, New Rochelle and 125th Street on the way to its midtown destination.

At fourteen minutes out of Pelham, Dolan slipped his hand into his jacket and pivoted the gun out of the holster. Hoag was still thoroughly engrossed in O'Connell's reporting, with an almost personal interest.

Dolan rarely knew much about his prey. This one was no exception. He seemed nice enough. A few weeks earlier he had followed him to work at a major publishing firm on 54th and Avenue of the Americas. Hoag was a business manager with travel perks. Dolan learned that he spoke a few languages and regularly flew to international divisions in Europe, Asia, and the Middle East. The guy liked First Class and knew how to spend both his money and the company's. What a business manager actually did was beyond Dolan. Hoag was obviously successful at it, though. Probably taking down 180 to 200-K a year, he imagined.

Dolan also looked into the man's private life. Married eleven years. BMW and a Lexus. By checking the garbage he discovered that they liked travel magazines and ran a five-grand-a-month credit card bill. They drank French Bordeaux exclusively and had season tickets to the Met. All of this garnered from sifting through trash.

He and his wife, Irina, had no children. It was probably better he didn't, considering what Dolan was there to do. By his estimation, the man was about 46, give or take a few years. Whatever his age, he wouldn't be celebrating any more birthdays.

Dolan chose the train because he liked the noise and the darkness. The noise and the darkness were about to work very well for him.

The 416 blared its horn as it entered the Bronx tunnel on the way to Grand Central. Instantly, the train plunged into darkness. The engineer was always late throwing the lights on. He didn't disappoint this time.

When the lights were restored Hoag was leaning against the window, *The New York Times* at his side. Dolan was gone.

The 8:10 arrived exactly on time at 8:59 and everyone got off except Steven Hoag. No one noticed he was dead. It was New York and everyone was in a rush.

Steven Hoag hadn't voted yet. He had planned to do that after work. Another 2,534,101 of the state's 5,892,617 registered Democrats would make it before the polls closed at seven. Typically, the presidential primary would bring out fewer than one million voters. This day, there'd be a record showing. Democrats were making a definite statement about who they wanted to see run against Morgan Taylor.

BURLINGTON, VERMONT
9:00 A.M.

The congressman stood stone cold throughout the minister's eulogy for Jenny. The Cathedral Church of St. Paul on Cherry Street was packed. Out of respect to the congressman, the press agreed to pool their camera coverage inside. However, outside 63 cameras focused on St. Paul's, feeding three dozen remote vans sent from New York, Boston, Albany, Philadelphia and Pittsburgh.

The minister, a soft-spoken man in his 30s with a slow and deliberate delivery, was instantly becoming a national figure with a congregation of 100 million.

"We mourn a sweet soul and a good friend who brought such light to our lives. Those of us who knew Jennifer admired her unbounded strength and character. Those who didn't are now just learning what she could have given to this country. So much for so long. We shall miss you, dear Jennifer. Your promise in this world shall be fulfilled in another."

Reverend Frederick Hamilton genuinely touched everyone. He offered a prayer for Jenny and the hope that Congressman Lodge would remain safe. "We have all seen the news. A fraction of a second was the difference between who we mourn today. We can only pray that the authorities will not give such a lawless, godless man a second shot. Let us now pray together."

He asked the assemblage in church and those watching to find their own words of solace in silence. He bowed his head and for nearly a minute the only sound heard was sobbing in remembrance of Jennifer Lodge.

The congressman used the quiet to take the four steps from his chair to the dais. After close to a half minute surveying the faces of the friends, colleagues, fellow parishioners, and dignitaries who had come to honor his wife, he drew in a long breath.

"If you'll allow me. 'Sonnet #43,' written by Elizabeth Barrett Browning. 'How Do I Love Thee.'" He proceeded to slowly recite the words by heart, with his eyes closed.

> *How do I love thee? Let me count the ways.*
> *I love thee to the depth and breadth and height*
> *My soul can reach, when feeling out of sight*
> *For the ends of Being and ideal Grace.*
> *I love thee to the level of everyday's*
> *Most quiet need, by sun and candle light.*
> *I love thee freely, as men strive for Right;*
> *I love thee purely, as they turn from Praise.*
> *I love thee with a passion put to use*
> *In my old griefs, and with my childhood's faith.*
> *I love thee with a love I seemed to lose*
> *With my lost saints,—I love thee with the breath,*
> *Smiles, tears, of all my life!—and if God choose,*
> *I shall but love thee better after death.*

Teddy Lodge concluded and walked back to his seat looking even more like a leader.

THE WHITE HOUSE

"Louise, get me Roarke!" the president snapped into his intercom.

Morgan Taylor was one of the millions watching Congressman Lodge. Midway through the Browning poem he put his coffee down on his desk. He had no stomach for it now and he needed to talk to his man immediately in the middle of an already busy morning.

The president had a pile of briefings to read, an interview with the BBC in ten minutes, a report on Japan's further economic slide to digest, and an update on the India-Pakistan front. Talking to Roarke suddenly went to the top of the list.

Louise Swingle dialed the cell number that only a few people knew.

"Hi honey, there's someone who wants to speak to you. I'll put you right through."

"Mr. President, Scott is on line five."

"Thank you," he said before punching in Roarke.

She didn't know what the president needed, but she had worked with him long enough to recognize this was not going to be a good day around the White House.

"What do you have?"

"Well, nothing much more than what we've read."

"I want to hear everything." He didn't tell Roarke what he was really thinking—that he was going to lose the damned election if he didn't stop Lodge. And now, goddammit, even his wife Lucy had a soft spot for Lodge.

Roarke talked in relatively innocuous terms. The digital line was secure from most eavesdroppers, but even the government's own National Security Agency and the CIA made listening to the chief executive a favorite diversion.

"Well, I can't really give you anything concrete," he concluded. "I'm on my way to a law firm to see about his parents' trust."

"Okay," the president said. "But call if you find anything. Nothing is unimportant."

"Got it. But you'll probably get more out of *The New York Times*. They have a reporter up here. We're nearly bumping into each other."

"Scott," the president offered softly. "Anything in your gut?"

"Too early, sir." But without thinking he patted his Sig and said goodbye.

CHAPTER 14

NEW YORK CITY
9:12 A.M.

Benny Larson was cleaning the Metro North coach before it headed back upstate. "Another guy who didn't get enough sleep last night," he said barely over a whisper. Typical for a busy Tuesday. He reached over and shook the man. "Rise and shine, mister." The man appeared to be in a deep, deep sleep. "Hey fella, get to work," he said, shaking him harder. That's when Steven Hoag slumped over. The newspaper slipped to the floor and Benny saw the blood-soaked shirt.

"Jesus H. Christ!" he proclaimed. Then he dropped his trash bag and ran out of the train.

"We got a dead one on car three," he cried to the nearest Amtrak security officer.

The word quickly went up the line and within five minutes the commuter was off-limits to anyone but Transit Authority Police and the NYPD.

The first ranking investigator on the scene from homicide was Detective Harry Coates, a 52-year-old career officer. He'd seen a hundred or more heart attacks before. But a murder on a train? Now this was different.

Examining the body, Coates noted, "Close range. A foot. Maybe less."

Very carefully, Coates reached in the victim's inner jacket pocket and pulled out a wallet. A Connecticut license gave him the man's name and address. A business card identified where he worked. A few other phone numbers were on torn pieces of paper. The man carried $155 in cash and American Express, Visa, and Diners Club cards. A picture he also carried suggested he had an attractive wife or girlfriend.

"Why's a guy who works in publishing taken out on a train?" he asked the Transit Authority Police officer at his side. "Not robbery." He answered the question himself.

THE WHITE HOUSE

Morgan Taylor stared at the picture of the frightened teenager he clipped out of Monday's paper. For two days, he had felt a personal connection with her. He tried to place it, then it came to him.

Though he wasn't in Dallas in 1963, the news of President Kennedy's assassination had been devastating to the impressionable young boy.

A teacher had told Taylor and his classmates that this was a time to look for the goodness in the American character, to find people who could explain what America really meant.

Morgan had taken it to heart. While walking home one evening, he had been drawn to a gathering at his local VFW. Maybe he'd find some answers from these men. Inside, the World War II veterans warmly welcomed the boy, inviting him to listen to their experiences. Taylor heard B-17 crews talk about their attacks against the Nazis, how the Marines took Iwo Jima, and about the long carrier-based missions in the Pacific by the Navy pilots. The youngster felt at home. He returned many times over the years, developing a budding kinship with the vets; ultimately finding his own course in life.

In March of his senior year, he confidently marched into the Navy recruiting office. He was 18 and legally able to sign the papers. The day after graduation he belonged to the military. The recruiter called his parents to be certain. After all, the United States was engaged in a war in Vietnam and volunteers were needed. Morgan's mother cried. She explained that her husband, a house painter by trade, had served in Korea. Morgan was an infant when his father died. Cynthia Taylor saw greatness in Morgan and recognized she couldn't keep her son home. So she stood with him as he swore to defend America that day, and again years later on the steps of the Capitol when he vowed to uphold the Constitution as President of the United States.

As he looked at the picture of the young girl, tears streaming down her face, he realized two things: This was her political awakening, too—her life would never be the same; and as president, he might be the last man to hold the office who actually remembered JFK's presidency.

BOSTON, MASSACHUSETTS
10:22 A.M.

Scott Roarke, dressed in a tie for the first time in weeks, waited in the lobby of Freelander, Collins, Wrather & Marcus. The law office overlooked Boston Harbor with dozens of sailboats bobbing in the water and the summer lunch cruises loading up supplies on Long Wharf. From 21 floors above Congress Street near Faneuil Hall, he watched people strolling through the park that replaced the old elevated Central Artery. Fifteen years of The Big Dig had finally ended and most of Boston's north-south traffic now traveled underground.

The law firm was an amalgam of three distinguished companies. Roarke was only interested in talking with someone familiar with the old Marcus accounts. He explained what he needed to one of the three receptionists working the desk. After thirty-four minutes he was finally cleared. A secretary came down to escort him.

"You'll be meeting with Mr. Witherspoon." She didn't offer him coffee or engage in any further chit-chat.

Donald Witherspoon was a junior attorney. Roarke expected to do much better with his Secret Service credentials.

"There's not much I can tell you," said the officious 28-year-old Harvard grad who never rose from behind his desk. He had 'asshole' written all over him, and paisley suspenders to prove it. Roarke disliked him instantly.

"You haven't given me much notice. But I did find some information."

The attorney stopped. He wouldn't reveal anything without a direct question. Roarke recognized it as his cue.

"Tell me about the relationship between Freelander, Collins, Wrather & Marcus and Mr. Lodge."

"There is none."

"But I understand the firm represented the Lodge family estate."

"No, that's incorrect. One of the partners did, but before the partnership was formed."

"And that would be?"

"Are you asking me which partner, Mr. Roarke?"

"Yes, which partner represented the Lodges?"

"Haywood Marcus."

"And is he here?"

"Yes, but unavailable. That's why you're meeting with me."

Roarke hated this give and take. He just wanted some basic information.

"And what about tomorrow? Will he be available then?"

"Mr. Marcus has asked me to assist you with these matters."

"Well," Roarke said, becoming more direct, "why don't you then."

Witherspoon looked at him blankly and waited for another question.

"Can you tell me about Mr. Marcus' relationship with the family?"

"I don't understand your question," the lawyer stated.

"Was he a family friend?"

"He was their lawyer."

"Over how long a period of time?"

"He managed the estate until the son became trustee at age twenty-five."

Roarke was grateful for the little information he just got, but clarified his question. "I meant, how long before their death?"

"I don't know."

"Perhaps you can check. I believe you're the one holding the paperwork."

Witherspoon reserved the comment that he wore with his expression. He was pissed. But he did examine the files, going back and forth between a number of pages. "Here it is," he said. "Mr. Marcus was engaged in the 1970s."

"Can you be more specific?" Lodge urged.

"About what?"

"The date Mr. Marcus' services were engaged."

Witherspoon consulted the record again. "I really can't."

"Can you tell me what the will provided for?" Roarke asked as a follow up.

"I don't believe I can get into that either…" He shuffled through the pages of one file and noted something that made him suddenly close the folder. Roarke caught the change in attitude. "…without Mr. Lodge's permission. You understand. Legally, I'm prohibited."

"And this is the only will?"

"I'm not aware of any other," he said, fumbling a bit.

Roarke had seen men lie before. He had witnessed it under torture by enemies and at microphones in front of the press. Now he saw it in Witherspoon's eyes and demeanor. He was lying and he hid it extremely poorly.

"Thank you, Mr. Witherspoon, I appreciate everything you *have* been able to tell me."

No, Roarke's instinct told him. *This attorney would* never *become a partner*.

"I'll show myself out. That way you don't have to bother to get up. Just point me to the men's room first."

"Down the hall to the right, the third door on the left."

Roarke left and walked slowly, casually checking for motion detectors, surveillance cameras or other security measures. There were none. After leaving the bathroom, he intentionally made a wrong turn down the hall to survey the rest of the floor. He walked past Witherspoon's office and saw that he had already put the Lodge file in his "out" basket. The attorney, wearing a wireless telephone headset, was absorbed in a telephone call, his back to the hall.

Roarke rounded a corner and saw an alluring young woman pushing a rolling cart full of legal files. Just to watch her, he stopped to tie his shoe, which didn't need tying. She had a sensational figure and appeared to be 5'6." He pegged her to be 28 or 29 years old. She wore a gray skirt, black heels and a burgundy silk blouse. A necklace made of smoke gray freshwater pearls complemented the outfit perfectly. She had her black, curly hair up in a bun and walked with an air of self-assuredness. He wasn't sure if she even noticed him.

The woman continued down the hall and entered a room located in the interior of the floor. Roarke waited a few moments before following. It was a huge bullpen-sized space, much bigger than the normal office. Roarke noted at least twenty deep rows of filing cabinets stretching fifty or more feet. In less than ten seconds he had scanned for active and passive security measures. He noted that at near ceiling level an infrared beam played across the room from each of the corners. They were more for show than for practical use. Someone had sold the law firm a useless system. Roarke figured that Shaquille O'Neal could have triggered it, but most people got nowhere near the height of the beam.

Suddenly a woman's voice broke his concentration. "Excuse me?" It was the woman. "Excuse me?" she repeated almost accusingly. They were only a few feet apart. After returning a file, she had rounded one of the aisles, then had seen the stranger. He had an unfamiliar, though pleasing face, but she was definitely on alert.

Roarke's instincts came into play. He studied her motions and her beauty. In a flash he recognized that this young woman already exhibited more verve than Witherspoon did. *She* would make a good lawyer.

"I'm sorry, I'm a little turned around," Roarke explained with an innocent smile. "I'm looking for the lobby."

"Well, you missed it by a mile. It's back out to the left. Go to the end of the hall and then through the double doors. It doesn't have a sign that says *Records* like this room," she added slightly sarcastically. "Even *you* couldn't miss it."

He grinned. *Is she flirting?* He couldn't remember the last time he'd caught that kind of inflection; a personal playfulness. He also couldn't recall the last time he'd let his guard down. First, he wasn't as stealthy as he had hoped. He'd have to work on that. Second, he was definitely being sized up.

"Thanks," he stammered trying to recover. "I was meeting with Mr. Witherspoon and then hit the bathroom. And here I am."

"Here you are," she responded.

They stared at each other and laughed. He decided to get back to work for a second and actually try to learn something. "This place all files?"

"Years and years worth. Some newer work also comes in on disc, which makes it a lot easier. But you know how we love our yellow pads." She saw a frown drawing across his face. "Or maybe you don't," she realized. "You're not a lawyer."

"No. Just the opposite," Roarke replied too quickly.

"So, you're a criminal."

"No. I'm one of the good guys, but I try to stay away from lawyers."

"We don't all bite," she said with a smile.

"You make a good case for restoring faith in the profession," Roarke replied.

"Quite nicely stated."

Roarke was enjoying the banter, but he decided to change the subject.

"Need any help carrying all those?" This was not so much a question from a Secret Service agent. He really liked this woman. "I'm good at heavy lifting."

A seductive smile lit up her face as she focused on the stranger. He was extremely good looking and he did appear strong.

"I think I'm okay."

Roarke grinned, "Well then, the lobby? Out to my right and then…?" he asked.

"No, to your left," she said with renewed emphasis. "Left… that way."

She pointed and Roarke looked at her hand and then the direction.

"Got it. Thanks again. I hope you're around if I get lost again."

The young woman nodded. "I hope I am, too."

Roarke left. He'd be back soon and now he knew exactly where he had to go.

NEW YORK CITY
11:50 A.M.

The procedure was fairly straightforward even if the crime wasn't. Steven Hoag's body went to the morgue. Detective Coates first called Mrs. Hoag at home to break the news. He told her he'd drive up to Connecticut to talk with her in person. From there he would retrace Hoag's last hour. Before the trip, however, he had some more phone calls to make.

Coates sat at his dirt-encrusted desk in his Manhattan precinct office. He removed Hoag's wallet from a clear plastic bag and examined the contents. Credit cards, Connecticut driver's license. Business cards. And some random phone numbers written on various pieces of paper.

He wrote each of the unidentified numbers down and started dialing. Maybe one would lead him to a suspect.

The first number connected Coates to Park Avenue Wine and Spirits where he learned that Hoag regularly bought burgundy. *Nothing to gather there*, he thought. The second number rang at Town, an eclectic fusion restaurant at West 56th in the Chambers Hotel. The maitre d' knew the name. Hoag ate there fairly regularly. He ordered almost everything off the menu, and was partial to the escargot risotto. *More useless information.*

Coates went on to the next number on the list. It had a 201 area code. New Jersey.

The number rang twice. A man curtly answered, "Yes?" It was a cold, official sounding voice; the kind of impatient "Yes" that a police chief gives a subordinate or a high ranking military officer gives to an enlisted man. Coates automatically sat up straight. The voice repeated, "Yes?"

Coates began just as authoritatively. "This is Detective Harry Coates, NYPD."

Silence on the other end, but the line stayed open. "Your number was in a wallet we found today…" He stopped, but the voice remained quiet. He completed the sentence. "…on a dead man."

The phone line went dead. Then the dial tone returned.

Coates leaned back in his uncomfortable wooden desk chair. He'd been hung up on. He tapped his pen on the paper and circled the number three times. "Now it's getting interesting," he said aloud.

He redialed the New Jersey number. It rang 15 times, but no one picked up. Then he called a precinct extension."

"Sarah. I have a number I need you to track down." He rattled it off. "I'll call from the road. Get me everything you can."

He thought about the voice on the line again. A thousand possibilities raced through his mind, none of them good.

HUDSON, NEW YORK
11:55 A.M.

Lt. Brenner was feeling way out of his league. The FBI had totally taken charge. Their fingerprint experts were crawling over every square inch; their photographers were creating a multi-image portrait of the scene that could rival a high-priced David Hockney lithograph. "Hell, it looks like they have an analyst for every goddamned towel," he complained to his chief.

Chief Marelli wasn't exactly happy either. First, a murder seen around the world happened right in front of him. Second, he felt he had been lax. And third, he didn't prevent the assassin from escaping. *The Register-Star* raised the same questions for two straight days.

Brenner was in the middle of complaining about the feds when Marelli asked him to be quiet. An idea was bouncing around in his head and he wanted to clear his mind. The chief looked outside his office window at 327 Warren Street.

"Talk to me about the parade. It got thrown together pretty quickly?" Marelli asked never taking his eyes from the cars below.

"Yes," Brenner asserted. "We got the word ten, no eleven days ago. The 13th, I think. Wednesday the 13th. The State Police called us."

"Thursday the 13th. It was Thursday, in the afternoon," Marelli said, correcting him.

"Right. Thursday. It'll be on the phone log. But I remember, because I'd just come back from the dentist."

Brenner began to outline the events. "The call from Albany. The District Commander. Then I alerted the mayor's office. He got Randy Quinn at the Chamber of Commerce involved and they began planning the parade. There were all sorts of things going back and forth. Which direction to march. Up or down Warren? Where the speeches would be? At Promenade Hill or at the park? Finally, Lodge's advance man or campaign manager, someone, looked at the park and thought it was too small. He wanted the platform right in the intersection of Park Place and Warren so more people could see. After that it was all the coordinating."

Brenner paused, keenly aware that Marelli was playing with a notion. He still hadn't taken his eyes off the window. "Where are you going with this, Chief?"

"Thursday the 13th," he repeated.

"Thursday. Right. The 13th."

"Terrific."

"What's terrific?"

"Your memory."

"I'm confused."

"Don't worry. I'll fill you in when I make more sense out of it myself," the chief said. Marelli left and walked up the three blocks to the St. Charles.

MARBLEHEAD, MASSACHUSETTS
THE SAME TIME

Michael O'Connell really enjoyed digging. The writing, which he was great at, still didn't touch the thrills of the legwork. He loved reaching into the past through the eyes of witnesses, helping them see things they didn't even realize were there.

He spoke to Teddy Lodge's piano teacher about his music lessons, his Boy Scouts leader about his merit badges, and the town librarian to see what he used to read.

With what he had, O'Connell pieced together an article of an all-American in the making. A standout. The athlete. The public speaker. The daredevil. The Eagle Scout. The neighborhood kid who delivered *The Boston Globe* on his bike at six in the morning. He helped his father at the office and his mother at home. About the only thing he ever gave up was piano.

All of this was going into his Wednesday story. He'd be short on personal pictures. He'd take heat from his editor on that. But he e-mailed digital shots of everything else he could put his hands on— pictures of the schools, Teddy's teacher Pat Sullivan, his Marblehead hangouts, the church where he met for Boy Scouts. The profile of the congressman as a youngster was filling out nicely.

Depending upon what happened in the New York State primary today, there'd be even more interest in Teddy Lodge tomorrow.

HUDSON, NEW YORK
LATER THAT AFTERNOON

It only took Anne Fornado a few minutes to check the records for Chief Marelli. The original file cards had been sent to the FBI crime labs at Quantico, but Anne had the computer reservation and the check-in confirmation.

"Here it is, Chief," she paused as she scrolled the screen down. "The reservation was originally made on June 13th, yes, the 13th at 8:34 at night."

Her face was buried in the computer screen, so she didn't see Marelli's disappointment. "And he checked in on June 14th around midnight."

"Damn it," the chief let out.

"What were you looking for?" the St. Charles Hotel manager asked.

"I don't know. I had a hunch," he said, emphasizing his disappointment. "And it was wrong."

He started out of the hotel office, then stopped.

"What has me confused is how he checks in the next day after his reservation and gets the very room he needs to pick off the congressman? What's the chance of that? This place is always booked this time of year."

Anne threw her hands up. She'd seen a lot of disappointment over the past few days. Nothing she'd done had helped anyone. She returned to her computer and studied the reservation again. The chief's question was a good one.

WASHINGTON, D.C.

"We have trouble," the man said over a secure line. "Book Man was taken out in New York this morning."

"What?" answered another.

"Shot twice on his train. NYPD is on it."

"Contained?"

"No. Book Man had our number in his wallet. A local detective called."

"Jesus Christ! You'd think he'd memorized that," the man complained. "So what does NYPD have?"

"Don't know. I'll get an asset inside to check for sure. No doubt though. It was a hit," the man making the call said.

"When was Book Man's next contact due?"

"Soon. Three weeks. We were arranging a meeting on his next trip. He'd been hinting that he might have something for us. He had to think about it. He didn't rush it and," he paused realizing his mistake, "neither did we."

"Any idea what it was?" the second man asked flatly.

"He said it was about school."

"School? Jesus."

"I know. We should have pushed this up."

"And the cop? What do you think he gathered after calling the number?"

"Depends on how good he is," the first voice answered. "It won't lead him anywhere. We pulled it. But I'd say there's a better than average chance he'll narrow the possibilities and come knocking on your door."

"That may be a little hard."

The last time the director checked, the CIA was still rather difficult to get into.

BURLINGTON, VERMONT
SHERATON BURLINGTON HOTEL
9:30 P.M.

It was official 30 minutes after the New York polls closed. But reporters had predicted it all day. Congressman Teddy Lodge was the winner. He swept the state taking 205 of the state's 294 delegates. Lodge also captured 28 of Rhode Island's 33 delegates.

Two days ago, the primaries belonged to Governor Lamden. As the McLaughlin panel conceded, the press liked Teddy, but pollsters put him in second. Now, all that was history. Democratic voters made another decision on Tuesday. They liked the way Teddy handled himself. He was the man they wanted to represent their party.

However, there were no celebrations at campaign headquarters; nothing more than quiet gratitude. Everyone waited for a statement to come from Geoff Newman.

At 9:33, Newman stepped in front of a bank of microphones and cameras in the ballroom of the Sheraton Burlington Hotel.

"Ladies and Gentlemen, I have a brief statement."

That was camera-speak for 'get your cameras and tape machines rolling.' He waited an extra beat to make certain the crews were feeding picture and sound.

"Congressman Lodge genuinely appreciates the outpouring of support today. To the citizens of New York and Rhode Island he has asked me to convey a most heartfelt thank you. And to the rest of the nation, he also wants you all to know how much the phone calls, e-mails and expressions of sympathy for Mrs. Lodge have meant to him. He will never forget your caring. Thank you."

With that Newman spun around and walked away without further comment.

For a split second no one could speak. What did he say? What was that? He appreciated the votes. What the hell did that mean?

Suddenly a dozen voices replaced the silence in a barrage of questions. The reporters shouted over one another. A few tried to follow, but local police held them back.

"Mr. Newman, will the congressman accept the Democratic nomination?"

"Is he going to stay in the race?"

"Has he decided to drop out?"

"Geoff, when can we talk to him?"

Newman heard them all and smiled. However, he wasn't going to feed the wolves anymore tonight.

PART II

CHAPTER 15

TRIPOLI, LIBYA
WEDNESDAY, JUNE 25
2140 HRS LOCAL TIME

Omar Za'eem walked through the narrow streets of Tarabulus, known to Westerners as Tripoli. He passed the poster-sized portraits, too numerous to count, of General Jabbar "the Almighty" Kharrazi. As he strolled toward the centuries-old souk, or bazaar, Omar wondered what other Middle East capital cities were like. This is the only one he'd ever seen.

Tripoli, though spread out, is walkable. The city, built on the ancient ruins of Oea, was founded as early as 7th century B.C. by the Phoenicians, captured by the Romans in 1st century B.C. and then taken by the Arabs in 7th century A.D. It served as an important trans-Saharan trading route, and a strategic Mediterranean port. As such, Tripoli was long sought by imperialist European nations.

The Spanish took it in 1510, then granted Libya to the Knights of St. John, who held it until the Ottoman Turks captured it in 1551. From 1711 until 1835, Tripoli was the seat of the Karamanli dynasty, which ruled most of the land encompassing Libya. For years, a lawless Tripoli became the refuge of the Barbary pirates who engaged the U.S. from 1801-1805 in the Tripolitan War and gave rise to the lyric in the Marine Hymn, "to the shores of Tripoli."

In 1911, Tripoli transferred into the hands of the Italians, and later became capital to the Italian colony of Libya. The Axis-controlled country was seized by the British during World War II, which eventually brokered a deal for Libya's independence. In 1951, under the leadership of King Idris, Libya established a federal monarchy and a constitutional democracy.

Libya began to prosper when oil was discovered in 1959. Exxon found rich deposits of exceptional quality crude, which shifted the entire economic picture of the land. Considering that the country's principal port lies just across the Mediterranean from Europe and close to Gibraltar and access to the Atlantic, Libya suddenly had the money to solve its long-standing problems.

But the money became attractive to others, too. Particularly a young army colonel named Mu'ammar al-Qadhafi.

When King Idris left Libya for medical treatment in 1969, Crown Prince Hasa ar Rida was left to watch the homefront. He was ill-prepared for Qadhafi and his followers who led an almost effortless coup.

At first Qadhafi helped Libya, a nation he called *Al Jamahiriya al'Arabiya al-Libiya ash-sha al-ishtrakia* or the Great Socialist People's Libyan Arab Jamahiriya. He fostered nationalism over religion and developed a system of free education for all Libyans. He also wiped out the existing social and political system, established a dictatorship of his own making and fostered state-sponsored terrorism.

Qadhafi became an enemy of the United States, an ally of the Soviet Union, and a pariah within sectors of the Arab community. Kharrazi's rule improved Arab relations after he ousted Qadhafi, but he did nothing to further the lives of the people of Libya.

A decade before Omar was born, Tripoli was emerging as a world-class city with a growing middle class moving into new homes that couldn't be built fast enough. An improved public works system brought running water in to people who had never known it and took sewage out. Super-highways, similar to American interstates, paved the way for more urban sprawl, while international businessmen flew into a modern airport. But things were different these days, thought Omar. *Dangerous. Even worse under General Kharrazi.*

The lights were on now. But there was no guarantee they would be in another few hours. The government controlled the electrical grids and provided power to Tripoli on an on-off basis.

Restaurants, shops, hotels, television—never knew when the power would flicker out. That's why the outdoor markets were still the center of life in Tripoli.

This bankrupt capital, once considered the "white bride of the Mediterranean Sea," was in decline. Citizens who once owned their own businesses, more than one house, and a second car, found such things banned by edict.

In a country formerly known for its fine medical schools and college scholarships, students now went to schools that lacked electricity, heating, books, and even desks.

Salaries were frozen according to law. Wages were generally paid every four to six months and only lasted a few days. Loans were literally impossible to secure.

Towns outside of Tripoli suffered from even more neglect. Sewage puddles backed up from clogged drains. In many apartment buildings, elevator shafts were cemented in because no one could afford the equipment or the upkeep.

Food was often rationed in this country rich with oil. People waited years for telephone lines. Inflation pushed 30% annually. The transportation system had collapsed and public services remained neglected. Only the older generation spoke foreign languages.

Omar Za'eem continued his walk through the workshops of the al-Harir souk where weavers hunched over their timeless looms, fashioning striped cloth in vibrant colors. Where proud Libyans sold cherished family heirlooms to buy food. Where children no older than six begged drivers to let them clean their windshields in exchange for a few dinars.

He nodded to men in the teahouses who sat inhaling their narghile, a honey-scented addictive tobacco smoked through a water pipe. The high was stimulating and masked the pain of day-to-day life. This was as it had been for hundreds of years; something beyond Abahar's power to change when he assumed control. But other things would.

Omar knew the first rule of personal survival. Everyone had to be extremely careful about what was said in public. As they drank their heavily sugared green mint tea and lulled themselves into fantasies with puffs of the narghile, patrons constantly looked over their shoulders. Trust could be bought and sold for little more than a pack of cigarettes. Many countrymen who didn't follow that rule disappeared.

Omar knew their lives weren't the same today. The family structure, long ago an essential part of the Libyan national character, had broken down, and he knew that many of their children lay dying in hospitals; with useless Arabic proverbs over their beds proclaiming, *"Martyrs are better than all of us."*

The General would soon die. His reign pitifully but fortuitously short. And Omar believed that Abahar, not Fadi, deserved to sit in his place. That's why he risked his young life, spying on one member of the first family on behalf of the other.

HUDSON, NEW YORK

Bessolo closed down the parking lot at the St. Charles on Monday. He was pissed that he hadn't done it earlier. By Sunday night there were literally hundreds of scuff marks and dusty imprints on the blacktop surface. The FBI field agent in charge called the hotel manager after he noticed a security camera focused over the corner of the building. The camera fed a five-inch monitor at the front desk, but no tape deck. Then he remembered seeing cutaways of the crowd in the news tape. There must have been dozens of people with home video cameras. Maybe someone's coverage would include shots of the parking lot. Maybe they'd get really lucky and see video of the killer leaving.

By Thursday morning he had six tapes in his hands that contained other angles of the podium and the confusion after the shooting. An unexpected surprise in one of the tapes was a shot of the St. Charles parking lot. Beth Thomas recommended that the desk match up the cars with the hotel patrons. Check-in required that they list the make and model of their vehicles. Seven cars belonged to Hudsonians who were on hand for the congressman's speech. Six belonged to the firemen on duty at J.W. Edmonds Hose Co. #1. Nine were hotel staff. That left twelve more cars to identify. They were able to put a name to ten of them. Two more were unknown. None, of course, belonged to McAlister.

Beth was working in the parking lot where the two mystery cars still remained. Fortunately, it hadn't rained in a few weeks and there was a significant layer of dust on the ground.

"Roy. Get on down to the parking lot. I have something for you to see," she keyed into her walkie-talkie. "And don't even think of coming within ten feet of me!"

"Roger that," Bessolo said. He radioed his senior photographer to get up on the roof. "I want this fully recorded. You get everything she's doing on tape with the closest shot you can."

"Beth," he said, calling back on the run to the parking lot, "we're going to get some shots from above. You let us know when we can come closer. This thing has to be recorded. Now what the fuck do you have?"

"An indentation that looks like it's off the same shoe in 301. Looks like," she repeated. "Not sure yet. I need to isolate this. If there's so much as a mild breeze, this thing is lost."

Everyone froze for ten minutes as Beth leaned over the imprint. She took her time, like a jeweler adjusting the works of a fine watch. Few others would have had the patience to explore the ground in such detail. Beth liked to earn her money and she didn't mind the attention. Bessolo's team watched and waited for her signal.

BURLINGTON, VERMONT

"It's Lamden," Newman announced to his boss. "You should take his call now. It's been four days."

"I suppose so."

Newman held the phone for him. Theodore Lodge took measured paces across his living room. He hadn't spoken to anyone except his campaign manager since his New York press conference. Not even the president.

"Hello, Henry," he said softly.

"Hello, Ted."

Henry Lamden was a well-respected career politician. And he was a maverick. Of course, coming from Montana, such things were allowed. He talked like a cowboy, walked like a cowboy, wore a Stetson, and often spun yarns instead of holding conversations. The grizzled 66-year-old lawmaker could ride and rope. He also could fight hard, as he had on the Gulf and in the campaign.

"Hello, Ted. I'm so sorry."

"Thank you. I hope you understand why I wasn't up to taking your calls before," Lodge replied.

Lamden pushed ahead without further personal comment.

"Of course, but you've got a decision to make. There are a lot of people waiting to know what you're gonna do. And I'm at the top of that list."

"Yes, I'd say you are."

"You've got the numbers, Ted. What are you going to do?"

Lodge closed his eyes. "Would you like me to concede?"

"Jesus, don't ask me that. You got most of New York and Rhode Island. The nomination is yours if you want it. It's got to be your decision, not mine."

Newman couldn't hear what the governor was saying, but he knew from Lodge's comments that this was a seminal deliberation.

"I've been trying to find meaning in all of this, Henry. It's been a difficult week."

"If there's anything I can do to help…" The governor's words trailed off. He really did hate losing. It wasn't part of his character. He had won every seat he'd ever run for and he had been just one primary away from narrowly winning the party's nomination for president.

"What was that, Henry? You were saying?"

The mood was changing. The governor could feel it. It was pure business now.

"What are you going to do, Congressman?"

Lodge walked the wireless telephone over to a green leather arm-chair in his study. "That's a very good question, Governor. I know what the convention would like to see."

"You'll have to help me with this," Governor Lamden stated.

"A unified ticket," Lodge explained. "Unbeatable in my estimation."

The governor understood from friends on the Hill that

Congressman Lodge could be coldly direct. He was now experiencing it first hand. Lodge had turned on a dime from the grieving widower to the calculating politician.

"And who's on top?"

"Yes, I suppose that is the big question," Lodge added. "Who's on top? But for purely argument's sake, Governor, if you're not, what would you do?"

Lodge heard a prolonged sigh. "If you're asking me to join you as vice president, I'll have to think about that."

"You do that, Henry. It may be as close as you'll ever get to the Oval Office."

CHAPTER 16

TRIPOLI, LIBYA
THURSDAY, JUNE 26

Omar Za'eem sat during a break from work at a table in a teahouse near the al-Zahar Hotel. Some of the patrons played dominoes. Most people sat and smoked. His drink was served in a small, clear glass, one-third filled with a rough form of sugar. It went down well with the apple-flavored tobacco he puffed from a three-foot long pipe. Well into his second drink, a man greeted him. "*Al salaam a'alaykum.* Peace upon you." Then he asked if the seat next to him was taken. Za'eem offered a polite no, and gestured for the customer to join him.

The man removed a pack of cigarettes from his shirt pocket and offered one to Omar. As he leaned over to accept the light, the man whispered, "I understand you have something for me."

Walid Abdul-Latif lit Omar's cigarette and waited for a response.

"Yes. Something interesting," he replied under his breath.

The two men puffed as Walid waved for the waiter and ordered a peach tea. He was stockier and more solidly built than Omar.

After the tea was served, Omar continued in whispers. He explained what he had memorized, concluding, "There's more I did not get to. *He* has it in his office." Za'eem emphasized the "he" for impact, not daring to say the name in public. Za'eem didn't have to. "What little I saw worries me."

Walid looked equally concerned. "We must learn more, my friend," he commanded more than stated. Walid Abdul-Latif was, after all, Za'eem's superior.

"I will find out what I can."

The teahouse was filling up. A few minutes later Za'eem thanked his companion for the cigarette loudly enough for nearby customers to hear. "A pleasure to meet you," he added for good measure. He counted out barely enough money for himself and left. He had communicated what he had known to his contact, a lieutenant in Abahar Kharrazi's secret police. On his way out he prayed to Allah that he had picked the right brother to support. If he hadn't he would pay the price for his poor choice.

BOSTON, MASSACHUSETTS
9:01 A.M.

Roarke timed his move. He wore a new four-button suit he bought on sale from Filene's Basement and juggled his briefcase and a cup of very hot coffee from an espresso stand on Congress Street. He easily blended into the crowd of six lawyers coming to work. The steaming coffee pulled any onlooker's eye. All they saw was the cup, not the man. It was a classic diversion. And, true to form, they steered clear of any guy who could spill hot coffee on their expensive suits.

Roarke strolled past the receptionist without a problem. He moved in step with the wave of lawyers making their way to offices and meetings. Far down the hall, Roarke peeled off. No one paid the least bit of attention to the Secret Service agent. He now looked like one of 132 lawyers billing clients for hours at Freelander, Collins, Wrather & Marcus. He was probably the only one actually wearing a gun.

His destination was the Records room. Because of the coffee cup and briefcase, he struggled a little with the heavy mahogany door.

One attorney, already deep into research, peered up but didn't offer any help. Typical, thought Roarke. Two other associates didn't even glance at him. Then again, neither would Roarke once he got settled in. He promptly found an out of the way corner, searched for five large volumes from the shelves, nothing really in particular, then he created a false workspace for himself. He pulled a dozen yellow pads from his briefcase and spread them out. As people came and went he lost himself in made-up work for the next eight or so hours.

TRIPOLI, LIBYA
1445 HRS LOCAL TIME

Writing was becoming a dying art in Libya, as it was in the rest of the world. But not because of the Internet or cell phones. Import bans often limited paper supplies. Those who could get their hands on good paper usually used both sides. It was a surprising residual effect of the trade sanctions renewed by the West against the Kharrazi regime. Government offices also felt the paper shortage. But some things were better not put on paper. The information that Walid Abdul-Latif had been told was classified as that.

He booted up his aged computer in his office on the third floor of the Office of Internal Security. No Pentium chip. It was painfully slow by Western standards, but the nearly ancient desktop was still a wonder to him. He typed up the recollections of his talk with Za'eem, created a folder and stored it. He wasn't proficient with computers, so he didn't really know how to do things efficiently or secretly. So after saving the file he re-saved it on a prehistoric floppy disc to take to his superior, Major Bayon Karim Kitan, who would, in turn, take it to his boss, OIS Director Abahar Kharrazi. First he called the major's assistant.

"I need to see the Major immediately. I have something important."

"You'll have to wait."

"I said this is important."

"You'll still have to wait. He's busy."

Sami Ben Ali, another assistant on the floor, overheard the conversation from his desk a few feet away. He knew Abahar wasn't busy. This was just "the way." He laughed, barely loud enough to be heard, but enough to encourage Walid to talk out of turn.

"Arrogance everywhere. Never ending," Walid said disgustedly. He didn't like answering to Katan's assistant and he wished he had more access to Abahar himself. This information deserved it. He showed his discontent in the way he grabbed the floppy disc and shot out of the room.

Sami Ben Ali shook his head. He'd have to agree. Arrogance was everywhere.

BOSTON, MASSACHUSETTS

Okay, Roarke rationalized. *I'm not really breaking and entering. I'm not walking out with anything.*

Nonetheless, Watergate kept coming to mind. He was planning on examining confidential documents without permission. And if caught, he'd have an impossible time claiming any National Security privilege. The more he thought about it, the more he considered he'd made a mistake. But he was certain there was something in the file that Witherspoon kept close to the vest.

Then he remembered the woman with the frizzy black hair. Perhaps there was another way. Later in the day he'd find out.

At 6:45 Roarke decided to close up the law books he had in front of him and pack up the yellow legal pads. *What was the chance she'd still be here on a Friday evening?* he wondered. *Pretty good*, he assumed. *She's dedicated.*

Roarke became invisible again merely by carrying four volumes of "Massachusetts Supreme Court Cases 1934-1937" in his arms and the legal pad under his chin.

He didn't know her name. Maybe that was a good thing. Look confused and needy. He stopped the first young male associate he could find—a hungry predator type wearing a blue shirt with a white collar.

"Excuse me, need your help for a second. I'm looking for a woman," he stammered. Roarke hid his build by hunching over. "Great hair, curly black. Really attractive. About five-six. Say 28." He paused to play the next line right. "On a fast track. I bumped into her the other day and I need her help with these." He held up the books. "Didn't get her name."

"Research stuff?"

"Yeah."

"She's good at that," White Collar said. Roarke always gave unknown people a descriptive name. "You're talking about Katie. Katie Kessler. Wouldn't mind her helping me, too."

Roarke had sized up this lawyer correctly.

"Wrong floor, though," White Collar added. "She's one flight up. You new here?"

"Just here for the day. But it sure would be good if she were still around."

"Probably is. The elevator, no, take the stairs. They're just up ahead. Go to the right, she's got a small office next to the lunch room."

"Thanks," Roarke said. "This way?" he nodded with his head.

"Right down there. I'll get the door. You're pretty loaded down."

Roarke unfolded his body and took the stairs two at a time even with the books in his arms. Once upstairs he resumed a haggard posture and proceeded down the hall. Twenty paces later Roarke was at Kessler's door. He looked in. She was a quarter turn away from the door, busy on her computer.

Roarke cleared his throat. She didn't respond. He did it again, more noticeably. "Pardon me," Roarke finally said to get her attention.

Kessler slowly swiveled in her chair and looked up. It took a moment, then she recognized him. "Ah, it's the lost soul. Still looking for your way?"

"No, your directions were impeccable. Am I interrupting?"

"Are you interrupting? Now, no. A moment ago, yes."

"A lawyer's detail to facts. Do you always work so hard?"

"Do you always ask questions?"

"Not always," he answered.

"And I'm not always working."

He felt that playful spirit in her again; an attractive quality, quite out of place for a young female lawyer. Roarke closed the door.

"Excuse me, this is a little sudden," she said standing up. She saw that he was carrying books. "Pretty heavy reading for someone who's not a lawyer."

"Or a criminal."

"Right. So exactly who are you? You don't work here. I already asked."

"You did?"

"Yes I did."

She was interested in him. That was a pleasant discovery. But she was heading for the door to reopen it.

"And you do work here. Which is why I need to talk to you." He politely, but firmly blocked her way. "You may not want to help me, but I need to find out."

Kessler and Roarke stood face to face. She was no longer playful.

"You're a reporter."

"No. I'm a Special Agent for the Secret Service."

She held her gaze and he was keenly aware how much her eyes sparkled.

"I don't understand. I think I better call my office administrator." She started for the phone.

"Wait. Please." The first request was business. The "please" sounded very personal. She turned to face him again.

"Look, I need your help."

"Me? Why?"

"To research some family history. One of your clients."

"Who?"

"Teddy Lodge."

The candidate's name hung in the air and her expression soured. "You've got to be crazy, I can't do that and you're going to have to..." He interrupted before she said "leave."

"It may be for his own safety," Roarke added.

"And you're with the Secret Service. For real?"

"For real."

"I suppose you can show me some identification?"

She hadn't moved for the telephone or the door for a few moments. "Certainly." Roarke produced the necessary evidence, complete with the unmistakable red and blue logo set over a five-point gold star.

"The Secret Service," she said, noting the obvious.

"The Secret Service," he repeated.

"And you're interested in exactly what again?"

"Congressman Lodge's personal safety, or haven't you been following the news?"

With that remark Kessler coldly handed him back his ID.

"Go on."

"I'm part of the investigation team." He didn't explain that he was operating on direct orders of the president. "I understand that his family's matters were managed here. The other day I came by to discuss the family history and I got a stone wall from an asshole named Witherspoon."

Katie Kessler laughed, apparently agreeing with his view of the arrogant young attorney.

"We had a fairly one-sided dialogue. My side. I believe he was holding onto information that may be important. He didn't show me. I want to see what it was."

"Have you ever heard of a subpoena, Special Agent...Roarke?"

"Yes. I've also heard of cooperation in a federal investigation."

"But it appears that you were willing to subvert that process and take it upon yourself to locate confidential client-lawyer materials."

"Your words, counselor. A moment ago I said I needed your help."

"While posing as a clerk, or a lawyer, or someone who's supposed to be here. I'm sure your name's not on the sign-in register."

She was quite right, but he didn't answer. Instead, Roarke fixed his eyes on her, ending the debate. "Are you willing to help me?"

She blinked hard. "Why me?"

Roarke let a smile lighten the moment. "You have a nice face."

"That's how the Secret Service works? Compliments?"

"No, that's more me. May I ask your name?"

"Katie Kessler," she said without giving in to his warmth.

He held out his hand. "Scott Roarke, and it's nice to meet you."

"Why, am I not so sure," she added, trying to figure out what surprises had just entered her world.

CHAPTER 17

It's not that the CIA didn't want to place someone within General Jabbar Kharrazi's inner sanctum. They couldn't. As in the Qadhafi or Saddam Hussein regimes, Kharrazi filled most positions of merit with relatives. They kept their jobs until their dying day, whether natural or unexpected.

However, there just weren't enough relatives to spread around to staff the General's sons' competing empires. That's where the agency had slowly begun to make some headway.

In September 2001, Yemen-born, American-raised Farouk Azzarouq defied his father's wishes and answered an intriguing ad in the *Detroit Free Press*.

"Help wanted. United States needs brave men with the desire to travel. Ages 22-35. Arab-American citizens only."

He really had no idea what he was walking into until the most serious man he'd ever met in his life introduced himself as an FBI agent.

"Are you a U.S. citizen?" he asked in the downtown Detroit interview.

"Yes," responded Azzarouq.

"Have you lived in the United States for the past five years?"

"Yes sir. My family moved here 19 years ago."

"Fill out these forms please." The FBI agent handed him a clipboard with five pages worth of additional questions to answer.

"Can you just help me out with one thing, sir?" Azzarouq politely asked. The agent peered at him. "What am I applying for?" The agent gave him a twisted smile and pointed to the clipboard.

There were questions on personal health and family illnesses, on American history and comic book characters, on baseball teams and the cast of "Friends." After forty-five minutes of writing, Azzarouq put his pen down. "Finished. I think I'm ready for the final Jeopardy question now."

The agent did not laugh. Instead, he quickly scanned the paperwork and raised his eyes in a sign of approval.

"Mr. Azzarouq, what is your feeling on terrorism?" he asked in perfect Arabic.

Suddenly everything became clear to the 23-year-old computer programmer.

Just eight days after the horrific attacks on New York and Washington, D.C., President George W. Bush mandated that the Federal Bureau of Investigation find candidates who could speak fluent Arabic and infiltrate terrorist cells in the U.S. and abroad. America would "fight against terrorism on all fronts," the president declared. As a first step toward accomplishing this, the FBI's newly appointed director Robert Mueller initiated a comprehensive job search.

Very few applicants made the grade. Those who did severed their ties with family and friends and began a new life with a new identity. Farouk Azzarouq was one of them. After two years of intensive training he graduated as Sami Ben Ali. He worked for 18 months for the FBI, specializing on Libya. His understanding of the internal politics as well as the Kharrazi family struggle made him a valuable asset to penetrate internal Arab cells. But someone else had their eyes on the man now known as Ben Ali. For the sake of the ongoing war on terrorism, President Taylor's FBI director, Robert Mulligan, was willing to send his trainee across town.

"Farouk, I want you to meet a friend of mine," Mulligan said.

"Yes sir." As Ben Ali he now had a beard, a history, the right dialect, and hopefully the wherewithal to stay alive in Libya.

Mulligan pressed a buzzer on his phone and a moment later a man entered the room.

"I don't believe you've ever had the opportunity to meet Jack Evans."

The young man turned around. He stood face to face with the head of the CIA.

"Hello Farouk."

"Hello sir."

"I understand that you're quite a quick study."

"I try."

"Well, Bob tells me great things. We need a man who can do great things."

"I don't understand," he said.

"I'd like to invite you to come to work for me."

"Sir?" he asked Mulligan over his shoulder.

"Same government, different agency," Mulligan answered.

Evans chimed in, "More perks. Better pay."

"Better chance of getting killed?" Farouk added.

"Only if you fuck up," Evans responded.

Azzarouq had grown up on Bond and Bourne. The idea of being a real spy appealed to him.

"Well?" DCI Evans asked.

"Where?"

"Say yes and I'll tell you all about it, son."

Two years later, after a great deal of complex trickery, Sami Ben Ali was deep within Abahar Kharrazi's OIS, reporting as best he could on the aspirations of the potential heir.

BOSTON, MASSACHUSETTS

"You don't look like a secret agent."

"Secret Service Agent," Roarke said lightheartedly, correcting the young woman.

"Clarification noted, but aren't you supposed to talk into your sleeve?"

"I'm not on a presidential detail."

"But you work for him."

"Yes."

"You realize, Agent Roarke, even he needs a subpoena to get in here. And I still think he'd lose out to client-lawyer privilege."

"Yes, he would. So would I. But you don't."

There was a long pause between them. During that time Roarke peered straight into her brown eyes. And through them, he saw beauty and life and honesty. In the world he lived, he didn't see much of that.

"I'm sorry," he said suddenly standing up. "I shouldn't have come here. I had no business asking you to…"

"Wait," Katie offered. "Please." She touched his arm. "I need to know more. What are you looking for? Is it political? If it's political I can't…"

"No, it's not."

"Then what is it?" she asked.

"I really don't know."

"You don't know what you're looking for?"

"Well, not really," Roarke admitted.

"Oh, and you're one of the guys who's supposed to protect the president."

"Scary, isn't it," he joked.

This made her laugh. *A sense of humor.* She liked that.

"Look, to be perfectly honest, there was something about Witherspoon's attitude *and his manner* I didn't like."

She laughed. "You're not the first."

"And it told me he was hiding something."

"Not hiding, protecting. We're a law firm. That's one of the things we do, Agent Roarke," she said, not smiling anymore.

"No, it was definitely *hiding*, Ms. Kessler. And one of the things I do is find things people are hiding, particularly when it comes to national security."

"Are we being snippy?"

He closed his eyes. She was absolutely correct. "I'm sorry, but the congressman barely survived an assassination attempt and now he is under Secret Service protection."

"You for real? Gun and all?"

"...and all," he answered.

"And I suppose you can just get Morgan Taylor on the telephone and confirm all of this?"

Roarke smiled and took out his cell phone from his right vest pocket and held it out to Katie. "Press the number 5 button three times and wait."

Now it was a chess game. The telephone was there for her to try, but even Katie Kessler was a little too timid to cold call the President of the United States.

"Maybe I'll take a rain check on that." He returned the phone to his pocket.

"I'll say one thing, Agent Roarke. You certainly get to the point," Katie said.

"So I'm told, Ms. Kessler." She smiled. "So what will it be? Will you help?"

"You haven't told me what I'd be helping you do."

"Find the truth."

"About what?"

"Maybe we'll discover that by starting."

Katie shook her head and picked up a folder from her "Out" basket. "I'm going to regret this, but why don't you take a walk with me, Mr. Roarke. I have some files I need to put away in the Records Department."

BURLINGTON, VERMONT

"Geoff, it's time I called Neill."

Newman smiled at the congressman. "I'm sure Lamden has already downloaded him by now."

"Get him on the line and we'll have a heart-to-heart about the next few months."

The Democratic Party chairman was having a bad week. Governor Lamden, the favorite son in the old boy network, was abruptly the also-ran. "Dammit," Neill had complained to Lamden when he called earlier. "This was supposed to be your year."

The nomination now belonged to Teddy Lodge and this would be Neill's last hurrah.

"He's on the line now," Newman announced. He handed the phone to Lodge.

"Hello Wendell."

"Congressman, I hope you received my message of condolence."

"Yes, thank you. I appreciate it from the bottom of my heart."

"It's such a difficult time for you. For us. I gather no breaks in the investigation yet."

"Nothing yet. The FBI is keeping me informed."

"They'll find the guy. Give 'em time. And Teddy, I commend you on the way you handled New York and Rhode Island. Showed real dignity."

"Thank you, and frankly, that's why I'm calling. I had a chat with Governor Lamden the other day." Lodge paused, but Neill didn't acknowledge he knew anything. "And I've decided to continue.

That said, I believe that Henry would make us stronger. I think he'll do it and I hope you'll sell it to the party leadership. You *will* do it, Wendell?"

Neill didn't like the tone he heard. Not one bit.

BOSTON, MASSACHUSETTS

Katie Kessler stood up on a footstool and pulled open a cabinet above them. Roarke watched her from behind and was pleased by what he saw.

"You're looking," she noted, as if having eyes in the back of her head.

"I'm admiring," he corrected.

"Here, steady this stool, I need to get this one out in the back. It's pretty damned thick. Oh, and by the way," she said looking down at him, "when we're finished, you're taking me out to dinner, mister."

"No problem, counselor."

There were eighteen file folders in all. She handed them one by one to Roarke who deposited them on a long work desk near to where he had put his things. Roarke tried to look over her shoulder when she opened them, but was chastised. "Uh-uh. Lawyer-client. You stay over there. Other side."

He obeyed and sat at one of the workstations. Katie scanned through the files for fifteen minutes. "This is interesting," she offered at last. "The Lodges already had a will. Drawn by a small Marblehead law firm, Woodruff, Stuart and Nunes on Washington Street. Signed two years earlier. Nunes is noted as his executor. Everything looks in order. Then in '75 they wrote a new one with another North Shore attorney, Haywood W. Marcus, who ultimately joined our firm in 1985."

"Do you have the new will?"

"Let me see."

She leafed through more tabs on more folders. Many more than Witherspoon had in his office.

"Hold on," she said. "Well, yes. This might be it." She read quickly to herself.

"What's it say?"

"This is fairly boilerplate until here." Katie tapped on page three, midway down. "Interesting. Marcus got pretty much irrevocable dictatorial powers."

"Isn't that what an executor is normally granted?"

"Well, someone must have sold Mr. Lodge a bill of goods. His old Marblehead law firm was suddenly out of the picture as executor. Marcus was in. And as far as I can gather, Marcus just walked in off the street."

"People change attorneys all the time?" Roarke asked.

"Well, yes, but this required a great deal of paperwork. It's not a bad document. Let's see, in the event of death," she read on and shared the bullet points, "burial at sea, memorial monuments at Waterside Cemetery in Marblehead. Trust funds for Teddy. Seems everyone was taken care of. Even Alfred Nunes." She finished scanning the will, then found another document. "Wait a second. There's something else here. It appears that Nunes contested the new will. There's a notation. But it doesn't explain much." She looked up from the documents and asked, "What happened to the family?"

"Teddy was in a horrible traffic accident when he was in high school; the only one to survive. It nearly paralyzed him. A day later, probably due to all the stress, his mother collapsed at home and died of a heart attack."

"And his father?"

"He died a year earlier." Roarke wanted to get more information, but he paused a moment, not wanting to appear insensitive. After clearing his throat he continued. "What grounds did Nunes use to contest?"

"Well let's see." After a minute she found another extract.

"Okay, here it is. Nunes said he had no prior knowledge of the change of assignment of executors. According to this letter he was furious." She continued reading and paraphrasing, "But the County Court declined to hear his complaint since he was not harmed by the terms of the new document. It ended there."

"So maybe they had had an argument or something and Oliver Lodge changed his mind."

"Or Marcus made a great pitch. He's a brilliant lawyer," she said trailing off. Katie was now lost in a clipping of Oliver Lodge Jr.'s obituary. She returned to a previous document. Then back again to the newspaper clipping. Then back and forth again.

"What are you doing?"

"Looking at the dates."

"The dates?" Roarke asked.

"The dates on the will and obit of Teddy's father."

"And…"

She looked directly at him. "You do have a nice face, Mr. Roarke."

"Why thank you. Now what do you have?"

"Maybe something worth finding."

She put the paper down. "Mr. Roarke, the new will is dated just three weeks before Oliver Lodge died."

Beacon Hill is known for its intimate, romantic restaurants. Katie picked one of her favorites. 75 Chestnut Street offered a delicious menu with a French Normandy influence. The ambient light was low enough to hide some of her exhaustion and yet accent her eyes, which she realized, almost with embarrassment, were constantly on her companion.

Katie and Roarke sat in the back, with Roarke taking the wall facing out. She hadn't been aware of the move, but it was part of his training. Not so much Secret Service, but a residual effect of his other assignments. None that he would be sharing with Katie. His trip to the restroom and the kitchen also followed his training. He always familiarized himself with all of the exits, wherever he went.

Katie ordered a Lemon Drop Martini. Roarke called for a margarita on the rocks with salt. "Jose Cuervo," he emphasized.

"That's not quite a proper Bostonian drink," Katie maintained.

"I don't think I'd qualify as a proper Bostonian," Roarke added with little reflection. "Are there still any left?"

"The old days of the Back Bay Society and Boston Brahmins with their aged scotch and brandy are history. Now it's exotic martinis. Martinis, Mr. Roarke. Not margaritas."

"Okay, okay. Two Lemon Drops," conceded Roarke. "But make sure the rim's coated with sugar."

"Thank you," she offered, then turned to the waiter. "And I'll be ordering dinner as well for 'The Hulk.'" She batted her eyes at Roarke when the waiter left to get their drinks. "Let me see if I can get you right."

Roarke took the challenge. "Okay. No one's ever tried before. Go ahead."

She studied the menu for only a moment. It was obvious to Roarke that she knew the restaurant's best dishes.

"I'd peg you for a lamb chop man," she said putting the menu down. "But I'm not going to let you have it tonight."

Was that a devilish smile?

"No, we're going for something lighter. Something more me than you, Mr. Roarke."

This woman got to him, quieted him, and touched him unlike any he had ever met. He permitted himself that fleeting whim he had in Washington. *Maybe it's time to start leading a normal life. Leave that other one behind.*

The drinks came. Katie was about to offer a toast, but he interrupted.

"No, you're choosing dinner. The toast is mine. To…to," he paused to weigh his words, "to the Supreme Court. They don't know what they're in store for, counselor."

"Why Mr. Roarke, you flatter me."

"Thank you. You deserve it." He stared deeply into her eyes. And for the first time since they met, she didn't have a fast comeback. Katie Kessler blushed.

"Tell me something," she finally said. "If you hadn't talked me into pulling the files, would you have gotten them yourself?"

"A very good question. A legal one?"

"A personal one."

"An honest answer then. No," Roarke admitted.

"That begs the question: What if your boss claimed National Security?"

"On what grounds?"

"Now you're asking the questions. Very clever, Mr. Roarke."

"Thank you, but I was counting on you."

"Why would you even think I would help you?"

"The one thing I know for certain—trust my instincts."

"And you can say without a doubt that none of this is political?"

"It's not."

"That you're not trying to dig up some dirt to help in November."

"No."

"That you're not messing with Lodge's principal law firm?"

"No," he said sharply. His body tensed and his voice grew completely serious. "Look, here it is. Real straight. I came to Boston after an assassination attempt of a presidential candidate."

"And the murder of…"

"His wife. Yes. And the fact that the Secret Service was not attached to Lodge yet was the law. Now he's under our protection. And he could get the job. So, I'm here and your law firm *interests* me."

"*Interests*? Such an interesting word, Mr. Roarke," she said, trying to keep it light. "What's that mean?"

He took a deep breath, not knowing what he meant. It was an honest response based on nothing more than instinct. "Just that," he continued more softly. "It *interests* me." Roarke let the inflection remain.

She peered into his eyes. A moment later, not even realizing what she was doing, Katie slid her hand across the table, finding his fingers. After a long silence she said, "Maybe we should visit records again."

All the tension in his body left and he softened to the feel of her fingers and the sound of her voice. Dinner tonight would be fine no matter what she ordered.

TRIPOLI, LIBYA

Sami Ben Ali took his time. During his training at Langley he had learned about two agents who hadn't been patient enough. The CIA even had file photographs, smuggled out of Kharrazi's Abu Salim Prison, showing what was left of their bodies after being riddled with electrodes, stoned, and beaten until they were put out of their misery with a bullet between the eyes.

Ben Ali liked living more than anything else. He earned a miniscule salary from Libya, and generous hazard pay from the U.S. Since he wanted to be around to enjoy it in his old age, he moved with utmost care.

On Thursday, the eve before the Muslim Sabbath, he found what he needed the most. Opportunity.

Like clockwork, Walid Abdul-Latif ducked out for a late afternoon cigarette break. Earlier, Major Karim Kitan had departed angrily. And since his assistant had reported in sick, no one else was around. Ben Ali had what he calculated as just seven minutes to log onto Walid's computer. Seven minutes—the time that it took for Walid to go down the hall, take a piss, smoke a cigarette as he always did on the balcony, and return. Seven minutes. That's all he had.

Ben Ali cursed General Kharrazi for the lack of better technology in Libya. They were decades behind. The damned computer required more than two minutes to boot up. Two-and-a-half to be precise, out of seven. And all of his next steps were slow, too.

First he needed to check the pull down file and write the exact order of the last four files that Walid worked on. He figured that would take thirty more seconds. He quickly ran through the rest of procedure in his mind: Allow another ninety seconds to locate the file that Walid had typed. Add a minute to insert a disk, copy and close the file. Another ninety seconds to call up each of the last four files in correct order to cover his tracks, thus hiding his work on the pull-down file menu. Finally, forty-five of the slowest seconds of his life to close each file in the correct order and shut down the computer.

If Walid smoked at his typical rate, his margin of error was only fifteen seconds.

He began. The computer churned, sputtered and flashed the start-up icons. And as he had planned, he was into the program at the 4 minute and 32 second mark. If only there was time to read the file, he wouldn't have to leave with a disc. He hated having evidence on him. But in this case, even the slow computer was faster than his ability to scan and absorb the report.

Then it was time to save the file. *"Shit!"* he screamed to himself. He had grabbed a floppy disc that was completely full. He scrambled to his desk and rifled through the top drawer. *Where the fuck is a disk!* Another ten seconds. Fifteen. He hated making stupid mistakes. This was one. At thirty seconds he found a disk, and prayed to Allah and anyone else who would listen that there was room to store the file. He inserted the 3MB disk, imported from the U.S. via Saudi Arabia, clicked on *Save As* and highlighted the A Drive. Now he was getting nervous. He had never been this careless before. Ten seconds, 20, 30, 40, 50. At 60 seconds, the computer was still saving the file. He was now six minutes into his operation and the damned computer wasn't finished yet. At a minute-fifteen into the process, it finally completed its task. *Now to quickly, if such a thing existed on this piece of crap, call up the old files.* He checked his list.

Just as he opened the last file he heard footsteps down the hall. Walid. He wasn't finished and he had another forty-five seconds to close down.

In a moment he'd be caught spying in the office of the Libyan leader's most accomplished son.

"Walid!" he called out, running into the hall.

"Yes, I'm coming, what is it? What is it you fool?"

"I just received a call—a car bomb in the plaza! We have to get out of here. Now!"

"Who called? The last time it was some idiot trying to scare us all."

"I don't know," Ben Ali answered, grabbing Walid. "But this sounded real."

"Okay, okay. But let go of me, you moron."

Ben Ali apologized. "Better take the stairs." As they ran past other offices, he yelled for people to evacuate.

Midway down the flight of stairs Ben Ali stopped. "Shit! I left a cigarette burning on my desk. I have to go back. I'll be right down." He bounded up the stairs three at a time, ignoring the foul outburst from Walid.

Back in the office he shut the computer down, lit a cigarette that he supposedly had been smoking, burned a brown stain on his desk, then crushed the butt on the floor. One task remained. He pulled his disk from the computer and stuffed it in his pocket.

He ran down the hall and rushed into the lobby just as Walid and the others were exiting. He was completely out of breath, ever so much looking like a fool. A *living, breathing* fool.

BOSTON, MASSACHUSETTS

Roarke walked Katie up to her Grove Street apartment. She lived in a condominium on the third floor of a converted 1889 brownstone.

"I have a view of the Charles River," she announced at the doorstep. "But you're not going to see it."

For all of his skills, Roarke dreaded this part of the evening. He had pretty specific erotic thoughts at the moment, but felt like a schoolboy. After all, this was a first date, with a little bit of danger of discovery at the law firm adding to the excitement. And as first dates went, he found himself thinking about a second and a third.

No, he had said to himself on their walk to her condo. *A kiss on the cheek will be fine.* And yet, Katie had telegraphed some fairly inviting signals that she was interested in him. That was until now. He was actually relieved.

"Another night maybe," she coyly added.

He felt those stirrings again.

"If you call me."

Roarke didn't take orders from very many people. The president. Yes. A few commanding officers along the way; but rarely women. "I will," he answered, meaning it.

Before he could kiss her on the cheek, she kissed him.

"Now be careful. I'm going to see what else I can find for you."

"You don't have to do that."

"I know I don't. But I liked your toast before dinner. It felt like a little career boost."

She turned, wiggled her fingers over her shoulders and pressed the key code to unlock the front door. A second later she disappeared up the stairs.

Roarke walked down Grove Street to find his car and a cold shower.

CHAPTER 18

BOSTON, MASSACHUSETTS
FRIDAY, JUNE 27

Haywood W. Marcus thanked Witherspoon for the information. "You handled everything quite properly and professionally, young man. I'm certain there's no reason for concern. You are to be congratulated," he said through his blindingly white teeth. Marcus was the most well put together partner in the firm; perfectly groomed and immaculately dressed. He favored hand-made shirts and suits and started every morning with a shoeshine in the lobby. His fastidiousness placed everyone else in the firm on notice that neatness mattered. So did the accoutrements. Everything in his office—the rare Winslow Homer depiction of a New England fisherman, the Victorian antique furniture, and his two cherished Frederick Remington bronze statues celebrating cavalry charges—contributed to the ultimate focal point: Marcus' desk and Marcus.

"Thank you, Mr. Marcus," the younger attorney said. "After I saw your cautionary note on the file I immediately ended the meeting."

"Again, thank you," Marcus said.

Witherspoon gave himself a few gold stars. He didn't get the chance to speak to one of the senior partners often and in his estimation this had gone very well, even though he had taken a few days to make the appointment.

"Oh, just one thing. An opinion, my boy. Where do you think this man was going with all of his questions?" Marcus asked without any apparent concern.

"Just exploring. He really knew nothing walking in."

Marcus peered over his glasses. His eyes turned ice cold. "And walking out?"

"Oh, nothing. I cited lawyer-client privilege."

"I'll ask you this just once. Answer as if your life depended on it. Are you *absolutely* certain?"

Witherspoon, acutely aware that this was no longer a friendly conversation, felt real terror. He had never been asked a direct question so intently. And this was not the kindhearted 62-year-old man he'd been conversing with a moment earlier. Here was a lawyer whose legal prowess proved the undoing of many formidable courtroom opponents. He was ruthless and calculating. Witherspoon realized he was way out of his league.

"Did you say anything?" Marcus demanded.

"No, Mr. Marcus," Witherspoon answered, revealing why he would never become a good lawyer.

"And the materials?"

"I had them returned to Records."

"Get them and bring them here. And do it quicker than it took you to decide to speak to me now."

"Yes, sir."

"To me. No one else. Do you understand?" Marcus demanded.

"Yes, sir," Witherspoon repeated, conscious of how cold the office suddenly felt. Not just physically, but emotionally. It was void of the typical personal touches; no family photos, no memorabilia, no clutter. Just Marcus holding court.

"Now!" Marcus' eyes had not blinked once and Witherspoon was frozen by the power of his boss' stare. "Now."

Ten minutes later Witherspoon returned with all the Lodge files. He quietly put them on Marcus' hand-carved 19th-century oak desk. Marcus was reading the latest edition of "The Robb Report."

"It's all here, Mr. Marcus."

"Thank you my boy," the partner said as if nothing had happened.

"There is one thing, sir."

Marcus lifted his eyes. "Oh?"

"They're a little out of order."

"And that's a problem?"

"They're not the way I left them. Someone's looked at them since me."

Marcus' law practice brought him many wealthy clients from around the globe. On any given day it was not unusual for him to bill major Fortune 500 members as well as industrialists from foreign capitals. He also had a select private list, which he didn't bill. Nonetheless, money found its way into special bank accounts far from Boston. At the top of the list was a very good client who resided on Miami's renowned Fisher Island.

He needed to think about what to tell him. This wasn't going to be easy. But he had to do it. He'd been *handling* the Lodge estate for years. He probably should have shredded the file, but he never saw a reason to do so, until now. He thought about what he had been promised more than thirty years ago and realized this required a personal conversation, not a phone call.

Haywood Marcus did something himself that he always gave to his secretary. He called the airlines.

CHAPTER 19

TRIPOLI, LIBYA
SATURDAY, JUNE 28

The fact that Sami Ben Ali even had a laptop would have raised serious questions.

He certainly couldn't afford a decent one on his salary. But he had a cover story that might hold up. Old computers like his 1990s Sony Vaio were readily available on the black market. His looked beaten up and barely working, yet it was a wolf in sheep's clothing; fast, state-of-the-art, and full of the most modern built-in firewalls and security blocks that the "Company" developed. The Company was the CIA.

The ordinary start-up programs took five minutes to load unless bypassed with the proper keystrokes. His main programs were not labeled. They were hidden four layers deep; triple password protected. The wrong combination of function keys, letters, and numbers, entered without proper authorization would trigger a lethal virus and fry the entire memory in seconds.

Ben Ali didn't discount that he'd have a great deal of explaining to do if his laptop was found in a search. But ultimately all of his excuses should stand up against the weak technological expertise of Abahar Kharrazi's secret police, the OIS. *They better.*

Nonetheless, every time he booted up, he worked in his closet and made sure that he had a radio blaring to cover the sounds of his keys. Sami, like everyone with a computer, knew that it was easy to lose track of time. So his final rule was to limit his work to under 30 minutes. He kept his watch next to him to make sure.

These were the hard and fast rules he followed as he inserted the 27 KB disk copied from Walid's computer.

Sami pushed his clothes aside in his closet and crouched to type. His computer rested on a makeshift desk, two cardboard boxes loaded with books. He ran power off the battery charge, and always worked when the electricity was turned on in his building. Israeli-made infrared scopes, in the hands of Abahar's intelligence squads, could spot the glow of his computer even through some walls. So it was important to have bright lights on directly in front of his closet. It wasn't hard to do. He lived in a small one room flat.

The prompts came up on screen. He jumped through the masked programs by typing the complex codes he'd memorized. Next he clicked on what would be the A drive in English. In an instant the file typed by Walid Abdul-Latif loaded.

Ben Ali read it with great interest. He discounted his colleague's misspelled words and bad grammar. It was typical of a Libyan education. At first, the report itself made him laugh. He read a self-inflated account about Walid's masterful control and handling of his contact. He followed the details of the contact with Omar and how Walid's mole discovered the file from Fadi Kharrazi's office. *Nothing but pathetic drivel*, he noted until getting halfway through the report. There, past all of the cloak and dagger hyperbole, was the gist of the summary.

Spying, Sami came to believe, is like a children's game of telephone where a message is whispered down the line. This information had gone from the hands of Fadi to Lakhdar al-Nassar, to Omar Za'eem, to Walid Abdul-Latif. Ultimately it would go to Major Bayon Karim Kitan and his boss Abahar Kharrazi. *But did Walid report what was first communicated? Did he get it right?* That's what Sami Ben Ali wondered as he began.

Ashab al-Kahf proceeding. Cryptic or direct? Ben Ali didn't know.

He read of Syria in the early 1970s, the late Hafez al-Assad and his son Bashar. Iraq and Uday Hussein. *Another leader's son.* Then something called Andropov I and "Red Banner." *Russian? Probably.* He realized that there wasn't a snowball's chance in hell, or Tripoli for that matter, that he'd actually figure out what any of it meant. He'd have to pass the information on.

MARBLEHEAD, MASSACHUSETTS

Roarke quickly discovered from the phone directory that the law firm of Woodruff, Stuart and Nunes no longer existed. A few neighbors told him that the old professional building housing lawyers had been demolished long ago and everyone had moved away or died. No one knew about Nunes.

A call to the Justice Department filled in the details.

The firm dissolved in 1981. Stuart died of a heart attack two years earlier. Woodruff retired to West Palm Beach and died in 1998.

Alfred Nunes, age 77, and the youngest of the partners, had a registered address in Boxford, Massachusetts, but spent most of his time on the road in a 340-hp Winnebago Chieftain with his wife.

Roarke picked up the trail from there. According to his inquiry at the Boxford Post Office, Nunes' mail was held for forwarding once every month to a pre-arranged location across the country. Thanks to his credentials, the Secret Service agent was allowed to examine the mail being held for Nunes. Along with the junk mail and bills were a half dozen fishing magazines. The next scheduled address was a box in Sisters, Oregon; the delivery due in ten days. He talked to the local mailman on the lawyer's route and learned that Nunes loved visiting Civil War and Indian battlefields and photographing national parks.

Next he visited the Registry of Motor Vehicles. They gave him Nunes' license plate number. Roarke called Shannon Davis, a friend at the FBI, for help in actually locating the lawyer. "He'll either be on the road or listed with a national park. I have a hunch he spends a lot of time fly fishing so you might want to check parks that handle RV's and have good streams," Roarke explained.

Davis looked at a map and estimated Nunes could be anywhere

from Oregon to Washington State, California, Idaho, Wyoming or Colorado.

"Just find him," Roarke stressed.

"Why? Did he forget to catch and release an under the limit trout?" the FBI man joked.

"I need to talk to him. This isn't an arrest. You don't even need to bother him. Just tell me where he is and I'll be out."

Roarke counted on hearing quickly.

WASHINGTON, D.C.
NBC STUDIOS
SUNDAY, JUNE 29

All the Sunday morning talkers wanted him. *Meet The Press. Face the Nation. This Week.*

Geoff Newman wanted *Meet the Press*, for strictly historical reasons. John Kennedy used the show to his benefit. When the call came in from the show's producer, Newman made an unprecedented proposal. "You get the congressman this week, and promise one appearance per month up to the election, and I'll give you exclusivity. If it's a 'no,' tell me right now and I'll be happy to call CBS, ABC or Fox."

The producer put Newman on hold. Ninety-seconds later he was back with a one-word answer. "Done."

Newman had his deal and *Meet the Press* had its booking. Such was the world of television and politics.

"Good morning, Congressman Lodge. First our sincerest condolences," offered the host at the top of broadcast.

"Thank you," Lodge responded quietly. He was wearing a dark blue jacket, light blue shirt and a conservative burgundy tie with thin blue stripes. It was a TV friendly ensemble, carefully chosen by Geoff Newman who was now picking all the candidate's clothing.

The host reviewed the particulars of Lodge's ordeal for anyone who had spent the last week under a rock. "I know this is painful to talk about. Seven days ago your wife was killed. Two days later you resoundingly won the Democratic primaries in New York and Rhode

Island." The host now relied on his notes. "By our NBC count you have 2,371 delegates out of 4,339. To capture the nomination you needed 2,170."

Lodge nodded politely to the assessment.

"And yet, you have not announced your intentions, though we have heard from Democratic Party Chief Wendell Neill that the nomination is yours for the taking. We appreciate you joining us today, and like all Americans, we hope you can tell us what you're thinking."

Geoff Newman watched from just off stage. Scott Roarke watched in Peabody. Michael O'Connell in Marblehead. President Taylor had his set on a few blocks away at the White House. And in Tripoli, Fadi Kharrazi caught the broadcast off his satellite dish.

Teddy Lodge began slowly. He focused directly on the host and talked to him like an old friend, avoiding the camera and any semblance of speech making.

"It was a week ago. One week." He closed his eyes, paused and shook his head. "You have to understand, this is very difficult for me." He stopped again to collect his thoughts. Tears formed in his eyes. He wiped them away, then apparently found the strength to continue. His voice cracked at first, then got stronger. "People are wondering what I'm going to do. First, let me focus on the crime. A killer who had his sights on me, shot Jennifer." Newman had reminded him to always refer to his wife by her first name, for emotional impact.

"He shot her. He killed Jenny. She was no further from me than you are. She was a lively, vibrant, beautiful, loving partner. Now she is gone." Lodge looked down. His voice cracked.

No guest in the history of *Meet the Press* had ever taken such pauses. Usually, reporters were quick on the uptake to get in their next questions. Not today. Neither the host nor his panel of three other distinguished journalists pressed the Congressman.

"Jen's killer is out there. The President of the United States has assured me that he'll be found. But he hasn't been. Not yet."

Political pundits writing about the appearance scored Lodge first blood. He openly attacked the president and, for that matter, the FBI.

"I want this killer brought to justice. And you can read into that whatever you'd like," he said raising his voice. "I want him brought to justice."

Lodge still held the floor. No one else jumped in.

"Now, I want to thank the voters of New York and Rhode Island," he said in a warmer tone. "They didn't have to come out on my behalf. But they did. They expressed their rights as Americans in the proper way. At the ballot. Not with a bullet as some damned coward did last week."

Americans like real people. And with his last angry utterance, Lodge earned more fans.

"So I thank everyone for your kind letters and for your renewed confidence and belief in me. And now I will tell you what you may already suspect." He looked past the moderator and directly at the camera. This assured Lodge that the sound bite would be used by all of the networks. "I *will* go to Denver. I will seek the nomination of the Democratic Party. I will accept, if nominated. And I will ask Americans to make me their president."

There was enough copy to be committed to front page stories, features, editorials and news reports in the first three minutes of *Meet the Press* to level a forest full of trees.

Theodore Wilson Lodge laid it all out. The spread between the congressman and the president evaporated.

TRIPOLI, LIBYA
MONDAY, JUNE 30

"Bullshit! This is bullshit!" Abahar Kharrazi screamed at Major Kitan. He slammed Walid Abdul-Latif's report on the desk.

The major stood rigidly at attention through his commander's rantings.

"You *are* going to find out what this is all about or I will see to it that my father sends you to paradise before your time! Do you understand me?"

"By your command, sir," Kitan declared, looking ever the obedient soldier. That's how he had survived to age 44. He had managed to get promoted to the rank of major in Colonel Mu'ammar Qadhafi's army and so far lived to serve General Jabbar Kharrazi and his son Abahar.

He didn't have much job security, but he used his status to pilfer whatever he could, hoping he'd enjoy the spoils someday. As he sucked in his belly, he realized that he had gotten soft and Kharrazi's fearsome son would somehow take advantage of his weaknesses. If he lived through this episode he would harden his body and his soul. If he lived.

The head of the Secret Police read the report again, pacing the floor and swearing at his younger brother.

"He's up to something. I know how his mind works. But what is it?"

"There are key words, sir. But it is the reference to Hafez al-Assad that concerns me. What is a dead Syrian president's name doing in a file of his? And Uday Hussein? Another puzzle."

Abahar shared the worry, but it remained unspoken. For years his moles informed him that his brother had a secret meeting with Saddam Hussein's son, Uday, before the fall of Iraq. *About what? About this?*

Abahar knew that the modern concept of "inherited office" originated with Hafez al-Assad. In Egypt, President Hosni Mubarak made his younger son, Gamal, a key member in the ruling National Democratic Party. Yemini President Ali Abdullah Saleh prepared his son, Ahmed, to take his place. Saddam groomed his tyrannical sons to replace him, just as Mu'ammar Qadhafi had. The same was true for Jabbar Kharrazi.

For Hafez al-Assad it was an easy ascension. There was only one son to consider. But Jabbar had two.

One day soon, Libyans would have an election after the father/leader's death, but it would be a one-man race with either Abahar or Fadi as the nominee. Conventional wisdom had it that Abahar would get the nod. And yet, here was a report that linked Fadi with Uday Hussein in the last years of his life, and in a roundabout way al-Assad of Syria. He came back to the nagging thought again. *Two other sons of Arab leaders. One who had aspirations; one who succeeded.*

"Be patient. We will discover more," Kitan promised, "or my man inside your brother's office will meet the Prophet Muhammad."

Abahar fixed a cold stare on his subordinate. "And you will be there to greet him." There was no equivocation in Kharrazi's voice.

Fadi Kharrazi sought an answer to a trick question. "Do you see me as the 'trouble maker' my father and brother do?" he demanded of Lakhdar al-Nassar over apple tea in his office.

Kharrazi's aide sipped his drink, stalling as he considered a safe, but proper response. But Fadi laughed before al-Nassar formulated an answer.

"That is an unfair question, my friend," he continued in a coldly calm voice. "Of course I am a trouble maker. And why not? I am my father's son. I tell them what to think. I provide them with the shows they want to watch. They love the American movies I give them. Yet, to my family I am nothing more than the playboy killer."

Fadi's tone intensified even as he fought to control it. "And who deserves to be the next president when the General meets Allah?"

Lakhdar swallowed hard.

"He dares consider Abahar. Abahar! A joke. Even the meaning of his name is a lie. *More brilliant? More magnificent?* A petulant child who lives only because of the guns around him."

Al-Nassar simply nodded. He knew Fadi's tempestuous speeches could not be interrupted. They were applauded with loyal listening and undying agreement. The assistant laughed inside. Undying was what he spent a lot of time working on around his beloved mentor.

"No, Lakhdar, Abahar will not replace my father. Not when the Great Satan itself rises in support of the new Libya and all people of the Arab world turn to me in thanks."

The younger Kharrazi brother was finished pontificating for now. Lakhdar suspected that Fadi had some sort of "arrangement" but he couldn't possibly fathom the strings that Fadi manipulated beyond Libya's Mediterranean shores. Lakhdar wasn't smart enough to figure it out or smart enough to keep quiet about what he did know.

Barely out of Fadi's office he gossiped with Omar Za'eem. By day's end, Za'eem carried the vague message back to Walid.

BOSTON, MASSACHUSETTS

Katie Kessler arrived early at Freelander, Collins, Wrather & Marcus, a good hour before most of her colleagues began their day. She wanted to review the Lodge files again. The other night she had given the papers only a cursory scan. Now personal curiosity drove her. She had no reason to meddle in campaign affairs. Katie still believed that's what it was about. But as an attorney for the firm, she did have access to the privileged information. *So why not see what else is there.*

The Records Department was dark and quiet. She flicked the lights on and casually pulled the rolling step stool over to the shelves containing the Lodge family papers. Katie climbed up, repeating what she had done before, laughing aloud at the image of Roarke studying her butt. Katie was lost in that idle thought as she opened the drawer. It slid a bit more easily than the last time. It soon became obvious why.

Three files were missing. The heavy ones labeled Oliver Lodge, Theodore Lodge, and Lodge Estate.

In that single instant Katie felt exposed. The files were pulled for a reason. That meant someone probably knew she had been looking into something that was none of her business.

"Getting a head start on some pressing case?" a voice asked in the doorway.

CHAPTER 20

"And pray tell, what are you working on, Ms. Kessler?" Haywood Marcus asked in the friendliest of terms. He then added, "The truth, Ms. Kessler. We work with the truth here."

Katie slowly backed down the steps and smiled.

"I didn't get back all of my work last week. I'm juggling research for a few cases."

"All beginning with the letter 'L'?" Marcus asked.

"Only one." She realized she could not beat such a skilled barrister in argument, so she decided to give him the truth, though stretched a little.

"The Lodge file."

"Oh?"

Katie climbed down and walked the eight steps to where Marcus stood. "A Secret Service man came in asking about our work on it. I'm sure you heard. He met with Witherspoon. He bumped into me and asked for directions out. Then he wanted details about the Lodges. In my estimation he was too forward." That was the truth. Katie just combined two separate encounters. "I got concerned someone might come back, without permission. So I went for the files." Still the truth. "I may be too late."

Marcus read her face for the telltale signs. He had an acute ability to detect lying. Liars revealed themselves in the ways their eyes avoided direct contact, how they shifted their weight when they stood, the uncontrolled nervous twitches in their fingers. This woman exhibited none of these tendencies. Somewhat satisfied he softly said, "They're quite safe. I can assure you."

Without hesitation Katie answered, "Good. It's better that they're out of circulation."

"Thank you for your assessment, Ms. Kessler." He studied her more. He had a smart lawyer here. He hoped she wasn't a dumb one, too.

"Well, if you'll excuse me, I have some other cases to pull."

She confidently walked to a cabinet and pulled the first name she recognized. Her back was turned away from the senior partner.

"Ah, one more thing, Ms. Kessler," Marcus asked. "If you don't mind?"

"Yes," Katie said without facing around. She bit her lip.

"A relevant point about the file you're reaching for." His tone grew cold. "Without looking at it."

Oh God! Katie slowly lowered her eyes and scanned the name on the tab. She lifted it out of the cabinet, inhaled deeply and pivoted on one foot. Her face was only inches away from Haywood Marcus.

"I beg your pardon, sir?"

"That file in your hand. Tell me about it."

"May I ask why?"

"Call it a test, Ms. Kessler. A test of your skills as a lawyer."

Katie handed the two-inch file over to the coldest hands she'd ever touched. "Mr. Marcus, I believe it's a case that you're intimately familiar with: Mercantile Associates v. Brockton, MA. Toxic waste. We represented Mercantile. State Superior Court dismissed the plaintiff's motion. But I've watched cases similar to this come back through Civil. And the plaintiffs are looking for a favorable judgement based on Super Fund legislation. If you remember the Woburn case, sir. Shall I go on?"

Marcus glanced at the paperwork. "Well, well. I see we have a proactive attorney in our midst. I'm quite impressed. You passed my test. Thank you."

"Oh no, thank you, Mr. Marcus. And if you'd like, I'll brief you on actions we can take to prepare Mercantile. Billable hours, I'm sure," she said with confidence.

"That would be good."

Katie Kessler left feeling lucky. *Damn lucky.* She just beat the legendary Haywood Marcus in direct rebuttal thanks to nothing more than luck. She had put her fingers on a case she studied in law school.

As she rounded the hall Katie realized two things. From now on she'd have to be much more careful. And she needed to visit *The Marblehead Reporter* archives on her own time.

Haywood Marcus also came to a realization. He'd have the girl watched.

NEW YORK CITY
NYPD MIDTOWN PRECINCT

The phone rang.

God please let it be something positive, Harry Coates begged. It had been days since anything had come up. Positive or negative.

The New York City detective ran the odds at solving this murder. Slim to none: No apparent motive. So far no witnesses had come forward. And worse, the gnawing feeling that somewhere people were working as hard to keep it unsolved as he was to solving it. The ballistics report determined the weapon as a Sig P229. That was not good news. A lot of police departments used P229's. So did the Secret Service.

He picked up on the third ring.

"Hello."

"Got news for you on that number…" He felt a twinge of relief. Sarah, his computer guru, lived on the net. She could use the system or subvert it to get almost anything. "…but it's not good."

Then again, there were some things that even Sarah couldn't find.

"Shit," he said.

"But I have an opinion. Want to hear it?"

"Give me anything."

"Okay. I started with your number. Should have been no big deal. But it was. Right away it was disconnected. I mean right away. Disconnected at the request of the customer. 'So who's the customer,' I ask. Well, I go around and around with the people I know at the phone company who know people who know people and I finally get a name. Nitrogen XL LTD., which as names go doesn't say a damned thing."

There was the sound of Sarah taking a sip of water on the other end. Coates wrote down the company name and underlined it.

"Keep going."

"All right. Then I went digging for anything on the company. The whole Internet, the business profiles, Wall Street, foreign corporations, dba's, you name it."

"And?"

"And now I give you my learned opinion. No amount of checking is going to come up with Nitrogen XL LTD. because there is no fucking business in the whole goddamned world called Nitrogen XL LTD., which leads me to believe that you got yourself a contact number for a handler."

This is exactly what Coates was worried about.

"Looks like you dialed a phone run by the mob, the military, or the government—ours or somebody else's. I'm presuming that only one other person was supposed to call that number, unless of course they got one of those miserable dinnertime randomly dialed solicitations. You called and they pulled the plug. That's just my opinion, of course."

Coates didn't say a word. But the news fit his growing suspicions. This could be a government hit.

"You there or am I gonna have to run through this all over again?"

"I'm here. Thinking," he offered.

"You better be. Cause I'll tell you something else. You don't know who they are. But they sure do know who you are…now."

"Thanks Sarah. You're always so reassuring."

"No problem. Tell you what. I'll see if I can hack my way into billing and come up with anything."

"And that would be illegal," Coates said for the recording that he now feared was being made *somewhere*.

"Yeah, you're right." And Sarah hung up.

Coates stood and walked to a corner window overlooking 42nd Street. The room was small, awkwardly broken up by a support post. He leaned against it and looked through the window below. Crosstown traffic was moving pretty well for midday. People outside were enjoying the sun. Political posters dotted the lampposts. From his third floor window he could just about make out the headlines at the corner newsstand.

This is where he came to think things through. If Sarah was right, then the guy on the other end of the line was sitting at a desk occupied 24 hours a day. Which meant more than one person was at that phone. And behind that desk had to be another desk, maybe with a closed door or maybe at another location. That's where the call would be transferred. But who sat at that desk? Someone important enough to kill the phone line after a quick call from NYPD.

Coates walked to his captain's office and told the secretary, "Goin' to Stamford. I'll call in." He picked up his copy of *The New York Times*. Lodge was all over it. He realized he'd forgotten to vote.

The article was simply headlined, Being Lodge. The nearly daily reports on the Lodge campaign underscored how Michael O'Connell was emerging as his unofficial biographer. He apparently owned the left-hand column of the *Times* more days than not.

He lives in the haunting presence of death and disappointment, yet time after time, Teddy Lodge emerges victorious over the forces that would bring a lesser man down—not by choice, but by the face cards life constantly deals him. He is a composite Kennedy, with hardships that strengthen him and experiences that harden him. This is the man who runs for president. Or more precisely, the man who doesn't run away from being president.

O'Connell provided readers with a sense of historical perspective, pointing out that should Lodge move into the White House in January, he'd be the first president since the 1880s to enter as a widower. In all, four presidents were widowers: Jefferson, Jackson, Van Buren and Garfield. He concluded with one simple fact:

None of the widowed presidents ever remarried while serving in office.

STAMFORD, CONNECTICUT

Harry Coates had three men in Connecticut. They worked with the local police to identify commuters who could have traveled on the 8:10 with Hoag. They talked to everyone at the Stamford station on a morning commute, starting with the 5:40 to Grand Central until the 9:15 A.M. train. They did the same with everyone returning in the late afternoon.

"Were you on the 8:10 today? Yesterday? Last Tuesday? Wednesday?" The police questioned travelers every morning since the shooting. A "no" got them a name and address for the file. A "yes" merited immediate follow-up starting with a picture of Steven Hoag. "Do you know this man? Did you see him on Tuesday morning, the 24th? Did you notice anyone talk to him? Were you sitting next to him? Did you ever spend time talking to him?" And on and on.

It took Coates and the Stamford police three days to identify and interview the fifty-three passengers who boarded the 8:10 with Hoag the day he died.

The inquiry ultimately narrowed to six people standing near Hoag at the station. Three recalled seeing a stranger with him talking about the news.

The descriptions varied. "Tall with a gray suit." "Medium build, tan pants." "Light brown hair. No, he was blond." "Piercing green eyes." "Blue eyes." "5'10"." "Definitely 6 feet."

The contradictions got the investigators nowhere until a Stamford policewoman flagged one man: a Korean doctor named Kim who spoke an affected, precise English. Coates was the third police officer to question him.

"Yes, I remember clearly. I had not seen this man before. He brushed by me impolitely, as I remember. He seemed to know where he wanted to go."

"And where was that?" Coates asked.

"Close to Mr. Hoag."

"Are you certain?"

"Oh yes, quite certain."

"Did you talk with Hoag often?"

"On occasion. He kept to himself. He was often gone for long stretches. I believe he said his business took him to Europe and Asia. But he always seemed to relish coming home. That's primarily what we talked about when we did talk. Travel. He had an ear for languages, French, German, Russian."

"And his work? Did Hoag talk about that?"

"Sure. But the normal stuff. Complaining about the things everyone complains about. The commute, the noise. But really never about his work."

"Let's get back to the man who brushed by you. How would you describe him?" Coates continued.

"I've told this to the police before."

"I understand, but I'd appreciate it. And be as detailed as you can."

Kim closed his eyes as if to conjure up a complete picture. He began his description with his lids still shut and his hands outlining the man in question.

"Taller than me…and you. I'd say 5'11", just shy of six feet. One hundred eighty-five pounds. Solid. That was apparent to me. He had more of an athlete's build than an executive's," he said as he opened his eyes. "Yes, that was obvious."

Kim closed his eyes again and continued. "Blond. Blue shirt. Red tie. The jacket was blue, double-breasted with gold buttons. And he wore tan pants."

Coates wrote it down unnecessarily. His men had gotten it all before. "Oh yes, one other thing."

"Yes?" Coates raised his eyebrow.

"He wore boots," Kim said without any hesitation. "Boots. It didn't fit the look. I remember thinking that. Big. Not Western, but they were boots. I'm quite clear on that."

Coates had to ask. "What kind of physician are you, Dr. Kim? You are particularly adept at your descriptions."

"Ah, very astute question. I'm a plastic surgeon. I have an office at 84th and 2nd. I notice things in people."

"I guess you do," the detective laughed. "And do you listen to what they say as well?"

"I'm better with visual cues, I'm afraid. I didn't overhear much. But I did catch a name. I forgot to mention this before. He said it quietly. But I heard it. Remember he pushed by me and I was rather upset."

"And the name you heard him say?"

"Dolan." He had trouble with the 'L.' Coates had him spell the name to be certain. "I'm sure it was Dolan. I'd never seen him before. And I haven't seen him since."

Coates would question Dr. Kim again. But now he excused himself to call his office and dictate the description and name of a possible subject. By the end of the day everyone with the name Dolan from Stamford to Pelham would be checked out. The information went on the wire to police departments throughout the Tri-State region covering New York, Connecticut, and New Jersey. And there it would sit, getting cold.

THE WHITE HOUSE

"Mr. President, do you remember our briefing about a man named Hoag?" the Director of the CIA began.

"Why don't you help me with this, Jack. I'm not really in the mood for game shows."

"Certainly, sir. Four years ago a long-time Russian agent, a KGB then SRE, operative came in. He had an American wife, a job here. I think he found that the best part of the USSR was the U.S. part. Lived up in Connecticut. Worked in New York."

"Yes, yes," Morgan Taylor chimed in. "The sleeper."

"Well, the sleeper is resting in peace...for good."

The president wrinkled his brow.

"He was killed on a train out of Stamford. It was a professional hit," Jack Evans explained.

"Why?"

"We don't know. But we had heard from him recently. He tipped us that he might have something. We were in no rush. I'm told we never got much from him. As far as I could tell, he wasn't active, maybe never was much of a player. Just a relic of the Cold War. I suspect that he was of no use to Moscow after the collapse of the Soviet Union. We were only minimally satisfied."

"Again. Why was he taken out?" An obvious question from the president.

"I don't know. But we may not have been the only ones tapping into Hoag's phone."

"Oh?"

"As I said, we heard he wanted to tell us something. Something someone else didn't want him to talk about."

"What?"

"Based on the tone of his last communiqué, it was more of the 'who' he knew."

"Another Russian agent?"

"Could be. The message was, 'I need to talk to you about someone from *school*.'"

The president stood up and poured himself a cup of coffee.

"Want any?"

"No thanks, Mr. President. I'm already wired. Four cups by eight this morning. My normal dose."

Jack Evans was a career investigator. Unlike many of the men whom he succeeded, he hadn't come up through the ranks of the company, the Central Intelligence Agency. He never posted in far-off capitals or had to deal with dead drops. Evans worked his way up from beat cop in Albany, New York to Supervising Investigator for the state's Civil Service Department. That put him on a fast track for political appointments. The governor liked him and eventually made him Civil Service Commissioner. From there he went to Washington, a Bush appointee, to evaluate civilian objections to the military tribunals. The job required thorough research of American history. He learned how the Army, during World War II, arrested and convened a war tribunal against six Nazi spies. They were subsequently put to death for planning to sabotage American factories. He read about President Roosevelt's willingness to sidestep normal due process in the name of national defense. He found similar cases dating back to George Washington's time.

Evans' work earned him the respect of the administration and he was rewarded with an appointment at the Central Intelligence Agency. Within six years he was named DCI.

At age 68, he still looked trim, voraciously read American and world history, and never lied to a president.

Morgan Taylor liked him a great deal. They hunted and fished together, watched the big playoffs and bowl games as friends, and helped each other through crises. Taylor felt one was definitely developing.

"It's the reference to 'school' that raised eyebrows," Evans continued.

"School?" Taylor asked the obvious. "What school?"

"Not a good one," the Director of the CIA began. The president listened intently to the explanation. After ten minutes he finished his lesson in Cold War history.

"Not a word of this outside," the president stated. "Not to the Bureau, not to anyone."

"Yes, sir," Evans answered. "Oh, and there is another thing, Mr. President." As if his tutorial on Hoag wasn't troublesome enough, Evans had another surprise. "We received a message from a deep cover in Tripoli, an agent called 'Sandman.'"

Lodge phoned his secretary at his Capitol Hill office. Francine hadn't talked to the congressman since before Jenny's death. She'd barely left the office, fielding condolence calls and going through the e-mails that flooded their computers. The 36-year-old assistant had really grown to love Jennifer Lodge and she took the loss extremely personally. They had been like sisters, going out for coffee and dinners, sharing books, shopping together, dishing about everyone in the office (including the dreaded Geoff Newman), and thinking about how they'd help run the world once Teddy Lodge became president.

They even looked liked sisters, if you discounted the fact that Francine was African American. Jenny had olive skin and Francine was fairly light. They were the same height, they both had inviting, open faces, similar cheekbones and the exact same smile and laugh. Jenny often gave Francine her old clothes, which added to their sisterhood. Now she feared the congressman would want her to take the rest.

Though not college educated, Francine had a graduate degree of sorts from Chicago's Cabrini-Green. She had experienced a great deal of the worst first-hand in the projects, and Francine Carver, the daughter of a Baptist minister, desperately sought a hero to make things better.

She had enough typing skills to get a decent office job. But any job wasn't good enough. She wanted to work in Washington, D.C. So Francine moved on her own, the same year that Congressman Lodge won his first term. After kicking around for a few weeks she knocked on the door of the young representative and applied for work. Since he was new and not many people were clamoring for him, she was a welcomed sight. An aide assigned envelopes to stuff and mail. Within six months she became the congressman's secretary. After years of loyal service she looked forward to following him to the White House and making her father proud.

The FBI had spoken to her and she vowed to help if she could. But of course, there was nothing she knew. The murder was far out of her reach, and so, for that matter, was the congressman. She understood that. However, she wanted to be at the office when he was ready to call.

"Congressman Lodge's office," she answered.

"Frannie. It's Ted."

"Oh my god. It's you. I've been so worried. I saw the news. I saw you. I saw Jenny. It was so awful."

"Yes, Frannie. Horrible. But I'm all right. And Jenny's with God now. We have to go on."

"And find the man who did this."

"Of course. And we all have to help each other."

"Yes, Congressman."

He allowed her many liberties, but referring to him as Teddy or Ted was not one of them.

"And I'm so sorry I wasn't at the funeral. I…" She burst into tears.

"Frannie," he said softly.

"I wanted to. I couldn't. I couldn't. Please forgive me."

"Of course. I understand. But now *I* need you."

She stopped crying, but sniffled as Lodge continued.

"We're going to the White House, Frannie. But I can't do it without you."

"You can count on me."

"Are you sure you're all right? Because this will be hard on you."

"Yes," she said forcing her tears away. "I'll be okay."

"That's good to hear, Frannie. Now tell me, what has the mail been like there?"

"Well, it's unbelievable. We're probably getting three or four thousand letters a day. You should see the bags." She actually wished she hadn't said that.

"What about the anthrax screening?" Lodge was referring to the required irradiating of all mail destined for Capitol Hill.

"They've made an exception for you and set up a special area to handle it," she said excitedly. Then Francine collected her thoughts. "Under the circumstances…"

"And the e-mails. So many. They're all going into a database."

"Good girl. You're way ahead of me. Because I want to answer them. All of them."

"I thought you would. That's what Jenny would have done."

Silence on the other end.

"I'm sorry Congressman," she said, realizing her gaffe.

"Oh, Frannie. No need," he seemed to struggle to say. "I'm lucky to be alive. It should have been me."

"Please don't say that. It shouldn't have been anyone," she offered. Tears welled up and streamed down her cheeks. She fought to compose herself for him.

"Frannie. I'm going to try to answer every single letter. But I promised Geoff that I'd sign a pre-printed card. As much as I hate that, it's probably the best way. I'll use the Montblanc pen Jenny gave me. The one with the gold tip. At least we'll have that connection." He choked up. "Better make sure I have boxes of refills."

"Of course, sir," she said through her own crying. "And Frannie," he continued, "I need you to be strong. You're a lot like Jenny. You can do this."

He had paid her the ultimate compliment. "Thank you, sir," she bravely said.

"Geoff will call and talk to you about the exact wording, some paper choices and font styles. But see what you come up with. Fax a proof sheet. We'll okay it." He meant Newman would. "Then get, say, 30,000 printed up."

"You'll need double that, sir."

"Okay, order up whatever you think. Then get them up to me as quickly as possible. We'll send them from Burlington."

"Certainly Congressman. It'll be very quick."

"And for goodness sake, Francine, go home. I heard that you've been living at the office."

"I will. I promise. And thank you, sir."

They both hung up and Francine started to cry again. She did grant herself one happy assumption. Soon, she would be secretary to the President of the United States.

MIAMI, FLORIDA

The summer rain fell in sheets. Ibrahim Haddad cursed the Miami weather. Stifling humidity made for oppressive heat. He never got used to it. While he had lived in the United States for more than thirty-five years, he always missed the arid desert air and the land of his father and his father's father.

In fact, Ibrahim Haddad's father was a successful Jordanian exporter. However, his mother was Eastern European. As a result, he could make both worlds work for him. Business and politics completely came together after a 1973 meeting with Syrian President Hafez al-Assad. Al-Assad made a proposal that changed Haddad's life and provided him with unlimited financial security. It required constant travel to the Soviet Union, high level negotiations with the KGB, the establishment of many secret Swiss bank accounts, and a search for the right talent to execute the Syrian president's ultimate plan.

He reflected on the beauty of it all and the years it had taken to nurture. How thrilled his old friend would have been to see it come to fruition. Pity he had died too early.

Haddad had spent the better part of his adult life as a puppeteer. His strings were invisible, but very well attached. He pulled some, loosened others, manipulated the motions and made the figures he handled very real-to-life. Even his puppets didn't know his name or where he lived. But they owed their success to the man behind the curtain.

"Mr. Haddad, I have a call from Turkey. Line two."

The call from Ankara originated nowhere near the Turkish capital. It had passed through routers in Paris, then Copenhagen, having started its faster than light trip 1,580 miles further south in Tripoli.

"Hello."

"Hello, Mr. Haddad." The language was English, the accent distinctly Middle Eastern. "I hope you are having a fine day."

Haddad instantly recognized the voice. *How can he be so stupid? The call violated all the rules.* But he stayed on the line.

"I am most pleased with your progress and I congratulate you on your remarkable accomplishments. And..."

"Thank you for your kind words," Haddad curtly told the caller. He dared not speak his name. "But I fear you have called quite mistakenly." *You stupid ass.* Speaking on any open line, even one that could not be easily traced, was incredibly dangerous. "Good-bye."

With that he ended the call.

Five thousand miles away Fadi Kharrazi slammed down the phone. He was not used to being hung up on, but like the child that he truly was, he craved attention. After all, such a grand plan was no fun if he couldn't talk about it with somebody.

CHAPTER 21

Bashar al-Assad made three important decisions after his father, Syrian President Hafez al-Assad, died in June 2000. He intended to stabilize Syria. His country would co-exist with Israel and he would fill a void in Middle Eastern leadership. Finally, he would abandon a three-decade-old political plan formulated by his father.

Bashar al-Assad replaced his father in a well-orchestrated succession. The party had unanimously nominated Bashar for the presidency; an endorsement that Hafez dictated from the grave. Each of the 250 parliamentarians serving in the single-chamber legislature, the Majlis al-Sha'ab, considered it a good idea for their health and well being to obey the wishes of their former president.

The so-called peaceful transfer of power underscored the hypothesis that hereditary succession is better than a bloody power struggle. The region was rife with religious fundamentalists ready to send countries truly needing 21st-century resources back into 17th-century chaos. So family continuity, under the veil of a democratic vote, actually provided some security to the region.

But years before the changing of the guard, President Hafez al-Assad sought other guarantees to his powerbase. He believed that if he was viewed as a peacemaker—the world leader who would get the Golan Heights back from Israel—his political stock would rise. The fact that he had lost the land in the 1967 war was not to be spoken. His attempts failed.

He subsequently tried to win concessions from Israel and curry favor from American presidents beginning with Nixon. Again, with little success. So al-Assad established close ties with the Soviet Union. It was in Moscow, during a secret 1973 meeting with Leonid Ilych Brezhnev over an arms transaction, that Hafez al-Assad asked through his translators if he could propose something that was not on the agenda. "Of course," he was told without sincerity. The Soviet Premier did not like surprises.

"I come to you with an idea for which I need your help."

Brezhnev read this introduction as a foundation of a financial transaction. "Please. Continue."

Al-Assad began to outline a plan, which on the surface was close to what the KGB had done for years. Brezhnev clearly appeared interested. "You have the means and the experience that we lack. And I, Mr. Premier, have the funds."

"Such things can wait, my *friend*," Brezhnev said, waving his hand in feigned displeasure over even the suggestion of talking money. "Is there more?"

Al-Assad smiled. "Of course." He continued to outline his long-range scheme with great enthusiasm; pacing the room, punctuating each new element in his timeline with broad gestures. Brezhnev silently and politely watched. But the more his visitor talked, the less credence he gave al-Assad's basic conceit. Finally, after twenty minutes, the Syrian president finished. Brezhnev stood up and lied.

"Your notion is creative and brilliant."

"Then I can count on your country's experience?"

"With great certainty." Then without a hint of awkwardness talking about money with *a friend*, Brezhnev quoted an amount double what al-Assad had been prepared to pay. The Syrian president didn't blink. He decided, well out of character, that this was not a time to negotiate.

"Agreed. Two hundred million U.S. dollars."

As they shook hands, Hafez al-Assad conceded that everything could fall apart for any number of reasons. However, he had the patience to see it through after the Soviet Union's incubation period and moreover, he had the man who could run the operation once it moved to America. In success, the United States would abandon its support for Israel and Syria would become a major power broker in the world.

Patience was not what al-Assad ultimately needed. It was more years to live. The Syrian president died in June 2000, at the age of 69, well before his plan fully matured. His son, Bashar al-Assad, was patently less patient a man. He quickly sold the plan to another government as if it were a loaf of bread.

TRIPOLI, LIBYA
TUESDAY, JULY 8

Sami Ben Ali received his instructions at a dead drop in the heart of Tripoli. They were written in code on a one-time pad, scrolled up in a thin tube, and hidden on the underside of a wooden fruit cart. Sami had seen the signal; an almost undetectable black shoe polish smudge on a tree at the corner. A right slash meant recover a message. A double slash meant urgent. He could take his time.

Sami waited three days, passing the cart in the souk numerous times on his way to work and again to his apartment. Once convinced no one tailed him or took notice, he approached the cart, stooped down to tighten his shoe laces and using the smoothest of motions learned at the CIA's training facility in South Carolina, he removed the small, thin, two inch-long tube.

Sami knew he shouldn't rush anywhere. *Take your time*, he told himself. Nothing out of the ordinary. Anyway, the electricity is off. He stopped for tea, read the fiction disguised as a newspaper in the candlelight, chain-smoked four cigarettes, and sauntered back to his apartment. Even there he did nothing unusual.

An hour later, with the radio running and the lights on in his room, Sami shut himself in his closet and began to decipher the code. Today's key was embedded in a dog-eared copy of a biography of the French ballad singer, Jacques Brel, that he'd picked up from a bookseller.

The work was never quick. But he had his 30-minute rule. After three hours of stopping and starting he was finished. He took the lit butt of his ninth cigarette and pressed it to the side of the orig-inal sheet. It flashed and disappeared in under a second. He did the same to a corresponding piece of flash paper that contained his deciphered message.

Sami was given a specific assignment. Find out exactly where Fadi kept his files on the thing called *Ashab al-Kahf.* There was only one way. Abahar's man Walid Abdul-Latif. He was a complainer, a gossip, and another Libyan bureaucrat with an inflated sense of self. The more he talked about his own importance, the more he'd spill whatever he knew. Walid would lead him to the location of the files based on what he learned from his contact Omar Za'eem. The CIA obviously wanted to read them first hand.

"Good morning, Walid," Sami Ben Ali said in greeting at the beginning of the new workday.

"What's good about it?" the lieutenant complained. He slumped over his desk and looked as miserable as he sounded.

"Ah, your wife has heard about your mistress?"

"No. But she wants new clothes. How can I buy for two on my salary? And what does she need it for anyway?"

"Maybe to look good for someone else?" Sami joked.

"I should be so lucky."

"Well, come with me tonight. We'll commiserate. At least you are getting some. Me, it's been months. And a witch with horrible teeth at that. We'll go out. You can advise me on my studies." Sami had said many times earlier he wanted to go to the University.

Walid shook his head. "No, no. Not tonight." He was negotiating.

Sami picked up the signal. "I'll pay. And maybe you'll have money to buy your girlfriend something on the way home."

A CAFÉ IN TRIPOLI

"They're all incompetents," Sami began over red tea. He wished he was sipping a tall, cold Bad Frog Amber Lager from home. But that wasn't possible. There was no beer or wine in Libya's cafés and restaurants. Alcohol was banned on orders from General Kharrazi and his adherence to strict Muslim law. "But do you think if Abahar was in control, we'd be drinking this swill?" Sami continued. "No. Libya would be more progressive. We'd be part of the 21st century. And we'd be talking with the West, not watching for their planes. We'd have our medicine. And we could grow an army in the sunlight rather than try to build our forces in the dark."

"Be careful what you say, my friend. For the sake of your job and your life."

"I know," he continued whispering completely under the din of the café. "But what if Fadi, that goat, seizes power when the General dies. Or worse, before?" This was the bait. *Will he take it?*

Walid sipped his drink and re-lit his cigar. A minute passed, but Sami did not press. Finally, Walid leaned forward.

"While we sit here, I can assure you that Abahar considers this too." Two more puffs and Walid spoke again. "There is something afoot. I don't know the details. Neither does Abahar, but Fadi is behind a plan designed to ensure him leadership."

"You must be mistaken, Walid. He doesn't have the means or..."

"You're blind to the world around you. He met secretly with Uday Hussein years ago, and others. He sits on his eggs and waits for them to hatch."

"What are you talking about?" Sami showed real concern. He encouraged Walid to go on.

"I don't know much. But I will find out for our boss. And it will fail."

"You?" Sami taunted. "What can you do?" *That will get him to talk more.*

"There are things you don't know and will never learn."

"Forgive me. But..."

"*We* have our ways," Walid hinted.

Sami recognized how Walid egotistically included himself. He also knew not to pursue the answer directly. Better to wait. Walid was talking openly. He would come back to it. A few puffs on his cigar and a little more tea and Walid was ready to continue.

"Even now we're close to discovering more. The answers are in Fadi's office and in that traitorous brother's head."

"Oh, you make up stories like Arabian Nights, Walid. You help pass the time."

"These are not stories, you fool."

"Careful, I said I would pay."

Walid ignored the comment. He enjoyed bullying his subordinate.

"I'm happy for the drinks, but you are a naive fool! These are not stories. Fadi is treacherous and plans something. I have seen some of the proof."

That was an exaggeration. Sami read his report. There was no proof in what Omar Za'eem presented. Not yet.

"And Abahar has entrusted me to uncover more."

Another overstatement. "Then what will you do? How will you find out?"

"I have means. Eyes and ears inside Fadi's world."

Walid Abdul-Latif betrayed his boss by speaking to Sami. But he was an overconfident, self-possessed tyrant. How else could he laud his importance if he didn't share the confidences of his position.

"You are not to utter a word of this…"

"Of course, Walid."

"…or I will personally slit your throat."

Undoubtedly, it was the same thing Abahar said to him.

"I pray to Allah for the day when Abahar will lead our people," Sami said. He signaled for another glass of tea and dedicated the rest of the evening to the details of their slutty conquests.

CHAPTER 22

CLAVERACK, NEW YORK
MONDAY, JULY 14

Chuck Wheaton made a considerable day's pay with his footage of the shooting, although personally not as much as he could have.

Long ago he learned that all of his freelance work depended on the strength and quality of his relationships. This was no time to burn bridges. He also lived by the credo that "No good deed shall go unpunished." So Wheaton neither over-charged nor gave away the footage. After a good deal of thought, he settled on a per-second fee of $30. A minute's worth would get him the going rate of $1,800. And he had a good eight minutes of parade, five minutes of the speech up until Jenny was killed, and another thirty minutes of the aftermath and interviews. Of course everyone wanted all of the footage. CNN, ABC, CBS, NBC, and Fox. He permitted each news division to license it for one year on a non-exclusive basis. The networks could also telecast it on any of their other sister cable channels or local affiliates. Since he immediately approached them on a conference call, none of them decided to steal the footage off one another. They agreed to his terms. Most outlets wanted all of his footage. In addition to some foreign sales and domestic news services, his one roll of videotape earned him more than $541,000.

He quickly donated $150,000 to Hudson High School, probably the biggest donation they'd ever received, and another equal amount to his alma mater, Emerson College in Boston. Chuck knew the networks would be back in a year to re-license some of the footage, but he truthfully wished the whole thing had never happened.

He was 60 years old. He'd taught his Social Studies students at the high school about the impact of JFK's assassination. They'd studied the legendary Zapruder film. And he discussed the importance of the Challenger tape in understanding what happened on the fateful day of that disaster. Now, Wheaton had witnessed the most horrifying moment of his life through his own camera lens. It replayed in his mind's eye as it did on the video screen; a moment suspended for all time. He had rolled one tape after another without thinking; 30 years of pure instinct coming to bear on the biggest story of his life.

Now, more than three weeks after the shooting, Wheaton was still haunted by the tape. Night after night he played the footage in his garage edit bay, in slow motion, then backwards and forwards. With the sound down it unfolded like a hideous ballet. *Almost choreographed*, he thought. *There. Jenny Lodge. She's slumping backwards. The Fire Commissioner rushes to help her. Lodge holds Jenny. The crowd is stunned. Marelli snapping to attention now. He's looking for the sniper. And Madelyn. Poor Madelyn, just a teenager. Why did she have to see it?* Every moment was embedded in his memory just as it was on the tape.

Backwards, forwards. The sound up, the sound off. Zoomed in and zoomed out. He had his own Zapruder film. Now he realized what he was up to; precisely what the FBI was also doing—looking for clues, frame by frame.

Something didn't feel right. He couldn't put his finger on it, but he couldn't stop watching.

WASHINGTON, D.C.

Every day since he got back to the Hill, Teddy Lodge set aside three hours to sign his letters of gratitude. Each response was a vote. He preferred signing the notes with his Montblanc Writer's Series pen, a rare Thomas Moore edition with a low registration number. The pen, now valued at more than three thousand dollars, was proving to be even more valuable than money. The ease at which the ink flowed from the pen to paper saved his wrist.

"More ink, Frannie." Lodge's assistant heard the call on her intercom frequently. He scheduled his signing three times a day—an hour in the morning, again mid-afternoon and once more before he went home.

Francine worried about the congressman. He seemed like a man on a mission. But he told her he'd be fine. "It's therapy for me," he offered. "Gives me a break from campaigning and a chance to think about Jenny. This is exactly what I need to do," Lodge said with a sincere smile.

Francine doted over him. She was there with coffee. She made certain he exercised. She cared and she coddled. She successfully blocked every nuisance call from him except the chief nuisance of all, Geoff Newman. He always got through. She put a light blanket over him when he fell asleep in his chair. And she felt sorry for the congressman whenever she observed his fitful sleep. He always tossed and turned, mumbling. Mumbling unintelligible words. No matter how much she strained, she couldn't understand what he was saying in his sleep. Jenny once told her he was a dreadful sleeper. Now she saw it. So much on his mind, she reasoned. "So much on his mind," she fretted to her friend Ceil. She wished that damned Newman would let him rest.

Ceil Carson worked at State as a researcher. She had a compassionate manner. That was one of the reasons she was recruited. Ceil was everyone's best friend. And potentially their worst enemy. She was one of the dozens of people on the Hill who overheard things in corridors and street corners, memorized conversations and passed them along. Maybe she didn't know what they meant. But her instructors taught her to report rather than interpret; consider everything interesting and nothing unimportant. Her instructors worked for Jack Evans. So she worked for the CIA. As a consequence, Evans learned that Congressman Lodge didn't sleep well.

And who would under the circumstances? But Evans also knew to question the meaning of everything. He wondered whether this was indicative of how Congressman Lodge would act under pressure. He decided to talk to the resident Agency shrink.

Dr. Garrett Sclar put it quite simply. "His clock is all out of whack. He hasn't been on a regular eating schedule in months. He probably doesn't know what time zone he's in half the time. He falls asleep at the office. That's not usual. And his nightmares? You might say it's his brain doing the wash; cleaning out the anxiety and tension through subconscious activity."

"Does it give you any indication what his behavior might be as president?"

"You mean is talking in his sleep and tossing and turning going to mean he doesn't have the balls to drop a nuke?"

"For starters."

"I don't think I want a president who *wouldn't* be bothered by that possibility. The only thing I don't understand is the mumbling you mentioned. Most of the time we grunt. We shout 'No!' at some terror. We flail our arms to ward off a beast. In my experience, the people who talk unintelligibly aren't speaking words that can't be understood. They're saying things the person who's listening doesn't understand."

"Meaning?" asked the CIA director.

"Meaning, get me a recording and I'll be able to tell you more."

"You know I can't do that."

"I didn't think you could."

The description of a man named Dolan had gone out to police departments. But NYPD Detective Harry Coates didn't have anything more now than he had a couple of weeks earlier. Nothing came back from other law enforcement agencies. And no witnesses beyond the Korean doctor. "We're hoping someone comes forward," he told a reporter for the *Daily News*, not indicating he did have one solid ID of his suspect. "But I guess we have the country's smartest commuters. They're all into their morning newspapers. A murder occurred on their commuter train ride and thirty people walked right past the dead man."

Coates' interview wasn't even interesting enough for the *Daily News* to print.

Hoag's wife tried to help, but she had nothing to contribute. They basically kept to themselves and a few friends. And except for her husband's travel, she described his work as fairly mundane.

It was obvious to Coates that Hoag's death was a hit, not a robbery. The motive lay in what people didn't know about Hoag rather than what they did know. A secret life with no visible trail except for a phone number.

Every day he called the number from Hoag's wallet. And every day he got the same response. "The number you have dialed is no longer in service."

So Steven Hoag was buried. Coates counted twenty-three mourners at the service. Hoag's wife, some neighbors and friends from work. There was a 24th, but he was well out of sight, taking digital photographs of everyone with a 200-mm zoom lens. The pictures would be at the CIA via e-mail within the hour.

The CIA relied on Internet communication daily. So did Ibrahim Haddad. He spent a good four hours a day reading international newspapers online, conducting business, and embedding his own secrets in encrypted picture files.

Cyberspace put him at an advantage over counter-intelligence agencies. He could post an innocuous e-mail with an attachment on almost any website and surreptitiously communicate with people virtually in the open.

Millions were spent on electronic eavesdropping, utilizing systems such as the super-secret Echelon network. Yet, Haddad could still transmit and receive secret information via his own two thousand-dollar office PC.

Echelon reportedly was operated by the U.S., England, Canada, New Zealand, and Australia. The network, with its "sniffing" software, hunted for keywords sent over the Internet; words that would arouse suspicion. The programs monitored the servers of Internet service providers. However, Echelon and its spin-offs, sister programs, and distant cousins could never monitor all the cyber traffic. While encrypted messages are a red flag to such systems, audio, video or picture files are not. This is where Haddad effectively hid his messages.

The method is known as "steganography," the electronic equivalent of the dead drop.

The software was widely available. The process was simple. It merely required the addition of a single bit to each of the pixels that comprise a photograph. Only the sender and receiver would have the software code to decipher the message contained within the picture. Experts called it effective, available, and relatively foolproof. Haddad trusted his life's work in it.

And so, inside the artwork of an obscure Romanian movie poster nobody would actually bid on, Haddad sent a message intended for an audience of one. He knew that his man would have preferred a little rest given how busy he'd been recently. Nonetheless, it was critical that he get another job done. No need to be careless, especially these days.

WASHINGTON, DC
FRIDAY, JULY 18

In another office at the FBI Headquarters at 935 Pennsylvania Avenue, a friend of Scott Roarke's scrolled through his afternoon e-mail. Like everyone else in cyberspace, he plowed through seemingly endless butt-covering correspondences and reviewed the handful of pertinent communications. One was from the Idaho State Police. They'd located Alfred Nunes at a Sun Valley trailer park. The retired lawyer had prepaid the week, and in a few days he and his wife were scheduled to head on to California. The officer learned the information very matter-of-factly while strolling through the park. The e-mail explained that Nunes was extremely chatty. The policeman's simple questions raised no concerns and the correspondence ended with the notation, "Awaiting further instructions."

Shannon Davis couldn't reach Roarke immediately. So he left him a message. "Found your man. Call me. Davis."

An hour later, Roarke retrieved his messages from Boston. He phoned his friend back.

"Yeah, got it. Sorry it took so long," the young FBI agent said. "You only have four days unless you want me to have him detained."

"Probably no reason to do that. I can talk to him on the phone first. Then I'll see. Have that Idaho trooper pass along my number. Right away."

SUN VALLEY, IDAHO
SUNDAY, JULY 20

Dr. George Powder explained he was a retired professor of history and law. He'd taught ethics in ancient civilizations for some thirty-seven years at the University of Rochester and spent his five sabbaticals digging for ruins on the Greek island of Santorini.

The gray and weathered Powder walked with a slight limp. He appeared every bit the 73 years printed on his nearly expired New York State driver's license. He was mildly arthritic and ached a bit. But he wouldn't give up his fishing. Powder cast for steelhead or whatever was biting today, and struck up a friendly chat with the other man working the Little Wood River.

Alfred Nunes met him by coincidence shortly after he settled into his comfortable spot knee high in the water. It was about fifteen minutes up from his campsite, just beyond where the waters of Silver Creek flowed into Little Wood.

Nunes wore a red-checkered cotton shirt, shorts, and fishing cap with lures dangling on hooks. He sported a closely trimmed white beard that matched the bushy chest hairs pushing over the top of his shirt. His red cheeks and thin but tall body partially gave him away. The way he pronounced his "r's" reinforced beyond any doubt that he was a tried and true Yankee.

Nunes wasn't a particularly good fisherman, so there was little worry of ever dealing with a fish. He was simply out there for relaxation. Anyway, the possibility of getting lost in talk with his newly found companion instantly appealed to him. That's what they did. They talked for hours, forgetting the fish that weren't biting, exchanging stories about classic legal cases and the impact they had on societies throughout the ages.

Powder spoke of the ancient Greeks and their laws, written in blood, not ink. Nunes brought it more up to date with his perspective on Leopold & Loeb, whether the evidence was strong enough to truly convict the Rosenbergs of espionage, and the way Judge Ito presided over the O.J. Simpson trial. Nunes couldn't remember having a more stimulating discussion.

The towering mountains, vast forests, and crisp air made Nunes feel more alive than he had in years. They were debating complex issues in the largest expanse of wilderness left in the continental United States.

Powder challenged Nunes. He made him think. He questioned legal fundamentals he had abidingly followed his whole life. "Why hadn't they met earlier?" Nunes complained as they retried the great cases of the Old World and brought evidence of the last 100 years up for appeal. It was immensely stimulating.

They drank all of Nunes' coffee and pissed it all away. And then Powder poured from his thermos. And on it went until mid-afternoon.

After sharing sandwiches, Nunes caught his breath. "Alfred, are you all right?" Dr. Powder asked. It took a moment for the old lawyer to respond. He suddenly felt a wave of extreme apprehension pass over him. He looked up, as if he heard some far away sound and then shook it off.

"I'm okay now. I, I just felt displaced. I'm fine," he said slurring his words slightly. "Now where were we, ah yes, the courtroom performance of Edward J. Reilly during his defense of Bruno Hauptmann in the Lindbergh case."

Powder picked up the conversation, but stopped in mid-sentence when he noted that Nunes' face was twitching and his left lip drooped.

"Alfred, you really don't look good."

"Oh, nonsense. I haven't felt this alive in years." Which, of course, wasn't true. Nunes began to realize his face was simultaneously feeling numb and twitching uncontrollably. And his stomach was queasy.

Nunes hadn't even realized he had let a minute slip by before responding.

"You're not well, my friend. I better get you some help."

Another minute before Nunes responded.

"Yes, yes. You're right. Please go," he said, gripping his chest. "My heart. I believe I'm having a heart attack." His heart was pounding irregularly and powerfully.

Professor George Powder leaned closer. "Alfred, you do look terrible."

"Please, go now. I need a doctor."

"I'm afraid I can't do that," Powder declared rising up over his recent acquaintance.

Nunes doubled over, twisted his head and peered deeply into Powder's brown eyes. They were no longer friendly, no longer warm. He was vaguely aware that Powder, straightened up, looked cold and cruel, not a bit arthritic. And he appeared to have gained two inches.

"A unique sodium morphate compound." Powder began, "It's an absolutely wonderful substance to work with."

Nunes listened and watched through his increasing pain.

"You never came across it in one of your distinguished cases, Alfred? I'm surprised."

Nunes looked confused.

"Probably not the thing a country lawyer would. Anyway, Alfred, it's quite beyond the scope of most coroners. You see, the toxin is nearly impossible to identify. The symptoms it produces are most often associated with heart attacks. Just what you thought. And old men do get heart attacks, even when they're fishing."

Powder sat down again, directly opposite Nunes. "Sodium morphate is light and compact. You weren't aware of it at all in the coffee I served, were you?"

Nunes was writhing.

"Of course you weren't, Alfred. I like it when I'm not in a rush because it takes anywhere from thirty minutes to a few hours. And we did have such a lively discussion while I waited. Wouldn't you agree?" he added with a laugh.

"Well, once in your body, it goes after the active cells—the ones feeding your body chemicals. And then it expands to six times its mass. That means it stops your active cells from getting energy. The result, which you're currently experiencing, is that your heart and brain strain and eventually shut down. As sodium morphate does its particular dirty work it metabolizes into your body's natural chemicals. Voila. It disappears in the victim."

Nunes was in terrible pain. He started shaking.

"Ah, and you're the victim, Alfred. Feel the convulsions?" Powder said coldly. "I imagine they're very uncomfortable. You'll be interested in knowing that sodium morphate is quite historic. The Mafia endorses its use, though I can't quote exact cases for you. The British forces were rather fond of the drug for assassinations in World War II. But the Bay of Pigs conspirators screwed it up when they tried to kill Fidel Castro. Well, I can see I don't have time to go into that now.

"All in all," he added as Nunes was dying, "it's a marvelous substance. Wouldn't you agree?"

Nunes barely managed a faint, "Why?"

"Was that 'why?' Alfred? Why? Oh, it's all about an old client of yours we failed to discuss. I suppose time was not on your side."

Nunes died with an utterly confused expression on his face.

Powder gathered his things together. He washed his thermos bottle in the stream, removed all other visible signs that the old lawyer had had a companion, and left.

Like his vitae and his license, his name was a complete fabrication. He had picked Powder specifically for this job and rather enjoyed the humor in it. The stories he shared with Nunes were true, but they were not scholarly interpretations of the law by a retired teacher. They were the musings of an assassin with a great many identities who just read a lot.

CHAPTER 23

MONDAY, JULY 21

Haywood Marcus carried only his briefcase. He left Boston early in the morning and intended to return in the evening. Haddad was not pleased about seeing him after all these years, but he granted him a one-hour audience over lunch at his Fisher Island condo.

Marcus wore a lightweight cotton-linen blend three-piece pin stripe suit; the perfect summer travel outfit. It hardly showed a wrinkle.

The lawyer also loved the theatrics the suit provided. It did a lot for a man, especially a lawyer in court. He could take off his jacket in mid-argument and still look masterful. He could slip his century old pocket watch out, open up the gold case, slowly check the time, then return to a witness, while holding every member of the jury spellbound. The suit was also Marcus' armor. He felt more secure wearing it. It gave him the air of authority he wanted today.

Ibrahim Haddad's men were waiting for Marcus when his ferry docked at Fisher Island. They didn't identify themselves, but they stood out. They had on loose-fitting warm-up suits. Marcus assumed they carried an assortment of firepower under the zip-up jackets.

Marcus followed them to a golf cart. One of the two drove, the other sat facing backward. Watching. The ride took ten minutes and covered acres of picturesque Fisher Island. They passed condominium towers owned by television hosts and actresses, retired doctors, bankers and stockbrokers, and younger people with fast cash. They drove around launches that housed multi-million dollar yachts. One of them, a 64-foot Aleutian AC-64, with a top speed of 22 knots, belonged to Haddad.

Marcus had never sailed on it. And never wanted to. He'd heard stories; all rumor he hoped, but enough to tell him he didn't want to cast off with Haddad.

"Good afternoon, my friend," Haddad said welcoming the Boston attorney with outstretched arms.

"Hello Ibrahim," Marcus returned in a warm hug.

"How many years? Thirty. No, nearly 35. And you look as young and fit as ever, Marcus."

"Thank you. As do you."

"Oh no. But I don't expect honesty from a Boston lawyer. Just a good argument."

They both laughed. Haddad escorted the visitor into a pure white Florida room with a brilliant Southeast view of the harbor. "We'll be comfortable in here. July is not the time for outside conversation."

Haddad was also always concerned about any potential eavesdroppers, though there were none today.

As soon as they sat down Haddad rang for his chef. Almost all of his meals were cooked by a Frenchman on his payroll for two decades. "Louis has prepared exceptional fare for us today."

"Why, yes," the handsome 54-year-old chef explained through his accent. "Beluga caviar on a potato split in half no bigger than a quarter. Eggs Florentine swimming under a delicious Hollandaise sauce, followed by a pineapple strawberry sorbet. And, of course, coffees of your choice. Oh, to start, a peach sparkling wine." Haddad didn't want to waste good French champagne on Marcus.

"Sounds delectable," the lawyer said.

"Then we begin," the chef added.

The discussion covered years of nothingness while the men were served. Every time Marcus tried to get to his agenda Ibrahim Haddad chided him, "Oh not now, my friend. Let us eat and enjoy ourselves before business."

Finally, with only ten minutes left to the hour reserved by Haddad, he snapped his fingers. All of his men quickly left the room.

"Now that we are alone, listen to me carefully," the Miami businessman said sharply. "You will never call me again. You will never see me again. Today, we have talked—you and I—about a potential buyer I seek for my boat. But you have changed my mind. It would not be advisable given the tax issues. Do you understand."

There was only one possible answer for Marcus to give. His suit offered him no protection. "Yes."

"Now tell me in two minutes why you dared come here."

Marcus was a brilliant lawyer. He was usually the one intimidating others. Now he felt the power of a greater adversary. He choked on his first few words. "Ibrahim, I'm sorry if I violated our confidences. But I believed this was too important to discuss over the telephone."

Haddad looked at his watch.

"A Secret Service agent came to the office," the lawyer managed. "He may have seen some of the Lodge legal work."

"Stop," Haddad proclaimed. "You think I need you to tell me who is prying? There are actually two. One I read every day in *The New York Times*. The other I understand is, as you say, a Secret Service man."

Marcus was aghast.

"Don't be surprised, my friend. You're not the only one at your establishment that I employ. Or do you think so highly of yourself that you were irreplaceable all these years?"

Haywood Marcus, never lost for a word, could not speak.

"So here's what you do from now on. And pay strict attention. You will refrain from speaking with me *unless* I initiate contact. And only then in the proscribed manner. You will continue to do as I say, when I say it. And you will now leave."

Haddad stood, towering over the seated visitor. "Oh, and by the way," he added as an afterthought, "thanks to your failings, I've decided to take care of some loose ends. Tidying up some. Haywood, don't be one of them," Haddad said.

Haddad turned to leave and raised a finger. "One additional thing," he added. "My men will give you a tour of my yacht."

Marcus stiffened. Haddad smiled.

"Oh come now. It's not what you think. You'll need to write me a note about why I shouldn't sell. Leave it with my men. It'll memorialize our business today. Then go."

Marcus caught himself nodding well beyond the time that Haddad was out of the room. He was unaware that Haddad's men had entered.

"This way," the bigger of the two men demanded.

Marcus rose out of his chair, never so scared in his life.

CHAPTER 24

BOSTON, MASSACHUSETTS
TUESDAY, JULY 22

"Hey, Scott, can you come back up? I want to show off what I just got you," Katie said clearly.

Very few people had this particular cell phone number. Roarke had given her specific instructions. "Use it only if it's important. No, make that very important. Otherwise call the answering service. If it is business related, and it better be, keep your conversation under 18 seconds. And I do mean 18 seconds. Time the call. Those are the rules."

"But it's digital service. Nobody can listen in," she argued.

"Yeah, right."

"It all sounds so cloak and dagger serious."

"Eighteen seconds." And with that, Katie understood he was serious about his phone calls. Now she was on one. She watched the seconds tick by.

"Great, honey," Roarke answered from Washington. "Sounds like fun. Dinner usual place tonight. Eight. Bye." Click.

Roarke had an unmarked Secret Service vehicle drive him from the White House to Reagan National. Within ninety minutes of hanging up with Katie, he was on the shuttle to Boston. An hour later he was waiting for her at 75 Chestnut—the *usual* place. The only place they'd been together to eat.

Katie walked in precisely on time. She looked especially radiant in a navy blue suit from Ann Taylor that flattered her in every possible way. Her phone call provided the perfect excuse for him to come up. He wanted to visit anyway, but this made it all the easier.

Roarke had a Lemon Drop Martini waiting for her at the bar. She nestled up to him and surprised him with a gentle kiss on his cheek. He slid up to her ear, with a kiss in return and whispered, "Whatcha got?"

"I'm fine," she answered coyly pulling away. "And you?"

"Hungry. Let's get a table." Roarke put a twenty down for the tab and signaled to the hostess.

After some playful dialogue Katie leaned forward. "You asked if I remembered anything else that might be relevant in the Lodge files."

"Yes."

"Well, I did. Nothing legal. But something very interesting. Newspaper clippings."

"Yeah, I saw some of the headlines. Piano recital. Boy Scouts stuff. So?"

"Do you remember seeing when they were from?"

"No, they were just clippings."

"Clippings of headlines without stories and stories without pictures. And all torn raggedly."

Roarke perked up. "Why?"

"That's what I wondered. Things are removed because we *don't* want a record of them. This was intentional. They were ripped against the grain. Badly."

"Keep going."

"I figured they were from the Marblehead paper, so I went to their archives. I figured Teddy was around age 13 or so in the one I really remembered. I started with the papers in the fall of '73. I was a little off. He was 14. I found it. Page 11, from a paper on October 17, 1974. It was there on the microfilm."

"What was there?"

"You *were* looking for a picture, weren't you?"

"Yes."

"Well, I have one for you. A young Teddy Lodge at his Eagle Scout ceremony."

"Fantastic. What's it look like?"

"See for yourself." She took a manila envelope out of her leather attaché case and began to raise it up over her lap. Roarke shook his head "no" and pointed downward with his right hand and put his left under their table. She followed his direction and slid it to him.

He took it and squeezed her hand in thanks.

"Can you tell me why it's so important?"

Roarke hesitated.

She squeezed his hand back and rested them on his lap. He had an immediate reaction.

"Look," he said trying to resist the wave of pleasure he was feeling, "I can't tell you what's going on, because I don't know. All I have is a vague feeling. And feelings are signals to me. I listen to them. But the picture may help."

"How?"

She inched her fingers up his thigh. "What are your feelings telling you now, Mr. Roarke?"

He slowly let out a breath of air. She knew exactly what he was feeling.

"You do listen to your feelings?"

The young waiter came to the table, in Roarke's estimation, just in time.

"Would you like to hear the specials for tonight?"

They hadn't even looked at the menu yet. "A few more minutes if we could," Roarke said.

"Sure. Take your time." The waiter noticed that Katie was leaning forward and her hand was under the table. "No rush."

He started walking away and Katie stopped him. "Actually, we'll start with some appetizers." She told him what she'd like and he left.

Roarke smiled. "He saw where your hand was."

"No he didn't."

"Yes he did."

"Well, I'm sure he's seen worse."

Roarke laughed and focused on her eyes. They were sparkling.

After enjoying the moment Roarke said, "Well then, back to work. Do you have anything else?"

"Oh my God, I forgot to tell you," she said. "Marcus removed the Lodge folders. All of them."

She saw his expression drop.

"Oh, come on, silly. He found me in the archives. I had a perfectly good reason for being there."

Roarke stopped listening. Shivers rippled through his spine. She was compromised. Katie smiled at him, trying to make the moment easier. Roarke's senses heightened. He looked past her eyes, over her shoulder, to the bar behind her, about twenty feet away. Reflected in the mirror was a man who looked out of place at 75 Chestnut. He was leaning over a short drink that hadn't been touched. For a split second he appeared to be studying them in the mirror. When Roarke locked on him, the man hastily disengaged. It was enough of a sign to convince Roarke one of them was being followed.

The appetizers arrived. A country pâté full of flavor and a delectable Maryland crab cake, prepared with a spicy remoulade and in a crispy but flaky crust. The crab cake in particular bordered on the erotic. It was deliciously moist and succulent inside. They both felt a certain sexiness about the texture, yet from entirely different points of view. After the first bite, Katie decided to add to the moment. She cut a portion with her fork and fed it to Roarke. He automatically closed his eyes and no longer simply tasted the food. He lost himself in the sensuality of the flavors and where it was taking him. He returned the favor to the equal delight of Katie.

As he fed her, Roarke watched the man at the bar. Dark. Maybe late-30s. Solid body. Very solid. He wore a black crew neck shirt and black loose fitting linen sports coat affixed by the middle button. Black pants. Dark glasses. He went back to the jacket. It was probably one size too big for him. Enough to hide a gun.

Roarke put a name on his adversary. Giving the man an identity made him human; someone he would take seriously, even deadly seriously. This man would be Crabbe, in honor of the first course.

"Katie, excuse me. Gotta make a quick trip to the bathroom. I'll be right back."

In one motion, Roarke rose and slid the manila envelope under his jacket. He ignored Crabbe and walked to the back of 75 Chestnut and into the men's room. He went to the only stall, opened the envelope and removed the microfilm print of the photograph. The quality was questionable, but there was young Teddy Lodge getting honored as an Eagle Scout. He wore a proud smile with his chest puffed out and his shoulders raised. Lodge's merit badge sash was filled with the honors he had earned on his way to Eagle. He looked like a soldier whose ribbons distinguished his battles, only these were for such achievements as swimming, lifesaving and good citizenship. Roarke realized he never wore the commendations he'd earned in the service. Like this one now, most of his assignments were never formally acknowledged.

He put the photograph in his inside jacket pocket and ripped up the envelope into small pieces. It took three flushes to get it all down. When he finished, he returned to the table, catching Crabbe peripherally. He hadn't moved or touched his drink.

"Sorry. So, what are we having for dinner?" he asked Katie.

"Well, this time, I have my eye on the lobster lasagna," she said. "The waiter took one to that couple." She nudged her shoulder toward a table to the right. "Looks scrumptious." She paused, "Like you."

"Well, the lobster it is."

"Lobster lasagna," she corrected.

He missed the compliment, his mind was elsewhere; figuring and planning what to do about Crabbe when it was time to leave.

The dinner was a delight. Katie's recommendation was superb. The lobster's shell was placed on top of layers of pasta filled with lobster amidst an ocean of tomato-cream sauce. If it was too rich, neither Katie nor Roarke minded. It was the way they fed each other that made it so enjoyable. For dessert they chose another appealing creation, the tiramisu. Katie considered the evening quite romantic, except for times when Roarke seemed distracted. The dinner was filled with soft and sensual foods; intentional choices that she hoped would serve as the appetizer for the rest of the evening.

As they ate, they talked about themselves and what filled their lives.

"I worked too hard at college," Katie explained. "I never had any free time at Smith. Everyone else spent weekends in New Haven or New York. I lived in the library for four years. I gained weight, forgot about friends, and ignored men."

"Something changed. You're tanned, you obviously exercise and I don't feel ignored," Roarke said.

"Thank you, Mr. Perceptive. I sort of came out of my shell at Harvard Law School. I met a med student who was the polar opposite. Everything came easily to him. He could touch a text and come away knowing the material. And that's what he did to me. The trouble was I stopped studying and started playing. I guess I'm catching up for lost time."

Katie took a sip of Dolce, a delicious late harvest dessert wine from Far Niente vineyards in Napa. Roarke preferred his port, a 20-year-old Fonseca. "A long story short, it took me an extra year to get through Harvard."

"And your med student?"

"He became a doctor and as far as I know he's now practicing on someone else," she said laughing. "But he did teach me a thing or two. I picked up sailing because of him. I exercise pretty rigorously. And I developed into the woman who sits before you."

"Who is most delightful," Roarke dared to say.

"And you, Mr. Roarke. Is there anything you can tell me about yourself?"

The question he always avoided answering.

He hesitated and looked everywhere but at Katie.

"Oh come now, it can't be that hard."

His eyes met hers. He smiled. He actually wanted to tell her.

"You're something. You know that?"

"I know. But we're not talking about me. Now where were you born?"

Roarke took a big sip of his drink and gave in. "I was born in Phoenix." And he stopped.

"Well that clears it all up." She made a gesture in the air jokingly and said, "Check please."

"Okay, okay," he laughed. "You win. My father was a long haul truck driver and my mom did every odd job imaginable during the year so she could take off summers. We'd all drive back and forth across the country. I have vivid memories of those great stretches of road—through Utah, Colorado, Wyoming. I loved it. A lot of country music and laughing together.

"When I was ten, my father's company went under and he took another job at a company based in Canoga Park, California, just outside of Los Angeles. We moved and it was pretty hard on me. The neighborhood was rough and we lived in a shitty tract house. My father always said it was temporary. But we never left."

"They're still there?"

"My dad is. Retired. My mom died," Roarke said sadly.

Katie watched his whole physique, totally contained a moment ago, change. She sensed the presence of a young boy inside this hardened man.

"I'm sorry," she said taking his hand.

"Me, too. Cancer. She was a two-pack a day smoker. It was awful."

"How old were you?"

"Fourteen. Not a fun time. Of course, my dad had to keep driving. He was away about twenty-five days out of every month, so I kind of became a latch key kid and a surrogate son to neighbors down the street. They basically took over and it wasn't quite good enough."

"What do you mean?" Katie asked.

"I lived in gang territory."

"Oh, Jesus."

"Hispanic and black turf. Block by block. And I couldn't ever seem to get to school or back home without trouble. I did learn how to run fast," he added with a chuckle. "But a lot of times I didn't get away. So, just to stay alive, I took up with some white kids I'd never otherwise hang around. And I picked up all the bad things you can imagine."

Roarke paused. He was ready to stop, having told her far more than he ever felt possible.

"You really want to hear this?"

Katie squeezed his hand and caressed his fingers with her thumb, encouraging him to continue.

"Summers were okay because I'd go on the road with my dad. Before I had my license he had me driving the semi while other truckers kept an eye out for police and radioed us if I had to pull over and switch seats. Hell, I think I was only fifteen. And it was the most fun I ever had. I got damned good at driving the thing at 90."

"During my junior year at school the gang stuff got worse. I'd been a decent student up until then, but it all went to shit. One day I got caught running out of a 7-11 with some awful donuts I lifted. Donuts. A big heist. Well, I ran right into a police car. I mean right smack into it as it was pulling up. The clerk came screaming out of the store. I threw the donuts at him and tried to take off. Now here's where it gets interesting. A cop got out, grabbed me by the arm, got my right hand and put me in some sort of hold. Not a hard one, but I couldn't move. I'd never seen anything like it before. I was completely immobilized. He told me to give him money for the donuts, which I did, and then he asked me to get in the back of his cruiser. He wasn't really asking. I'm cleaning up the story a little."

"I'm sure you are. Go on," Katie pronounced with real interest.

"Well, I got very, very scared. Scared about what my dad would do. And scared that I had blown it. Basically, I wasn't a bad kid. Maybe he sensed it. The cop just watched me in the rear view mirror. We must have sat there for ten minutes before he turned around and said something."

Katie followed the story word for word. "What did he say?"

"He gave me a choice. Go to jail, where he figured I'd be rather unhappy. Or drive across the valley to see a friend who he said would straighten me out.

"Now I didn't know who the 'friend' was, but the idea of jail wasn't on the top of my list. He said I had to make up my mind by the time he returned to the squad car after giving the clerk my money."

Roarke's lips were dry from all of his talking. He finished his glass of port, wiped his mouth and asked, "Are you sure I'm not boring you?"

"Oh, no. Tell me. What happened? Who's the friend?"

"He came back with a coffee for himself and a donut for me. Jesus, that surprised me. And he asked if I'd made a decision. I was slow on the uptake. I saw his eyes in the mirror close. 'Sorry, kid, you're going to jail.'

"I said, 'Wait, wait! Please!' We sat there for another few minutes. Finally he said, 'A few minutes ago you wanted donuts real badly. Not hungry now?' Well, I started crying. 'Okay,' I said. And I had a bite. We still sat there and then I gave him, what do they call it, the magic words?"

"'I'm sorry?'"

"That's exactly what I told him. I saw him crack a smile and then we left. After about a mile I asked who we were going to see."

"Who was it?"

"He didn't say a word. We got on the freeway and drove for a good twenty-five minutes. A few blocks before stopping he told me, 'You can take a bus to here.' He pointed to the intersection. 'It's about ninety minutes each way. Twice a week. If I hear you're not coming and you don't have a fucking good reason, I'll throw your ass in jail so fast you won't know what happened.'"

"So where?"

"An academy for martial arts."

"Karate."

"Actually Tae Kwon Do. And it changed my life.

"We walked in and he spoke to an Asian man about 5'8" who didn't look particularly strong. I learned differently. He walked over to me and bowed. Not knowing what to do, I automatically bowed back. 'Very good,' he said in a Korean accent. 'He'll make a good student.' He bowed to the policeman and went to a display counter where he pulled out a traditional white uniform for me. 'Here, put this on. It will fit.' Apparently he was used to the cop hauling in students."

"This is incredible," Katie said excitedly. "Who was he?"

"His name is Jun Chong, and he's one of the leading martial arts masters in the country. His Tae Kwon Do classes are based on respect, discipline, character building and, oh yes, self-defense. And he is incredible."

"So you did it? You went right into it?"

"Instantly. And was I ever bad. But I went there every week. Not twice a week, but four times a week. I trained every chance I had except when I was on the road with my dad. And my grades went up. I developed confidence. And word got around, too. The townies stopped messing with me. I never even had to fight to prove myself."

As Katie listened she became more aware of the strength and power of the man opposite her. His muscles pushed at the seams of his shirt and jacket sleeves. His face appeared rugged and tight. She imagined him naked and became breathless at the thought. But his eyes still gave him away as the sensitive boy who got caught by the policeman. Katie leaned across the table and kissed him.

"What's that for?"

"That? That's for *starters*," she said with a coy smile. "Now go on. You're still only, what, seventeen?"

"Right," Roarke said smiling. "That was nice. Thank you."

"You're welcome. There's more where that came from, but go on."

"Well, okay." He was flustered and liked it. Recovering, he said, "Let's see. During a demo my senior year I saw an Army guy talk to Master Chong. I didn't pay too close attention until my Master signaled for me. I'd just broken three separate boards with three kicks while jumping in the air and not touching the ground. Two were held to the side, another higher up. I ran over and bowed and he said, 'Mr. Roarke, meet Lieutenant Cutler. He wants to talk to you.'"

"I didn't know it then, but apparently he was from a place called 'The Fortress,' Fort Bragg, North Carolina," Roarke explained. "A fairly foreboding location I came to know quite well. Army Special Operations Command. Abbreviated USASOC. Apparently my martial arts training gave me a leg up for his particular line of work."

"Which was…"

"Same question I asked."

"And he said?"

"'None of my business unless I made it my business.'"

"Oh that answers everything."

"He told me I had to accept the job offer on faith. That I was ready and that he wanted me. I said I needed to talk to three people first."

"Three?"

"My father. Master Chong. And a policeman in Canoga Park."

"What did they say?" Katie begged.

"My dad said he was sorry he hadn't been there for me, but I should do what I needed to do. Master Chong bowed at the waist, put his right palm over his left fist in greeting and said I should serve my country. And the policeman, Jim LaRosa, hugged me like I was his own son and cried. He had paid for all of my studies. All of them."

Tears formed in Katie's eyes and soon spilled down her cheeks. Roarke reached over and kissed them away. He continued quietly. "Two years later I went into the field and there wasn't a desert hole or a jungle high hide where I didn't think of LaRosa and how much he helped me."

Katie fought back more tears and flashed a confused look. "A jungle what?"

"A high hide. A place to hide, way up. Usually waiting for animals. But I tracked the two-legged kinds. The ones with guns."

"Where?"

"That's one thing I can't really talk about."

"What did you do?"

"That's another. But I can tell you one thing. I saw a lot of the world for free."

"Oh you," she said pulling one hand away to dab her cheeks with the napkin. "Well, now you've settled down for a nice safe job like protecting the President of the United States."

He laughed. "Yeah. But it comes with a really great 401(k)." Roarke leaned across the table again and kissed her. This time on the lips. And this time they both lingered, exploring each other's senses, tastes and smells.

When he opened his eyes he asked, "Ready, Katie?"

"Oh yes," she said, answering a number of questions at the same time.

CHAPTER 25

Roarke stood and casually glanced in the direction of the man he dubbed Crabbe. Even through his story telling he had been aware of Crabbe's mannerisms and mood; everything about him was suspect.

Using the simple distraction of putting his wallet away, Roarke allowed himself a moment to study Crabbe's features. In an instant he was convinced he could provide a complete and accurate description. He also noticed the man was also prepared to leave. His bill was paid. Cash. And most importantly, he never touched his drink. Crabbe was sober and ready to move. If he came in following Katie, he was definitely going to leave with Roarke.

Outside, Roarke and Katie made a left up Chestnut Street toward Beacon Hill. A few paces took them to Charles Street where Roarke knew he'd quickly be able to hail a cab. At the corner he casually moved his arm around Katie, turning her body slightly. She smiled, but Roarke's motives were purely professional. He maneuvered himself to look back down the street. Crabbe was no more than twenty paces behind them. Their eyes briefly met and Crabbe slowed down and checked his watch in a highly transparent diversion.

Roarke angled back to Charles Street and struck his hand up to signal a cab. Katie smiled more. *No walk home up the hill. Tonight we'll get way past the front door.*

But when the brown and white Boston Cab pulled up, Roarke quickly opened the door, let Katie take a seat and then whispered, "You go home. There's a man following us." He handed her a twenty. "I'll call you later." Roarke tapped the roof twice. The cab began to roll even before he closed the door on his startled date. Now he searched the street for Crabbe.

"Okay where are you?" Roarke whispered. Crabbe was gone.

He retraced a few steps, looked into an empty alley, and then back down Chestnut Street. *Damn.* The authentic Back Bay street lamps actually offered little illumination. Primarily they were there for the ambiance. Roarke could have used more right now. That's when he caught a shadow crossing under a tree at the corner of Chestnut Street and Mugar Way. He dashed down the street only to realize he had made an error and lost time. He had pursued a man walking his dog.

Roarke focused his senses. Footsteps behind him. *Too short and deliberate*, he thought. He was right. He stepped aside to let an elderly woman pass.

Roarke double-backed again up Chestnut. That's when it happened. From his blindside, behind and to the right.

Roarke was lifted off his feet and slammed against a parked van with the full force of the Crabbe. He fell to one knee with a pain racing through his left shoulder. The assailant had emerged with a running start from between two brownstones. Seconds ago Roarke was on the offense. Now he was off balance, unable to quickly steady himself. He felt cold steel pressed into his side; a thin rod, probably a silencer in the hands of a hired killer. Roarke knew it would be a painful mortal shot, but from where it was held, not an instant death. His mind raced through purely defensive moves and then to something more practical. *Get Crabbe to talk.*

"You're not going to want to make a mess here," Roarke said with no fear in his voice. "Witnesses are all around."

"Shut up!"

Crabbe had a deep, dangerous, cold-blooded voice. "Let's see," Roarke said daring to continue his taunt. "You followed me? No. You followed the girl. Right?"

"Shut the fuck up!" Crabbe said louder than he should have. The outburst told Roarke what he needed to know.

"So you know she talked to me. That's what Marcus wanted to find out. But you weren't supposed to be noticed. So you fucked up. And now you have to do something about it."

Roarke struck another nerve because Crabbe bore the gun further into his side. The Secret Service agent winced at the pressure.

"I'd say you have a problem."

"Get up," Crabbe demanded. He stepped back giving Roarke room to rise, but the gun was still on him.

"And now we're going to go somewhere," Roarke said as he slowly got to his feet.

"You bet your sweet ass."

By rising Roarke had been able to reposition his body so the gun, in Crabbe's right hand, was more on his back, no longer pressing into softer flesh. He could maneuver.

In those few seconds, Roarke had enough time to size up his enemy. He sensed that Crabbe was worried. He'd blown it. He should have disappeared and he didn't. Now he had to do something about it. Roarke assumed they'd take a walk across Storrow Drive to the Esplanade along the Charles River. In the moonless night, Crabbe would cover his tracks. But he wouldn't get that chance. With one swift move, Roarke stepped slightly forward and to the side. He pushed his right elbow back sliding Crabbe's gun off its mark. He swung his body around to the right, bringing his left hand down on Crabbe's wrist.

Roarke's right hand also went for the gun. He could have done it blindfolded. It was a classic move. With his thumb on Crabbe's palm and his fingers on the top of his hand, he drove the gun back towards Crabbe's body in an unnatural and instantly crippling way. The pressure of the two hands working against Crabbe's fragile bones, and a corresponding twisting action to the right, and the weight of Roarke's forearm coming down on his wrist, forced Crabbe to release the weapon. They both heard the bones split.

Crabbe felt the excruciating pain pulsate through his body.

Roarke then kicked the gun into the street, but that allowed Crabbe to get a half a step jump on him. Crabbe was in no position to fight, at least until he had the advantage again.

Cars honked as he darted between a VW and an Explorer on Mugar. Roarke hesitated, allowing the cars to pass before he followed.

Crabbe jumped a two-foot fence onto Storrow Drive. He raced around six or seven cars, getting side-swiped by one, but he continued with about twenty yards on Roarke.

Roarke was in great shape. So was Crabbe. The man ran through his pain until he got about midway through an open expanse of the Esplanade in front of the Hatch Shell where the Boston Pops play during the summer. Roarke saw him stop and kneel as if trying to remove something from his pant leg.

There were only ten yards between them now. The light from a car heading around a curve on Storrow Drive squarely hit Crabbe. For barely an instant Roarke saw the glint of metal from a snub nose gun.

Instinctively, Roarke dove to his right, counter to where he bet Crabbe would shoot. Crabbe's perspective was left to right and he would almost assuredly expect his adversary to move the same way. His mistake. The bullet missed him by three feet.

Crabbe responded to the sound of Roarke rolling and immediately adjusted his aim. Another bullet struck the ground near him. Too close; only inches away. During his roll, Roarke reached for his Sig Sauer P229 under his jacket, then reconsidered. Crabbe got off another shot. Three misses, not unexpected since he was firing with his left hand.

Roarke knew he had one chance; two at the most. But if he fired and missed in the dark, Crabbe would see the flash and know exactly where he was. With the cars speeding by in the background it was hard to sort out forms in the foreground. But Roarke calculated where Crabbe would be. He reached inside his left vest pocket and put his hands on a pen, a special order from BingShot, an Internet site. The functional blue ballpoint had dual purpose, which became obvious with the twist of the top. A two-and-a-half-inch 42052 stainless steel blade extended. For $5.00 Roarke had a silent weapon which he didn't hesitate using.

Roarke needed one distraction, if only for a moment. He grunted, ducked, and rolled to his right. Crabbe heard the sound and shot wide and behind him. Roarke rebounded with a silent back flip to a crouching position. He dove low and fast directly into Crabbe's blind side and stuck the knife into his side, twisting as he pushed. With his other hand he applied a penetrating pinch to Crabbe's wrist, which released the gun. Crabbe tried to reach for it, but this was his fourth mistake of the night. It only drove the knife deeper, severing vital arteries. The assailant crumbled to his knees, looking at nothing in particular. Then he slumped to the ground, dead.

Roarke quickly searched the body for identification. He discovered a wallet. It was impossible to clearly see what was inside, but it appeared that Crabbe carried different identity cards. Roarke put it in his pocket and ran down the Esplanade toward the Longfellow Bridge.

Roarke would have a great deal of explaining to do. But he preferred to talk to the FBI over the Boston Police.

Roarke slowed down when he reached Cambridge Street. He

caught his breath and called FBI Director Robert Mulligan's direct line, dictating the names he found in the wallet for the Bureau to run.

A few minutes later Roarke called Katie who nervously answered the phone on the first ring. "Scott?" It had been twenty minutes since Roarke rushed her into the cab.

"Yes," he answered.

"Are you all right?"

"Yes, yes, I'm fine. Look, I'm heading back home. I'm awfully sorry about tonight. I really wanted to spend more time with you, but I had to say goodbye to our *friend*."

Katie listened carefully. He was not all right. Something was wrong, but she took his cues and waited.

"I'll give you a shout. Okay?"

"Okay," she offered tentatively. "And you're sure you're—"

"I'm fine. I'll be back in town soon, let's play then. Let me know if anyone says anything about our *friend*."

An awful possibility abruptly struck her. *Did Scott kill the man?* Then she thought something more worrisome. *The man could have killed Scott.*

"You be careful," she pleaded.

"I will. I promise. Talk to you soon. Bye."

He ended the call and watched her pass by her front window three stories above Grove Street. He wasn't leaving. Not yet. He decided to watch Katie's apartment for the night. This last episode came a little too close for comfort. He considered the possibility of pulling her into an FBI safe house, then decided against it. Crabbe had followed Katie, but he got what he wanted. He saw that she was having dinner with the Secret Service agent. That's what he would have reported. Better she simply go back to work and not raise any suspicions by her absence. Crabbe's death would read like a robbery to everyone except Haywood Marcus. And Bob Mulligan would get a judge to approve a wire tap.

Katie peered into the night sky, then slowly closed her curtains. She looked beautiful in silhouette against the backlight of her room. Roarke watched, longing to be with her as the lights went out.

BURLINGTON, VERMONT

"Thanks for coming by, Governor," Lodge replied. "Burlington isn't the easiest of commutes."

"No problem Teddy. I've been looking forward to sitting down with you."

"Anything to drink?"

"A beer will do. Coors if you have it."

The congressman nodded to Geoff Newman who gave him a high sign that he'd be back with the beer.

"And take your time, Geoff," Lodge said.

"He's always around," the Congressman confessed. "Sometimes it drives me crazy. I still don't know where I'll put him once *we're* in the White House."

"'Once we're in,' Congressman?" Governor Lamden observed. "I've heard that you've spoken to a number of potential running mates."

"For show, Henry. The job's yours. Like I told you and Wendell, I know we can win *together*. We can beat Taylor and we can beat him good. I'm not so sure if anyone else could make it as my running mate. Maybe Reeves from Kentucky. But just between us, I doubt it. The two of us—that's a different story. *We can* take the country. We can help the party and bring more Democrats into the House and Senate. And we can really change the world."

"Are you giving me one of your campaign speeches, Congressman?"

Lodge didn't like being lectured. All manner of friendliness evaporated.

"Henry, I'm giving you the chance to get your fucking name on a political button," he shouted. "You can be Vice President of the United States. Take it or leave it."

Newman entered the room. "Excuse me, gentlemen. Your drinks. Or would you prefer pistols at dawn?"

"Oh, I see you've been listening. We're fine, Newman," Lamden declared. "The Congressman is just insistent that I become the second most powerful man on the face of the earth. I had my sights set on being number one."

"What do they say, Henry?" Newman said. "One heartbeat away. It's still closer than anyone else."

The governor forced a smile. He glanced at Newman wondering, *Who really will be number two?* Then he said, "You have yourself a running mate, Congressman."

Lodge smiled. He'd won again.

"Tell you what. Let me propose a toast," Newman added as he passed the drinks around. "To the next President and Vice President of the United States. Lodge and Lamden."

Lamden faced both Newman and Lodge. There was awkward silence, then the governor lifted his glass. "It does have a nice ring to it."

BOSTON, MASSACHUSETTS
WEDNESDAY, JULY 23

The bell chimed as the elevator door opened to the main reception area for Freelander, Collins, Wrather & Marcus. Katie Kessler stepped off with three other people. She breezed past the reception desk and walked down the hall toward her office.

"Good morning, Miss Kessler."

The voice belonged to Haywood Marcus. *Oh shit!* He intercepted her near a conference room; an intended encounter that Katie read right through.

"Good morning, Mr. Marcus," she said with a grin. Katie juggled her pocketbook and briefcase to free up a hand for shaking.

Marcus took it, and studied her for a moment through an insincere smile. He didn't read any nervousness in his associate. She was calm, friendly, and perfectly relaxed. Apparently she had a quiet evening. But he'd wait for the report from his man to find out more. *Odd though, he hasn't called yet.*

It would be another day before the news of the Back Bay killing made the City & Region section of *The Boston Globe* or *The Boston Herald*. That's when Haywood Marcus would really begin to worry.

THURSDAY, JULY 24

The man logged onto his computer. He'd been working harder in the last two months than he had in years. Business was good. His various bank accounts, divvied up in four countries, had swollen by millions. And now there was another message embedded in some eBay ads for first edition Frederick Forsyth novels.

He'd have to think about this offer and how he wanted to handle it.

As the antiques dealer he used hair dye, glasses, clothing, and dialect to effectively change his identity. As the Connecticut commuter, theatrical pigmentation makeup and appropriate business attire did the trick. And as the old lawyer casting for steelhead, the wrinkling cream proved positively amazing. It slowed the blood flow to his face, helping his facial muscles sag. He added decades to his features. His character came together with more hair dye, a loose fitting wardrobe, and great acting.

Every disguise began organically. He created full biographies for his roles, understanding who they were, where they grew up and where they lived and worked. He gave them personal idiosyncrasies, particular tastes in food, and how they satisfied themselves sexually. Some of his characters were good family men, one was gay. He could pass as an Arab, however he admitted to himself that he had difficulty perfecting a credible Asian identity. Curiously, he did play a woman once with deadly success. His victim's last realization was how wrong he'd been about the woman he took to a hotel room.

He enjoyed everything about his job; so much more than his teachers could have imagined. Amazing, too, that it had been his goal since losing a leading role in his high school play. Of course, he had directed the very real death scene of his old drama teacher and, by last count, forty-three other men and women since.

Forty-four would be a Boston lawyer. He'd have to give some real consideration to how he'd do it.

CHAPTER 26

HUDSON, NEW YORK
FRIDAY, JULY 25

"Chief, Anne Fornado wants to see you at the St. Charles right away."

"Did she say why?"

"Thought you'd be interested in something."

Chief Carl Marelli was hot and annoyed. This mid-summer Hudson Valley humidity was brutal. Not as bad as what Manhattan and DC were getting. Still they sure could use a little break. As a matter of fact, so could his investigation. He wiped the sweat off his forehead with his sleeve, drove his squad car up Warren Street but didn't even bother with the AC for the short drive.

The reporters were all gone. No more satellite vans; no more visits from first tier and wannabe anchors. The story started in Hudson and that's also where the trail got cold.

Marelli and Bessolo talked every day or so. If the FBI had anything in Washington, they weren't telling the Hudson police. And Marelli had nothing that would merit calling the Bureau back.

The last field agent left a week earlier. And he was having more luck scoring antiques on Warren Street than any more leads around town.

"So whatcha got, Anne?" Marelli asked as soon as he pushed open the side door.

"Come on back," the hotel clerk said. She'd been two years behind Marelli at Hudson High and still tried to catch his eye.

Anne Fornado opened the door to her office. Thankfully the air conditioning was blasting refreshingly cool air.

"Remember a few days after the shooting you came by to ask about McAlister's reservation? You really were disappointed with what I gave you."

"Yeah, nothing," he remembered.

"But Carl, there *was* something. I just hadn't found it yet."

"Go on," the police chief implored, now thoroughly engrossed.

"I needed to dig a little deeper. And there it was."

"There was what?"

"In the record. The reservation, the booking *and* the notations. Here."

Marelli was feeling more comfortable and it wasn't the air conditioning. He circled around Anne's computer screen. She smelled nice. Funny, he hadn't noticed that in years.

"Let's go to McAlister's reservation on the 13th. The night he called it in." She typed the words "McAlister" and "check-in" and pressed enter. A two-page list of hotel guests named McAlister came up. She moved her mouse down to "Sidney McAlister," highlighted the item and hit enter again with her right pinky.

The full registration immediately appeared showing McAlister's name and his credit card number, since found by the FBI to be a pre-paid Visa credit card covered by cash. A few lines down was the hotel short hand: Ckn tm, rmchrg, rm#.

"What am I looking for?" Marelli asked. Fornado helped him by moving the cursor to the last line and highlighting "Room #207."

Marelli straightened up but never took his eyes off the screen. Anne looked over her shoulder and smiled. "Interesting."

"207, on the side, second floor," she said unnecessarily.

"207? But he was checked into 301."

"Not right away. Someone else was in 301. And look at this." Anne scrolled down to a further notation on McAlister's record. "Request frt rm, 3rd, 301, when avail."

"That was added by Sam Martell, who was on the night desk on the 15th. McAlister must have called it in. See, it's all right here."

Marelli read it all.

"I talked to Sam. He remembers it. McAlister even offered to buy him a drink, which Sam turned down."

"And when did the room open up?"

"Three days later. The 18th. That's when McAlister got his room."

"And if the guy in 301 didn't leave, then McAlister would have been up shit creek."

"Guess so. But the odd thing is," she said as she typed in another few words, "the guest in 301 left early. He wasn't supposed to leave until June 25th."

"The FBI never ran any of this down?"

"Not a bit. I wouldn't have either, but I wanted to help you." She flashed a warm smile. "Somehow."

"Annie, I don't know what it means, but the coincidence is overwhelming. Do you have a name to go with the room?"

"Right here," she proudly volunteered. "I've got everything printed out for you."

Anne handed him a file with all of the pages.

"Thank you, Anne. Thanks a lot," he said on the run. When he got back to his desk he was going to track down this man who had 301 and why he left. He had a phone number in Connecticut and a name. Dolan.

BOSTON, MASSACHUSETTS

Roarke made the noon shuttle out of Logan. Getting through security with his gun was always a potential problem. He preferred to take care of these "unpleasantries," as he called them, away from the crowds. Arriving at the terminal he identified himself to a uniformed guard who escorted him to a holding room. There he voluntarily turned over his Sig while the federal security guards checked and rechecked his Secret Service credentials.

Everyone on the president's payroll remembered the 2002 case involving an armed Secret Service agent who was removed from a Maryland-to-Texas American Airlines flight. The pilot was concerned that the man posed a potential security risk, and he acted accordingly. In light of that, Roarke believed that rushing these people was not a good idea. The airport guards had been federalized for years, which simply meant they could fire first and ask questions later. And the captain of an airplane, like the captain of a ship, has complete responsibility for the safety of his passengers. According to security specialists with the Airline Pilots Association, when dealing with a perceived threat, the pilot has the authority to return a plane to the gate and have passengers removed.

Roarke preferred anonymity in public. He provided the security team with a number to call at the White House to confirm his credentials. While they were waiting for a response, Roarke's cell phone rang.

"Roarke here," he answered. The news was not good and he automatically turned his back on the guards. A few moments later they heard his side of a testy conversation. "A heart attack? When? He didn't get the message?"

They instantly knew he was real. The fact was confirmed by the fax coming in now. The senior of the two guards took it out of the machine, scanned it and gave the other a thumbs up just as Roarke sharply stated, "Have that trooper seal off the scene immediately. And Shannon, get a team out there. Find out who can do a complete toxicology workup before some local funeral director shoots him full of anything. I'll be back in town by ten."

Roarke pocketed his phone. "Is everything okay?" he asked the guards.

"Is it okay with you, sir?"

"Not in the least."

They returned his gun and identification and escorted Roarke to the gate. The lead guard whispered something to the ticket agent. She flagged him on the plane with a polite wave of her hand.

The one thing Roarke did request was the privilege of being seated first. He liked to study everyone who boarded. But today he was tired from his vigil the night before. The flight was delayed for thirty-five minutes because of air traffic patterns. Roarke used the time to rest.

When he opened his eyes again he was on the ground in Washington. The landing jolted him awake. Once permitted to use his cell phone, he dialed his friend at the FBI. But Davis had done him one better. He was waiting at the gate for Roarke.

"Well, this is service," he said when he saw the FBI man. Davis, a blond version of Roarke, was rock solid. He projected a *don't mess with me* attitude in his 6'2" frame. He looked tough, but sophisticated in his navy blue suit and designer sunglasses. Shannon Davis had served with Roarke in the Army Special Forces. They remained close friends and they helped each other in ways well beyond what the rules allowed.

"I figured you deserved a little TLC."

"And I get you. Where did I go wrong?"

Roarke took Shannon's right hand when they met and wrestled his neck with his left. The two friends exchanged small talk until they got in the FBI Town-car. The Bureau driver had absolutely no problem keeping it waiting at the curb.

"Okay, here's what I can tell you," Davis began. "It does look like a heart attack." Roarke was about to jump in, but Davis continued, "I know. I know. And we'll get a full autopsy. But I'm telling you he had all the signs of a heart attack."

"What about where he collapsed?"

"Sealed off like you asked. Jesus, Scott, the man was in his late seventies and he was out there alone in the woods. People do die of heart attacks."

"Yeah, but one day he's a critical link for me and the next day he's dead."

"A link to what, Scott? What are you into?"

"I can't explain now."

Davis paused. "You better be careful, buddy. You work for a high profile guy."

Roarke nodded. *The highest. But for how long?*

They drove for another twelve minutes talking baseball to pass the time. Once inside the FBI building, they went up to Shannon Davis' office.

Roarke asked him to get the Idaho State Trooper on the line. While the FBI man placed the call, Roarke phoned the White House. "Louise, I need to see the man today," he said. Morgan Taylor's secretary put him on the calendar for 5:50. "Ten minutes, Scott. No more. He's scheduled for a dinner at six."

Davis had his man on the phone by the time Roarke was finished talking to the president's secretary. "His name is Duke Hormel. He's cooperative," he explained with his hand over the mouthpiece, "so for God's sake, don't piss him off."

Roarke flashed Davis the finger and pleasantly said, "Hello Officer Hormel, this is Scott Roarke. I'm with the Secret Service. Thanks for your willingness to assist." He smiled to Davis as if to say, "Aren't I being good?"

"Hello," was all he got back from the Idaho trooper.

"Listen, I know you've gone over this before, but can you run through it again for me. Please," he added for Shannon's benefit.

"Secret Service? What's this got to do with…"

"The vice president might be visiting the area. It's routine, officer. But keep that to yourself, if you will."

"Sure. Okay. Well, what happened is that we received a 911 call from a woman who said her husband hadn't returned for dinner after a day fishing up river. It's not the best country to be out in after dark, so we take these things pretty seriously."

"I understand."

"We get these calls fairly regularly and usually the person in question turns up a bit drunk. Too many beers."

"This was different?" Roarke asked.

"Actually not, pretty routine. We got the general idea from his wife where Nunes was supposed to be and about 10 P.M. on the 20th we found him. He'd been dead about nine or ten hours. A heart attack. I guess it turned out to be a bad fishing day for him. Not even a bite on his line."

"Any visible signs of distress on the body?"

"No, the coroner pretty quickly determined it was a heart attack."

Roarke felt some attitude back, but he had to ask the next question. "Any signs of a puncture wound? Even a needle to his heart or under his armpit?"

Roarke could feel the officer getting mad. He heard a deep sigh over the phone.

"It was a heart attack."

"Look, Trooper Hormel, I didn't say it wasn't a heart attack. But heart attacks can be induced. And as I explained, it's my business to make sure your neck of the woods is safe for the VP."

The Idaho officer lowered his voice. "Sir, we had the place cordoned off like Agent Davis requested. Now the body's being held at St. Luke's Wood River Medical Center."

"Did his wife say Nunes had any history of heart problems?"

"No, I asked. Aside from asthma he was in pretty good health. No heart problems."

"Come on, Trooper. No suspicions? Isn't there anything that doesn't strike you as right?" Roarke demanded. He was showing his anger. After all it took almost five days before the troopers notified the FBI that the heart attack victim was the man Roarke sought.

This time the young trooper didn't jump right in. He weighed his answer for a few moments, then started. "Mr. Roarke, I'm usually running down fishermen who were supposed to catch and release, but didn't. I write up a lot of drivers who smash into a deer and I'm always giving some teenage campers a good warning after finding them in possession of some grass. We have wolves, coyotes, and even a few bears to scare away from campsites. I don't have much to do with criminals. This is way over my head."

THE WHITE HOUSE

"Hello, Mr. President."

Morgan Taylor nearly spit out his sixth cup of coffee of the day. Roarke never referred to him as "president." Ever. Usually "boss," but never "Mr. President."

"Sorry, but such protocol, I'm just not used to it, Scott. Glad to see you."

The president closed the door to the Oval Office and invited Roarke in. "I understand that you've been a busy, busy boy."

"Oh?"

"Your stroll through the Boston Esplanade last evening. That was your handiwork?"

"Yes sir."

Mulligan had obviously briefed the president in person. Nothing more needed to be said about it directly. Nothing more would ever be said.

"Louise told me you need to get to a dinner, so I'll get right to it."

The two men remained standing. The president stood behind the Jefferson chair.

"You sent me up to Lodge's hometown to ask a few simple questions. Quietly. I don't think it's quiet any more. I'm getting a really bad feeling."

"Which is?"

"Well, I don't have enough to make any kind of professional assessment yet, but I want you to put in a good word for me with Mulligan. I need to talk to one of his people. Maybe that will give me something concrete." He clutched the photograph, not certain if he should show it to the president yet.

"Okay, but you could have called that in. There's something else. What is it?"

"I'll share what my gut tells me."

"Please do."

"I think you're being fucked over."

CHAPTER 27

HUDSON, NEW YORK
MONDAY, AUGUST 4

Carl Marelli typed up exactly what Anne Fornado told him and then dialed the number the man Dolan had left with the hotel.

"Hello. Hold on," roared the woman who answered. Marelli heard clanging in the background and a cacophony of voices. "Yeah, what can I get you?"

"Dolan. I'm looking for a man named Dolan."

He heard her yell into the room, "Hey, anyone here named Dolan? I got a guy on the phone." When nobody responded, she came back. "Nope. No Dolan here. You want anything?" the woman asked again. "I'm in a hurry, bub, so let's have it."

"Excuse me, but where have I dialed?"

"Pizzalla. If you're not going to order, then so long."

"Wait a second. Let me check the number again." Marelli read it off to the woman.

"Yup. Right number. That doesn't change who you got. This is Pizzalla."

"Okay, I understand that, but…"

"Hold on a second," she said. The call went on hold. Marelli presumed she took an order. A minute later she returned, just as gruff. "I'm back and like I said—"

"Look, I'm Chief of Police in Hudson, New York, and I'm trying to find a man named Dolan. He's not a customer. This was supposed to be his phone number."

"I told you, there ain't no Dolan here."

"But this was the contact number he left."

"Then you've been snookered. You reached a pizza place in Stamford, and I'm damned busy. So with all due respect, so long."

The woman hung up. She was right. They'd been snookered, which told him that this Dolan was definitely part of a team. He added the information to his report. Then decided to check the computer for Dolan name matches.

Marelli logged onto NYSPIN, the New York Statewide Police Information Network. The system, maintained by the New York State Police, communicates messages internally among police departments and other law enforcement agencies and provides users direct access to NCIC, the National Crime Information Center. Police can share information, add comment or updates, and link to systems in other states through cooperative agreements.

Four names came up on the NYSPIN police web. One in Buffalo, a spousal abuse matter. The second a DWI from Gilderland. The third match was a car theft in Syracuse. The fourth caught Marelli broadside. It was filed by the Manhattan Police with a cross-reference to another police department—in Stamford, Connecticut.

Dolan, Frank. Wanted possible suspect. Homicide.

The description that followed matched Anne Fornado's ID. The contact was an NYPD detective named Coates.

Carl Marelli made his second call. This one counted.

"Coates. Homicide."

"Detective. My name is Marelli, I head up the police department in Hudson, New York."

Hudson was very much on the map these days and Harry Coates immediately gripped the phone headset harder.

"We need to talk about a man named Dolan."

"Say that again," Coates asked. He rolled his chair forward to get closer to his desk and write.

"This is Carl Marelli, I'm…"

"I got that part. But it's about?"

Marelli spoke slowly. "Dolan. A man named Dolan. Frank Dolan."

"You have my undivided attention, Chief Marelli," Coates proclaimed.

Marelli told his story and then listened to Coates as he explained about the death of Steven Hoag.

"So, we both have a guy named Frank Dolan," Marelli added. "Their descriptions match pretty well. And they were both around murders. What's the chance that there is just one Dolan?"

"I'd say about 100 percent. Send me your report. I'll get you what I have. And let's stay on this, Chief."

"I have to talk to my contact at the Bureau. Then I'll fax you," Marelli said.

"I don't know where this is going to lead, but I have to tell you, it's the best news I've had in awhile."

Marelli was actually feeling excited. So was Coates. If Dolan was also involved in the assassination attempt on Lodge, then it raised even more questions about the phone line that had been disconnected. The New York cop thought for a moment. The possibilities were unnerving. For now, he didn't even want to go there.

The people silently listening on the line recording the exchange looked at one another. This was an interesting development to them, too. Their boss would have to hear about it. Before they were off the line, Evans had been notified.

It was the constant eating that President Taylor hated the most about the job. At least four nights a week he hosted a dinner at the White House, spoke at an embassy function or traveled to one dais or another halfway across the country. And all the food was bland. Where were the spices he discovered on duty in Asia? Or the delicious meals in the Caribbean ports? Unless he was visiting Los Angeles and Wolfgang Puck catered the meal it was all fairly uninspired.

Rather than eating, the president moved the food around on his plate: from left to right, up and down and sometimes creating food artwork in patterns. An aide confided that his predecessors had basically done the same thing.

By Taylor's count he had to endure another seventy-eight dinners before leaving the White House.

Teddy Lodge led by twenty-three points now. He'd get another boost at the Democratic primary. Then, Taylor would enjoy a predictable bump following the Republican primary. Maybe they'd be 50-50 for awhile. But by Labor Day, Lodge would move ahead again. The president needed to deliver a command performance in the debates to achieve any advantage. That is unless he really wanted to call it quits after another seventy-eight state dinners. Funny how the most important job in the world came down to limp vegetables and dry chicken breasts, the staples of the "rubber chicken" circuit.

While Morgan Taylor chatted with a Brazilian ambassador, he noticed that the Secret Service agent closest to him cupped an ear to block the room noise. A communication was coming in. The agent nodded, and tapped "Top Gun," the handle the Secret Service gave to Morgan Taylor.

"Gotta go, Mr. President."

"No argument from me," the president said through a relieved smile. "What is it?"

"The Chief needs to speak with you. Pronto." The reference was to the president's chief of staff.

Twenty minutes later Morgan Taylor was back at the White House. John Bernstein was waiting for him in the Oval Office.

"What's up, Bernsie?"

"Jack Evans is on his way. He'll be here in a couple of minutes. There's been a development."

"More," Taylor asked not understanding.

"The Lodge shooting."

This was just the kind of news that made Taylor realize he could put up with another thousand bad presidential meals.

THE WHITE HOUSE

"Sit down everyone," the president commanded.

"Give it to me straight, Jack." The President of the United States lit up a Partagas against all Federal smoking regulations in the building. "Straight."

"Pieces right now. But enough to paint a disturbing picture."

"As I'm sure you've heard, I'm all ears."

The CIA head and the president's chief of staff laughed. They were very familiar with the cartoon caricatures of the president, which overly emphasized his ears.

"It's about McAlister, the man who shot at Congressman Lodge."

"Shouldn't Bob Mulligan be in on this?" the president asked.

"Oh, I think he'll be here all on his own very soon. He's got much of the same information."

"What is it?"

"We think that McAlister may know the man who took out Steven Hoag on the way to New York."

"What?" exclaimed Bernsie. "The man who tried to kill Lodge is involved in the death of a Russian, too?"

"Maybe," Evans said.

"Do you know what you're saying?" Bernsie said. His voice cracked like a teenager's. "This could be a hit by the Russians? Retribution for turning their man. Or…"

"Easy, Bernsie," the president said.

"But there are legal ramifications. National and international. I can't begin to stress…"

"Later, Bernsie. When it's time to notify the AG we will. But by the look on Jack's face, I don't think he's quite finished yet."

"No, I'm not." He directed his comments to the president, who had been right about both the seriousness of his expression and the need to continue. "McAlister was the shooter in Hudson. But McAlister is an alias. There's no such person. A few days after he checked into the Hudson hotel, this McAlister moved from one room to another. Into 301, exactly where he needed to be to set up his shot. Initially that didn't raise any concern with the FBI. Now it does, thanks to some heavy lifting by the local Police Chief. McAlister had direct line of sight from there. He just blew it."

"If killing Jenny Lodge was blowing it," Bernsie interrupted. He showed his anger.

"Okay," Evans apologized, "Poor choice of words. Anyway, agents say Room 301 gave him the percentage shot. And the room became available to him right when he needed it. Right when someone else left the hotel earlier than he indicated at check-in."

"I assume you're saving the best for last, Jack."

"Quite right, Mr. President. The man who checked out? His name was…Dolan." Evans paused to allow the president to process the first part of his story.

"And…" Taylor said, encouraging further clarification.

"And according to a statement the police took from a witness in Stamford, Connecticut, the man who shot Hoag was also Dolan."

"Dolan," the president repeated.

"Dolan. With a description that matches the man who checked out of 301, allowing McAlister—who had requested it—to move in."

"How do you know this?" the president asked.

"I just know it."

"That's it?" Bernsie blurted.

"And Mulligan?" the president asked.

"I'm sure you'll hear from Robert this evening."

"This is ridiculous," the chief of staff protested. "We have spies spying on the FBI? Is that it?"

"We learned this through a telephone call. That's all you need to know, sir."

"Are we not playing together nicely in the sandlot, Jack?"

Evans took a few steps closer to his boss. He respected him a great deal and didn't want to see Morgan Taylor defeated, personally or professionally. "We're not playing, Mr. President. We're not playing at all."

Evans took a breath and then added, "And there's more. We received another report from Sandman."

The president stood up and walked to the bay window facing the Rose Garden. "Go on," he said to the DCI. Taylor definitely wanted to hear more about their deep cover in Abahar Kharrazi's OIS.

"Abahar is hell bent to find out about what his brother is up to. He knows where to look. So do we, now. Neither of us have detailed intel. Not yet. But it's big enough to make Abahar fear for his succession. It involves Bashar al-Assad and his father before him. And if that's the case, I'll bet it also means the Russians have their fingerprints on this. And I'd like to lay the groundwork for a mission to find out."

"Oh shit," Bernsie said under his breath.

The president continued to gaze outward into the darkness. Two pictures instantly came to mind. The photograph of Bobby Kennedy consoling his brother Jack; exhausted looks on their faces during the fearful days of the Cuban Missile Crisis. And Lyndon Johnson at the same window mulling the catastrophic effects the Vietnam War was having on his presidency. Now he was here contemplating the unknown himself. He was grateful no photographer was around to capture the moment.

Taylor walked back to the couch. "I want Roarke."

"With all due respect, Mr. President, that's not possible," Evans answered. John Bernstein cleared his throat trying to telegraph that this would not go down well, but he was too late.

"He has no history with Sandman," the intelligence chief continued.

"He has a history with me."

"Quite honestly, Mr. President, I'm not comfortable. He's not one of mine." Evans realized he might have misspoken. He put it a different way. "I would feel much better if we used one of the Agency's assets."

Anyone who worked closely with Morgan Taylor understood that he was a good listener. He rarely interrupted. It was his military training and his Jesuit upbringing. He was polite. But he was also President of the United States. A man who made his own decisions.

"Thank you, Jack. Of course, you're right."

Evans smiled.

"But, I want someone in there who can explain everything to me in terms that I will understand. I want to know exactly what my options are. Roarke will do fine. Just have the mechanism to spring them if there's trouble."

Evans sighed. He wouldn't win this round. "Then I'll need him by the weekend, Mr. President."

"Agreed."

John Bernstein was not happy. "If you'll allow me a moment. We should have something concrete before we send a man like Roarke in. He might know every last sand dune in Iraq, but this is new territory for him. He could compromise the whole…"

"He won't."

"But if he does, Mr. President?" the CIA Director asked solemnly over his shoulder. "If he gets caught?"

"Then you get them out," the president stated emphatically.

"Morgan, please," said Bernsie. "This is no walk in the park."

"He'll be ready. Trust me," the president responded calmly. Then he turned back to Jack Evans. "Jack, put Roarke with anyone you want. Anyone."

"I have a man in mind."

"Good. Now tell me, when Bob comes in, how surprised should I be by what he tells me?"

An hour later, Robert Mulligan got his appointment and went through what he knew. The major difference was in the details he'd gathered from Bessolo's conversations with the Hudson Police Chief. The president didn't disclose what he had learned from Evans or that the CIA had their hooks into Hoag. This was a classic example of "need to know."

When Mulligan finished, Taylor graciously thanked him and asked for a favor.

"Yes sir, what can I do?"

"Bob, I need you to open some doors for me at the Bureau."

"Anything, sir. I believe you own those doors. What is it?"

"Scott Roarke. He needs some Bureau help."

"Sure. What's it for? Part of his little Boston escapade?" he added. "The one the police would give anything to figure out?"

"He's got something else on his mind. He doesn't ask for much. Make it so, Bob."

"Done. Have him at my office at 8 A.M."

They wrapped up their meeting with a nightcap of scotch.

When Mulligan left, the president telephoned Roarke with news about his morning meeting. Then he said goodnight. The president held off telling him about a little trip he'd be making soon. Better he get a few good nights' sleep.

CHAPTER 28

WASHINGTON, D.C.
TUESDAY, AUGUST 5

"I need to work with that photo expert of yours up at the Academy," Roarke said.

"Which one?" FBI director Robert Mulligan replied between bites of his onion bagel.

"You know, the Identikit guy. The nerd," explained Roarke.

"Touch Parsons."

"Touch?"

"Touch, like 'touch up,' but it's really Duane Parsons," Mulligan explained.

"Okay. Can I see him today?"

Mulligan made the call. Within minutes Roarke was on the way to the FBI Academy at Quantico, Virginia.

The ride was slow going. The weather bureau forecast a 60 percent chance of rain. But along 1-95, 100 percent of it was coming down in sheets, slowing his way. Roarke had an idea and no time to waste. He'd once seen what the Identikit could construct in the hands of an expert. And by all accounts, Touch was the best.

Mulligan cleared Roarke ahead of time at the gate, but rules still required officers to thoroughly search the underbelly of Roarke's Jag with mirrors, pop the trunk and check under the hood. An officer in charge scanned his photo ID with a government bar code reader, counted the ten seconds it took for computer confirmation, and then asked Roarke to place his hand on a palm print scanner.

In the past decade all of the security regulations were buttoned up, and as a result, the FBI Academy was becoming as secure a facility as the CIA and NSA. It was all necessary.

After going through another checkpoint at the front desk, Roarke was given a plastic card to pin on his jacket. It contained a microchip programmed with specific clearances; where he could walk and where he couldn't. For Roarke it meant the elevator to Parsons' floor, the hallway and the men's room. Any place else and a readout at the security desk would scramble officers to Roarke's exact location.

Roarke was met by a young secretary, barely out of school, who failed to take any interest in Roarke.

"This way," was all she said as she escorted him to the elevator and down a hall to a waiting area.

He laughed to himself. He was probably too old for her. But it did make him think about Katie and that powerful attraction they felt for one another.

"Have a seat here. Mr. Parsons will be right with you."

"Thank you," Roarke said.

Five minutes later Duane Parsons burst through the door.

Roarke had imagined that he'd be about 55 years old, a sloppy dresser with a goofy laugh, tape holding his glasses together; a dweeb.

Instead, a tall, trim and fit man came out.

"Hello there. I'm Parsons." His handshake was as tight as the rest of his body. Roarke had to squeeze back just to get him to lighten up.

"Roarke, Scott Roarke. Mulligan called."

"Yes. Yes. I was expecting you. You realize it's not everyday Mulligan calls personally. To tell you the truth, it's the first time. You must have friends in high places, Mr. Roarke."

"Just one."

"Well, from the little I heard your project is fairly straightforward. You could have gone to any number of people."

Roarke looked him straight in the eyes. "That wasn't possible."

It was then that Parsons realized that this man was deadly serious. "All right, I'm honored. So whatcha got?"

"Inside."

Parsons appeared surprised.

"Inside," Roarke insisted, this time pointing to Parsons' office. He was inside the FBI's labs, but that didn't mean everyone could be trusted. He didn't know Parsons' secretary or anyone else on the floor. He closed the door behind them.

Parsons' office was typical government issue—a stark metal desk and matching filing cabinets, computers, a small round table for conferences, and a photograph of the president. The photograph made Roarke laugh. It was Morgan Taylor in a classic Brooks Brothers suit. Only he appeared to be around eight or nine years old.

"Oh, that?" Parsons offered. "Some of my work." With that, Roarke realized Touch was good, really good.

Instead of stopping in the office, Parsons hit a button on the top of his desk. A file cabinet moved aside, exposing a high tech computer photo lab. "This way."

"Very 'Bond' of you," Roarke joked.

"Well, not really. It just allows me a certain degree of isolation while I work. What I do takes time and concentration. Mulligan gave me everything I wanted."

"Including extra security," Roarke suggested.

"Yes, a bit extra, and lots of toys. As a result, I've been able to put new faces on some old crimes. I earn my keep.

"Now for your particular project."

Roarke removed an envelope from his pocket and silently passed it along to Touch.

"May I?" he said, blowing air into the envelope to create space. He removed the newspaper photograph, a cropped copy that Roarke had made on a Kinko's Kodak photo machine.

"A newspaper. Loose dot matrix. Not much gray-scale to work with and a bit out of focus. But I've started with worse. No caption?"

"None," Roarke lied. He intentionally cut off the caption and all other hints to its origin.

Parsons placed the picture on a scanner and before Roarke fully realized what had happened, the photograph appeared on a 19" flat computer screen.

"Now I can work with it."

With a few keystrokes Touch enhanced the sharpness, thereby improving the focus. He added more contrast, cropped out the superfluous portions and enlarged the subject.

"Well, what do we have here. A Boy Scout. Troop 134. See," he said as he zoomed in on the boy's shoulder patch. "I'd say your little fellow here is about 13, maybe 14. Tall for his age." He studied the face, moved the cursor around and immediately filled in some pinpricks that the microfilm negative had transferred to the positive image. "I have to be honest with you. This is going to be hard. But luckily, the features are all developed; enough for a first pass."

"First pass?"

"Well, I can age his face to whatever you want. But I really don't have enough visual data with just this photo to genealogically age him accurately."

"What do you mean? Isn't this what you do?"

"It is, Mr. Roarke. But how good do you want me to be? That's more in your hands than mine. Let me explain. Age progression has become an important part of crime solving. I imagine that's why you're here. Some sort of crime. Kidnapping?"

Roarke didn't give any ground.

"Kidnapping is why we often age children. To see if anyone recognizes them as adults. We also use the process to age adolescent criminals on the run. We've been able to capture them five or ten years out. Of course, that's mostly for capital offenses. What's your Eagle Scout? A killer or did he squeeze a Girl Scout's tits at camp?"

"Neither. Call it *research*. I need to age the boy into his late forties," Roarke said. "Can you or can't you do it for me?"

"I haven't finished with my explanation. Given that this is somehow important to you, you'll soon understand why I'll need more."

"Go on," Roarke said more politely. He sat down and watched Parsons at work.

"Look," Parsons said, clearing his screen. He went to a file and clicked on a picture of a young girl. He quickly cycled through various stages of her life through 75. "Amazing, isn't it. An individual's basic look holds relatively true through the years. The eyes hardly change. They're a signature to me, just as fingerprints are to other investigators. Certainly the subject will mature, but I can extrapolate some of the variables—the distance of the eyes to the nose, eyebrow growth. Shape of the nose through puberty. Things like that. It's the other changes that make it a real challenge. How much will the lips thin over the years? Or the hair recede? What happens to the jaw line?

All of it is indeterminable. Of course, I get a little help from computer models. The programs were developed and refined in Louisiana at FACES."

"'Faces?'"

"Short for Forensic Anthropology and Computer Enhanced Services Laboratory at Louisiana State University. We learned a lot from them in the early years of age progression portraiting technology. We still share a great deal of information with—"

Roarke cut him off. "Not this time. You. Just you."

"This is serious business."

"Very."

"Well, then, there is something that can make it far easier for me."

"And that is?"

"Family photos, Mr. Roarke. If I have photographs of brothers or sisters during different stages of their life, and parents younger and older…"

"Not possible."

"Come on. Parents?"

"I don't have any."

"Then find them," Parsons demanded. "Get me pictures of this boy's mother and father at ages 45 to 50. Better yet, get me a whole slew of pictures representing different years. Then the percentages dramatically increase for me to spot and track family characteristics. Oh, and health records of the parents. Get them, too. Invaluable information."

Parsons switched to another program comparing an aging montage of a boy with his father who, as Parsons explained, suffered from diabetes.

"This case—missing persons—required determining what a boy might look like at age 35. His father had diabetes and gained a good deal of weight. Knowing that, and the boy's genetic predisposition to diabetes, we added some pounds to him that we might not have otherwise considered." The montage ended on the boy at age 35. It dissolved into an actual photograph of a man who had gained weight and looked exactly like the computer model. "We found him, Roarke. We found him because we added the weight. We can find them because of their health, their personalities and what we can predict that they'll wear. All of it goes out to the FBI or police departments, or on TV. And it all helps.

"It's truly forensics, Roarke. We quantify growth data to predict the natural changes that a face will likely undergo through life. I can manipulate grids within the face to refine, or more specifically, redefine facial features. Knowledge of the distinguishing family facial characteristics is key to predicting the spatial arrangement over time."

Roarke was impressed by Parsons' knowledge. "How do faces change? What are the variables?"

"Faces grow downward, also outward. The bridge of the nose rises. The face broadens and lengthens. The eyes will narrow slightly, the mouth expands. Hair color will darken, then gray. There are transformations to the cheekbones. They tend to become more prominent. And there's facial-cranial growth. It's all, no pun intended, *relative*. Which is why I need family pictures.

"Do the parents wear glasses? Are they smokers? Do they battle with depression? Drugs? Alcohol? Everything is a factor."

"His parents have been dead for decades," Roarke said. "Pictures were destroyed."

"So what are you trying to do? Locate this kid now?"

"Oh, I know where he is," Roarke stated.

"Then why do you need to know what he looks like? Can't you just take a picture yourself?"

"There are ample pictures of him, Mr. Parsons. Let's leave it at that."

Roarke stood up and stared directly at the computer artist. "Come on, Parsons. I know your reputation. You get shit to work with and you end up with fucking Rembrandts. I'm sure you can…"

"You said one friend in a high place?" Roarke nodded. "Okay, let me see what I can do." He moved his computer mouse to the open file of the Boy Scout and zoomed in to the eyes. He worked quietly for five minutes, typing computer instructions, shading the picture in a Photoshop program and manipulating the image a little at a time.

Parsons sat back in his chair and considered his work. "Once more for me, Roarke. You know what he looks like, but you need me to create an accurate picture for you."

"Exactly."

"Then get me the other pictures. This is complex work. Without additional resources I'll be relying on my own presumptions. And I can easily miss the obvious. Give me what I need and I'll show you exactly how your Scout ages 33 goddamned years. I'll nail him within six months if you'd like. Now go get yourself some target practice and come back in a few days. And bring those medical records and parents' photographs I want!"

Roarke liked it when people got mad enough to prove their worth. He actually smiled. "Touch? It's Touch?"

"Yes," he answered.

"I like that. Nice and descriptive." Roarke offered his hand. "Most people usually call me 'Asshole.'"

Parsons laughed. "Well, Asshole, get moving." He took Roarke's hand and firmly shook it.

They both had a hell of a task ahead. Only Roarke knew why.

On his way out, Roarke's cell phone rang. The president's secretary asked him to hold. He stood in the large parking lot of Quantico, took a deep breath of the rain soaked air, and prepared for either a question or an order. He never expected answers from his boss. The answering part was all up to Roarke.

"Here you go, Scott," Louise said as she connected Roarke to President Taylor.

"Scott. Was Mulligan helpful?"

"Very."

"Then you got to see who you needed?"

"Yup," Roarke simply responded.

"Good."

"I've got to head back up to Boston and get my hands on a few other things."

"Put a hold on that. I have a little side trip for you first. Up for some more Navy frequent flier miles?"

"The food service sucks."

The president laughed. Roarke was absolutely right. He'd be flying in a cramped F/A-18, refueling midair courtesy of a KC-10 tanker, and eating a miserable boxed lunch. The only things worse than the food were the toilet options.

"Yes, but you can avoid all the lines at the airport. Why don't you come by, I'll brief you and send you on your merry way."

"And exactly where is that?"

"Can't say now. But get rolling. The plane is leaving at 0300."

"Any movie showing?"

The president considered the question, then said, "*Lawrence of Arabia.*"

CHAPTER 29

WEDNESDAY, AUGUST 6

Roarke liked the ground a whole helluva lot better. The two-seater F/A-18D delivered slamming, bone hammering g-forces as it climbed through the clouds to 40,000 feet. The president might consider the fighter cockpit his second home; Roarke thought a beach house in Malibu was right where he wanted to be. But there was no arguing with his boss on travel accommodations. Taylor ordered him to join Evans' operative in Libya and evaluate the possibility of a covert action. Ordinarily he would chomp at the bit to get back into the field. Not this time.

He tried to sort through his thoughts, but instead he fell asleep.

While Roarke was in the air over the Atlantic, the country woke up to another article on Teddy Lodge by Michael O'Connell. It combined straight reportage with the prose that was quickly becoming his signature. Though he never admitted it to anyone, O'Connell believed that every front-page story brought him closer to a book deal.

This year voters won't be choosing between the lesser of two evils, or the evil of two lessers. Either one of the two front-runners can effectively run the country.

Both candidates are distinguished by strong intellect and unwavering dedication. Both emerged as leaders at an early age.

One a warrior. The other a scholar.

A president who was prepared to die by the sword. A congressman who makes war with words.

The Navy flier who learned how to deliver death and destruction from above. The nuclear scientist who understands the physics of how efficiently it is delivered.

Ultimate power in the hands of a mortal man.

Either could press "the Button." In November, the voters will pull the levers. They alone will decide who deserves the awesome responsibility to lead the nation into the uncertain future on January 20th.

O'Connell's sources included military experts, political friends, and academic observers. They helped him construct a picture of the president's achievements as a Navy pilot in the Persian Gulf. He recounted recorded heroics and speculated on some rumored missions. He wrote of how, as a downed aviator, Commander Morgan Taylor survived alone in the desert and barely escaped alive. Unknowingly, he got part of that story wrong. Yet, for every sentence of praise for President Taylor there were two for Congressman Lodge. Most readers could not mistake the emphasis.

Off-and-on for almost thirty years, the U.S. Department of State warned American citizens against traveling to Libya. According to published advisories, the country is again "*hostile and unsettled.*"

Since the Kharrazi revolution, Americans generally had to wait months to be granted a special visa, granted through a Libyan Embassy in a third country.

Requests ordinarily were submitted with supporting documentation and only granted to people specified as being eligible in one of four categories: American Red Cross, for which the applicant must establish that he or she is a representative of the organization and traveling on an officially-sponsored mission; humanitarian considerations, which allow people into Libya who can provide compelling reasons for family unification or critical illnesses; national interest, which recognizes Americans if it is in Libya's national interest; and finally, professional reporters.

This category includes full-time members of a newspaper staff, magazine, or broadcasting network whose purpose is to gather information about Libya for dissemination to the public. Roarke and Evans' characters would go in as journalists, slightly outside the bounds of the overall criteria, but arguably close enough. They would be on assignment for a respected Oxford academic publishing house, Collingsworth Publishers, with a contract to photograph and chronicle Tripoli's famed mosques. The assignment came with a fast deadline and a black mark. Collingsworth, or at least one CIA plant inside, claimed to need an update of their North African architectural texts for the following fall.

The paperwork went in via the British Embassy in London and was walked through the Libyan side in days.

That was the plan devised by the U.S. Army Special Operations Command (USASOC), operating out of Fort Bragg in North Carolina and hence the "black" mark. According to a 1977 Executive Order signed by former CIA director, Admiral Stansfield Turner, agents were banned from posing as journalists for cover. The regulation was the result of a Senate study on clandestine activities, but it did allow some wiggle room. Within the order is a directive that permits exceptions to be made, if authorized by the director of the CIA or his deputy. In this case, Jack Evans made the exception himself.

USASOC is the nation's largest command component of SOCOM, U.S. Special Operations Command, which has a wide range of worldwide responsibilities under presidential authority, from covert counterterrorism activities to full-out 7 P.M. news in-your-face wars.

Although not called into service for this Special Reconnaissance Mission (SR), USASOC has a full assortment of boy toys at its command, including the famed UH-L Black Hawk, the MH-47D/E Chinook and its baby brother the MH-60K/L Pave Hawk, and the super secret "Little Bird" or A/M/TH-6 helicopter built by Boeing. Each of the heavily outfitted copters is flown by the 160th Special Ops Aviation Regiment. The formal abbreviation is SOAR, but the 160th prefer to be known as the "Nightstalkers."

Their ultimate boss is the President of the United States. The money comes from the Department of Defense, under Title 10 of the U.S. Code. Their operations do not require Joint Chiefs consent for money, training, operations, equipment, or upkeep. In short, they're Morgan Taylor's private army.

And the man who runs USASOC is General Jonas Jackson Johnson, or J3, to his friends. The Iraqis, in particular, had other names for him.

"J3," the president said on the secure line, "Roarke is yours."

"Got the word," the general answered over the phone. "Vinnie

D'Angelo is already on the ground at Heathrow. They'll hook up at 0400 Zulu. We're ready."

"Good."

"And your man knows what he needs to know?" the general asked the Commander in Chief.

"Nothing more," Taylor answered.

Their SR was divided into three parts. Insertion, initial recon, and extraction. The insertion was going to be completely out in the open on a commercial airline. So was the recon. When the mission was finished, they'd get out quickly. Their cover stories weren't elaborate. Roarke was going into the country to write about some of Tripoli's classic architecture, D'Angelo was his photographer. Before they would withdraw, Lt. D'Angelo, a skilled Special Forces officer and an expert amateur photographer, would make one side trip into downtown Tripoli.

Roarke's military jet landed on time and quickly veered off Heathrow's main runway, far from observers, and taxied to a privately leased general aviation hangar. It rolled in, the doors closed behind, and Roarke disembarked without incident. A ground crew immediately refueled the jet; a new pilot climbed in the cockpit and after a pre-flight check, the F/A-18D was out on the runway and in the air. Total ground time clocked at fourteen minutes. A polite young man, an American, led Roarke to a shower.

"I'm sure you're ready to clean up, sir."

"Am I ever!" Roarke stripped, hung his clothes in a locker, and drowned himself in a hot, refreshing shower. While lathering up, Roarke heard a familiar voice boom across the shower tiles.

"Well, you old son of a bitch, looks like you're lettin' your gut slip!" Vinnie D'Angelo called out to the stark naked Roarke.

"And you're hanging around in men's showers too much," Roarke easily joked back.

"I like to check out my competition for the ladies. Looks like I'm way ahead of you," D'Angelo added.

Roarke flicked the soap at him and D'Angelo tossed the towel back. "Dry off and meet me in fifteen. There's a change of clothes on the bench in front of your locker. I'll have a cup of joe for you in the hangar. We'll go through everything. And then we're on our way again. Oh, and for goodness sake," D'Angelo said eyeing the naked Roarke, "Don't play with yourself. You may need your energy."

The Secret Service agent liked D'Angelo. The two grew up together in SOCOM, took some hard knocks in Afghanistan and came out alive. Roarke felt better just knowing that D'Angelo would be in the field with him.

There wasn't a lot Roarke could actually recite about Vinnie. He was one of the best at what he did. And no one claims to know all of what he did. The 39-year-old, prematurely gray hulk, was undoubtedly one of Jack Evans' men. However, even Roarke couldn't say for sure. And no one else was talking. Roarke just marveled at his abilities and figured that his chances of getting out of any jam alive were far better with Vinnie D'Angelo around.

Roarke appeared in fifteen minutes, refreshed and ready. His F-18 was already back over the Atlantic. In its place in the hangar, a stretch limousine with blackened windows.

"Come on, we'll talk," D'Angelo began. Once inside, they got caught up on their personal lives. That took ten seconds each. Then it was down to business.

"It's a basic op," D'Angelo said. "You're a writer named Adam Giannini. There's so many ways to spell your name, it'll drive any bureaucrat crazy and no two files on you will be the same, especially if you keep giving it to them differently. I'm your photographer Tomás Morales."

"So far so good," Roarke said. "Geez you're ugly," he added.

"And the shower doesn't take your stink away."

They traded more small talk and then D'Angelo focused on the briefing.

"We're on the morning BA flight direct to Tripoli. About a four hour trip." He handed Roarke the tickets and validated paperwork for the writer named Giannini.

"They'll ask if you're from Italy originally. Libya was an Italian colony. You tell them your grandparents left in the '20s. If they ask you something in Italian, don't worry."

"Not a problem. I wouldn't understand it anyway."

"By the way. You had a good time in London over the last couple of days. Some fine dinners, a meeting with me at Collingsworth, and you took in a delightful performance of 'The Mousetrap,' like a good American tourist."

"Did I have row 12 seats, center section?"

"No, as a matter of fact. But I'll give you five points for the question. Pretty sophisticated coming from a social ingrate like you," D'Angelo joked. "You were in P15, off to the side. But you didn't complain. I have a copy of the play for you to read on the plane."

Of course, all of this was done with a look-alike who established Roarke's presence in England. D'Angelo pointed out his double in the hangar who looked a good deal like him.

"Tell me something, Vinnie. For such a basic operation, why me? Why such a complex insertion plan? What's this all about?"

"You'll have to ask the big guy when you get back. He obviously wants you along to give him a personal report. Meanwhile, all you need to know is history and read up on the play. So here." D'Angelo tossed him three books and tapped the window for the driver to turn on the motor.

"Wait. I'm not armed."

"And you're not gonna be. Red flag. Oh, and expect surveillance everywhere. Hotel. Telephones. Restaurants. Nothing, absolutely nothing gets mentioned, written down or passed between us. It may look like an open city, but believe me, it's not. It's as bad as the worst days under Qadhafi. And for goodness sake, don't get sick. They don't take American insurance and I know you don't want to pay $50,000 for a battery of tests. So nothing but bottled water."

"I'll be good."

The limo drove them to the British Airways terminal where they boarded, BA898. Commercial air service between America and Libya was prohibited by U.S. sanctions.

Roarke counted the Libyan dinars he'd been given. The published exchange rate was around .47 to the U.S. dollar, but in reality people valued the green-backs much more than their own currency. That's probably why Libyan law required all visitors to travel with a minimum of 500 U.S. dollars which had to be converted to dinars before they could pass customs. This wouldn't be a problem for Roarke. Like his companion, he traveled with 5,000 dinars. "Better to have the cash," D'Angelo told him. "Most places won't take Adam Giannini's MasterCard."

D'Angelo also carried twenty-five chips for his digital still camera, another ten rolls of Kodak film for his traditional 35-mm camera, and the paperwork that confirmed he was Tomás Morales.

SUN VALLEY, IDAHO
THURSDAY, AUGUST 7

"We're gonna need a photograph of this footprint," the first year FBI field agent called into his walkie-talkie. His Denver supervisor, Jake Messenger, ordered him to walk upstream from where Alfred Nunes died and check around.

After barely twenty minutes trudging through the shallow water and thoroughly ruining a new pair of FBI issue shoes, he found a single footprint in the dried mud about a quarter mile away. But rain threatened the integrity of the imprint. Thunder rattled off in the distance and he knew he didn't have much time to work.

Whoever made it had been walking in the water, came out and took one step into the mud, then disappeared through the brush.

The field agent had no real reason to suspect any foul play. After all, it was fairly apparent the dead guy had a heart attack and the footprint was totally unrelated. But he'd spent years trying to get out of his State Trooper uniform and into the plain clothes of the FBI, so he wasn't about to piss off his boss on his first real investigation.

"Get that photog here fast," he added for good measure. "And bring some umbrellas!"

The rain started falling. The photographer, a very serious-minded woman from the Denver office, had to work fast. She set up her 35-mm Nikon on a tripod above and slightly behind the footprint. Next, and with great care, she put a 6" plastic ruler with a color chip chart to the side of the impression. The photographer adjusted the f/stop, enabled the flash, connected the remote shutter cord so she wouldn't shake the camera when taking her pictures, and zoomed in so the footprint and ruler would fill the frame.

She snapped three rolls of film with varying shutter speeds. By the time she packed up, the rain began wearing away the impression. Small streams flowed from the higher banks to the nearby river. Five minutes later the evidence was gone.

TRIPOLI, LIBYA

Vinnie D'Angelo shot some innocuous pictures on the airplane. He figured that when guards questioned him at customs he should have photos on his digital camera to show for his time. He also encouraged Roarke to make notes so that he could speak authoritatively about their destinations. In addition he had quietly reminded Roarke about some important basics. "Just like binoculars, the lens can see things closer than we can. The camera remembers more about a scene than we will. People expect a photographer to take pictures and a writer to make notes. We can do things in clear view if we just look normal."

Roarke had used his time to best advantage. He filled twelve pages with notes and completely read the play that his double had seen on his behalf. It was a good thing. They were completely scrutinized clearing Libyan customs. They were separated from the other passengers, then from each other and suspiciously questioned for nearly ninety minutes.

D'Angelo was the first to get released. He waited for Roarke, greeting him without their normal joking.

"I'm famished. Let's hop a cab to the hotel and then get a bite."

Their first indication that they were being watched by Abahar Kharrazi's OIS came at the British Air terminal curb. They hailed a cab. Two old black and white taxis skipped them. A third rolled up, sputtered and stalled. When it started again the muffler let out a loud bang which caught the attention of airport security forces with their automatic rifles.

"Not to worry," the cab driver said in halted English. "I get you there okay."

Considering he spoke English and two cabs were somehow told to pass them by, Roarke figured they were already under observation.

"I'm glad you speak English. We're going to the Bab Al Bahr Hotel," D'Angelo said.

"Fine, fine. I get you there." The cabbie popped the trunk and tossed in the bags rather unceremoniously. Roarke didn't get into the cab until he was certain the trunk was closed and locked.

As they made their way to the city their driver provided a running commentary that was difficult to understand. But it took pressure off of the two men to talk. After awhile he got to the real agenda on his mind.

"This is your first visit, no?" *A question a cab driver would ask. But so would a spy.*

"Yes," D'Angelo said taking the lead. "We're here for work. Journalists with an academic publisher in Great Britain." D'Angelo knew that this would get reported back as soon as they exited the cab.

"Ah, good, good," the driver said. "The Great Socialist People's Libyan Arab Jamahiriya welcomes members of the press who will report the truth."

"And we're pleased to be here."

Once they arrived at the Bab Al Bahr, paid their driver, and got their bags, D'Angelo asked Roarke to pose for a few pictures at the entrance. "The tourist thing," he explained.

Roarke stood at the entrance. At only 15-stories high, the white cement structure still towered over the Mediterranean coast. The principal driveway was lined with well-manicured trees and flowers. The fresh sea air wafted over him. Roarke took in a breath and looked around. While he was checking into what otherwise might qualify as a seaside resort, authorities could arrest him at any moment.

"Smile," D'Angelo said.

"Right."

The two Americans strode to the front desk and announced themselves as Giannini and Morales. They produced their passports, visas and credit cards, but they'd pay in cash.

"Good afternoon," the desk clerk said in fair English.

"Hello."

"Let's see, Mr. Giagani?"

"Giannini." Roarke spelled it out.

After a minute the clerk found it. "Ah yes. Here you are. Italian?"

"Italian descent. My grandparents."

"Italy controlled us for many years."

"Yes I know."

"Like their Roman fathers before them," the clerk added. "May I ask the nature of your business?"

Of course he could, Roarke said to himself. *I've got my story down.* "Yes, we're working on a new university text about your mosques."

"They are quite beautiful, especially in the late afternoon light," the young male clerk said while typing.

Roarke believed, quite rightly, that this exchange would also be reported to the police within minutes, accompanied with photocopies of their identification papers.

"I recommend the Small Room over the Single. It has more space."

Roarke didn't follow the logic, but agreed. He was told the price, approximately the equivalent of $94 in U.S. currency per night.

"If you prefer we also have the Presidential Suite and many other choices. We are not fully occupied."

The American reasoned that had been the case for years.

"No, the Small Room sounds perfect." Roarke signed the register and thanked the clerk.

"And now Mister?" the clerk asked.

"Morales. Tomás Morales. Miami, Florida."

"Well, Mr. Morales, I hope you enjoy your stay. You would like the same accommodations?"

"That would be fine. Thank you."

"Certainly. On the 6th floor. Four doors from your friend. You know, we don't see very many Americans. Oh some from your universities. But not many individual travelers, unless, of course, they're correspondents or government agents. You wouldn't be working for your government, would you?"

Morales looked at Giannini. They both offered an unrehearsed half laugh.

"Not with our record of paying taxes," the man named Giannini answered.

"Well then, you'll have a wonderful time. I see you're both staying for four nights. We are here to serve you. 24-hour room service is available and we have three notable restaurants. The Zahra which specializes in Asia cuisine, Shahrazad with a variety of offerings. But for late night or the early morning, you must try the Sea Wave Cafeteria. You will like it a great deal. Pizzas and cakes."

"Very nice," Roarke said politely.

"Of course, no alcoholic beverages are permitted according to Islamic law."

"We understand. Now our rooms?" D'Angelo said drawing the conversation to a close.

"Ah, yes." The clerk rang for a bellhop and then disappeared into a back room to call in the arrival of the pair.

They were led to their modest rooms, complete with bathrooms, television, radios and a telephone that could be used for either local or international calls. The Sheraton-esque structure would be home to the tourists. And, no doubt, everything they said or did would be recorded.

Roarke knew one thing for sure. The air conditioning worked and it was going to be more comfortable than camping in the desert as he had many nights in Iraq.

That evening they ate an acceptable Asian meal at the Zahra, though underspiced even for the Szechuan dishes, then called it a night. Roarke turned on his television set and took the opportunity and the cover of unpacking to calmly search for listening devices and hidden cameras. The telephone was certainly bugged. He didn't need to check there. One overhead light didn't work. When he called to the front desk for maintenance help and was told they couldn't get to it for days, he was convinced the bulb contained a lipstick camera, most likely with a fisheye lens. A radio next to the bed was another likely place for a monitor. And there was a suspicious looking vent in the bathroom. While Roarke washed his face he looked up and could clearly see sloppily laid red wires behind the grate.

He conducted his entire survey casually and without focusing on anything too long. Roarke expected D'Angelo had come to the same conclusions in his room.

After seven hours of sleep, a morning shower, and a breakfast of eggs, toast and juice at the Sea Wave Cafeteria, they began their walking tour. Roarke wore a navy blue T-shirt, a tan linen sports coat and khaki pants. His clothes were all wrinkle-free wear right out of the TravelSmith catalog, sharp contrast to the requisite camouflage uniform he had worn on his last mission in an Arab country.

Vinnie D'Angelo was also dressed casually, wearing a denim shirt and olive green pants with a camera bag slung over his shoulder.

D'Angelo got right into taking pictures like he really did it for a living. The Tripoli streets were inviting; completely different than the aerial recon photos.

Tripoli, or in Arabic *Tarabulus Al-Gharb* (The Western Tripoli), is one of two capitals of Libya. Benghazi shares the distinction as the other. However, Tripoli actually houses the administrative offices of Libyan government, the meeting-place of the People's Congress, and the full-time residence of General Kharrazi. It is the country's largest city, home to about 1.5 million people.

Tripoli has an old and new quarter. The new city includes the official buildings, Al-Fateh University, and the former royal palace. The old city—the medina—contains the historical structures that Roarke and D'Angelo would visit.

Roarke was quite taken by the charm of Tripoli and its principal sites: Green Square, the center of the medina; Al-Saraya Al-Harnra, the great Pre-Roman castle considered Tripoli's main attraction; and the Red Castle, for years the residence of Libya's ruling families.

The pair roamed through the labyrinth of courtyards and alleyways, soon realizing there was far too much to race through in the 140,000 square feet that comprised the Castle. They'd return later in their stay, if time permitted.

From the northern promontory they took in the real beauty of the city—seven distinguished mosques, each with distinctive architectural form. No wonder Tripoli also went by another name, *Arous Albahr Almotawasit*—The Jewel of the Mediterranean. It was a magnificent sight.

D'Angelo clicked away, effectively fulfilling the role of the Collingsworth Publishers photographer, but enjoying himself as well. Roarke noted the detail of what they saw, taking extra time to write about the 300-year-old Karamanli Mosque, the most splendid in all Tripoli.

They stopped working only when hunger overtook them. Lunch in the souk consisted of a delicious couscous bil-Khordra, dajaj maghli, and tajeen hoot.

Roarke and D'Angelo sat and relaxed as tourists would, watching how the warm room tones changed as the sunlight moved across the interior. The hotel desk clerk had been right. The mosques were glorious. And anyone reporting on their conversation would say the Americans were acting as expected, two professional freelancers on assignment for Collingsworth Publishers.

For a moment, Roarke let his mind wander to Katie. He wished he was sharing the beauty of Tripoli with her during the day and exploring the mystery of her body at night. The vision of her stimulated his memories and aroused his appetite. Roarke hadn't spoken to her since he left Boston. She had no idea where in the world he was. And she wouldn't. With that realization he went back to being Adam Giannini in a world far away from hers.

That night they stopped for dinner at a small café in the medina, then retired early and exhausted. Roarke drew a long, hot bath. D'Angelo watched a soccer match on TV before falling asleep.

They started their second day by backtracking to the medina to tour the famed Arch of Marcus Aurelius, reportedly the oldest landmark in all of Tripoli, then on to the Great Mosque.

Their third morning was spent retracing their steps, getting more detailed photographs and making additional notes. First the Red Castle, then the Karamanli Mosque. After eating, they returned to En-Naqah and the Gurgi, a magnificent Ottoman structure.

The second visit to each location was as eye-opening as the first, with D'Angelo providing illustrative running commentary on Arabic history and architecture. Roarke had done his share of reading since leaving London. But he was thoroughly impressed with what D'Angelo knew. He could have taught a course on everything they had seen.

For a time both men forgot they were really there on a Special Reconnaissance Mission. D'Angelo, in particular, couldn't allow himself to get caught up in the moment too long. They were in enemy territory. And only he knew why.

CHAPTER 30

ABOARD AIR FORCE ONE
SUNDAY, AUGUST 10

The president's chief of staff and closest friend was normally a worrier. Now Bernsie was positively beside himself. He headed over to Morgan Taylor, who sat in the plush black leather seat aft on level two of Air Force One. They were making the 92-minute flight back to Andrews Air Force Base, the end of a long one-day campaign swing through Florida that took them to Miami, Fort Lauderdale, West Palm, Tampa, and Tallahassee. All quick stops; all necessary to court the senior votes.

And they were finding Florida to be like every other key state: infatuated with Teddy.

"What the hell's happening, Bernsie?" the president asked as he absorbed the latest polls. "This should've been a horse race with Lamden. This guy doesn't have it, for Christ's sake."

"Like I said before, that's the part we have to hit. But wait 'til September. He's still getting his bounce from June."

"And he'll get another so-called bounce at the convention next week with his acceptance speech," Morgan Taylor replied.

"…that nobody watches." Bernstein said.

"…that gives him a bigger lead." the president concluded.

John Bernstein poured himself a glass of water, gulped it down, then answered the president. "And you get to come back with your own killer speech two weeks later."

"…that nobody watches." Taylor said using his chief's own words.

Bernsie couldn't argue away the truth. Unless Taylor's team pulled a political miracle out of a hat, Morgan Taylor was going to have time soon to talk with architects about his presidential library.

BOSTON, MASSACHUSETTS
THE SAME TIME

It was really too late to be working. But for the first time in her legal career, Katie Kessler felt completely overwhelmed and behind. The firm piled a ton of research on her for a pending case. At least eighty hours of billable time in less than a week. On the other end of that impossible task was a summation she had to compose for a senior partner who needed to stand up to one of the toughest judges in Boston. A typical week for a law associate. Nothing could pull her away, with one exception. A phone call from Scott.

Where the hell is he? she wondered. *He'll call*, she said, comforting herself. What made her worry was her last thought before she returned to work:...*if he can.*

TRIPOLI, LIBYA

Fadi Kharrazi's office sat at the top of his new eight-story downtown media center. The modern construction paid no homage to the past and ignored any pretense of contemporary style. In point of fact, it was a modestly built thick hulk, barely noticeable in the skyline of a city that had real architectural identity.

On the street D'Angelo felt as if there were other eyes on him. There probably were. But he was doing such a good job as an academic photographer on an assignment that he was fairly confident his alibi was holding.

D'Angelo had left the hotel early in the morning of their fourth day while Roarke slept in. He planned on rejoining his partner at lunchtime, then visiting the less traveled mosques they hadn't seen yet.

Tomorrow they'd leave. Worst case, should his cameras be confiscated when they cleared customs, he would sketch the important details of Fadi's office building exterior he committed to memory. His work, paired with shots from the high altitude spy planes and satellites, would give SOCOM what it needed.

Sandman's report stated that Fadi's private offices were on the southwest corner of the top floor; in business parlance, the power suite with a partial view of the Mediterranean.

In the morning it was in the shadows. From midday on it would be directly lit by the sun, but D'Angelo couldn't wait for better time of day. Anyway, general "coverage" would suffice.

D'Angelo shot pictures of the nearby intersections. He'd need those later. He photographed the direction the traffic flowed, also for good reason.

Whenever he could he zoomed in on the eighth floor. He counted twenty-four windows across one direction, eighteen in the other. The exterior columns told him where the retaining walls were and where rooms were likely to be linked by internal doors. By his estimation, Fadi's main suite covered six windows by eight, for an area of approximately 1,600 square feet. Breaching it would be less of a problem than knowing exactly where to go once inside. That was going to be Sandman's job.

He didn't photograph everything. What he did included other things in his field of view. A corner ground floor shot included people shopping. Tilting up and widening out he focused on the skyline behind. For a front shot of the building he made it look like he was photographing a family walking by. It was all relatively innocuous, or so he hoped.

However, just when D'Angelo was satisfied he had enough, a nagging feeling tugged at him. Intuitively he knew someone's eyes were bearing down. There were no outward signs, but he trusted his instinct. D'Angelo automatically aimed at shopkeepers and pedestrians, picking off typical tourist shots. But as he focused his camera lens in different directions he used the viewfinder to confirm his suspicions.

Across the street a man in a crumpled suit leaned against a building. He smoked a cigarette and broke eye contact as soon as he saw the tourist's camera aim in his direction. *That was one.*

D'Angelo panned around in the opposite direction. *There.* Another trying poorly to blend in. He did the same thing. *Two.*

The third was likely to be down the block, triangulating on him. And if experience taught him anything, a fourth coordinated the surveillance over a walkie-talkie.

Vinnie D'Angelo's heartbeat quickened. He was more pissed than surprised. Shooting mosques posed no concern. An American taking photographs in front of a building owned by Fadi, a son of the

Leader of Libya and perhaps an heir to his father's rule, was another thing entirely.

Options? D'Angelo's mind raced.

"Mr. Morales?" The voice came from behind him in perfect English.

Damn! Number four! The interruption answered all of his questions. Now the best defense was to be startled and unprofessional.

"What? Who?" He turned to the man who now had a firm hand on D'Angelo's shoulder.

"Mr. Morales, you'll have to come with me," the voice continued in a deep register. OIS. He appeared to be north of fifty; a hardened military type. *Definitely OIS.* He wore plain clothes, which meant nothing. D'Angelo pegged him as the supervisor of the younger men who had been tailing him.

"Excuse me. What do you mean, 'Come with you?' Who are you? I'm just…"

"I'm Major Yassar Hevit. You might think of me as a," he paused, "policeman."

Yeah right, D'Angelo thought. His English was extremely good; his description of his duties all wrong. The man was Secret Police, no doubt about it. *A senior officer who reported directly to Abahar Kharrazi.*

"What have I done?" D'Angelo protested predictably.

"Oh that's what we'll talk about." He glanced at the cameras. "Nikon and a Sony digital. Very nice. I'll take those." He snapped his fingers. Man #2 appeared. He brusquely removed the two cameras from D'Angelo, breaking one strap, and handed them over to the Major.

"Be careful with them. They're worth a lot."

"Of course. We don't want to ruin your fine work."

"Do you have any identification? I've heard of kidnappings."

"Oh, come now, Mr. Morales. Despite what your media reports, we are a friendly country. Nonetheless, if it makes you happy, here is my identification." Hevit flashed it. It was in Arabic. It looked official. And it told D'Angelo little.

As Hevit closed his wallet and returned it to the pocket of his frumpy jacket, he continued, "And tell me, Mr. Morales. If I hadn't shown you my identification, what would you have done?"

The man was obviously taunting him; already showing suspicion and looking for a reason to test his captive.

"I, I don't know," D'Angelo said. "But the books say be careful."

"Books?"

"Tourist books. And the Internet advisories."

"You're either a very, very experienced liar, which if true is something I *will* find out…" He paused for further emphasis. "…or you are an extremely naïve American. Personally I'm hoping you're the liar. It'll make my day so much more interesting."

The major's entire body grew stronger as he gloated. He grabbed D'Angelo's arm and nudged him forward. D'Angelo offered no resistance, though he could have killed him with one blow. Now Man #1 joined on the right side, and #3 fell in beside him on the left. Tomás Morales, the American photographer, was now in custody. With one more shove from Hevit they began walking toward some god-awful interrogation room.

THE WHITE HOUSE

"D'Angelo's been picked up, Mr. President." Jack Evans always cut to the chase. Especially on the telephone.

"Situation?"

"He was taking pictures near the target when he was apprehended. One of our company assets saw him. No commotion. He stayed cool. With luck they'll release him after listening to his story and looking at the digi pictures."

"And without luck?" Morgan Taylor asked.

"We'll have a major *embarrassment* on our hands."

"Possibly worse. What about Roarke?"

"As far as we can tell, he's all right. We'll know shortly. We think he's still at the hotel and D'Angelo was on his own. If he has any inkling, he'll seek out his contact and get our instructions."

"Do we know where they took him?"

"Not yet, but as soon as I hear anything I'll tell you."

The president hung up without a thank you. He looked out the windows onto the South Portico where the birds flew freely. His thoughts went to his trusted men in Libya and not to the overnight poll reported on CNN. It was turning out to be another shitty day.

CAPITOL HILL

Teddy Lodge was happy. Very happy. "I like this speech. It's the best thing I've seen since Jenny's writing," Lodge told Newman. "Where'd you find this guy?"

"This girl," the campaign manager said snidely.

"Oh?" Lodge smiled.

"A poli-sci grad from GW. Mid-20s. Has a nice way of phrasing things. I thought you'd like her work."

"Doesn't completely have my voice yet, but it's fresh. Forward thinking."

"She's missing some of our message, of course," said Newman. "But she picked up on your basics. I like where she's going with that biblical reference, '*As we forgive those who trespass against us.*' It's right on target."

Lodge took the speech and began to pace through the office, mouthing the words and gesturing for impact. He smiled as he began making the text his own. Ten minutes later he ended up right in front of Newman. "Will this be in shape by the convention?"

"With time to spare."

The congressman returned to the speech and began projecting now. Newman was very pleased it was working out; better than he had first imagined when he heard about the girl from her "sponsor."

BILLINGS, MONTANA

Governor Lamden hit mute on his remote control.

The screen, already crowded with chyron information, news headlines, and bullet points, told the story perfectly. Lodge was ahead. In a few days Lamden would deliver a keynote address at the Democratic

National Convention and later Lodge would officially bring the Montana governor onto the ticket as his running mate. He tried to feel happy about it but couldn't.

Deep down inside Lamden didn't trust Teddy Lodge. From that same place in the pit of his stomach he believed that Morgan Taylor was the better man. Part of his affinity for Taylor was their link to the Navy. Lamden served as a lieutenant aboard the USS *Enterprise* during the last year of the Vietnam War. Taylor, a few years younger, did most of his service in and over the Persian Gulf. The Navy bond united them more powerfully than their different political parties separated them.

Now, Washington was coming his way more easily. But not the way he intended. He did what he'd been meaning to do for a long time. He telephoned his old friend.

"Well, you old sea lion. Calling to lob a torpedo into a sinking ship?" the president said after Louise Swingle announced the call.

"Not me. I'm smart enough to know that Morgan Taylor doesn't go into battle unless he's got enough ammunition to shoot his way out."

"Okay, now that we've established that I'm not flaming out, how the hell are you Henry? And how's Samantha putting up with all of your shit?"

"Feeling okay. She's excited; already packing up the mansion for DC. I told her to wait a bit. We haven't even hit the convention yet."

"I don't think this town's ready for her, Henry. I might have to call up the guard and post them at all of the stores."

"Tell me about it."

Governor Lamden quieted for a moment to collect his thoughts. The president sensed the mood change.

"Morgan, I wanted you to hear this directly from me."

"Yes, Henry," the president said patiently.

"I really was up to take you on. It would have been a grand old fight. And in the end you probably would have won again and I would have made my grandchildren proud."

"You would have done better than that, Henry."

"Thank you. But now there's a real chance you're gonna lose this thing."

The president cleared his throat, getting serious. "Your point, Henry."

"I can't really say what my point is. Except that we've been friends for too goddamned long. And I have to be honest with you. There's something that bugs me about Lodge's guy Newman. The man's dangerous."

CAPITOL HILL
THE SAME TIME

Michael O'Connell's next article was going to be about the elusive Geoff Newman, the man who maneuvered in the shadows cast by Teddy Lodge.

O'Connell made his final notes outside of Lodge's Capitol Hill office. Initially Newman refused to see him. But O'Connell sent a hand written note to the congressman that got the desired results.

"Hello, I'm Frannie. Welcome, Mr. O'Connell," Lodge's trusted assistant said as she entered the waiting room.

"Thank you, Frannie." He made a mental note of her name.

"Mr. Newman will see you now, Mr. O'Connell. Right this way."

"Great."

As they walked, Frannie whispered, "You know, he hates doing these kind of things."

"Oh?" the reporter answered.

Realizing she had already said too much to a reporter, she tried correcting herself. "Mr. Newman believes that it's not his job to get attention. But recently it's been so difficult for the congressman. He hasn't wanted to be out much in public."

"Of course."

By now they had arrived at Newman's office. Frannie led him in. O'Connell didn't wait for an introduction or for Newman to stand or notice him. "Mr. Newman, I appreciate the time. Michael O'Connell." He held out his hand.

Newman stood, nodded and took his hand as if it were an inconvenience.

"Sit down." Almost painfully, he added, "Please."

"You're not comfortable being interviewed," O'Connell stated as he took out a digital recorder, a pen, and a reporter's notepad.

"I prefer working behind the scenes, Mr. O'Connell. But I do appreciate all that you're doing for us on the campaign."

"I'm not doing anything for you, sir."

Newman realized his faux pas. "I meant to say you've taken such care to present an accurate picture during a difficult time."

O'Connell tipped his pen as an acknowledgement and went to his questions. The recorder quietly memorialized the interview.

"You met Teddy Lodge at Harvard Essex. What did you see in each other?"

"Very good question, Mr. O'Connell. You know how they say opposites attract. That's what we were. I wasn't an athlete or an outgoing kid. I kept to my books and pretty much had no friends. I probably wouldn't have even known Teddy except for the fact that I wrote him after his accident. Eventually I went to see him. We became friends. It's as simple as that."

"How often did you travel to Vermont to visit?"

"Weekends, generally."

"Every weekend?"

"Not every weekend."

O'Connell pressed. "Most weekends?"

"Many weekends. I think we can leave it at that."

"And no one else came along?"

"He didn't even want to see me, at first. He didn't want any friends to come by. The state he was in. Pretty badly hurt. His parents were gone. I'm not telling you anything you don't already know."

"But why you?" O'Connell pressed. "No offense, Mr. Newman, but why did he bond with you?"

"I was there," Newman answered sternly. He had obviously taken offense.

"Only you?"

"Yes."

O'Connell was aware the answers were getting shorter and the atmosphere was becoming more charged. He smiled to lighten the mood and hopefully encourage more.

"Is that why Mr. Lodge cut off contact with everyone else from those days?"

Newman seemed to force himself to look directly at O'Connell. "I'm not aware he had."

"And you became close. You must have been a big help to him during that period."

"I tried. Again, I wasn't the sort of person who made friends easily. Maybe I felt good because I was needed. But that's far too psychological for me. It just worked out."

"What worked out?"

"Our friendship."

"Teddy never went back to Harvard Essex?"

"I'm not certain. He had a long recovery," Newman said staring directly at O'Connell. "He finished high school with tutors."

"He abandoned all his old friends."

"As I explained. He'd gone through a lot. Maybe everyone reminded him of the past."

"Let's talk about Yale," the writer said.

"Okay."

"You went there together."

"We attended Yale at the same time. We had other friends and Teddy started expanding his realm again."

"But you always remained in it."

"We had developed a strong relationship and by then we had common interests."

"Can you amplify those, Mr. Newman?"

"Politics. Science. History."

"The Middle East?"

"Yes, thank you. We both studied Middle East politics."

O'Connell became acutely aware that, in person, Newman looked older than the congressman. There were more lines around his eyes. His forehead was full of creases. The veins in his hands flared.

He scribbled down a single word on his note pad and circled it. *Age?*

"All of those disciplines are the basis of our work in Congress, Mr. O'Connell. It's the basis of what makes the congressman such a vital candidate for president."

"It's as if you've been preparing for this for a long time," the reporter observed.

"Your words, Mr. O'Connell."

The president and Henry Lamden were well into their phone call.

"Talk to your party leadership," Taylor proposed.

"Christ, Henry. Tell them to get rid of Newman. He's supposed to work for the Democratic Party. You don't like him, dump the bastard."

"It's not that easy. He's Lodge's fucking right brain function," Governor Lamden complained.

"Look, I'm not the one to play shrink here. This is only going to come back and bite me on the butt. Remember, I'm running against you."

"Morgan, for Christ's sake. Listen to me. Newman is bad news. And if we get in, Teddy Lodge is going to give him a nice big job. Like Secretary of State. Or Defense. Or Chief of Staff."

The president audibly exhaled. "Like I said. Take it to Wendell Neill."

"On my opinion? Now what do you think he'd say? 'Let's not upset Teddy. He's on a roll.' I'd be slitting my own throat."

"Then I have no idea, Henry."

"I need something I can use," the governor pleaded over the phone.

"We're not having this discussion, governor. I will not use this office to further your political aims."

"And risk a sociopath having the ear of your successor?"

"He's your problem. Not mine."

"No, Morgan. He's our problem."

CAPITOL HILL

"Let's discuss *your* childhood for a few minutes," O'Connell proposed. "Very little has been published and—"

Newman didn't wait for *The New York Times* reporter to finish. "That's because it's no one's business."

"Perhaps not now. But if Congressman Lodge wins in November and appoints you to a senior level position in the administration, as is rumored, then it is, in fact, everyone's business. So if you please, Mr. Newman."

Newman looked rattled. He didn't like pointed questions. He was skilled at helping Lodge, but not shaping responses or measuring words for himself. For that matter, he wished he hadn't agreed to the interview. Once Lodge won he would only speak to the press through official flacks.

"I truly am not good at this, as I expect you've noticed, Mr. O'Connell. But I'll try."

The reporter pointed his pen at him again. "Thank you."

"I grew up in Europe. Primarily military bases. My father was in the Army and we shuttled between his assignments in Germany, England, and some in Saudi Arabia."

"Yes. And your parents? Brothers or sisters?"

"I was the only child and my mother died from cancer when I was nine. My father raised me, or rather the service raised me. It was hard for him."

"He died as well while you were in Saudi Arabia."

"Yes," he said. "I see you've done your homework."

"A little."

"It was a helicopter accident. One of those damned Pave Hawks. The MH-60 K/L, I think. It went down in the desert."

"What happened?"

"An explosion. That's all I was told. I still don't know for certain. The Army. It's hard to get information out of them. Maybe they'll find a reason to give it to the congressman in January."

"Point well taken," O'Connell said as he made another note and underlined it. *Helicopter.*

"How old were you?"

"Just turning fourteen."

"And who raised you after that?"

"I stayed for three months in a school in Germany, and then at fifteen I was sent to Harvard Essex Academy by my father's uncle, who acted as my guardian."

"Is he still alive?"

"No. He passed away shortly after."

O'Connell tapped his pen and thought for a moment, then offhandedly said, "You and the congressman seem to share something of a common background."

"Oh?" Newman responded.

"Both of your parents gone while you were the same age. Someone else in charge of your well-being."

"I never gave it much thought," Newman stated through an uncharacteristic smile. "But now that you mention it. Yes. It must have been one of the things that brought us together."

CHAPTER 31

TRIPOLI, LIBYA

"Mr. Morales. Why are you in the Great Jamahiriya?" Hevit circled D'Angelo who was being tied to a chair with his arms behind his back. His shirt, pants, shoes and socks had been removed. The major allowed him to keep his briefs on, but only after submitting to a cavity search. Hevit's officers pulled the ropes tightly and D'Angelo grimaced. This he couldn't hide.

"I'm a photographer." *And I've got some great real estate for you in the Everglades,* he didn't say aloud. "Photographing your mosques and museums for a British book company. For Christ's sake, it's all in my papers."

"You are a liar, Mr. Morales. But tell me more lies. Are you working alone?"

D'Angelo took his time. Giving up Roarke was not a risk. They knew he hadn't come into the country alone. "Of course not." He did avoid adding, *Like you don't know.* However, D'Angelo volunteered, "My writer is with me."

"And his name?"

"Adam Giannini. He's back at the Bab Al Bahr. Hopefully still sound asleep." He struggled with his ropes. *If he knows what's good for him.*

Hevit nodded to someone on the other side of what D'Angelo figured was a two-way mirror.

"And tell me about these photographs you take," the major asked sharply. The cameras had been examined for any secret components and given back to Hevit.

"Beauty shots. Architectural sites."

"Oh, with such good storytelling, I'd think you were the writer, Mr. Morales. Mr. *Tomás* Morales," Hevit said emphasizing the first name. "I suppose you speak Spanish, too."

"Fluently."

"And this morning? Exactly which mosque were you photographing this morning?" the major asked sharply.

"I wasn't."

"Then what did it have to do with your work?"

"City streets. People. I always overshoot. I'm a freelance photographer."

"Freelance?" Hevit was unfamiliar with the term.

"I sell pictures. This is how I earn my living. One client sends me to take pictures. But I take advantage of every situation. I'm always shooting. Maybe I can sell a picture to someone else."

"Like your government?" Hevit shouted right into D'Angelo's face.

"No. Like a magazine or another publisher!" D'Angelo locked his eyes on Hevit. "It's not every day an American gets a visa to visit Libya."

"This is the Great Jamahiriya!" Hevit declared. "You will kindly refer to it by its proper name." The major's manner was anything but kind. He paused in thought, then continued stone cold. "An American photographer for a British book company. That doesn't strike you as odd? It certainly does me."

"Call them."

Hevit slapped D'Angelo hard.

"You are not to tell me what to do," he yelled. "Do you understand?"

D'Angelo wanted to rub the side of his face but he couldn't. This bastard had really hurt him. When he didn't answer quickly enough, the major hit him again. Harder.

"Do you understand?"

The tactic was fairly standard. The interrogator pushed his suspect, hoping to provoke him into either committing a chargeable offense or revealing himself. D'Angelo wouldn't give him the pleasure of either.

"Yes."

"You have no rights here, Mr. Morales. Not you or your friend. You can't go running to your embassy for sanctuary. You have no embassy. So you will answer my questions one by one."

He continued. "Isn't it odd? You an American?"

"No, sir," D'Angelo said looking down, forcing tears. A soldier would face his enemy. A photographer would be scared.

"And why would they hire you then?"

"They like my work. They've hired me before. I'm a damned good photographer."

"You are indeed damned," the major laughed. "A photographer, I'm not so sure."

"Please believe me," D'Angelo said, promising to himself that one day he would get back at the sadistic major.

"Why should I? You are a worthless spy to me. I could kill you now."

"Sir, please call my employers," D'Angelo pleaded. He hoped his sincerity would be convincing enough. Of course the Libyans would call Collingsworth in Oxford and in time they would be connected to a specific executive who would confirm his cover and ersatz history. But no doubt he'd be made to suffer before that would happen. D'Angelo was prepared.

"And these photographs," Hevit demanded, dangling the cameras in front of him. "I suppose if I develop the film I would see exactly what you say is here?"

"Yes..." *You fucking shithead.* "But you can look at some now. One of the cameras is digital. You can scan through the shots. They're stored on the computer chip."

"Ah, modern technology. We are not so lucky here," the major added. "All right, then. Show me your pictures." He tipped his head to an officer to untie his hands.

Roarke rang D'Angelo's room for the fourth time since lunch. Something was definitely wrong. The night before, D'Angelo told him not to worry if he didn't come back by 1200 hours. He'd be out shooting around town. But it was already past 1400.

When he went to the lobby to look for his partner, he noticed two men checking his movements. He didn't acknowledge that he saw them for fear it would reveal his own expertise. However, he could tell that things had changed for the worse. He believed that D'Angelo was in custody for some reason. He might even be compromised. If that were the case, then so was he.

Roarke approached the concierge. "Excuse me," he said loud enough for the others to hear. "I'm looking for my friend Mr. Morales. Have you seen him?"

"No sir. Not this afternoon."

He got the same answer from the desk clerk and a bellhop.

"Thank you," Roarke said politely. "If he does come in, tell him I'll be back around 1600 hours." He tipped them both.

"Of course, Mr. Ginney." D'Angelo had been right about one thing. They still couldn't get his name straight.

Roarke stepped outside. The two men casually followed him, spacing themselves by about thirty feet. At the first intersection he got a good look at Number One, whom he called "Laurel." The man was thin, dressed in a white linen suit that was a size too big for him and desperately needed a cleaning. Midway down the street Roarke bought a pack of gum from a child and caught sight of Number Two. This character was a sweaty, little man with a gut that hung over his belt. He would be "Hardy." Both underpaid cops or members of Kharrazi's security force.

They tailed him badly. But Roarke made it easy for them. If D'Angelo were in trouble he'd do better to look all the more innocent. He did have an emergency contact and he casually made his way to the location.

NEW YORK CITY

O'Connell's editor at *The New York Times* read his four-page story about Geoff Newman sent via e-mail. He complained in a quick reply that it didn't contain enough new information to make the paper. He'd seen most of it before. "Michael, you have to do better."

O'Connell didn't like missing a good by-line. The coverage in the paper was one thing. The checks when his articles rolled out to the syndicate were another. As far as he was concerned, Newman blew a nice payday for him.

The reporter dated and filed the article in his Lodge campaign bin and turned to his notes. He definitely needed more. Maybe the party's chief, Wendell Neill, could help him out, or Governor Lamden. Or maybe the U.S. Army.

CHAPTER 32

TRIPOLI, LIBYA

"Mr. Morales, your pictures leave a lot to be desired," Hevit complained. He ran through the digital camera's memory chips, criticizing the American just for sport. "You do a fair job on our revered mosques, but your street shots are deplorable. So again I ask you. What were you really doing?" He paused for a second and corrected himself. "No, no. Let's start with who you really are,"

So far, D'Angelo's Office of Internal Security inquisitor, through all of his theatrics, hadn't gotten anywhere after three hours. They developed the film in the Nikon, and although Fadi Kharrazi's office building was in some of the pictures, it clearly was not the subject of the shots. When officer Number Three came into the sealed room and whispered in the major's ear, D'Angelo presumed that they had made the call to Collingsworth and his story checked out. It wasn't going well for Hevit and he looked mad. He slapped his prisoner harder than before, only to see a frightened photographer shrink into a ball to protect himself, not a defiant spy.

"Please," D'Angelo pleaded. "My name's Morales. Just like it reads on my identification. I'm from Miami, Florida. My parents are Cuban. They emigrated from Havana. But you are right about one thing." Hevit raised an eyebrow. "I'm not a particularly good photographer. That's why I do books. But I'm into art history. I'm a pretty fair amateur archeologist and I wanted to come to Tripoli and see your buildings."

D'Angelo gave him something. *Now let's see what happens.*

Hevit circled his quarry's chair three times. Then he pressed right into his face. "I don't like you, Tomás Morales. What's more. I don't believe you."

Hevit swung his arm back ready to slap D'Angelo again. Then he smiled and dropped his hand. "An archaeologist, you say."

"No, just a history buff."

"A what?" Hevit asked not understanding the colloquial term.

"A buff. It's just a hobby." *Keep it going awhile,* he thought.

Hevit drew up another chair, swiveled it backwards and sat face to face with his captive. "No, no. That's not what you said. Your words were a pretty *fair archaeologist.*"

"Amateur. I said amateur. It's just a pastime."

"Oh, well, let's see what you know. Consider it a test, shall we?"

Now it was going to get interesting.

It was called a newsstand. But that was a misnomer. There were newspapers, but not ones that reported any actual news.

Roarke stopped at the kiosk near the hotel located on the edge of the souk, leafed through a few glossy German magazines, then opted for a Cuban cigar. He took it to the salesman, a haggard old man with a toothless grin.

Over the man's shoulder was a broken down art deco clock; its face stained from years of cigarette and cigar smoke. There was nothing particularly distinctive about the timepiece except the time. It was an hour behind.

Roarke handed the man 200 dinars. He spat openly on the ground and handed back the wrong amount of change. Roarke looked at the amount, recognized that he was being stiffed, but left.

The wrong time on the clock and the wrong amount of change told him two important things.

Change of plans. Don't count on your safety any longer.

Roarke strolled back to the hotel, casually smoking his cigar while watching his watchers. Once back, he'd wait until midnight. If D'Angelo hadn't returned by then he was to proceed to a pre-selected location. From there everything was pre-arranged.

"So, tell me," Hevit began. "Tell me all about our heritage you admire so much. Let's start with Karamanli Mosque."

And so amateur archaeologist Tomás Morales began reciting everything he knew, those things he learned in the past few days, and his personal impressions. He got into the details of the exterior walls, the building materials, and the poor patchwork done over the years. He threw in just enough facts to sound authoritative. He even covered the smog damage. All of it served to deflate Hevit. But the officer was not through.

"Such facts can be memorized by a talented spy, especially when you have learned exactly what pictures to take." Hevit stood up and went to a door that opened when he knocked twice. "I will be back."

"May I go to the bathroom?"

"Piss in your shorts if you'd like," the major said. "There are no bathrooms for American spies."

D'Angelo made a good showing in the last round. No doubt, he'd be asked to play "Final Jeopardy" when Hevit returned. He silently hoped he'd remember enough to talk his way out of the mess.

Twenty minutes later the door opened again.

"Mr. Morales, a few more questions. It seems you do have friends who confirm that you are a photographer for this Collingsworth book company. But I remain skeptical. Not because of your recital about our great treasures, but your photography near the offices of the son of our Brother Leader. So one more test for the amateur archaeologist. Something you're unprepared for."

"Look, my job checks out. Just let me go."

Hevit ignored the wimpy request. He removed a folded sheet of lined yellow paper from his jacket pocket, opening it meticulously. Hevit read it to himself and smiled. "This shall determine your guilt or innocence."

"I'm not on trial here."

"Shut up," the major shouted louder than before. Then he pulled his voice back. "Perhaps you're right. This is not a trial." He lurched forward with his face no more than an inch from D'Angelo's. "There is no judge or jury. But you are facing your executioner, Tomás Morales. So think carefully before answering my next and very *last* question."

D'Angelo feared that he might have pushed the sadistic major too far. He took a deep breath and locked onto the cold eyes.

"I just want to go home, Major. I want to see my wife." That was his most truthful answer of the day.

"Mr. Morales, your interest in ancient architecture must include Greece," Hevit said ignoring the plea.

D'Angelo blinked and looked away.

"Well, we shall see. This took me some time to get. I am so sorry for my delay. But not being a student of archaeology myself, I needed to make a few calls. But you, on the other hand will be able to educate me on a place called Isthmia."

D'Angelo gritted his teeth and met Hevit's eyes again. They were still no more than an inch from his face. "So Mr. Morales. Tell me all about this rare archaeological site."

"Isthmia?"

"Isthmia, Mr. Morales. As if your life depended on it." Hevit leaned back and removed his service pistol from his shoulder holster. He flipped off the safety and repeated, "Isthmia."

"Isthmia," the American whispered, then cleared his throat.

"Louder!"

"...is along the old Scironian Road from Athens to the Peloponnesus." D'Angelo's voice strengthened and now his expression grew colder, more hateful. "It was home of the temple of Poseidon, a landmark to travelers in the first and second century A.D. Adjacent to it, I believe, was the sanctuary of Melikertes-Palaimon," he paused in thought. "From the Roman period? Perhaps that's why you asked? The Romans controlled your land for some time." Then he stopped and corrected himself, "No, no. I'm mistaken. It definitely was not Roman. Melikertes-Palaimon. But Isthmia is best known for the Panhellenic Games, which was very popular in the Roman colonial period."

Hevit was fuming. Every word undermined him more.

"The principal dig was in 1952, by Oscar Broneer and in the mid 1970s...."

"Enough. I should kill you right now!" He raised his gun toward D'Angelo when suddenly the door flew open. Another officer, a few years older and probably higher ranking than Hevit, entered and spoke in Arabic. Vinnie D'Angelo could actually understand them, but he didn't let on and it didn't matter. Language was no barrier to what was being said. It would have been apparent to anyone. The superior officer was dressing down a subordinate.

The major saluted and left, glaring at the man who defeated him.

The senior officer allowed Number Two to untie the prisoner's hands.

"Thank you," he said to the corporal without acknowledgment. "Thank you," he then said to the man, memorizing his face.

"I suggest you and your friend, Mr. Gino, leave Tarabulus and the Great Jamahiriya as quickly as you can, Mr. Morales. You are no longer welcomed here," he said in poor English. "And Major Hevit is not a happy man."

Roarke acted increasingly concerned through the rest of the afternoon, making sure the hotel staff noticed. He constantly went up to the lobby to ask the front desk clerk if he'd heard anything from his colleague. The word was always no. Roarke figured the more annoying he appeared, the more his cover story would hold. Eventually, he laid out his clothes and put his suitcase on the bed knowing that microphones undoubtedly picked up the sounds. He had to assume cameras were trained on him as well. It was now 2030 hours; the night before they were scheduled to check out, so packing would not be unusual. But inwardly he was planning an immediate escape, traveling as light as possible. He set 2200, ninety minutes away, as his target.

Better start winding down. Roarke hummed a made-up song for the sake of the microphones, intentionally sounding nervous. He yawned, then he killed the lights and turned on the television set to one of the pirated films on Kharrazi's movie channel, Schwarzenegger in *Total Recall.* The film was more than half over. He pushed his suitcase out of the way and stretched across his bed. He lowered the sound twice during the next forty minutes to check again with the hotel reception desk.

When the movie ended he shut off the TV and closed his eyes. In another thirty-five minutes he would sneak out, hopefully after his watchers got bored listening and watching.

Roarke tuned his senses to the dangerous work ahead. He mentally ran through the backup plans. He felt it would be dangerous only until he slipped into a café two blocks away. Once there he would order a coffee, wait an appropriate amount of time, maybe twenty minutes or so, then go to the bathroom. From there he would exit through the window, one with a broken latch over the far stall. After dropping down into the alley behind the establishment his instructions were to turn left and just before the corner find a rotting faded blue door and knock three times. *That's the signal,* he recalled. *Three knocks.*

Three knocks. Roarke bolted forward. Had he fallen asleep? The sound seemed so real. He checked his watch. 2153. Then he heard knocking. *The door?* He automatically reached under his pillow for his gun. It wasn't there. Roarke stopped fumbling and remembered that they'd come into the country unarmed. *Shit. Shit. Shit,* he mouthed but did not say aloud.

Three knocks again. He checked the window. *No escape there. Too high up.* He decided to approach the door cautiously.

"Come on, wake up and open the damned door!" came a booming voice from the other side. Roarke took in a huge breath and sighed with relief. "Time to get out of Dodge!" He was never happier to hear a wiser-ass voice than D'Angelo's.

"Where the hell were you," he called out to D'Angelo, expecting not to hear an honest reply. "You're gonna get us both fired."

CHAPTER 33

The two Americans went straight to the airport and waited standby for the next BA flight out of Tripoli. It wasn't the prescribed emergency route, but better to do it in public. They were able to fly to Cairo, make a change of planes to Amsterdam and then on to Heathrow. Neither of the men talked about what had occurred earlier that day until they had landed and rented a car to take them to Crowley Road in Oxford, home of the Collingsworth Publishers. However, the bruises on D'Angelo's face had already told Roarke everything he really needed to know.

They arrived at 2015 hours and said their goodbyes. The building was still open. D'Angelo remained at Collingsworth for another hour in the research department, biding his time in the archeological department, reading up more on Isthmia, the ancient city that saved his life.

Roarke, on the other hand, wanted to get back to Washington as fast as possible. After nursing a Coke from a vending machine for twenty minutes while perusing Collingsworth's winter catalogue, he ordered up a lift to the train station for the 2 hour 45 minute ride to London. He checked in at Grosvenor House as Giannini, slept for two hours, then discreetly left through a service entrance. His double from Heathrow, still in London, would check him out three days later.

Roarke made his way to Devonshire Terrace changing cabs three times, taking the Underground, and walking two blocks before finding another cab. He liked the hotel, a popular three-star establishment with a comfortable bar. It was not known to most tourists and the location afforded him any number of ways to disappear through Hyde Park and Kensington Gardens.

It was now 0500. After settling in he dialed up Shannon Davis at home.

"Hello," Davis answered.

"Hi. It's Roarke."

"Jesus, it's about time. Where the hell have you been?"

"Getting a tan."

"Well, get the fuck in here. I've been trying to reach you," the FBI agent complained.

"I'll see you tomorrow, late afternoon."

"Good, because I've got some stuff you're going to want to see."

WASHINGTON, D.C.
J. EDGAR HOOVER FBI BUILDING
MONDAY, AUGUST 11

"So, where were you?" asked Shannon Davis.

"Out."

"Really, Roarke? Out? Out of the city? Out of the district? Out of the country? I couldn't get bupkis from the White House. So…"

"I was just out. Busy."

"I see nothing much has changed. I ask questions and never get an answer. You ask me to get information for you and I never know why."

"And your problem is?"

"Oh nothing. It's just good to see you."

"You, too."

The FBI man gave him a genuine bear hug. They both counted on each other. If the situation were reversed, Roarke would be the first to help Shannon.

"Well then, let me bring you up to date. I'll start with Alfred Nunes. He's still dead."

"Very funny, Shannon."

"But you'd be interested to know that he may not have died from a heart attack. Come with me to the lab. We'll walk and talk and see if there's anything new on the toxicology report."

They left Shannon's office on the 5th floor and walked down the hall to the elevator that would take them to the basement lab.

"No visible puncture wounds, no trauma to his body except when he fell off the rock he was sitting on. But we're looking into the possibility of drugs. Honestly, I didn't give it a second thought even though you were suspicious, until one of our guys, a fairly aggressive rookie, found a footprint downstream."

"A footprint? Not much to go on," Roarke said.

"No, but we're running it anyway. Looks like a boot. A man's. Size 12ish."

"You have a file of boot prints? Like fingerprints?" Roarke asked.

"Some, not many. But you go with what you have. We're running it for potential matches now."

They changed the subject in the elevator when two other people joined them. They were in the headquarters of the FBI, but as recent history had shown, they might as well be telling the Russian president directly. Secrets were hard to keep and security was always playing catch up to spying.

While most of the toxicological work was done in facilities at

Quantico, the FBI still kept a lab in Washington. This is where a sample of Alfred Nunes' blood was analyzed.

"Anything showing?" Shannon Davis asked a technician.

"Very hard to tell, Shannon." He acknowledged Roarke with a nod.

"It's all right. This is Scott Roarke, Secret Service. He started us on this science experiment."

"Thank you for your help," Roarke offered.

"Don't thank me yet. But I may be getting some positives for Sodium morph."

Roarke stopped him. "Sodium morph?"

"Sorry. Sodium morphate. It dissipates into the body damned fast so it's hard to read this far out. I'm still working the probabilities since there's no clear evidence left."

Shannon leaned over and whispered to Roarke, "Sodium morphate is lethal stuff. The kind of thing used by the mob and others."

"Others?" Roarke said curiously.

"Assassins. From *all* countries. You fill in the blanks. We've got a list as long as the Washington Monument is high on suspected hits using the drug."

"It's nasty," the technician offered while working on a computer model of Nunes' blood compared with the characteristics of sodium morphate. "Painful and slow with all of the outward signs of a heart attack."

They continued to talk about the deaths attributed to SM and those that were hinted about in the halls of the agency. After another fifteen minutes, the technician pulled back from the screen as two overlapping pictures merged as one.

"Yup," the technician offered. "Your boy should have lived another good five to ten years. This was no natural heart attack. In my estimation, he was poisoned. I'd say he probably got a hefty swig of sodium morphate in something he drank."

Roarke sighed. "What's all this mean, Scott?"

"It means my life is going to be sheer hell for the next few months."

The president's mouth was full of prime rib when Roarke walked into the White House dining room. Morgan Taylor acknowledged him with the wave of his hand. Roarke automatically turned to the first lady.

"Hello, Mrs. Taylor," Roarke politely offered. "Mr. President."

"Hello, Scott," Lucy Taylor answered.

Mrs. Taylor invited Scott to join them for dinner, which he gladly accepted.

"Well, you look like shit," the president finally said.

Mrs. Taylor didn't flinch. She was used to her husband's language.

"Nothing that an early retirement wouldn't solve."

"Tell me about it," the president said reaching for a roll.

Through the next few minutes they traded sports stories and caught up on movies the president and the first lady had seen, since neither man could discuss the more sensitive work issues yet.

"Morgan tells me that you've met a woman in Boston."

Roarke gasped. He wasn't used to personal questions.

"Well, yes." Roarke said.

"And?" Mrs. Taylor continued.

"And what?"

"And do you like her?"

"Well, yes," he answered positively squirming. He hadn't spoken with Katie since he left Boston. She probably hated him, or worse yet, she forgot about him.

"Look honey, Scott's obviously not quite ready to talk about this. We've got to give him time," the president stated. Roarke appreciated Taylor letting him off the hook. "Anyway, we've got some business to catch up on, so…"

The first lady took her cue. "And I have some reading to do," she said as she stood up. "You take care, Scott. And let me know when I can meet her."

Roarke looked down, embarrassed.

"Oh, and take care of my husband, too," she said. Roarke looked at the president. He telegraphed a look that seemed to say Mrs. Taylor had her sources as well. She kissed Roarke goodbye and they waited to speak until the door was closed.

Roarke looked at the president for an explanation.

"She probably just put things together, my boy."

"It seems to run in this family," Roarke joked. Then it was time for business. First he covered his trip to Libya, then a different topic, the likely cause of Alfred Nunes' death. As he ran through the facts, the president did his normal pacing across the floor. He lit a cigar, smoked it, often stopping to examine the ashes as they accumulated at the end. It was a habit of the president's whenever he listened intently. Roarke knew what would come next. A barrage of questions. Some rhetorical.

"Nunes was the attorney for the Lodge estate?"

"Yes sir."

"And he lost representation to..." he trailed off allowing Roarke to fill in the blank.

"To Haywood Marcus in Boston."

"Yes, your lady friend's boss."

"Yes."

The president studied the ashes and flicked them in a crystal ashtray, the gift of the Chinese premier.

"Nunes dies. What does that suggest to you, Scott?"

"The end of a trail. Quite intentional."

"Perhaps so. But from what you say, not completely provable."

"Yet," Roarke stated.

"Stay with the facts for now, Scott, because I have another interesting tidbit for you."

The president wasn't playing it out for theatrical sake. He was weaving meaningful pieces together himself.

"The gentleman you *encountered* in Boston along the Charles? You remember him, Scott?" the president remained intentionally vague.

"Yes," Roarke responded.

"Apparently he was from out of town with prints that brought up a nice long record. Well, not exactly nice."

Roarke laughed at the president's delivery. He was obviously having fun but saving the best for last.

"He carried a cell phone," Taylor said, again pacing. "Which led to his telephone records, which have proven very enlightening to the FBI, and will soon be in the Attorney General's hands. We know for sure who called him and set him on his merry way."

"A Mr. Haywood Marcus?" Roarke volunteered.

"Give the man a cigar."

BOSTON, MASSACHUSETTS

"Scott Roarke. No, I don't think I've ever met anyone by that name."

"Well then, perhaps you should. I just arrived from abroad and I understand that you're the sexiest woman in the Boston law community."

"Well, you heard right," Katie Kessler said through a chuckle. "And you, Mr. Roarke, have quite a compelling voice. I bet you make all the girls cry."

"There's only one on my list," he bravely added.

Katie prided herself on being quick on the uptake. This time she stuttered and then confessed, "Scott, where were you? What happened?"

"Not over the phone. I have one stop first, then I'll see if my boss will give me a few days rest."

She smiled to herself. "You come up here, but I guarantee you won't get much rest."

QUANTICO, VIRGINIA
FBI LABORATORIES

Duane Parsons typed in his password, jumped over three security fences he'd built, and called up his finished jpegs. Roarke peered over his shoulders.

"I think I have a pretty good extrapolation here, based on the predictable variables," he told Roarke. "But I still need those other pictures I told you about."

"I'll try to come up with something," the Secret Service agent answered. "I've just been busy."

"Family, the kid's family at various ages. Anything that would help me input some…any genetic influences. Anyway, here it comes."

Roarke watched as the image of the original Boy Scout picture appeared on the 19" flat screen.

"Okay, here's your newspaper clipping." He typed in a command and an enhanced picture appeared, which Touch Parsons then added to a split screen with the first.

"You see I cleaned up the picture. The grain's gone. It's sharpened. I've doubled the pixels and played with the gray scale. Next, I zoomed in on the boy's face and cleaned it up more."

Another pair of images appeared on the screen as Parsons quickly moved his stylus. These were close-ups with enhanced facial detail. Roarke could just about see the pores.

"This is the one I modeled. The real challenge is not to impose my aesthetics on the subject, but to focus on what's unique in the character. Otherwise, the individual would disappear during the digital aging process."

Touch blew up the clear picture on the right and then slowly put it through a series of dissolves. In an extraordinarily dreamlike progression, the boy aged, with the face elongating, then broadening, his hair growing, then thinning, the eyes narrowing, the nose expanding. "Honestly, there's no software that can guarantee we'll come up with 'the' most accurate picture, but the developmental characteristics should be within a range of acceptable. I use Photoshop on a Wacom tablet. The files use a helluva lot of RAM and a project this complex takes hours to render. After I saw where I was going, I added other variables like stress, possible weight gain, the effect of exercise or the lack of it. You name it. I threw out some of the choices the computer offered and took some guesses on the features including eye and hair color."

The age progression continued. Roarke watched in amazement. The face aged from the teenager to college student to a twenty and thirtysomething in slow two-year increments. At last it dissolved to a 47-year-old man wearing a suit and tie of Parsons' choice.

"I thought you'd like the clothes. They say they make the man."

Touch hit Ctrl-P on his computer and an Epson Stylus Photo inkjet whirred. A minute later, a full-color glossy 8x10 photograph sat in the tray. It depicted a strikingly handsome man with a broad distinctive smile, high cheekbones, and slightly almond eyes.

Roarke silently examined it for what seemed like an eternity to Parsons.

"Well?" the photo expert asked.

"This is absolutely incredible. Are you sure you've got him nailed?"

"Am I sure? Well, no. You've got to get me more family pictures.

But I think I'm within striking distance. Anyway, it's the best I can do for now."

Roarke continued to look at the photo in amazement. "Thank you, Touch. Do you have an envelope I can put this in?"

"Sure and I'll throw in another print or two."

As the images printed out the FBI photo expert asked, "By the way, you know what's a lot of fun to do?"

"What?"

"Going in the opposite direction. Taking an older person and regressing him."

"What do you mean?"

"Going backwards. There's not a lot of call for it. But it's fun." Roarke laughed. "I bet."

When the photos were completed, Parsons slid them in an envelope, backed by cardboard. "You don't have to come back in. You know you can scan and email me whatever other pictures you find."

"That'll help. And thanks again. I had no idea how this whole process worked."

They shook hands and Roarke left with the age progression photographs of a man he had never seen before in his life.

CHAPTER 34

BOSTON, MASSACHUSETTS
WEDNESDAY, AUGUST 13

They came together like a furnace. So much heat and intensity had been building for weeks. No longer able to deny one another, Katie and Roarke melted together, seeking each other's tastes and finding unknown pleasures. The two individuals as one in total, exquisite rapture.

Katie surrounded Roarke in every imaginable way; first with her arms and with her legs. And then with all of the tenderness she had.

He was lost in her deepness, and she felt how he expanded within her. Roarke explored her feelings, taking Katie to the edge and holding her there with delicate moves and long kisses.

Katie's breasts cupped perfectly in his hands. Her body, beautifully matched to his, moved rhythmically and sent waves of excitement through both of them. She tightened around Roarke and was aware that he seemed weightless above her; his arms supporting his sculptured body, making loving effortless.

She whispered to him, "You're a perfect fit." It was the first complete sentence in more than an hour.

Neither partner had ever experienced such pleasure, with an insatiable desire to give more. Four hours went by suspended in time and outside of reality. Finally, Roarke fell asleep inside of Katie, snuggling from behind her after an intense explosion. But Katie would not let him rest for long. She woke her lover by gently pressing against him and he grew to love her again.

At nine o'clock they showered. It gave them the opportunity to use their eyes and feast on their bodies another way. This brought more gratification and in turn, satisfaction as their gentle caresses turned to petting and rubbing. Scott had never known such a woman. Katie had never given herself in such a way to any man.

They hungered for each other, but Katie insisted on preparing some actual food, which they ate, while dressed only in T-shirts. The pasta was complemented with a Kendall Jackson Cabernet. They didn't finish any of it.

"I love getting lost inside of you," Roarke said as he slid back.

"You're not lost. You're found," Katie whispered. She pulled her legs tightly around him, transferring all of her pleasure to Roarke. This wasn't just sex. She experienced beautiful sensations when he was inside her, but more than that, she could feel his love. With the intensity of both she came again.

The next morning they showered once more and had fun applying lotion on one another's hidden places. After getting dressed, Katie kissed Roarke goodbye with unreserved passion.

"There's an extra key in the top right hand drawer of my dresser. It's there for you to use when you come back later." Then she softened her voice. "You will be back later." It was a statement, not a question.

"This afternoon. I need to go to Marblehead while you're at work. But I'll be home with dinner on the table."

"My goodness, the man cooks, too." She kicked up her heel and left. Roarke realized he needed another hour's sleep.

THE WHITE HOUSE
CABINET ROOM
THURSDAY, AUGUST 14

"Good morning," the president said cheerfully as he entered the Cabinet Room from the door leading directly to the Oval Office. He instantly read the room. He caught the long face from his CIA Chief. "Or is it?"

"I'm afraid not, Mr. President," the CIA Director immediately volunteered. "India test fired another short-range missile last night."

"Sweet Jesus. Give me more." The president looked to his chief of staff, John Bernstein, and shook his head.

"An Agni II, with a range of some 1,800 miles, capable of carrying a 200-kiloton boosted-fission warhead. It could take out a target almost anywhere within Pakistan. All in all, not good."

"Any warning to Pakistan this time?"

"No."

"They're all lunatics!" the president swore. "A few years ago they got so close to settling this thing. Now, they're back in the same fucking mess." Taylor made no attempt to hide his anger. "Okay, at least tell me they gave *us* a heads up. I don't care if it was ten minutes. Khosla promised me."

"Nothing," the DCI said.

"What the hell is he thinking?" he asked no one in particular.

The secretary of state entered the discussion. At 52, Joyce Drysdale was the senior woman in the Taylor administration. Though she let her hair go white, she gave the impression of a woman in her 30s. She was well-versed in contemporary American history, a dynamic speaker, and strong leader. As the former president of the University of Washington and author of a trio of books on the Vietnam War, she could command attention. Some people had her running for president in four years.

"Rest assured that Pakistan is bound to have a response. I'd say Sajjad will be launching his own tests within a few days. Right along the border. Hopefully not over it. We should notify the prime minister that the U.S. does not view that as a good idea."

With that, the meeting evolved into a twenty minute exchange of ideas. It ended when the president called for some specific thoughts. Jack Evans posed a possibility. "You're Khosla and Sajjad. How about accepting an invitation from the President of the United States to come to Camp David and hash this thing out?"

John Bernstein argued against it. "Like being called to the principal's office?"

"That bad, Bernsie?" the DCI questioned.

"Yeah, Jack. It'll look like an old-fashioned scolding. There's no way they'd walk into that."

"You all agree?" Taylor asked.

"Afraid so," added the president's secretary of state.

"Then maybe you could go there," the DCI noted. "It'll send a strong message that you're willing to get directly engaged. It wouldn't hurt back home, either." He didn't need to explain what he meant by the last comment. Though the CIA director stayed out of such things, the political upside was immediately obvious to everyone.

As the president thought about the idea, he saw that his SecState did not concur.

"Joyce, you don't like Jack's proposal. Why?"

"Mr. President, it's a risky step before we even exhaust exploring lower level talks through our ambassadors. They should be the ones to formally open the door."

"Which won't lead anywhere," Bernstein argued.

"Which *probably* won't lead anywhere," she asserted. "But it's a step we have to take. But borrowing from what Jack had to say, what if you call them. You ask Prime Minister Khosla to meet with Ambassador Shayne in New Delhi and for Prime Minister Sajjad to sit down with Ambassador Medinica in Islamabad. They communicate the gravity of the situation and carry in the president's message."

"And this message is?" Bernstein asked acerbically.

"That their actions endanger not only themselves, but the entire world," the secretary of state added.

"Oh, that'll make them stop. They'll say, 'Thanks for the call. You know we just forgot.'" Bernstein threw up his hands. "Come on, Joyce, they've got their fucking fingers on the button. You think a lecture from a United States ambassador is going to help? These are people who are hell bent on destroying one another."

"Precisely, and we cannot allow that!" she argued.

"Which means what?" Bernstein shouted.

"That the fleet parks in the Indian," added Secretary of Defense Norman Gregoryan as his first comment. "USPACOM shows some muscle. That's a message they'll get."

The president encouraged open discussion, but this was going too far.

"Thank you for all for that lively exchange. Now here's what *I* propose.

"Joyce, I want you to go to New Delhi and Islamabad to lay the ground work for a subsequent trip that *I* will make. And you will tell Dr. Khosla and Mr. Sajjad exactly that. That I *will* follow. But we'll meet on neutral ground, in Qatar. In your call to Prime Minister Sajjad you will indicate that this president would view his government's testing of its Ghauri or M-11 missiles as an unnecessary escalation. In other words, don't up the ante. Tell them both, as far as I am concerned, there is nothing more serious, with the exception of terrorist threats to the United States, than the dangerous course these two countries are proposing by their actions. Tell them that I will announce a trip to our military base at Qatar for no later than ten days from today to meet with our commanders in the Gulf and Qatar. But the purpose of this visit is to sit down with Khosla and Sajjad. We will do it in secrecy and we will stay there until we have a solution.

"Norman, I will see the troops there, too. You can set that up. But coordinate the dates with Joyce for this meeting. That is why I'm going. To Jack's earlier point, hopefully that will provide its own benefits. Bernsie, you'll have to get into the calendar. It's going to throw a big monkey wrench into everything."

"Including the convention," the chief of staff noted.

"Quite possibly."

"But Mr. President. You have to be at the convention."

"Let's hope I can, Bernsie. Now, Norman and Joyce, the only way this is going to lead to any meaningful result is if *we* put something on the table. This has to be worthwhile to each of them."

Demonstrating his detailed grasp of geopolitical issues, Morgan Taylor ran through the options. "You'll have to help me through this, but in terms of Pakistan, maybe we slack off on our insistence for a new election. Sajjad should welcome that. What was our last grant for education? Only around $5 million. That's pretty insulting. Work up a viable package."

"And if they want us to back pedal on our pursuit of their drug trade?" the secretary of state asked.

"That's not on the table," the president said without any equivocation. "But more money to fight the Taliban. Yes. More money for Emergency Relief and Migration Assistance. Yes. Whatever it takes to get them to see we're serious. This has got to be a visible win for Sajjad, given the threat from India.

"Now for Dr. Khosla. Same questions. What will it take? More assistance in non-military nuclear research? Determine the short-comings of the old Bush proposals? Can we improve upon them? More money for HIV/AIDS vaccinations? And market incentives? It's about time we face it, India is one of the six major powers in the world. We should publicly acknowledge that." The president laughed as he shared his next thought. "Nothing like telling somebody they've got one of the world's biggest dicks."

Everyone laughed, including Joyce Drysdale and Attorney General Eve Goldman.

"Okay, those are my general ideas. Give me the specifics and do it quickly. Maybe I can help stabilize this mess before the country puts us all out to pasture."

"Mr. President," John Bernstein insisted, "Please. Can't this wait until after the convention? State can start setting it up now. I'm sure Joyce could use the extra time. Then you go as soon as you've accepted the nomination."

"No," the president declared. "This can't wait."

Taylor allowed another few minutes of debate, however his mind was made up.

"One thing—for all of your memoirs. I'm not doing this for any polls. Got that?"

They understood.

"If necessary, Bernsie, I'll address the convention from the road."

"That's never been done before," the chief of staff added.

"Yeah," the president said as he concluded the session. "Maybe this time someone *will* listen."

MARBLEHEAD, MASSACHUSETTS

"I'm looking for old photographs for an article on the Lodges," Roarke explained to the Executive Director of the Marblehead Chamber of Commerce.

"Oh, you and everyone else," the 54-year-old full time spokesperson for Marblehead tourism replied in a thick New England accent. "I've had people from the networks asking and a reporter fellow from *The New York Times*. Wish I could help you, but we don't archive anything like that. Try the newspaper."

"Already did."

"Give the *Globe* a call. I don't have a contact for you. But they've got an extensive archive. And then there's Cronin at the *Herald*. Try him."

Roarke thanked the director and called the archivist at *The Boston Globe*. The librarian checked and came up with nothing. Next he called *The Boston Herald*.

He got the same message. "Sorry. Our photo library really starts with Mr. Lodge's visits to Boston once he was a congressman. We also have the typical AP pictures from Washington, but nothing from his Marblehead days," the archivist explained. "But you may want to check with BU. They've got the old *Record American* morgue."

"BU?" asked Roarke.

"Boston University. Down on Comm Avenue." Cronin gave him the contact number and directions.

After Roarke arrived, the archivist at the school listened to Roarke's pitch. He had Roarke wait a good ten minutes, only to return with bad news.

Roarke finally decided to check with the Lodges' neighbors. And the best way to do that was to drive back up to Marblehead to canvass the streets. That took the better part of the day. And everywhere he heard the same story. "We don't have any," or "We can't find any."

As he passed a newsstand he saw a copy of *The New York Times*. *The reporter, what's his name, O'Donnell. No, O'Connell. He may know.*

From a phone booth at a gas station on Pleasant Street, he called the paper, hoping to get O'Connell. The chances were slim considering how reporters used voice mail to screen their calls. On the fourth ring, a recording triggered and Roarke left a message.

"Hello, you don't know me," he started. "But I'm calling to ask a favor." The rest would all be a lie.

"I'm Reuben Putman, calling on behalf of the Democratic Convention and we're desperately looking for a photograph of Congressman Lodge's family for a documentary that will be running before his speech. It's scheduled for Thursday during the convention. I'd appreciate a call if you have anything or if you could steer me in the proper direction. I'm in Boston and I'll be checking into the Parker House. You can leave a message for me there after three today." For good measure he added, "And maybe I can help you, too." That should guarantee a call back.

Roarke was about to hang up but then added an irresistible compliment. "And by the way, great job on your articles. Fascinating backgrounders. Bye."

He returned to Boston and drove, up and over Beacon Hill to the Parker House, one of the city's famed hotels. Roarke produced an ID and credit card in the name of Putman, a rarely used alias, and checked in. After programming the room telephone so he could call in for messages, he decided to grab another hour's rest before returning to Katie's. He figured he'd need it.

Just before 5 P.M. the phone rang waking him up from a deep, heavy sleep. In his disorientation, Roarke almost missed the call. "Hello," he said in the strongest voice he could muster.

"Hello, Mr. Putman?"

Roarke had to think a moment. "Ah, yes."

"This is Mike O'Connell. You asked me to give you a ring."

Roarke forced his eyes open and focused. "Yes, yes. Thank you. I'm so sorry if I put you out. I know it's not quite regular to be asking for help like this."

"Well, it's a bit unorthodox, but under the circumstances, I understand. And as you said, maybe you'll have something I might need."

Roarke smiled. He took the bait. "Possibly," Roarke said aloud.

"But in answer to your question, I'm having the same problem. It's the damnedest thing. I can't find a picture to save my life."

"Yeah," Roarke agreed.

"Or his family."

Of course there was one photograph, but Roarke decided not to offer it up. "I've gotta finish this doc with sketches. It's impossible."

"We're both in the same boat, then." O'Connell suddenly had another idea. "But while I have you on the phone, maybe you can help me out with some solid info on Lodge's head guy, Newman."

"What do you mean?" Roarke asked. He shook off the tiredness. *This could prove interesting.*

"Newman."

"Yeah? What about him?"

"He just sort of came out of nowhere."

"What do you mean?"

"I interviewed him and got a bit of his history. But not much. I'd sure like to be able to write a solid backgrounder on him. But I don't have enough to fill a column. And the man may be the next chief of staff."

Roarke scribbled the name *Newman* on a hotel pad next to the phone.

The reporter continued. "The Army's been pretty tight-lipped about his father and the helicopter crash and I don't have time to run the Freedom of Information Act up their fucking asses to get at it. Maybe you can feed me something. Not for attribution, of course, unless you want it."

Roarke added *Army, father and copter crash* to his paper. Certainly he could open doors where O'Connell couldn't.

"Look, keep me out of the papers. But here's the deal. I'll look into it. I have some connections, but you have to find me a picture."

"Give me a day."

"You got it," Roarke said. "And I'll see what I can deliver, too."

He didn't feel one bit guilty using the reporter.

O'Connell had been fueling Lodge's campaign for two months. It was about time that Morgan Taylor got something in return. "You can reach me here for the next few days. Let's talk tomorrow, say at five o'clock."

"Oh, and one more thing, while you're at it."

"Yes," Roarke said.

"Newman's date of birth. Can you get that, too?"

"I'll try."

O'Connell agreed and hung up. Roarke immediately dialed the office of the Secretary of the Army at the Pentagon. With luck he'd have his information well before twenty-four hours. He hoped that, in return, O'Connell would press his sources to find a photograph. Touch Parsons needed more.

O'Connell liked having someone on the inside. He was proud of himself and didn't question how easily Putman fell into his lap. Unfortunately, even though he was a top-flight journalist, he failed to double-check the veracity of his new source. He probably wanted to believe Reuben Putman because they struck a deal. Possibly it was because he still thought far too much about writing a bestseller on the election. Whatever the reason, it blinded him. Which, of course, Roarke counted on.

O'Connell logged onto Google and began a series of searches, which constantly narrowed. He typed in "Marblehead" and added additional parameters: restaurants, fire stations, hot dog stands, clubs, and organizations, anywhere he might find photographs of the Lodges. He also cast a net for high school yearbooks. He was surprised he hadn't tried that before.

He printed out 53 telephone numbers of possible contacts and began calling.

At the same time, Roarke was on the phone with the Pentagon. He spoke with an old friend, Captain Penny Walker, a tireless bloodhound who could dig into the deepest hole and come up with gold. She worked with the Secretary of the Army and Roarke knew all of her skills first hand. In an internal investigation six years earlier,

Walker and Roarke had discovered a white supremacist faction that had been recruiting members at Fort Bragg. Roarke had infiltrated the group and continued to work undercover with Capt. Walker, but in an entirely different manner. They ended their affair early, yet remained devoted to one another.

She worked online while speaking to Roarke on the phone. "Newman, William. 2nd Lieutenant. Deceased. Let's see what comes up. And I'm not talking about you, honey," she said punching in the last variable to her initial entry.

"That's a relief," he said. "I'm not sure if I even could."

"Oh, has Mr. Happy been busy recently?"

"Captain!" he chided her. "Stick to your search."

"You're no fun anymore. But okay. Here we go."

She began reading the results. "Newman, um, only 6,411. Give me a sec, I'll cut through this."

She typed in "Germany." Next, the approximate years of service.

"Got it down to four. Anything else I can use?"

"Yeah. Add helicopter accident—some sort of crash, I don't really know, as the cause of death." He heard her fingers race across the computer keys.

"Bingo. I got your man. Let me track his file and I'll call you back in the morning with an update."

"You've got my number."

"Had it," she added for good measure in her sexiest voice. "And by the way, congratulations. Hope she's good."

"What are you talking about?'

"You have a sweetheart. I heard it in your voice. What you said."

"Oh, you are good."

"You used to think so. Anyway, I am Army intelligence."

"I'll say."

"Good luck, Roarke. Maybe it'll be *this* time."

"Thanks, Penny. Thank you."

Roarke had barely enough time to pick up groceries for dinner. He dashed to DeLuca's Market near the corner of Charles and Beacon Streets, bought two fresh bluefish, enough greens for a salad, one tiramisu because he thought they could find a fun way of eating it, and a bottle of Mt. Eden Merlot. With the bags in hand he walked up Beacon Hill to prepare dinner like a regular Bostonian.

Meanwhile, O'Connell worked on a soggy tuna sandwich left over from lunch while he continued to run down his phone numbers. He'd started late in the day, so there were at least two-thirds of the calls left over for the morning.

At 10 P.M. he called it quits. At 10 P.M. Roarke and Katie were lost in each other's arms.

Teddy Lodge read the draft of his acceptance speech. It was pure poetry. Newman was right. This new girl had real talent; like Jenny's. Not that he was surprised. He knew it was no accident. Nothing in their world was.

"A few word changes, a phrase here and there. I've redlined them. Otherwise it's great," Lodge told Newman. "I want to meet this woman."

"All in good time, Ted. Keep your eye on the prize. Maybe after Thursday," the campaign manager and chief of staff insisted.

The congressman didn't like being told what to do. It was in his voice when he snapped back. "Thursday night. At the reception."

"Okay. Okay. And you won't be disappointed."

FRIDAY, AUGUST 15

"Hello, this is Michael O'Connell. I'm a reporter for *The New York Times*. And I'm on a deadline."

He liked to begin his calls with a sense of urgency. It made people feel important; especially the ones who wanted to see their names in print.

But call after call delivered the same response. He scratched out names and numbers all morning until, through a restaurant owner in Marblehead, he found an old man who remembered a man, who might know a woman, who had a friend, whose uncle was a barber in Marblehead. "Call Ciccolo's. He always put pictures of the kids on the wall. Maybe one's still tacked up."

O'Connell considered it nothing short of a miracle that the shop was still around. The 65-year-old son of the original barber, Nick Ciccolo, now ran it.

"Teddy Lodge, you say. Jeez, you mean the one running for president? That one?"

"That's the one," O'Connell answered.

"Hold on a minute. I'll check," the barber said. The minute was actually seven, filled with the worst Mantovani renditions imaginable, all filtered through the phone lying next to the radio.

"Hello. You still there?" Ciccolo asked when he came back.

"I'm here. Any luck?"

"It was pretty high up. That's why it took so long. One of my customers had to help me. Thanks, Shelley," he threw to the man at the shop. "I had the feeling that we had something."

"And?"

"This goes way back. But I sort of remembered the old man coming in with his kid. I got a mind for that sort of thing I suppose."

"And?" O'Connell demanded.

"And I found one."

"Great!" The reporter showed his excitement. "What's it look like?"

The barber laughed. "Well, it's like a hundred other pictures of first haircuts. But it's sure him. Dated and everything. The kid was bawling his eyes out. His father is standing behind him trying to quiet him down."

"I love it. Can I borrow the picture?"

"Well, it does leave a weird spot on the wall. The paint's all faded around it."

"Sorry. I can get it right back to you."

"Yeah, I know but," the barber stopped and O'Connell felt what was coming. This was all about money now.

"One hundred?" offered O'Connell quickly.

"I dunno," the barber replied.

"We normally don't pay anything. But since it's a presidential candidate, how about two-fifty."

"Five hundred?"

"This is really pretty far out there, but five hundred. Deal. If you throw in a haircut on my next trip."

"And a credit for the shop?"

"Done."

"You got a picture, Mr. O'Connell."

"Thank you. A friend of mine will come by to pick it up. Probably tomorrow."

"With money."

"Yes, Mr. Ciccolo. With money."

"I close at five sharp."

"He'll be there. His name is Putman."

An hour later, O'Connell also scored an old high school yearbook from the daughter of a classmate. It was tiny; a group photo, but Lodge was there. He'd give Putman the addresses for both.

Penny Walker was also on a roll. She found Newman's military records, information on his wife and kid, and background on the MH-60 K/L Pave Hawk that crashed.

"Take some notes. I can email you the rest," she told Roarke.

"Ready."

"When Newman died, the Army convened a panel. There'd been a rash of Pave Hawks going down. Generally fuel leak problems. They were constantly being grounded. The only rub here is that Lt. Newman wasn't assigned to the aircraft. No orders to board. And it certainly wasn't protocol for him to hitch a nighttime ride to nowhere. So I made a few calls. There was an NCO who remembered seeing a colonel yelling at Newman to get into the chopper. Newman didn't want to go. He was supposed to be off duty. But he was being dressed down pretty badly and he obeyed."

"And the colonel?"

"No record of him signing in."

"Any inquiry produce this guy?"

"No. A description in the record. That's all. No positive ID. Someone fucked up ordering him on and then apparently had the rank to cover the thing up after the accident."

"And the boy?"

"Shuttled around until he got back to the States. The airlines actually lost him on his way between the KLM and American gates at Heathrow. He missed a connecting flight to JFK. Things were frantic for a while. An airline attendant was supposed to get the hand off at the gate, but somehow missed him."

"Give that to me again."

"Geoff Newman was lost at Heathrow. Missing for about an hour. He apparently had the presence of mind to get himself to the American gate. They got him on the next flight and he was met by his only relative, a distant cousin from Portland, Maine, he never knew. Right after coming to the States, his cousin shipped him off to private school in Massachusetts."

"Harvard Essex Academy."

"So you know some of this."

"Bits and pieces. Got any pictures?"

"One. The lieutenant in Germany. I'll scan it and email you."

"Nothing of the kid."

"No. And by the way, you wanted his birth date, too."

"Yeah, right," he said, actually having forgotten.

She told him.

"Thanks sweetheart. I owe you."

"You don't have enough to make it worthwhile," she laughed.

Roarke left a message for O'Connell. He got a call back in three minutes.

"What do you have?" O'Connell asked.

"You first."

"Two addresses for you. One a barber shop in Marblehead. The second, a house in Beverly. Pictures waiting for you at both. But I want copies. Try Kinko's and then FedEx them out. Or better yet, have them scanned and attached it in an email. The originals have to go back to the owners."

"Great."

"Not so great. Bring $500 to the barbershop and another one hundred to Beverly."

"What?" Roarke asked.

"The price of doing business, Mr. Putman. I figure you've got a budget." He gave Roarke the street addresses. "Now your turn."

Roarke explained that he also found a photograph—one of Newman's father, plus information on the helicopter accident and Geoff's birth date.

"Fifty-one?" O'Connell commented.

"That's right."

"That makes him a few years older than Lodge."

"So?" Roarke asked.

"Dunno, just a little odd." *Different ages in the same class?* It was odd, but he left it at that.

Roarke said he'd get everything out in an email after he picked up the pictures. All quid pro quo. "But keep me out of the papers," Roarke stated, "And I'll be good to you."

"A pleasure working with you Mr. Putman."

"Likewise, Mr. O'Connell." With that, Roarke recovered his rental car from the Boston Common garage and cruised up to the North Shore.

TRIPOLI, LIBYA

The report made it from Abahar Kharrazi's office to his brother Fadi's desk well after Roarke and D'Angelo had left the country. Each brother had infiltrated the other's offices at various levels. This time it paid off for the younger brother.

"Tomás Morales. U.S. national. Photographer. Suspected spy. Detained. Questioned. Released." The brief contained surveillance photographs, detailed reports from his tails, and the summation justifying his dismissal.

Fadi studied the images. He was troubled. Why would an archeological photographer be taking pictures of his street? And his building? Especially an American?

"I want to know who this Morales is," he shouted to his aide, Lakhdar al-Nassar.

"Find me this man."

Al-Nassar ran an Internet search. In time, he came up with Collingsworth Publishers in England. His call to Collingsworth confirmed the employment of the man named Morales. Simultaneously, the CIA was notified of a second backtrack from an accented man. In fifteen minutes they had determined that the call originated from Fadi Kharrazi's media center in Tripoli.

Al-Nassar typed up his findings and presented them to Fadi.

The younger heir immediately read the report and threw it back at his assistant.

"I said I want to know who this man is, not who he says he is! This man is not a photographer; he is a spy working for the devil."

Fadi considered dialing the man in Miami directly, but remembered his last warning. Instead, he encoded a message in a photograph and posted a special notice on eBay.

During one of his daily surfs through the net, Ibrahim Haddad saw the tickler. He downloaded the photograph of a 45-year-old Omar Sharif from "Funny Girl." Embedded within the pixels was a cryptic message from Fadi. As Haddad read it he considered how much Fadi was his father's son.

He wanted Haddad to know that the Americans had sent someone in. If his brother's OIS goons were too stupid to recognize it, he certainly wasn't. Haddad doubted the assumption. Nonetheless, he had long ago realized that their operation had more reason to fail than succeed, so he took everything very seriously, as if his life depended on it.

Haddad had one contact in the FBI so deeply placed he rarely called. Today would be the exception.

BOSTON, MASSACHUSETTS

At Katie's house, Roarke fulfilled his part of the bargain. Through a dummy AOL screen name he created, he emailed the photograph and information to O'Connell that Penny had sent him. Then he used Katie's scanner to make jpeg files of the photo of Lodge and his father he'd picked up at Ciccolo's and the admittedly poor yearbook picture from the daughter of the classmate. Roarke attached them to a note and fired it off to Touch Parsons at the FBI labs in Quantico.

Later, under the covers and between breaths, he told Katie he had to go back to Washington the next day.

"Not if you can't get out," Katie said playfully reaching down and pulling him between her legs. He responded instantaneously, as he had so many times over the past two days and nights.

"I really love having you here…and *there*," she whispered in his ear as they moved. He especially felt the *there* part as she squeezed her muscles around him. It was the first either of them used the word *love*. He knew what she really meant.

"Me, too. But I'll come again."

"And again," she said.

"And again, and again," Roarke replied.

"I can make sure of that." Which she did.

CHAPTER 35

DENVER, COLORADO
TUESDAY, AUGUST 19

"I call for the delegate vote," boomed Wendell Neill over the public address system.

Cheers filled the Denver convention center. Posters sporting pictures of Lodge and Lamden bobbed up and down in the aisles. The network cameras caught the wildly enthusiastic demonstration supporting the Democratic Party ticket.

Governor Lamden controlled a great many votes. Although he could have released them, too many supporters had worked too hard to just give them up. Even Lodge agreed. So until the state-by-state delegate count came to South Dakota, Lamden led. But when the Tennessee Democratic chairman stood a rumble began to grow on the convention floor. It started with stomping, then cheers, then the call for "Ted-dy! Ted-dy! Ted-dy!" The chairman tried many times over the next fifteen minutes to regain control of the hall.

Finally, Wendell Neill's voice cut through. "Will the delegation from Tennessee please cast your votes," Neill called out.

"Mr. Chairman. The great State of Tennessee, home to the king of rock 'n' roll, Elvis Presley; the National Football Champions, the Tennessee Titans; and the finest family values in the nation; proudly pledges all of its eighty delegates for the next President of the United States, Theodore Wilson Lodge!"

Before he finished, the room erupted. Teddy Lodge was now the official candidate of the Democratic Party.

WASHINGTON, D.C.

Vigran missed the delegate count. He was working late at the FBI.

The senior researcher had computer access to most of the official cases and a few of the unofficial ones. Tonight he searched the data bank looking for any information on Tomás Morales and Adam Giannini; keywords that he'd learned through a discrete telephone answering service.

The request had been urgent, the first one in years.

Vigran cursed the day he first gave in to the caller and his money. Now with his retirement only three years away, he was particularly nervous. But the man, who always remained anonymous, quoted a figure that made the risk worthwhile. He hoped.

DENVER, COLORADO
WEDNESDAY, AUGUST 20

Governor Lamden gave a rousing speech on the third night of the convention. The platform had been ratified to Lodge's specifications. The party called for increased spending on public education, health care reform, alternative energy partnerships with oil producing nations, and a number of initiatives for women, the poor, and the cities. He addressed each of them in his remarks and proclaimed Teddy Lodge as the president who would accomplish them all.

The broadcast networks covered the governor's speech; their first live telecast from the convention floor since breaking in for the South Dakota-Tennessee vote. The cable news channels offered more. Tomorrow, when Teddy Lodge walked to the podium at approximately

8 P.M. Mountain Time, 10 P.M. on the East Coast, the networks estimated an audience of 150 million viewers in the U.S. alone.

It was Newman's idea. "You're going to be introduced by a woman born on November 22, 1963."

Lodge figured the date was important. Then it came to him. *Holy shit, it's brilliant!*

"And she's from Dallas. You'll be swept along like a second Camelot."

THURSDAY, AUGUST 21

The congressman loved it. Newman was a brilliant strategist, but this was pure genius. A woman born the day President John F. Kennedy died. November 22, 1963. The anniversary always resonated with Democrats. Well over forty years after the assassination, it still carried incredible emotional impact. "Hell, after she introduces you they might as well swear you right in."

Alma Franklin, a black city counselor from Dallas, delivered the keynote address summoning the ghosts of the Kennedys and the promise of the future. When she finished, the crowd erupted in cheers for twelve minutes. Alma won them over and no doubt earned a secure place for her own political aspirations.

Scott Roarke watched on MSNBC from his home in Washington.

Morgan Taylor gathered with Republican Party strategists in the pressroom. He followed CBS's coverage, but five networks were turned on.

Katie Kessler tuned to ABC with a glass of her favorite summer wine, a '97 Kendall Jackson Merlot.

Chuck Wheaton recorded the speeches on NBC while he was out shooting reactions in Hudson for the Albany affiliate.

Ibrahim Haddad drank champagne and raised his glass in toast to the conservative Fox News Channel for its restrained commentary.

Michael O'Connell roamed the convention floor watching faces and writing notes.

And Haywood Marcus sat on a stool at Locke-Ober, the famous

Boston restaurant that catered to people who still wore suits. A TV set was tuned to WBZ, the local CBS affiliate.

At precisely 8:01 P.M. in Denver the overhead lights dimmed in the convention hall and the Verilights shot their patterns across the ceiling. A full band struck up "Fanfare for the Common Man" and a single high-powered beam illuminated a deep navy blue curtain.

The intensity in the house built as curtains on the stage parted to reveal a rich red curtain behind it. The music built, then the red curtain opened to reveal another. This one stark white. Instead of parting, it raised as the light source switched from front to back, silhouetting the tall form of Teddy Lodge through a haze of smoke.

Lodge stepped forward like a conquering rock idol. At the proper timpani crescendo in the music, also perfectly timed, the spotlight hit him full front. Lodge shot his arms into the air in a majestic wave, stealing a scene from a Paul McCartney concert. He wore a blue pinstripe suit with a powder blue shirt and the same handcrafted red tie he had on the day Jenny Lodge died. Some eagle-eyed reporters would note it.

Teddy looked tanned and rested. Slimmer than he'd appeared last on camera. He had let his hair grow out and fans from backstage blew air frontward, giving more life to the moment. Amid all the lighting and effects Teddy Lodge appeared absolutely triumphant.

For fourteen minutes the cheering continued at an ear-shattering pitch. His speech would be secondary. These were the images that would lead the news for days and run on the front pages of newspapers coast to coast.

Like everything else in politics, it came down to who you were and what you believed.

Roarke viewed it as a circus. President Taylor's staff laughed at the ridiculousness of the staging. But the average viewer couldn't help but be drawn into the drama and emotion.

"Ted-dy! Ted-dy! Ted-dy!" reverberated throughout the room, cascading into a pounding rhythm.

"Thank you. Thank you. This is all so overwhelming," Lodge said motioning the conventioneers to quiet down. "Thank you."

The cheers continued unabated for another two minutes and the congressman cried. He took a handkerchief out and dried his eyes.

A news photographer for *Time* with a 200mm telephoto lens on his Canon camera pushed in for a close-up.

"Please. It's getting late on the East Coast. People have to get to work tomorrow," Lodge said playfully. "You're so wonderful. Thank you."

At last the convention hall hushed and Teddy Lodge nodded.

Looking to his right where the previous speaker stood, he blew a kiss and said, "I love Alma!" To everyone else he added, "Don't you?"

The cheers began again. This time for Alma Franklin. The statuesque woman came forward and Teddy Lodge kissed her, held her hand high, kissed her again showing his thanks and gratitude, and then kissed her hand and bid her goodbye. It was great theater, fully choreographed and rehearsed. Alma threw kisses to the crowd and left taking a seat behind Teddy. She'd be in all of the head to toe camera shots of the congressman; an intended reminder of what she brought to the ticket and a focal point where Jenny would have sat.

Teddy gestured a last "thank you" to Alma and then stepped up to the microphones. It was time to begin.

"I…" he looked around. The move commanded attention. "I have an idea," he whispered. The television, radio and Internet audiences caught the words, but the convention audience didn't. Newman's perfect staging.

"I have," he forced his voice louder, "an idea." He said it a little louder getting attention from the crowd. The media's microphones picked up the "Shssssses" and the congressman repeated, even louder, "I have an idea."

"I have an idea how we should live. Now let me share it with you."

A blanket of silence fell over the room.

"It's not a radical idea. But it's different. It's not a hard idea to grasp, but it will be difficult to achieve. It's not an idea for some, it has to work for us all."

From the wings, Newman smiled to himself. Alma's speech recalled Kennedy. Lodge now spoke to Martin Luther King. He bet the significance would not be lost on the commentators in their analysis.

"I," he paused with greater emphasis, "have an idea that *will* succeed. Not just because *I* want it to, but because *we* have to."

"America is at a crossroads. We can choose to live in the world we are given, or make the world we deserve. No longer can we shrink from accepting our responsibility as leader. We must lead. No more can we take from foreign markets. We must give back. And no more can we ignore reality. We must face up to it."

Roarke dismissed it all as rhetoric, but realized how effectively Lodge was coming off. He'd be impossible to beat, which wouldn't be so bad. He was already thinking of moving up to Boston.

"I have an idea," he paused. "I have an idea that we must demonstrate beyond a shadow of a doubt that we are prepared to enforce the law of society on those who would dare do us harm. Yet, we must show that the way out of the shadows is by illuminating those things we don't understand. The differences between women and men, black from white, rich and poor, and religion from religion, Arabs from Jews, Democrats from Republicans." He let the last words echo.

Haywood Marcus downed the last of his drink at the bar and slapped a fifty on the counter.

"You leaving, Mr. Marcus?" the bartender asked him.

"Yeah."

"But Teddy is still speaking." He tossed his head to the TV screen above.

"I'll catch it on the news tonight."

"I wasn't sure about it before, but he's gonna make it," the bartender added.

"He's been counting on being president for a long, long time," Marcus said as he folded his jacket over his arm. "See ya soon, Timothy."

The bartender didn't hear him. Like everyone else at the bar, his attention was on the TV.

Marcus closed the door to Locke-Ober as Lodge continued to mesmerize his audience.

"For only in the light will we see the path to tomorrow..."

Marcus was up for a satisfying walk. He quickly crossed from Boston's financial district into the North End and heard Lodge's speech as he passed open windows.

Normally in August, the North End was crowded with tourists or kids playing between the closely parked cars. Normally, people were on the streets celebrating festivals devoted to Madonna Della Cava,

Madonna Del Soccorso, St. Grippini, and St. Anthony. Normally there was music filling the air and old women leaning out the windows. Normally it was safe to walk along the narrow cobblestone streets that intersected Hanover. Tonight most people were inside watching the convention and their candidate, Teddy Lodge.

"Make no mistake, the swords of the United States will stand at the ready. But so will the pen to sign new declarations of peace."

He heard the thunderous applause echo off the buildings. And he smiled.

"We are a tolerant people, but intolerant of others who conspire against us. To those people and countries, I guarantee, you will fail if you attack America. But to those who want to join in a new age of reason, give us the reason to help you."

Marcus wondered, as he often did, how he would personally benefit. *A Federal Court judgeship? No, better. Three seats on the Supreme Court should come up in the next four years.* That's where he believed he belonged.

He was so absorbed in his own future that he didn't see a young man step out of the shadows. It could have been broad daylight and he wouldn't have noticed. The Supreme Court was such an awesome dream. It would be his greatest achievement as a lawyer.

The sound of Congressman Lodge's voice accompanied Marcus down Battery, Fleet, and North Streets. He caught phrases like *"the greater need to build nations up rather than beating people down,"* and *"finding the courage to fight isn't enough, being brave enough to forge lasting peace is…"*

He didn't sense the danger coming toward him. He didn't see the cruelty in the man's eyes. Now, even the words blaring out of TV and radio speakers in the apartments above didn't reach him. Haywood Marcus, self-absorbed, focused on his own destiny; the Supreme Court seat, the prestigious black robe, the austere bench, and his place in history.

"I have an idea," Lodge's voice boomed out.

The man approaching Marcus raised his arm. A glint of something shiny caught the streetlight. Then a compressed pop and a puff of smoke. It was over before Marcus was even aware that he was about to die.

The man, dressed in faded jeans, baggy boxers hanging over his belt loops, and an oversized sweatshirt, now held Marcus' lifeless body. He quickly slid him by the heels into a doorway and rummaged through his jacket and pants pockets extracting his wallet, credit cards and cash.

He'd use the credit card at a liquor store, then dump everything except the cash in the gutter. He'd done this before. This time he wore beaten up sneakers, not his usual boots. They didn't work with his outfit. This time he was a gang member. The next time, well, he just wasn't sure.

"...and my idea includes every living person on the face of the earth."

CHAPTER 36

WASHINGTON, D.C
FRIDAY, AUGUST 22

Coverage of Congressman Lodge dominated Boston's morning papers and early news. Nothing about Haywood Marcus made air until 11 A.M. Once it was out, word spread quickly through the office. The law firm issued a statement punctuating Marcus' esteemed accomplishments and his skill as a lawyer. Colleagues gathered in the halls, stunned by the senseless robbery and murder.

Katie Kessler believed robbery had nothing to do with it and the murder was anything but senseless. She reached Roarke on his cell phone.

"What?" the Secret Service agent shouted. "Say that again."

"Marcus is dead. Shot and robbed walking in the North End."

"Robbed my ass," Roarke interrupted.

"That's what I figured, too. Scott, what's this mean?"

"I'll get back to you, sweetheart. Gotta go." He hadn't answered her question.

Roarke called Shannon Davis' office at the FBI. "I need everything you can get on a shooting last night in Boston," he demanded. "Murder victim. The name is Haywood Marcus."

"Marcus? Like in the Boston law firm?"

"Same one."

"That's a coincidence," the FBI man said, not believing it.

"Yeah, right," Roarke said, agreeing.

On another floor, Roy Bessolo opened an e-mail on his computer. An agent working on a case in Idaho had a footprint match he wanted to discuss. Bessolo worked on so many cases he didn't give it much attention until a second e-mail popped up.

"Re: Latent print Sun Valley, ID—Hudson, NY 2nd analysis."

This time Bessolo went right to the phone.

"Bessolo. You e-mailed me."

"Yes, thanks," said Jake Messenger, the Denver field officer. "Figured you might be interested in this. I was running the evidence analysis on a possible heart attack that one of our people lifted nearby." He hadn't been privy to the news it wasn't a heart attack. "Well, I've been away on vacation and I just got back. After going through all of my messages, I saw the results of a routine search I put out to the Bureau. A case in Hudson, New York came up. Hudson was where the guy took a potshot at Congressman Lodge, right?"

"In a matter of speaking."

"Well, 97 percent likelihood the footprint you pulled is a match to the one I got. A right Frey boot, basic signatures are the same, except a few more on mine. Probably for the wear and tear since."

"Holy shit!" Bessolo shouted into his phone. "I want everything you have and every way to reach you. Cell phone, home phone. Your pager. Christ, I want to know that I can reach you even when you're banging your wife."

Forty-five minutes later, Bessolo had what he needed. He read through the file. Maybe this case would finally break. Of course, one boot print didn't mean he had a suspect. But it was a start. He read on. Now who the hell was this Nunes guy? He read further and saw that another agent had his hand on the file, too. Shannon Davis.

"All right, Davis. What the fuck is this all about?"

Shannon Davis recognized Bessolo's voice. He closed his eyes and imagined Bessolo towering over him; his head as bald as a bowling ball, his body wound tighter than an eight-day clock. He was an ass-hole, but a great agent.

"What are you talking about?"

"You've been asking about a guy named Nunes?"

"Yes."

"Well, seems that a footprint lifted near the recently departed Nunes comes up as a match for a little case I'm working on."

"That's nice," he said without trying to give away his interest.

"Cut the shit you son of a bitch. This links back to the assassin in Hudson. And I want to know your involvement in this."

"Well, now that the pleasantries are out of the way, why don't you come down and we'll talk about it," Davis offered.

"No. I'll see you in the director's office."

Davis gulped. This was escalating fast. "I'll be there."

Bessolo ignored the elevator and ran for the stairs. He beat Davis to Robert Mulligan's office where he treated the FBI Director's secretary to the same soft sell.

"Get me in to see Mulligan now," he stated. "Shannon Davis will be down, too."

She notified the director. Bessolo's name carried weight. He got his meeting.

By the time Davis walked in, Bessolo was already standing over Mulligan's desk, pointing to some papers. He looked pissed.

"Shannon."

"Bob, good to see you."

"I take it you know Roy."

"Yes. We met about three years ago. November. The Mystic Seaport security breach."

"The al-Qaeda break-in," Bessolo shot back.

"You did a good job."

"You got in the way," Bessolo answered.

"Enough, gentlemen," the FBI Director said. "Now that we've established you have a little history between you, let's talk about this."

Mulligan pulled a picture of Alfred Nunes. He tossed it in front of Davis.

"Both of you, take seats. Shannon, you're on."

Davis began. "Alfred Nunes. Healthy until a few weeks ago.

Apparent heart attack. Now suspected sodium morphate-induced murder."

"Come again?" Bessolo asked.

"Wait. Who is Nunes?" Mulligan asked.

"You'll find this interesting. Former family attorney for the Lodges. Congressman Teddy Lodge's family."

"This isn't your case, Shannon. Mind telling me why you're so expert in this?"

"Scott Roarke asked me for some help a few weeks ago."

"Roarke?" Bessolo boomed. "Who the hell is—"

"Secret Service," Mulligan explained. "Special detail."

The director made a quick decision. "Roy, will you excuse us for a few moments."

"What?"

Bessolo showed his displeasure, but left without complaint when Mulligan tapped his watch and held up five fingers.

"I'll be just outside." Bessolo said.

Mulligan waited until they had privacy then simply asked, "Roarke?"

"Yes, sir. But…"

"No 'but's.' You work for me. Not Roarke. Not his boss." The latter could be debated.

"Now think about this very hard before you answer. Do you believe he has any political motives? That he's acting on behalf of Taylor for any political reason?"

"None, sir."

"You're sure?"

"Positive." *I hope.*

The FBI chief thought about it through a deep sigh.

"Let's hope so. Because this whole thing is suddenly getting more complicated."

"Oh?"

"Yes, and now that you volunteered to join this goddamned party, let me tell you about a man named Dolan."

Davis packed everything relevant into his attaché case and headed to Roarke's White House basement office. On his way he called. "You got yourself a partner, so clear off your grease board, buddy. We need to sort out a bunch of stuff."

Roarke met Davis with a red marker in hand. He had already started writing after the FBI man's urgent call. At the top was *Teddy Lodge* and beside his name, *Jenny Lodge*.

"I have a few for you to add." Davis said when he got settled. He leafed through a note pad and began to dictate names that Roarke wrote down in block letters.

"Good, I need to see how this all lays out."

"Then below *Teddy Lodge* add *Sidney McAlister*, the assassin. Then further down, *Frank Dolan*."

This was a new name that Davis threw out to Roarke; a man known to have been in the St. Charles Hotel and involved in the death of a Connecticut commuter, Steven Hoag. Mulligan had offered it up to Davis during their earlier conversation and Roarke added it to the right side.

"Tell me about this Dolan character."

"I don't have much. But I do have a nagging suspicion that your boss can find out more from my boss. Or vice versa. The file is sealed. What I have gathered is this guy Dolan occupied the room that McAlister ultimately needed to get his direct shot. He checked out, McAlister conveniently checked in. Now it appears that Dolan can't be found. The number and address he gave to the hotel desk were fake."

Roarke put a question mark after Dolan.

"And Hoag?"

"A guy on a train. Killed two days after the assassination attempt on Teddy Lodge. Business manager at a publishing company. Beyond that, I can't tell you."

"And he's dead."

"Deader than a door nail. Now add *Alfred Nunes*, then *Haywood Marcus*. Do it above Hoag."

"Three dead guys on one side," Roarke said. "Let me move *Jenny Lodge* to the middle. And see what connections we can make." He drew his first line, the obvious one, between McAlister and Jenny.

"One," Davis said. "Now here's a new one for you."

"Oh?" Roarke raised his eyebrow.

"Hot off the wires. But not for publication. Courtesy of Roy

Bessolo, who's heading up the Hudson investigation. He called to find out why I was snooping around Nunes."

"Why would he…"

"Wait, it gets better. He got my name because the Denver office called him about a footprint they lifted upriver from our friend Alfred Nunes. Matched one his team had found. Guess whose?"

Roarke didn't need to look at the board. "McAlister," he said solemnly.

"Draw your next line, Mr. Roarke. McAlister to Nunes."

"I'll do you one better," Roarke said, "Connect McAlister to Haywood Marcus."

"Why?"

"Marcus' killer is possibly our very busy and talented assassin."

Roarke then put a line through the names of everyone now dead: *Jenny Lodge, Alfred Nunes, Haywood Marcus* and *Steven Hoag*.

"So what's the connection with this Hoag guy?" Davis pondered.

"I can't say. But considering that McAlister and Dolan are related, why don't we add lines between the two men at the hotel and carry it over to the late Mr. Steven Hoag."

Roarke finished and stood back to examine their handiwork, Grease boards helped him see the big picture. This was as big as they get.

Alfred Nunes
Jenny Lodge
Teddy Lodge
Haywood Marcus
Sidney McAlister
Steven Hoag
Frank Dolan

"Four deaths, two trigger men," Roarke noted.

"Seems that way. Considering the footprints in Hudson and Idaho. And Dolan also showing up in two places."

Roarke examined the board for a long minute. "You know, this requires an incredible amount of planning. Tons of coordination and money. An assassination attempt in Hudson, a successful hit a few days later in Connecticut. Then Nunes' poisoning out West and Marcus' death in Boston. What's intentional and what's the cover up?"

"And who's behind it all?" Davis asked.

"A very good question. I'd say it isn't McAlister or Dolan. Someone else. Somewhere."

"Someone wanted Teddy Lodge out of the picture. But he also decided to have two people killed who handled his parents' estate. Why? And instead of eliminating him from the election, his action has the opposite effect."

Opposite effect?

The words hung in the air.

Did they have the opposite effect?

Davis kept talking, but Roarke's mind was elsewhere—on Touch Parsons' photo locked in his desk.

QUANTICO, VIRGINIA
FBI LABS

"Thanks for the e-mail. I'll give you an 'A' for effort, a 'B' for results. Good shot of the father. Okay one of the screaming kid. And the yearbook shot's passable." Touch Parsons said.

The computer expert typed in some keystrokes and his work came up.

Roarke was more than curious. "And…"

"I got the refinement I needed. You can throw that old rendering out. This is it. And sometime I'd love to compare it against an actual contemporary shot of the guy and see how accurate I am. Feeds the ego. Do you have one?"

"Oh, plenty," Roarke affirmed, surprising the FBI computer expert.

"Well then, I look forward to seeing it. But presto change-o, here goes." Touch pressed the commands and the age progression began.

Five minutes later, Roarke had a hard copy in his hand.

"Not bad. Huh?" Touch boasted.

Roarke nodded. As he examined the computer rendering, he figured that Parsons was either the very best in the world at this or one of the worst.

The picture was different from the first. Based on what he had extrapolated from his family traits, the hair receded more gradually. The nose was now narrower, while the chin spread and the cheeks rose higher.

"The picture of the father gave me a whole new way to look at the way his face would widen in his late forties. Still, if I had his mother, I could do more. But even the high school photo helped out a bit."

"And you feel pretty damned good about this?" Roarke asked.

"I'd run it in the newspaper like it was taken yesterday."

Roarke could pull any number of pictures from yesterday's news coverage of Congressman Lodge and not one of them would resemble this man.

All he said in addition to "thanks" was, "I'll be back."

Outside on his cell phone, Roarke went right to the point. "Meet me back at my office. I have a new photo for you."

"Good," Davis said. "Because I have something else for your third column."

LANGLEY, VIRGINIA
GEORGE H.W. BUSH CENTER FOR CENTRAL INTELLIGENCE

Jack Evans closed the Tripoli report. The CIA analysts had satellite images of Fadi's building and D'Angelo's assessment of the objective. Now the job would go to mission strategists. How to get in, where to go once inside. How to extract the files in Fadi Kharrazi's office, and most importantly, how to get out. Evans couldn't predict whether such an operation would ever go active, but an operational plan had to be developed, even rehearsed.

TRIPOLI, LIBYA

"A week and no message back from Ibrahim. Who does he think he is?"

Omar Za'eem was used to the tirades through the flimsy wall. Fadi shouted all the time even when he didn't have anyone to yell at. His voice carried through Lakhdar al-Nassar's office and out to where Omar sat.

"Lakhdar!" he yelled. "Lakhdar, get in here!"

"Yes, sir." The aide rushed into Fadi's office. He knew the consequences if he dawdled. There was always another assistant in line to move up. Advancement usually came at a high price, so al-Nassar prayed daily that his position wouldn't suddenly become available to his own lackey, Za'eem.

"I'm here," he said. "What can I do?"

"This man Morales. I know nothing more now than I did a week ago." He started calmly, but his voice rose quickly.

Al-Nassar thought better of answering.

"I have incompetents everywhere!"

"Yes sir."

"Everything's going to change soon. Everything. Now get me a tea."

Lakhdar left and shook his head as he walked up to his assistant. "You heard him!" he shouted to Omar. "Get the man some tea."

Omar did as he was told and recited the words over and over that he had just heard. *Ibrahim and Morales.* Abahar would need to hear them, too.

COLLEGE PARK, MARYLAND

Vigran left a message on an answering service. He used a pay phone at a Denny's outside the District.

"Morales and Giannini clean. Credits in books. Recent entry 15 August. State Department inquiry on trip to Tripoli through London."

When he was finished, he wiped the phone clean of fingerprints and hoped he'd never get another request.

AL-ODAYDIA, QATAR
US AIR BASE
THURSDAY, AUGUST 28

President Morgan Taylor was doing what he did best—talking people off the ledge, calmly, clearly, and authoritatively. His hours in the cockpit under extreme pressure gave him the nerves of steel few opponents could match.

If he was dangerous at 35,000 feet and at 1,190 mph, he was positively lethal across the table. His eyes never swayed. They locked on his subjects the way his missiles found their targets.

Secretary of State Joyce Drysdale, herself presidential timber, met with the prime ministers of India and Pakistan individually. India's prime minister, Dr. Rajesh Khosla, and Pakistan's Zulfigar Sajjad got both an earful of warnings and a list of concessions. In the end, it was the promise of economic aid, not U.S. concerns over their weapons of mass destruction, that brought them to the negotiating table with the President of the United States.

Too much depended on these deliberations. Taylor remembered how close Clinton had come to forging a peace between the Israelis and the Palestinians, only to see it end bitterly. This was not going to happen now. Taylor laid out his offers to each of them with little poker play. The deal was this: An immediate military stand-down in the region. Agreement by each nation to notify the United States 48 hours prior to any future missile tests within 500 miles of the border. Resumption of air routes between the two countries. In return, the U.S. would guarantee aid in cash, services and goods; additional funding for anti-terrorism efforts; and perhaps most important to the economy of both countries, U.S. financial help through the restoration and full development of free trade zones.

After four long days, which began with obstinate posturing, Morgan Taylor had his peace. On the morning of the fifth day, the president woke early. At 0459 he stepped in front of a single camera in the base's briefing room. There was a lectern in front and an American flag draped behind as a simple backdrop. Outside, a portable satellite uplink beamed the video halfway around the world. Morgan Taylor wore a dark blue three-piece suit with a plain white shirt and a dynamic red tie. The American colors on the American president. He'd gotten little rest since he left Washington nearly a week ago, but his weariness was not apparent to the camera now.

It was seven hours earlier on the East Coast of the United States, 9:59 P.M. the previous night.

"Ready, Mr. President?" asked the network producer who had flown the distance.

"Let's do it."

The producer talked to the pool feed master control operator in New York and got the go. "Okay sir, coming to you. In ten, nine, eight…"

The president took his cue and began to address the Republican National Convention.

"Ladies and Gentlemen, please excuse me for not being there in person. My day job took me out of town."

Teddy Lodge hated any time Taylor used the presidency. This was one of them.

He watched the broadcast from Qatar and recognized that if Taylor had good news he'd get some political currency from what he'd accomplished. However, he also believed the benefits to his campaign would be temporary. The country had already begun its psychological shift away from the president. In less than three months, the voters would affirm it.

PHILADELPHIA, PENNSYLVANIA

Everyone in the convention hall watched Morgan Taylor on the huge plasma screen. It had been agreed that there would be no applause or cheering, spontaneous or planned, until the president concluded his remarks. So unlike the hoopla surrounding Congressman Lodge's speech, Morgan Taylor's was subdued and serious; an address from a statesman rather than a speech from a politician.

The result was quite mesmerizing and unlike any convention appearance on record.

"The possibility of war is much too real," the president continued. "Guns are aimed. Their safeties off. Missiles have their targets. The American political system will continue. But what of the lives of the people in these two countries? More than a billion in India alone. Another 160 million in Pakistan. That's why I'm here," the president explained. "That's why I am not with you to say thank you in person for honoring me with your nomination. But we live in perilous times where situations dictate how we must act.

"Today's winds of war carry more than hatred. They carry radiation far beyond the field of battle. They carry death to innocent people who can't draw the borders that are in dispute, who can't pronounce the names of the cities that will be destroyed, and who can't ask, 'Why have you done this to me?'"

The president grew even more serious. "There is nothing, mark my words, nothing more important than securing peace. There is no greater goal for a president or a citizen. And so, I am a world away because a majority of Americans put their trust in me four years ago. But I am here as your president for *all* Americans.

"At this time, I can report to you that we have achieved the peace I sought. India's Prime Minister, Dr. Rajesh Khosla, and Mr. Zulfigar Sajjad, Prime Minister of Pakistan and I have been talking candidly with one another. That is as it should be. Responsible leaders with their coats off, their sleeves rolled up, and their hands open in greeting. True, they are far from being close friends, but today they are not mortal enemies. We have peace."

The applause from the delegates began despite the ground rules. But the president, not hearing the return feed, pressed on.

"So please accept my apologies for my absence. I appreciate your confidence and, yes, I proudly accept your nomination."

And that's when the cheering for Morgan Taylor erupted and Teddy Lodge threw his glass, smashing it on the TV screen.

CHAPTER 37

WASHINGTON, D.C.
TUESDAY, SEPTEMBER 2

Predictably, the Qatar speech announcing a fragile peace accord gave the president a needed boost. By Labor Day, it looked like a good old horse race again.

The first debate was scheduled to be held in three weeks. Political analysts now believed the election would rest on how the candidates faired in their head-to-head confrontations.

In the meantime, while Morgan Taylor got down to the actual business of running for reelection, Roarke felt his own investigation slow down.

"Come on, Shannon. Give me some news," he pleaded over a drink at one of the Capitol's famed watering holes, the formally informal Tabard Inn.

"Stone cold, buddy," Davis said looking at his own reflection in the mirror lining the wall.

"What are we missing?" Roarke asked just below ear level of Sean O'Reilly, the bartender.

Roarke reached into his pocket for a piece of paper. Finding none, he grabbed a napkin from the bar and started writing.

"What are you doing?" Shannon asked. He held up two fingers for O'Reilly and mouthed, "Two more Coors." He figured they'd be there for a while. "And a couple of burgers, too," he yelled out.

"So what are you doing?"

"Taking another look at our chart."

Roarke jotted just initials representing all the names. Then he added the lines replicating the connections made on the grease board in his office.

"I'm still stuck on Hoag," he said.

He circled the abbreviations for Nunes, Marcus, Hoag. "These people knew something."

"No shit, Sherlock," Davis laughed. "A bungled job to get Lodge out of the running. And then the need to cover up. Hoag was connected, somewhere. But what did Nunes know that we should know? I say we go in with a subpoena and find out."

"By now nothing will be there."

"What do you mean?" Davis asked.

The drinks arrived and Roarke held off from answering. Davis thanked O'Reilly, then rephrased his question. "How do you know?"

"I saw them and now they're gone."

"Uh oh."

"Don't worry. I didn't break in anywhere."

"'And that, your honor, is my client's case for the defense.' So long!" Shannon held up his glass in a toast. "See you in twenty."

"Hey, asshole, they were sort of open on a desk in front of me."

"Sort of…"

"Look, I went in inquiring. Nicely. Through a *friend*."

"Then we can get a subpoena."

"Too late. My friend says they're gone. I gotta believe Marcus fed them all to the shredder."

"So we're back to suppositions."

"Right, which don't mean a flying fuck," Roarke concluded.

The two men ate their hamburgers, settled up the bill and walked in the fall air toward the Metro station.

"So who wants Lodge dead?" Davis asked, returning to the point.

"And why?" Roarke asked softly.

"Well, if we're trying to come up with names, I'd say your boss," Shannon blurted out. They stopped. Taylor would have had an easier run at the office against anyone but Lodge. A president certainly had the means. And this president had killed before.

"Not that I think he did," Davis added quickly looking over his shoulder. No one heard him.

"There's one basic problem with that notion." Roarke began to laugh. "If he loses in November it'd probably be the happiest day of his life!"

The two men continued to walk toward the subway. After a run of more jokes at the expense of Morgan Taylor, Davis turned more serious.

"So one more time, just for me. Who wants Teddy Lodge dead? And why?"

Once again Roarke asked, "Why?"

MIAMI, FLORIDA

Ibrahim Haddad programmed his computer so encoded messages were immediately expunged. He had another rule: No notes. Nothing that led to him on paper. Ever. And the phone call from Tripoli. *Incredibly stupid.* While he had no doubt that the NSA super computers were completely capable of matching the voice of his caller with a recording of the General Kharrazi's son, the chance of it being checked was slim to none.

So Ibrahim Haddad believed things were good. With the exception of Marcus, he hadn't had any direct personal contact with anyone involved in the operation for decades. The last time he could remember doing anything himself was when he wished a well-trained young man goodbye at Heathrow.

Haddad's only real worry was with the damned fickle American voters. They never seemed to stay with one man.

THE WHITE HOUSE
THURSDAY, SEPTEMBER 4

"Boss, you're pretty good at spotting targets from high up. I need some help here."

Roarke had gotten on the president's schedule with a simple call to Louise Swingle. He hardly ever thought about the immediate access he had to Morgan Taylor. Today he did, and he used it, almost afraid where the conversation would go.

"Depends on the terrain. Have I been over it before?"

"You'll have to tell me," Roarke said sharply. "And I need you to be truthful."

The use of the word "truthful" caught the president off-guard. He didn't say anything, but his mood definitely changed. He put his coffee down and watched intently as Roarke removed a legal pad of paper, a folded poster board and a small wooden easel from a black leather shoulder bag. Roarke unfolded the cardboard and set it up on the stand.

"Have a seat," he told the president. "This is going to take a little bit of time."

Taylor scanned the card, a flow chart with familiar names, but lines drawn between them, creating relationships and the basis for Roarke's explanation.

As Roarke began, he noticed that the president's eyes almost imperceptibly shifted to the name *Hoag*. Morgan Taylor was a very good poker player. He rarely showed his cards, but Roarke recognized a blink when he saw one. He completed his review of the chart and addressed the president.

"If I can put these names together, so can any diehard late night radio talk show conspiracy theorist like Elliott Strong. And you know what? The first person they'll point at is you."

"Now wait a goddamned second," the president huffed.

Roarke continued unaffected. "Look, I can't control what Strong or anyone else might pick up on. On face value, the man who you least wanted to run against was nearly killed. But he lived. And he even gets the nomination. Would he have if his wife hadn't died?"

The president looked over Roarke's shoulder into the eyes of Franklin Roosevelt. A portrait of the 35th president hung on the wall over the Adams chair. Of all the American leaders, Taylor admired Roosevelt the most. For a man who never served in the military, FDR was a brilliant strategist. His cunning gamesmanship combined with a ruthless desire to crush any enemy. Any. He disarmed political adversaries as well as nations. Roosevelt used his disability to lure foes closer, thinking he could not strike. And they were all wrong.

Roarke broke the president's concentration. "So you tell me, Morgan, were you involved?"

The president slowly turned to Roarke and without hesitation, without emotion, stated in one word the truth. "No."

Roarke accepted the answer from his friend and smiled. "You knew I had to ask."

"Yes, I did."

"Now, something you can't deny," Roarke noted. "One name on the board caught your attention."

The president looked as if he didn't understand the question.

"There's one name on the chart that you focused on. I saw it."

"Was there?"

Roarke pointed to the right hand column. "Hoag. Steven Hoag. How about you tell me what you know about him, boss?"

The president let out a small laugh, as if to say, *You're a smart sonofabitch.*

"I'm sorry, Scott. I'm afraid I can't."

"Can't or won't?"

"It's extremely sensitive."

"Like Jennifer Lodge's brain when the bullet shot through it? Like the kid's reaction in the crowd?"

Morgan Taylor sighed deeply. Roarke wasn't making it easy for him.

"Who is he, Mr. President?" Roarke said forcefully.

The president looked at the painting of FDR again.

"Who is he?" Roarke asked again one more time. "Fuck security! Who is he?"

"Want a drink?" the president said, rising to get one for himself.

Roarke declined, waiting for his question to be answered.

The president poured himself a glass of port from a bottle on a silver tray. "Jack Evans should be here for this. He knows more than I do."

"Who's Hoag?"

The president took a sip on his way to his desk. He pressed an intercom button on his phone. Louise Swingle immediately answered. "Yes, Mr. President?"

"Louise, have Bernsie take my meeting with the Secretary of the Interior. I'm going to be awhile with Scott."

"Of course, sir. I'll call him now."

The president invited Scott to join him at the couch.

"Many years ago, at the height of the Cold War, the Soviets created a specialized spy school for the most elite students. They called it Andropov Institute, after Yuri Andropov. It was the principal training ground of the FCD—the First Chief Directorate of the old KGB. That was pretty well known by us and British intelligence. But lesser known or not known at all were the closed Soviet cities. ZATO, as they were dubbed."

"ZATO?"

"It's an acronym. You're not going to make me try to pronounce it?" Roarke encouraged him.

The president went to his desk, pressed something underneath in a sequence which Roarke suspected was a coded lock, then opened a drawer. He removed a file that read "Top Secret." On the first page he found what he wanted.

"Okay, but it won't be pretty. *Zakrytye administrativno-territori-al'nye obrazovaniia*. ZATO."

"Thank you," Roarke said, stifling a laugh.

The president reclaimed his seat. "These cities were uncharted on maps and usually named after the closest administrative centers. A simple post office designation helped the mail get through." He looked at his report again. "Like Krasnoyarsk-26 or Chelyabinsk-45. Most of them were physically closed, surrounded by high concrete walls. Access was permitted only with the most stringent proof. Some of the ZATO cities were designed for the creation and testing of biological warfare. We figure there were at least 40, about ten were devoted to nuclear research and missile testing. But the Soviets ran another 15 ZATO for other purposes. We believe a few served as remote campuses for Andropov I."

"Which was?"

"Have you ever heard of Red Banner?"

"No."

"Few people have. Red Banner was a unique division of the Andropov Institute, with very unusual classes."

Roarke settled into the seat for what he gathered would be a complicated story.

"Red Banner graduated many people with special talents. They offered a variety of courses that couldn't be found elsewhere. Even Aleksandr Putin went through the school before serving in East Germany. Most relevant was a special curriculum nicknamed Red Banner 101. '101' for introductory. Students went in as Russians. They came out as Americans."

"I don't like where this is going," Roarke commented.

"This was total immersion training. The purpose was to graduate men and women who could pass as Americans," the president emphasized, "in America. That was the purpose: integration in American life; some as active spies, others as *sleepers* waiting for their assignments.

"The students never knew each other's real names and many never saw one another again unless they were sent into the field as couples. Oh, and they had a *no fail* policy. That's not to say you couldn't fail, but you wouldn't live long enough to get any remedial work. It was a killer course."

The president consulted his file before continuing again.

"Scott, let me give you a better picture of their success rate. For a long time, the Russians were pretty inept at getting the basics of American life. They could perfect an accent, drive an automatic, and disappear in a crowd, but it was the little things that confused them. The things that are so, so *normal* for us. Buying the right sneakers or toothpaste or jeans. They couldn't do it. Too many choices for them. They didn't even know where to begin. They'd try to haggle. Well, that's not the American way. They'd take one product not knowing the other is really what they needed. From what I understand, things were so culturally different, most of the spies didn't even have a clue.

"Just imagine landing here in a space ship and suddenly needing to apply for a house loan or buy a car. That's what it was like. Way beyond their comprehension. So eventually the KGB wised up and created a program designed to teach Russians the practical fundamentals of American life. Both men and women were enlisted. Sometimes the Soviets trained off site in Moscow apartments. People like Abel or London's Philby often lectured them. But Red Banner 101 was the main campus."

Roarke found the story totally fascinating.

"It was an acting job," the president continued. "The student spies lost their Russian accent, worked American idiomatic expressions into their speech, and became young Republicans or Democrats. Oh maybe they dreamt in Russian, but on the street you'd never know.

"Evans told me he heard from one former asset that a couple placed here as sleepers even raised a family in America. The wife was East German and he was a Czech citizen. They came to the U.S. from South Africa, via Canada, with a young son.

"Here's the worst of it. They made a spy out of their nineteen-year-old son while he was a student at Georgetown. Their other kid, born here, didn't know that mommy and daddy were Russian spies. But I can guarantee you the whole family would have been ready to serve old Mother Russia by the time they were through. And just string it out. The boys could have married and co-opted their wives…and then their children…and their wives. You see how insidious it is?"

Roarke followed the lesson. "This isn't going to have a happy ending, is it?"

"Well, in the case of this family, the older son was about to be sent back to Russia for more training, but the couple was brought in by the FBI. The DCI assures me we learned a great deal about Red Banner from them and the lengths to which they trained their actors for the roles of their lives.

"And now to your question. Who's Hoag? Much of the latest picture we have on the old Soviet intelligence apparatus comes from a man named Yuri Kusnitzoff. He learned to be an exceptional American at Red Banner. He blended right in, waiting a good twenty years to be activated. A leak in Moscow turned us onto him and I'm told that Evans' people had what you might term a 'come-to-Jesus meeting' with him.

"Kusnitzoff decided to share some information with us, a little bit at a time. Gradually we got the most complete picture of Red Banner we ever had. Through him we discovered that maybe one-hundred graduates remain in deep cover within our borders. They're still here, Scott. Still in America. Many of them have to be in their late forties or even much older. Who knows what their instructions are. Who controls them. Or whether they'll ever be activated."

The president paced. Heavy steps. "We were working on Kusnitzoff to identify other graduates, which so far he had been unwilling to give up, though he supplied us with other important information. But according to Evans, he recently called in. That's something he never did on his own. The CIA thinks he may have decided to report somebody else; a classmate. Or he had a change of heart on some other important information. But we won't find out from Kusnitzoff. You see, in the States he went by the name Steven Hoag."

The president stopped and smiled at Roarke. "Are you sure you won't take that drink now?"

Roarke went to get a glass. The president met him at the sideboard and poured the Tawny.

"Interesting when you consider it in context, Scott. What's a Russian spy got to do with an assassination attempt of a presidential candidate?"

"Shades of Lee Harvey Oswald," Roarke offered.

"Oh, that doesn't even scratch the surface, my boy," Taylor said. The two men stood side by side. "This runs deeper into American life. How deep, we don't know." The president handed Roarke his port. "Now, tell me what you're thinking."

Roarke took a sip and let the warmth work its way down. "You realize, nobody is who they're supposed to be."

The president frowned. "What do you mean?"

"Starting with what you just told me. Hoag is Kusnitzoff."

"And?"

"You're familiar with the name Sidney McAlister?"

"The assassin."

"What about Frank Dolan?"

"The man who shot Hoag."

"Yes. Well, as far as we can tell, neither of them exist, at least with those identities. So they have to be somebody else. *Who* is the question. But that's not all."

Roarke removed a manila envelope from his backpack and from within that, a photograph. "You tell me who it is."

He put the photo, not in the least looking computer-generated, on the art stand.

The president studied the picture and then asked, "I'll bite. Who is it?"

"It's an age progression photograph created by the FBI's top computer artist, the one you helped set up through Bob Mulligan. Touch Parsons. He's a wizard. He's able to take photographs of children and reliably predict what they'll look like later in life. It's proved invaluable for locating and identifying kidnapped kids."

"So who's this?" Taylor repeated.

"As far as I can tell, it's *nobody*."

"Okay," the president said looking closer. "It's nobody. Is it *supposed* to be somebody?"

"Mr. President, I believe it's supposed to be the man you're running against. Teddy Lodge."

CHAPTER 38

BURLINGTON, VERMONT
WEDNESDAY, OCTOBER 8

Teddy Lodge was ahead with Black voters, Hispanics, Jews, and most importantly in female demos. His crossover numbers were especially telling. Republican women openly talked about how good he looked to them. *The New York Times* poll had him ahead by nine percent, with a margin of error of three. If the momentum continued, he'd take the election by fifteen points. Lodge was going into the first debate on sure footing.

Geoff Newman ran Lodge through the mock debates as if they were real. He used law students as journalists and Madison Avenue consultants who critiqued him through real time sessions. They drilled him and coached him. And with every rehearsal, Lodge's responses drew sharper. He was prepared to answer the reporters directly and calmly and deflect any political salvo from the president.

In four days they'd both be tested. In one month the voters would decide.

At the end of the long day, Newman let Lodge catch up on his newspaper reading. He tossed him the *Times*. O'Connell's latest front-page article landed face up on his lap.

THE ICEMAN IN THE LODGE CAMP

A sub-heading clarified the point.

Geoff Newman: Cold and Calculating.

"The Iceman!" Lodge yelled out. "How did you let this happen?"

"Let it happen? I made it happen."

"What?"

"Classic good cop, bad cop. Makes you come off warmer. You were the only one who was interested in me. I was the only one who helped you. Read it."

Lodge did as he was told. O'Connell recounted Newman's early life in Germany, how his father was killed in the military helicopter crash, getting lost on his way to America, and his difficulties blending in at school.

The unusual fraternity he forged with Teddy Lodge gave him the ability to find himself through the success of another.

Lodge saw what Newman meant. While the reporter painted a personally acrimonious picture of Newman, he showed how their fellowship completed Lodge, helping him grow into a leader in school, in business, and in politics.

There were harsh words like "shrewd and calculating," but they were balanced with observations that termed Newman as "intense and determined." Altogether, O'Connell presented the most complete portrait of Newman to date.

Teddy Lodge may receive enough votes to become president, but if he wins, Geoff Newman is the one man who really got him elected. Come January 20th, the question may not be what Lodge will be doing, but which job he'll give to Newman. At times the two men appear to be inseparable parts of the same being, with the public potentially getting two presidents for the price of one.

The last line was not Lodge's favorite, but he clearly knew that the reporter had gotten that part of their story right.

A rare photograph of Newman's father in Germany accompanied the article.

"Nice picture of dear old Dad," Lodge said.

"Took me by surprise. But I give O'Connell credit. He did his homework. See the photo caption? 'Courtesy, U.S. Department of Defense.' Good digging."

Lodge nodded and continued. There were no other archival photographs, which wasn't surprising. There weren't any. Instead, the article relied on campaign photos and a still frame credited to Chuck Wheaton's video coverage from Hudson. The picture showed Newman consoling Lodge immediately following Jennifer Lodge's death.

"I can't believe it. The iceman melteth," Lodge joked.

"See, a picture is worth a thousand words."

HUDSON, NEW YORK
THURSDAY, OCTOBER 9

Chuck Wheaton's real paying job was teaching 20th-century world history to his high school students. Every autumn he ran one of his favorite films, Constantin Costa-Gavras' Academy Award winning 1968 conspiratorial tale, *Z*. He was absorbed in the intricate layers of the story, which masterfully fictionalizes the real life assassination of a notable Greek doctor and humanist. The movie's critical tension is owed to the subtle dialogue during the investigation. *Z* never failed to hold his students' attention.

The twenty-two Hudson High seniors watched the film over three class days. With only twenty minutes left the final day, Wheaton also sat mesmerized as if it were his first time screening the classic thriller. He'd seen it every fall for the last twenty-five years. The film was in French, but he could mouth the subtitles almost verbatim. There was a rhythm to the structure and to the dialogue. The key plot twist hinges on the conspirators using the same rehearsed phrase, "Lithe and fierce as a tiger." One government official and dubious character after another comes to testify before the chief investigator, played by Jean-Louis Trintignant. Each uses the same phrase that only they would know. Costa-Gavras cut the scenes together with an ever increasing pace, emphasizing the connection.

Suddenly Wheaton looked away from the screen. *The rhythm. Lithe and fierce as a tiger.* There was something utterly familiar to that rhythm. *What is it?*

He thought harder. *Something in the rhythm.* The audio of the French language film continued to fill the classroom; then without even realizing it, Wheaton was now mouthing English words to himself. Other words. He felt his palms perspire and his heartbeat quicken. He closed his eyes and pictured the movements that went with his words. Just as the words fit specific actions and gestures in the movie, so did the phrases echoing in his mind.

The film ended and the bell rang. Wheaton's students sat stunned, as they always did. But their teacher wasn't there to send them off to 5th period. He was already out the door to see an old friend.

"Carl, come on with me. I want you to watch the footage again."
The Hudson Police Chief had no doubt what footage Wheaton meant.

"Again?" Marelli asked putting down his coffee.

"Again."

"Without a hello?"

Wheaton realized he had pushed through the chief's door without an invitation. Both stupid and dangerous in any police station. "'Hello.' Now come. You've gotta see it. This time really closely. I can't believe I didn't catch this before."

"I've seen it a hundred times. What the hell are you talking about?"

"I can't explain it. Just come on."

Marelli stayed put. "This better not be about you playing cop."

The Hudson Police Chief knew that it was only Wheaton's football injury years ago that had prevented him from pursuing his earliest goal of becoming a policeman. In the fourth quarter of a championship game his senior year, a bulldozer disguised as a seventeen-year-old Albany Academy student blindsided him as he faded back to pass. Wheaton took the full force of the human Caterpillar in his knees. And his opponents took the game. Surgery and physical therapy ultimately restored much of the mobility he lost on the field that night, but it didn't give him the dexterity and strength required for police department entry.

Marelli was right, though. It was in Wheaton's DNA. Even after all these years, he wanted to think like a cop. Maybe that was why he slept with the police-band radio on and he was typically the first freelance cameraman in Columbia, Greene, and even Dutchess Counties to show up at a crime scene. Maybe that was why he couldn't stop screening the footage he shot.

"No," he answered. "Well, maybe yes. Who the hell knows. But don't give me any shit now. If you don't want to see it, I'll go directly to that FBI shithead. That'll look really good, won't it?"

"Alright already. I'll follow you."

"No tickets on the way?"

"No tickets. But don't push it." Marelli grabbed his hat and shooed Wheaton out the door.

After a near-record eleven-minute run, Wheaton was at his gravel driveway. He slammed his car door and tore into his studio to warm up his PC-driven digital edit bay before Marelli caught up.

"Coffee's over there behind me, just flick the switch. The water will start to drip," Wheaton said without looking.

"So what's got you all hot and bothered?"

"Today I flashed on something crazy. Here, watch." He pressed a green key on his keyboard and the video came up, well into Congressman Lodge's now fateful speech.

Congressman Lodge was speaking with great enthusiasm. *"We strike partnerships by sharing food and building up economies. We give. We get. We educate the world's uneducated, we make them intellectually stronger against dictators who would take advantage of their lack of knowledge."*

Marelli was surprised how much he had memorized himself. Lodge's complete speech was embedded in their consciousness.

"We give and we get. And yes, we share our knowledge of arms and our technological know-how to fight emerging terror in third world nations. So we won't have to rush in at an unacceptable cost of American lives. We give and we get."

"We build bridges to former adversaries and make them our friends," Lodge proclaimed on a close-up. Wheaton and Marelli heard the crowd, unseen at the moment, clamor, *"We Give and We Get."* They saw the congressman step back and smile, then approach the microphone again.

"Soon you will have to make a major decision," Lodge predicted on the playback. *"But it is not about one man over another. One candidate versus another. We are all responsible individuals, devoted to serving you. No, the decision is not about a person. It's about policy.*

"Walk with me to the future. We'll make a partnership for peace, celebrating all people of the world, with the United States of America as a full and valued partner.

"Better we go to welcomed arms than with arms unwelcomed.

"It will mean we take what we know to the world so the world will know more. And by so doing…"

And everyone cheered, *"We Give and We Get."*

Congressman Lodge peered over his left shoulder to Jenny then back, smiling to the crowd that continued to chant, *"We Give and We*

Get! We Give and We Get!" Over and over. *"We Give and We Get! We Give and We Get!"* Lodge raised his arms to quiet the crowd.

"It's time for a family of nations in a world apart," continued Lodge softly.

"Time for a family that will last into all of our tomorrows."

"Here's where I zoom out a little to include Jenny," Wheaton whispered during the congressman's pause.

"...a family for you...and," then another pause, *"and...a family for me."*

"And he'll bow his head forward in a second, just a little, and wipe his eyes."

Then the moment Marelli and Wheaton would never forget. The instant that Jennifer Lodge died in front of their eyes.

The policeman looked away. "Enough. I've seen this enough."

"You haven't begun to see it," Wheaton demanded. "Now again." The cameraman reset his computer with a thirty-second roll cue from the gunshot and hit play. Marelli took a deep breath.

"Really, no more, Chuck," the police chief complained.

But Wheaton ignored him. He slowed down the audio and video and described what he was seeing on screen.

"'And by doing so,' yadda, yadda, yadda. The next string of 'give and get.' Everyone's charged up. Now watch carefully, Carl. *Very* carefully."

He skipped forward a few seconds. The congressman spoke at one-quarter speed, the words stretched out. *"Time for a family that will last into all of our tomorrows."*

"My zoom out," Wheaton said again, then, "There." He pointed to the screen. As the camera widened to include Jennifer, Wheaton froze the shot. "His fingers. Watch his fingers on his right hand, by the side of his leg." He rolled more. Lodge finished saying *"a family for you,"* and the cameraman counted "one" aloud in sync with Lodge putting his index finger down and then "two" as Lodge added a second finger. Then the second phrase, *"a family for me."* And again Wheaton whispered "three" and "four" as Lodge repeated his action.

"He's counting, Carl. It's amazing. He's really counting the beats. I'll bet you a steak at Kozel's he's counting. Watch again."

Wheaton rewound the video. "Watch. The words have a rhythm

to them. So do the pauses. I swear he's timing the pauses. Two beats each."

As the tape played, Marelli moved closer to the screen.

"He's going to lean forward slightly to wipe his eyes. But now watch his count. Four seconds, Carl. Watch. He'll count it for you. One…two…three…four." And in the background Jennifer Lodge straightened her body never realizing that death had just gripped her.

Wheaton froze the shot on Jennifer. "He was timing it, Carl. Lodge was timing his move."

The police chief stared at the image, looking at the four fingers Lodge barely extended on his right hand. He looked down at his side. This time he had done exactly the same thing.

Wheaton's body shook and sweat poured down his forehead despite the air conditioning in his editing room. Marelli reached for a chair behind him. He swung it around, pulled up next to Wheaton and quietly said, "You may make rookie yet. Play that again for me, Chuck."

CHAPTER 39

FRIDAY, OCTOBER 10

The man hadn't worked in over a month, but on balance it had been a very good year. His offshore accounts had swollen by some three million dollars. All of it earned tax-free. The IRS wouldn't have approved of the deposits for any number of reasons, the least of all murder.

He read the news and surmised that his first shot had done as intended. The subsequent assignments fell more into the category of "insurance." Since he held no practical political positions and none of his various identities ever cast a vote, he really didn't care about any American presidents except the dead ones on U.S. currency.

Little got to him. Not even the urge to kill. Assassination was simply his profession. He could walk away from it, and happily would, if no other work came along. He did, however, answer his sexual desires. And one had been building for months. The hotel maid in Hudson, New York.

"Carolyn, it's for you," the front desk clerk at the St. Charles said. He'd found her cleaning a room on the third floor. "I'll put the call right through. Hang up. Here it comes."

"Hello," Carolyn Hill said a moment later. She didn't recognize the voice.

"Ms. Hill, this is Roger Waterman. I met you during the summer when I…"

"Yes, yes, of course." The call caught her off guard. "You haven't been here in months."

"Quite right. I've been busy traveling. Pennsylvania, Virginia. Scouting antiques. But I'm in the area, and I wanted to see if you had time for dinner?"

"Dinner?" This really surprised her. "Me?"

He instantly read it. "Absolutely, you."

She'd fantasized about this call. Now it had happened. "You're coming into Hudson?"

"Actually I'm not. I can't seem to get any further north than Poughkeepsie this trip. But, you could drive down, or better yet, just take the train."

"I don't know, I mean, I'm working…"

She wasn't. He'd memorized the schedules of everyone who worked at the hotel. "Don't you have Saturdays off? How about tomorrow afternoon?"

"Tomorrow? This tomorrow?" she laughed, knowing full well she hadn't felt this excited in years.

He instinctively sensed her interest. *One more thing will put her over.* "Well, yes. This tomorrow. I think we'd have a good time together. Besides, I have a pair of picture frames for you. Remember?"

"Oh my God, yes!" she replied. *He's really giving them to me,* she thought. Then she let her mind drift further, to where this all might lead. *He's good looking. He's successful. He's asking me out. Out of town!*

"I don't know, I guess I could have my mother baby-sit."

"I'm sure she would."

The twenty-eight-year-old single mother chuckled. "Yes, I know she would."

"There's a 2:40 out of Hudson that gets in at 3:16." Waterman had also committed the train schedule to memory. "I can meet you."

Carolyn Hill was so flustered she didn't even notice he never mentioned the train ride home. But Waterman had no intentions of getting her back that night. None whatsoever. He was going to have her. Risky as it was, it was also sport to him. Dangerous and exciting. Adding sex to the equation just increased the drama and his erection. Of course, he would make a surveillance pass through the Poughkeepsie station well before she arrived. If anything looked remotely suspicious he'd leave. If she had a tail when she disembarked, which he'd easily recognize, he'd never show himself.

"So what do you say, Ms. Hill."

"Carolyn. It's Carolyn."

He had his answer. He was going to get laid.

SATURDAY, OCTOBER 11

He was quite taken by the woman who got off the train. He'd only seen Hill wearing plain hotel whites. Now she had on a black cocktail-length skirt with a perfectly fitting red blouse, which allowed for his immediate enjoyment. She wore a red print scarf for accent and carried a black jacket on her arm. None of her wardrobe was expensive, but it all looked nice. She had her hair up in a sexy twist. A shiny red gloss made the most of her lips. And then he saw her legs. Carolyn had great legs and he immediately imagined them wrapped around him. He had all night to make it happen.

"You look wonderful," he said completely certain that she was alone. *No police.*

"Thank you, Mr. Waterman," she replied somewhat shyly, though her outfit had already given her away.

"Please. If you're Carolyn, I'm Roger. I'm not your guest now. I'm your dinner date." He kissed her on the cheek for emphasis and to see how she'd react.

"Mmmm," she said without pulling away. "Okay, Roger. You're my date. But you know we'll miss the first debate. It's on tonight."

"That's just fine. They say most people really can't do anything about politics anyway." And with that, Waterman smiled and led her to his rental car.

He was polite and classy, she thought. And he was obviously rich. He called her. That was the amazing part. During their drive, Carolyn felt like a teenager on a *really* important night.

"Well, where are we going?" she asked.

"I like Le Pavilion, a French restaurant fairly close." He glanced away from the road and at Carolyn. "It's romantic. At least you'll make it that way."

She took a deep breath. *Yes.*

"It's up Salt Point Turnpike," he said demonstrating his knowledge of the area. "I think you'll enjoy it."

"Well then, I'd love to go there." In truth she'd never had French food before, but on the way down to Poughkeepsie she vowed almost ironically, *What would be would be.*

"Then Le Pavilion it is. You're in charge," she said, moving her hand across the seat and letting it touch his thigh.

"We do have some time before dinner. Let's drive a little, get to know each other better. Does that sound good?"

Everything sounded good to her right now. "Sure."

After spending two hours sharing stories about their lives, his made up, hers limited, he pulled up in front of what Carolyn thought was a three story colonial home. But instead she discovered that this was Le Pavilion. They entered a warm, inviting dining room, where white walls broken up by gold curtains and freshly ironed tablecloths marked a degree of grace she'd never experienced. As they were led to their table, he told her that Zagat had given the restaurant a wonderful review awhile back. Not that it mattered; she was already impressed.

"Let me order for you," he offered, wanting to make certain that Carolyn enjoyed dinner.

He decided against mixed drinks and asked about the wines. He easily settled on a New York State Cabernet Sauvignon from Bedell Vineyard for $38. "Are you sure?" She had never tasted a wine that expensive.

"For you, yes."

She watched as he swirled the wine in his glass, took in the bouquet, then sampled the Cabernet. His approval led the waitress to pour a glass for Carolyn.

"I like it," she said taking a healthy sip.

"How would you describe it?" he asked. "A good wine, like a beautiful woman, deserves appreciation, comment, and savoring." *She'll like that*, he correctly surmised.

"I guess I've never actually thought about the taste much." Carolyn smiled then lowered her eyes out of embarrassment. She suddenly became aware she sounded unsophisticated.

"Try."

She took another sip, more delicate than the first. "Spicy? Maybe a little spicy."

He swirled the wine in his glass, then sipped it. "Very good. There is a spice to it. What else?"

"What do you mean?"

"The aroma. The nose. Smell it." She took a casual sniff.

"No, no, no," he explained, enjoying his performance. "Really put your nose *in* the glass. Like this."

"Okay," she replied, laughing as she followed his lead. "I think I smell a little cherry."

"That's called the 'nose.' And you're very close. Now sip again. There's a hint of raspberry."

"Mmmm," she added. "Yes. It's there." She was loving it. She was loving the evening.

"It's a Merlot blend. Helps to create a depth of flavors."

"What goes with it?"

"You," he said, his second seductive line of the evening.

"Roger, you're trying to flatter me."

"I'm complimenting a ravishingly beautiful woman." *Three's the charm.*

"Like a good wine?" she quickly responded.

"Oh, far better than the wine," he added. "Now, if you're asking about what foods it complements?"

She nodded.

"On tonight's menu...oh let's see. The sirloin steak au poivre. The grilled Bordelaise. Or we could switch to a fine white for the salmon sauté with shrimp, if you'd like."

"This is just fine," she said through a sensuous smile. Her first. "How do you know so much about wine?"

"I travel a great deal. I look for the character in everything and everyone. I analyze and I explore." At that moment he stared deeply into Carolyn's eyes. She didn't retreat. *No defenses.* He felt himself getting hard.

"To us," he proposed raising his glass. Carolyn liked that. They clicked glasses and after a long beat, he turned back to the menu. "I think the escargot may be too exotic an hors d'oeuvre, but how about starting with the trio of pasta with basil garlic and olive oil and, of course, the Hudson Valley foie gras. After all, we're here."

"I'd love it all," she said still focused on him. She didn't give the foie gras, which she had never tried, a second thought.

"You don't have to rush right home?" he said sensing the right moment.

"No, I told my mother I might be late." *Very late.* She moved her leg up to his under the table.

As the dinner plates were cleared, he ordered espresso and Grand Marnier. The caffeine to assure they'd stay awake. The liquor to level out any of Carolyn's lingering nervousness. There was none.

They drove for barely 11 minutes; the time it took Waterman to get to the Copper Penny Inn on New Hackensack Road. She made no objections when they pulled into the parking lot of the restored 1860s colonial farmhouse. When they stopped, Waterman faced her and pressed forward, kissing her forcefully. Very soon her legs would be completely around him.

Roarke decided to visit Katie over the weekend. They ate take-out from DeLuca's and watched TV, though only partially committed to the first debate. The president drilled down on his successful peace initiative which backed two nuclear powers away from the launch buttons. India and Pakistan were still within ten launch-to-detonation minutes of one another, but their WMD's were at stand down.

"The world owes a debt of gratitude to Morgan Taylor for his courage," the Democratic nominee proclaimed, never addressing him as president. Instead of attacking Taylor on his success, he chose to congratulate him.

It pissed off Taylor because he was ready to seize the moment.

However, he didn't show his anger to the cameras and Roarke and Katie certainly didn't see it.

"So who do I thank for us meeting?" Katie playfully asked while reaching for his shirt buttons. "The president or the congressman?"

"Umm," Roarke purred, pulling Katie's sweater out of her skirt. "Now that's an interesting question." He found the hook and eye to her bra and gently unfastened it. "I'd have to say the president."

He let his shirt fall off his arms onto the floor and lifted her sweater over her head.

"But you came up to the office because we used to handle the Lodges' affairs. So wouldn't that count some for the congressman?" Katie responded.

"I suppose so." He turned her around, kissed her neck and unsnapped her skirt. His fingers followed the path as it dropped down, stopping at her black lace underwear. Katie was doing the exact same thing to Roarke with her hands working behind her back. "But remember I didn't have an appointment. It was a cold call."

Her fingers found him under his boxers. "...that turned into something hot," she added seductively.

"What do you say we just thank them both." Katie nestled her head back into him. He answered her movements, walking his fingers down until they were exactly where she wanted.

The debate continued, but only on TV. Roarke came around to face Katie and kissed her deeply. After what was almost a minute, she took his hand and walked him from the living room into her bedroom.

"You know what I'd like?" she asked pulling him down and rolling on her side.

"What?"

"Your *special* massage."

He maneuvered closer to Katie, taking her from behind and letting his hands knead her back as he slid into a wonderful position.

"What a nice rub," she moaned.

"You know, I've never asked which way you're going to vote," Roarke whispered as he worked his hands over her back and moved slowly inside of her.

She answered to the same meter as his movements, "No, you haven't."

"So who's it going to be?"

"Normally I'm a Democrat," she cooed. "But I'm feeling some pressure right now."

The pressure continued through the night.

Carolyn's tongue explored Waterman's mouth. The sophistication he displayed over dinner had disappeared. Now he revealed to her a different kind of hunger; insatiable and rough. She was acutely aware of his strength. He was stronger than she first believed; his body much harder. Dressed, he looked bookish. Naked above her was a muscular, needy lover with none of the antique dealer's mannerisms.

He had an appetite like a wild animal that had stalked her. She had been alone for so long she was ready to be devoured. And then the animal instinct came out of her, too. Carolyn became the aggressor, as she never had been before.

Teddy Lodge thought Christine Slocum was wonderfully inventive in bed. She exhibited as much creativity under the covers as she did in her writing.

Lodge began his conquest the night of the convention. They had been extremely discreet, though Newman purposefully provided her with an adjoining room to the congressman's suite. Even his Secret Service detail didn't know they had begun sleeping together.

Christine was a wild and exciting blonde. And the congressman had been horny for months. He had no patience for foreplay and pushed right inside of her. As far as the public was concerned, Teddy Lodge was still a man in mourning. In the privacy of his own room, he was devoted to his own selfish pleasure.

Newman would send her away in another week. But for now he felt Lodge deserved a reward, especially after such a good performance in the first debate. This was the way Newman worked. He controlled the congressman's sex life, like everything else.

Roger Waterman wanted to fuck more. He finally let Carolyn sleep for forty-five minutes, but at 2 A.M., he found the means to wake her up. She responded instantaneously to his tongue between her legs. An hour later, they lay in bed together talking. Waterman knew he needed to seem interested in her, so while touching her breasts lightly he asked a series of innocuous questions he could care less about.

"Did life around Hudson change much since June?"

"No, not really. It's always the same," she answered. "Well, up until tonight." She leaned closer and kissed him, proud of herself that she could make him grow again.

"Oh, there are people still coming around asking questions about the shooting. That makes things interesting." She moved her hand up and down him, using long, ever tightening strokes.

"Really?"

"Reporters. The FBI. All sorts of investigators."

"And what do you tell them?"

"Nothing. But my manager came up with something."

"Yes?" he prompted.

"I think she really helped them out. You know, the killer, McAlister? He got the room he needed."

He pulled his hand away. "What do you mean?"

"Well, there was this other man who was checked in there, but he left early. And that meant that the McAlister guy could move into it. People request 301 all the time. But McAlister really needed it. So now they're looking for the man who had it before him. Frank something. Frank Dolan."

Carolyn now noticed that her lover had stopped touching her and that he lost his erection. "Heh, I'm sorry," she said. "Am I talking too much? Because if I am, I can…"

"No, that's all right," Waterman said. It was just the opposite. He *wanted* to learn more.

His mind flashed on the slip he made at the train station in Connecticut. He had to assume that someone had overheard him and remembered the name Dolan. Some smart investigator would connect the two if that hadn't happened already.

And then he began to think about Waterman. *He should disappear forever, too.* And the woman? *Maybe she was smart enough to put another piece of the puzzle together.* He had hooked up a pre-paid answering service to throw off the FBI last June. But he had let the payment lax and now his office number was disconnected. If Carolyn tried to call him after tonight and couldn't reach him, she'd ultimately tell somebody. He had played this out too far.

Maybe he should kill the woman right now.

"What are you thinking?" Katie said as she nestled into Roarke's chest.

"I'm just trying to sort some things out."

"They're far away," she said.

"What do you mean?"

"The things you're sorting out. They're far away. And you're already there. Come back."

"I'm sorry." Roarke began stroking her curly black hair onto her shoulder and breasts.

"It's very important, isn't it."

"Yes, I'm afraid it is," he admitted.

"You'll tell me if I can help again."

"I don't think there's anything you can do, Katie. I'm not sure if there's anything *I* can do."

He closed his eyes and held her tightly. Perhaps there was one thing. But he wasn't ready to ask.

Waterman weighed his immediate options. He decided that if he killed Carolyn it could give investigators another roundabout link to the Lodge murder. If he simply went away, she might try to find him, but his trail would lead nowhere. However, he would have bought extra time before she even admitted her affair to anyone.

As for covering his tracks, he didn't think she was smart enough to go to the police for a DNA analysis on his sperm. Besides, she'd been using a diaphragm. For good measure, he'd shower with her in the morning. Then he'd wash *his* evidence away. All things considered, he decided to let her live and reward himself. She was *good* and he wanted one more fuck.

When they dressed in the morning, Carolyn sensed his mind was elsewhere. He was quiet, but polite. They ate a simple breakfast of eggs and toast at a coffee shop on the way to the train station. They made it well before the 11:07.

She asked if he would call.

Waterman said he would, but soon there'd be no more Waterman.

Carolyn gazed into the eyes of the man she had loved all night long.

He looked right through her.

She snuggled into his arms before she got out of the car, still grateful for the time.

He counted the minutes until she'd be out of his life.

Teddy watched Christine's perfect naked body quietly slip back into her adjoining room. He said goodbye with the same fierce passion that brought them together the previous night. He wanted her again. Soon. But he would have to be careful. After all, he was a grieving widower.

CHAPTER 40

WASHINGTON, D.C.
MONDAY, OCTOBER 13

"You can be a hard guy to track down," FBI Director Robert Mulligan said.

"Well, sometimes I do turn my phone off." Roarke had been in no rush to leave Katie and get back to Washington first thing Monday morning. Their relationship was developing and would go further, he felt, if he gave into it.

"Actually, I could have disturbed you. But I thought better of it."

Roarke smirked. Of course they knew exactly where he was. One emergency call to the White House would have cinched it. *But if they were looking for me and it wasn't an emergency…?* Roarke was confused.

"Okay, what's important enough for you to find me, but not important enough to roust me out of bed?"

"Some asinine notion." He passed him a hard copy of an e-mail from Roy Bessolo to the Director.

RE: Lodge, Jennifer footage/Marelli phone call.

"I can't let you take it. But read it. It's vague. If you're interested, you tell me what you want to do."

Mulligan watched Roarke while he perused the memo Bessolo wrote up following his telephone conversation with Chief Marelli. When he finished he put the paper down. Mulligan was right on him.

"Well?"

"Sounds way out there, but what the hell. Let me meet this cameraman."

"You better know one thing going in. It might even save you the trip."

Roarke raised his eyebrow.

"We hear this Wheaton character couldn't make it as a cop. Bessolo thinks he's just trying to one-up everyone else. You know, double jump into the conspiracy theory sweepstakes."

"Eh, let me see him anyway," Roarke offered.

"Your time, not mine. I have a copter waiting to take you. Oh, and as long as you're going, I'll send Bessolo, too."

"I'd rather do this alone. Sounds as if he's already made up his mind."

"No. You work with him. This is his investigation. *His.*"

Roarke was not happy, but it probably didn't matter.

"You'll be up there by three." The FBI Director decided to add one additional thought. "I bet you'll be ready to head home by four."

The ride north on the Huey was noisy. Even the earphones didn't help abate the sound enough. With the exception of some quick questions and answers, Roarke and Bessolo couldn't compare notes. Not that they would have shared anyway. Roarke knew more than his new partner and Bessolo wasn't a talker.

The helicopter touched down in a field next to Chuck Wheaton's two-story Revolutionary era stone house. They were out of the door before the blades died down.

Wheaton stood at the doorframe. His two golden retrievers bounded out barking, looking about as ferocious as a pair of stuffed animals. Wheaton came after them, ducking under the rotors.

"Hello, I'm Chuck Wheaton," the cameraman shouted above the noise.

"Yes, I know who you are," Bessolo said impertinently. "We've met before."

"I remember. Bessolo, right?" Wheaton said. Bessolo nodded. Roarke offered his hand. "Scott Roarke." He didn't add "Secret Service."

"Thanks for coming up. Let's go over to my editing room," Wheaton said. "This way." He led them to a room carved out of an unattached garage.

Inside, Wheaton had all of the equipment needed to put together a television documentary or news story: a non-linear editing system, a microphone for audio, and a console to feed the footage out on a fiber-optic line.

"Let's see what brought us up here," Bessolo stated as warmly as he said anything.

"Have a seat?" Wheaton pulled some stools in. "I'm fine. Just play," the FBI man said. "I've talked with Marelli. You can dispense with the preamble."

"Okay. But first normal speed. Then slow motion. Stopping and starting. It took me months to start seeing it."

"We don't have months, Mr. Wheaton," Bessolo said.

The cameraman was beginning to dislike the FBI man, but he bit his lip and hit the play key on his computer key board.

Roarke remained quiet. Bessolo was the first to comment. "Again."

Wheaton used his mouse to click and point to the same start point. They screened it a second time and Wheaton now gave the description of what *he* saw.

"Again," Bessolo barked.

After watching it the third time, the FBI agent in charge straightened up from leaning into the screen and said, "Look, you're a nice enough man. So I'll give it to you straight. You want to see something, so there it is. You see it."

Wheaton hit the red stop key on his keyboard. He spun around. "Agent Bessolo, I didn't want to see anything," Wheaton shot back. "In fact, I wish I wasn't even goddamned there! I haven't had a good night's sleep since. Ask my wife!"

Roarke rested his hand on Wheaton's shoulder to calm him down. "Can you enlarge it, please?" he asked quietly.

Wheaton had forgotten to make the image bigger. They had screened the footage in only one quarter of the computer monitor.

"Yes, sure."

"Then play it again. I'm getting into the rhythm of the speech."

"That's exactly what you need to do," Wheaton said excitedly.

Bessolo gave it only cursory attention. As his team knew, he preferred physical evidence you could hold.

He ran it five times without comment, seeing if they would pick up on the motions in close up. On the sixth pass Roarke spoke up.

"Help me a little. More show and tell."

"Okay, there. See?" Wheaton said, pointing to the screen. He froze the picture. "Did you see that? His eyes. They darted around quickly. Just a little. But they look nervous. And his fingers are counting. One, two, three, now four fingers. It's right there!"

"Oh come on," Bessolo said. "If he's counting anything, it's for the place in his speech where he expects to get applause."

"No. He's nervous because he knows what's going to happen. Watch his fingers, dammit! He's counting; timing it to get out of the way!"

"Bull!" blurted Bessolo.

Roarke looked at Wheaton. "You realize what you're saying?"

"For Christ's sake, of course I do," he said facing both men, but ignoring Bessolo.

Bessolo reached past Wheaton and tapped his index finger on the television screen. "I want to make this very clear. You're suggesting, and I'll leave it solely in those terms, *suggesting* that a United States Congressman willfully knew that he was going to be shot at."

"Not shot at."

Bessolo's tone sharpened. "…Willfully knew a shot was going to be fired towards him? Is that clearer?"

"Yes."

"That he had been warned about the assassin?"

"Yes."

"And he knew when?"

"Yes. And he ducked." Wheaton jabbed his finger on the monitor right on top of Bessolo's. "Right at that moment!"

"Oh Jesus. He ducked. Why in this God's earth would he duck?"

"To get out of the way."

"So his wife would get shot?" Bessolo yelled.

The words hung in the air, as if suspended by the shock of being said aloud. The cameraman yelled back "Yes!"

Bessolo shook his head and stepped away. "I've been on this investigation from the first hour of the first day. I've seen all of the evidence that my team has pulled together and read thousands of pages of transcripts from eyewitnesses. And there is nothing, nothing that will support your theory!"

He turned to leave, but not before Wheaton defiantly said, "Except what I have on this videotape."

Bessolo slammed the door. Wheaton felt utterly defeated and was ready to turn off his edit system when he remembered that Roarke was still in the room.

"You going?" he asked Roarke. He heard the sound of the rotors beginning to turn.

"I don't know." He was thinking.

"I think your helicopter is."

"Maybe in a few minutes. Do me a favor," Roarke asked using almost the same words Chief Marelli had a few days earlier, "Play it again, will you, Chuck?"

The helicopter lifted off at 2212 hours. The long day, coupled with the intensity of focusing on the TV monitor all evening, left Roarke exhausted. He drifted into an unsettling sleep, with the noise of the helicopter melding into the sounds of a crowd.

He was in Hudson in June. Park Place and Warren. The people watching Teddy Lodge. The sound slurred, deepened by the sense that everything was in slow motion.

Roarke saw the candidate, the chief of police, the mayor, and Mrs. Lodge. All there, merely feet away. But he knew where to look—the third floor of the St. Charles Hotel. A rifle barrel inched out of the corner window. The shooter remained faceless behind it. He turned to the podium, to the congressman who paused and slowly leaned forward. His heart raced but everything else was painfully, terribly slow. Now back to the hotel window. He heard the bullet explode from the chamber. It traveled the 25 yards in slow motion. Roarke took a step toward the podium and saw Lodge's finger by his side. There was Jennifer, beautiful, smiling at her husband through her tears. Roarke moved closer, still in slow motion, desperately trying to race the bullet to its target. As he propelled through the air, he saw Geoff Newman off to the side, laughing at him. Roarke was single-minded now. He had to reach Jennifer Lodge before it was too late. He was getting to the bullet. He reached out. Closer. Feet. Now inches. And then the laughter of Newman again. He turned to the voice and lost his concentration. As he fell to the ground he heard a horrible sound. The sound of the bullet smashing against cranial bone. The sound of a life ending. And the sound of Bessolo waking him.

"Get up. We're home."

They'd landed on top of the FBI building.

CHAPTER 41

TUESDAY, OCTOBER 14

It was already 0230 when the FBI car dropped him off at his two-bedroom Georgetown apartment. Roarke lived at 2500 Q Street NW, in a brick building on a block of brick buildings next to the Dumbarton Bridge. It gave him a Georgetown address, which wasn't really important, but he enjoyed the convenience of living next to Dupont Circle. There was a playful message from Katie on his answering machine. It was much too late to call back, although he wanted to. So instead he opted for a shot of his favorite Macallan, the 12-year-old. After just one sip, he poured the scotch back into the bottle. *Not tonight. I have to stay alert.*

Four hours later Roarke was on the Mall, running in dark blue shorts and a matching T-shirt. He had let his exercise regimen lax and he needed to be in shape. The time also allowed him to think.

Nothing that he felt, nothing that he heard, and nothing that he had seen would stand any true test. That's why Bessolo so easily dismissed the video. But Roarke wanted to believe it. He was looking for something to give credence to his gnawing suspicions that had originally brought him to Touch Parsons.

On his sixth mile, just as the morning traffic was beginning to slow down along Constitution Avenue, he jogged past a bus stop with a vertical poster of a father and a 12 or 13-year-old son standing beside a new Mustang. The two were eyeing the car; the father seeing his youth reflected in the windshield, the son visualizing himself older and on his way to a hot date. Beneath the picture was the advertising line: *Mustang. See yourself in it.*

Roarke doubled-back. The father and the son. He looked at each of them. The resemblance was striking. The picture of the father as he remembered himself younger, and the boy as he saw himself older, were so much the same, yet different. *Older and younger, but the same man.*

A smile spread over Roarke's face. He cut across the grass, sprinting the remaining mile home.

"Mr. President, a new communication from Sandman."

The president was onboard Air Force One, talking on a secure com line to the DCI. Following the debate he had extended his stay and brought his campaign to three cities.

"Substance, Jack?"

"Keeping things in the simplest of terms, sir, his friends are paying undue interest in a certain political contest of note. I'll meet you at Andrews when you land. We'll talk."

Sixty-one minutes later, the most sophisticated 747 in the world touched down and came to a roaring stop. The ground crew at Andrews Air Force Base drove the stairway up to the plane. F-16's flew overhead and confirmed the airspace was clear before the president was allowed to exit.

Jack Evans waited in the president's bulletproof limousine. A minute later the door opened.

The president extended his hand. "Jack, good to see you. I've been looking forward to our conversation."

"Likewise, sir." However, they waited to talk until they were driving down the access road toward the highway. The partition was closed to the front compartment.

"Here's what we have. First the flyover. Internally we've been following all of Libya's coverage of the election. They're greeting Lodge like the Second Coming, predicting that he'll open the borders again and change the balance of power in the Middle East. It's unprecedented."

"Anything specific?" the president asked without comment.

"This took a helluva long time to get out. But it also has to do with the Kharrazi clan. You know how the General's boys basically hate each other?"

"I love it."

"Well, it seems D'Angelo started a family squabble after Abahar Kharrazi's men picked him up there."

"Oh?"

"Fadi got wind that he was detained. He was furious. An American, caught taking pictures of his building? Questioned, released, and allowed to leave the country? In a funny way, I don't blame him. He tried to back channel the photographer. But he didn't come up with anything he shouldn't have. The cover is layers deep. But Sandman has given us a name that may be related to the infighting. Someone outside of Libya; possibly here. He's not sure, but he thinks it's *Abraham*."

"Have we heard that name before in connection with Fadi?"

"Not to my knowledge."

"Do they talk often?"

"That's what we're trying to determine. But according to Sandman, when this Abraham hung up on Fadi, the little bastard was fit to be tied."

"Is that his first or last name, Jack?"

"Don't know. It may not even be right. But we'll run a check on every Libyan named Abraham living or working in this country."

"You asked me to bring in a picture of an adult."

"I did?" Touch Parsons asked.

"Yes you did," Roarke explained. "You said you particularly like taking shots of adults and regressing them into kids."

"Oh yeah, I did. But I'm a little busy now."

"You're going to have to do this for me."

"Look, Roarke. You're a nice enough guy with a gun. But I meet a lot of people like you. And I'm really on a deadline. I don't have time for any more family pictures right now."

"If you need a phone call to clear your schedule, I'm sure I can arrange that."

"Like I said. I'm busy."

Roarke bit his cheek. He stepped away and placed a phone call on his cell phone.

Parsons ignored him. The Bureau needed fast help on a murder case in Houston. He didn't care who Roarke put on.

A moment later Roarke held out the phone. "It's for you."

"Look. This was a fun diversion during the summer, but I've got real things to work on. So why don't you take your fucking phone and go protect the president?"

Roarke still held the phone out, angled it toward him more and nodded.

"You're going to want to take it," he said. "I guarantee you it'll be quick."

"Fuckin' better be," Parsons complained grabbing the cell phone. "Hello!" he all but yelled into it.

"Mr. Parsons. This is Morgan Taylor."

"Oh shit," was all that Parsons could get out.

"Mr. Parsons, Mr. Roarke tells me you have very special skills."

"Why thank you, Mr. President," he stammered.

"Not at all. Can I remind you of one thing, Mr. Parsons?"

"Yes, of course."

"Helping him is helping me."

"Ah, yes. I understand that."

"He also tells me you're a bit busy right now."

"I did tell him that, maybe not as delicately."

"But I understand he's come to you with another project. I recommend you take the time to listen to him. I think you can get my drift."

"Yes, sir."

"They call you Touch, don't they?"

"Some do."

"Well then, Mr. Parsons. Let's give whatever Mr. Roarke has for you today your special touch."

"Yes sir, Mr. President."

"Thank you," Taylor said. After a pause he added to the stunned computer artist, "You can hang up now."

"Yes sir."

He handed the telephone back to Roarke.

"Let me guess. Some time has suddenly opened up in your work day?" the Secret Service agent said, holstering his phone.

"A change in plans," Parsons said quietly. "What do you have?"

Roarke produced a glossy photograph, which Parsons perused for barely a second. "You're kidding?"

"No. Deadly serious, as a matter of fact."

"This is Teddy Lodge."

"Yes, I'm perfectly aware of that. I want to see what you come up with taking him down to say, age eleven."

CHAPTER 42

WEDNESDAY, OCTOBER 15

Parsons worked all night while Roarke slept on a couch in the reception area. When he awoke he bought two cups of coffee from the vending machine, offering one to Parsons.

"Good morning," he said good naturedly.

"Yeah." Parsons was still engrossed on the computer. "Go away. I need another hour." He smelled the coffee. "Does the java have milk?"

"Yup."

"Then leave it." Roarke tried to look over Parsons' shoulder.

"And go away."

CHICAGO

Lodge loved the sex again. But it was getting more difficult to arrange a rendezvous with the young speechwriter. Newman was keeping him running longer hours; a strategy that was paying off. The polls had him securely 14 points out in front of Taylor. What's more, the networks predicted that he'd take the state electoral count by as much as 69 percent. The number made him laugh, considering what he was doing at the present moment in the presidential suite of the Hyatt Hotel.

The knock at the door sounded urgent. "Congressman!" It was Newman. "Time to get up, congressman."

"You already are," Christine giggled.

"Go away."

328 | GARY GROSSMAN

Newman stood on the other side of the door and shook his head. *This will have to stop.*

Touch Parsons was ready when Roarke returned.

"Here we go, this time in reverse. I press the way-back machine, thusly," Parsons said lightly in an homage to one of his favorite classic cartoons. "Voila. The subject as presented." The picture of Teddy Lodge appeared on the screen. "I called up early archival photos to check against these, but guess what?"

"I give up."

"There weren't any."

"Really?" Roarke said offering nothing more. Parsons glared at him. "So I went on instinct and ignored every marker except some shots of him in Congress a few years back. Oh, and there was one picture from Yale on the web. I hope that was okay."

Roarke ignored the question. "Keep going."

"Now let's go back in increments. Slowly, regressing every two years over twenty seconds."

The years melted away at the rate of six per minute. Forty-eight years old became forty-six, forty-four, and then forty-two. During the second minute Lodge returned to his mid-thirties. Lines from his face relaxed, his body weight lightened, his hair filled out, more for style than aging. And his face narrowed.

"Now here's where it gets interesting. We're at thirty years old by the time we're through with the third minute. So far I remained pretty damned close to the pictures on record."

Roarke noted how handsome Lodge appeared. No wonder he was so popular with women. He had drop-dead good looks.

"And now I'm venturing into relatively unknown territory. The Yale photograph to compare my work against. Watch him in his twenties. His basic features are fully matured."

Roarke said, "He's still pretty recognizable."

In the fifth minute Parsons' sequence took away more years. Age twenty-two, twenty, then eighteen. He thinned out more, took on an awkward teenage appearance, but demonstrated where his signature bushy hairstyle originated. "It's in his eyes, lips and cheeks, too," Roarke observed. "Very distinctive."

"Let's go all the way to eleven now," Parsons said in the sixth and seventh minute. Here Teddy Lodge became a kid again, a boy with a cute expression.

"And there he is." Parsons turned to face Roarke as he continued. "Teddy Lodge at your target age. Of course, as I said, I ran out of archival photos around age twenty."

Roarke couldn't miss the "of course" part.

"And I took a little liberty."

Roarke raised an eyebrow.

"You asked me to regress the picture of the congressman to about the same age as the first picture you gave me to age. I told myself you must have a reason. So here."

Parsons keyed in another command. The age regression photograph of Teddy Lodge moved to the left and the original picture of the young Boy Scout appeared on the right.

"Your two pictures side by side, Roarke. My guess is you wanted to see them together at some point—shall I say *out of curiosity*." Roarke didn't respond. "To see if they looked alike."

Parsons dropped his voice and got very serious.

"And they don't."

Parsons typed in another string of letters and the screen produced a different comparison: The contemporary shot of Teddy Lodge and the age progression depiction of the scout as a forty-seven-year-old.

"Nor do these two," Parsons added.

One more command and all four pictures appeared on the screen.

"Care to tell me what this is all about?"

Newman pounded on the door again. "Let me in."

"Whoa, whoa…" Lodge protested as he flung on a hotel bathrobe. "I've got company."

"I know who's in here," Newman said. "Who the hell do you think is pimping for you, for Christ's sake."

Lodge opened the door and Newman pushed right past him. Christine Slocum heard the comment but chose to ignore it. She knew her job. Newman glared at her until she rose out of bed, completely naked, ignoring the fact that he was also in the room. She went to the bathroom and closed the door.

"Taylor wants to see you," Newman said holding a phone message slip. "Frannie got the call first thing in the morning."

"Why?"

"How the hell should I know? It's totally irregular."

"So what should I do?"

"I'll send your utmost regrets. No time in the schedule. Only two weeks left." Newman helped himself to orange juice from the hotel mini-bar.

"He's up to something."

"Screw him."

"Tell Neill to find out and then remind Taylor I'm busy running for president." He waved his hand in disgust and walked to the bathroom. Newman heard the woman laugh when Lodge entered.

Christine Slocum was beginning to wear out her welcome.

"How reliable are your renderings?" Roarke demanded.

"Are you asking how good am I?"

Roarke didn't reply to Touch Parsons' question. "I'm the best in the country. Maybe the world. Now if you're also asking me if any smart-ass attorney could rip me to shreds on the stand, I'd say I'm probably not your most credible witness. What I do is science; very useful forensic science, but it's impeachable. Age regression is a very useful tool for law enforcement. For finding kidnapped children, now grown up. But it doesn't carry anywhere near the weight that DNA evidence does."

"So what we have is just…?" Roarke let his words fade into a question.

"Some nice artwork that can get you shit-canned for sure; useless against a sharp lawyer."

"Forget it as evidence. Just tell me what *you* think," Roarke said defiantly.

"Oh, that's really easy for me. Our man Lodge, based on what I've come up with…"

"Yes?"

"You've got yourself a 100 percent dyed-in-the-wool fake." Then Parsons smiled devilishly. "It's out of my bailiwick, but I recommend you see a good dentist immediately."

CHAPTER 43

THE WHITE HOUSE
THE SITUATION ROOM
FRIDAY, OCTOBER 17

Roarke was back with his dog and pony act. His audience would grow larger today. As he looked around the Oval Office, he figured that John Bernstein, notorious for playing devil's advocate with the president, would be hard to sway. He couldn't count on any help from Bob Mulligan. And he had no idea what CIA Chief Evans would think.

Then there were the others. How would the usually reserved Vice President Stanley Poole react? *Skeptically, of course.* The president only recently told him that he needed to be brought up to speed on an important national security matter.

Next to him, Nathan R. Langone, a man who *had* to be concerned. He was the president's Secretary for the U.S. Department of Homeland Security. Roarke already knew that the silver-haired fifty-six-year-old ex-Marine, ex-Wall Street broker, ex-FBI Assistant Director started each day with the notion that every rumor could be true.

Arthur Campanis, Taylor's national security advisor, would surely be surprised. Here was his biggest challenge. Campanis was a short, stocky man, with closely cropped salt and pepper hair. His role model was President Lyndon Johnson's Secretary of Defense, Robert McNamara, and he lived up to the tough image. As a former under secretary of state, Campanis earned the reputation of a hard-ass negotiator. He cultivated it in Taylor's administration. The president warned Roarke that Campanis wasn't going to be an easy sell in the meeting. *No shit.*

"I think we're ready to begin, Scott," the president said.

"Okay." The meeting was "by invitation only." The participants had been briefed in general terms. Nothing specific. Roarke gauged by their expressions that it wasn't exactly a friendly crowd. "Hope you don't mind if I stand and walk around a little," he said. There were no objections. He had the floor. "In a bit, I'll show you a flow chart and some footage. But let's start with the players. Then we'll go to the video." It was an old sports joke that didn't work.

"Recapping first. June. Hudson, New York. We have a trigger man killing Jennifer Lodge. His name is Sidney McAlister. Beside the hotel register and a cancelled credit card account, there's no record of him. He's merely a name. Other than that he doesn't exist. But what he did is seen around the world. In turn, we know how the fortunes of Congressman Lodge change with the death of his wife. There's a better than even chance that before the killing he would have lost the New York primary. Because of it, more people come out for him. He pulls in the sympathy vote and he secures the nomination. Are we somewhat agreed on that point?"

Roarke received the nods he desired.

"Moving on. McAlister got away. Amazingly quickly. We still don't know how. He leaves his sniper rifle, not even caring. It's clean as a whistle. Like his entire room. No residual evidence that Bob's team could submit for DNA testing. Can we agree that this was a professional hit?"

"Don't you mean attempted hit?" the vice president asked. "Intended for Congressman Lodge."

Roarke looked to the president for guidance. "It's your show, Scott."

Thanks for nothing, he thought. "I'd like to skip that just for now, if I could."

"Fair enough," Poole answered.

"However, the FBI was able to lift a latent footprint from the wall of the hotel room and another impression from the hotel parking lot. We suspect they are the killer's. That same footprint shows up later in the summer thousands of miles away. This is most interesting. It's in the woods, near where a man is found dead."

This earned the vice president's interest. He loosened his yellow print tie; always a sure signal that he was getting engaged in the content. "Who? I didn't know that."

"A retired lawyer by the name of Alfred Nunes, on a fishing trip out near Sun Valley, Idaho, Mr. Vice President. A heart attack, according to the coroner. However, a further toxicology report strongly leads us to suspect he was poisoned. And this particular lawyer happens to have been a founding partner in the original law firm that represented the estate of a prominent Massachusetts family. A family named Lodge."

"Well imagine that," the vice president managed.

Poole, balding and always looking grim, was a former senator from Maryland and renowned as a sharp debater on the Hill. Little facts meant big things to him. This was one of them.

"Now what about the law firm that eventually took over the estate?" Roarke asked. "Lo and behold, one of its senior partners shows up dead this summer, too. Haywood Marcus. The press reports it as a robbery-homicide by a gang member. There are no witnesses."

An audible "hmmm" from the vice president. Langone and Campanis remained silent.

"I take a personal interest in this one," Roarke offered. "I tried to meet Marcus. I wasn't allowed. As a result I couldn't question him on archival files that might have been pertinent to our investigation." Roarke neglected to say that he had actually seen some of the confidential paperwork. "If you want my personal opinion, I don't think any subpoena could produce them now."

"Mr. Roarke, for the sake of argument, there are other explanations to everything," Vice President Poole argued. "You're even providing them. A heart attack. A robbery. Even the whereabouts of old files. Things do get misplaced. I presume you *are* leading up to something?"

"Yes, I am. The good part. But to summarize, can we agree, based on what I've covered so far, that people connected with the Lodge family were killed in a short period of time?"

"'Killed?' Mr. Roarke. I don't believe you've established that," the national security advisor said, joining the discussion. "You'd have us believe that on faith."

"Point well taken. If I substitute 'died'?" Roarke asked.

"Assuming this can be substantiated? 'Died' it is," conceded Campanis.

This technicality disrupted Roarke's logical progression. He had to try another approach to make the connection.

"Does it seem coincidental to you that Mrs. Lodge and two senior partners of *two different* law firms that represented the old Lodge estate died within three months of one another?"

"I'll grant you *coincidental*," the vice president allowed. "An interesting coincidence."

"Then for the sake of argument, is it possible their deaths, if not all natural—could be related?"

Campanis and Poole didn't give any ground. Langone poured a glass of water from a pitcher on the coffee table in front of him, an indication that he was now involved; simultaneously the president put his hands together, a signal to Roarke to tie things up.

"Gentlemen, I maintain that we have a professional assassin and he isn't working alone."

"Just one moment," Nathan Langone said. He scribbled some notes on a pad; his first since Roarke began.

When the secretary of homeland security indicated he was ready, Roarke continued. "Now back to the hotel in Hudson. A short while into the investigation, the FBI establishes that Mrs. Lodge's killer may have had an accomplice who helped him secure the specific room he needed to take the shot. As I've understood from Bob's briefings, that same man, identified as Frank Dolan, then shows up days later and kills a commuter on a New York bound train. Another hit."

"Who's that?" asked the national security advisor. "Jack, maybe you can take Arthur's question," Roarke said deferring to CIA Director Jack Evans, knowing that he'd have the answer.

Evans leaned forward in his seat and whispered, though he didn't have to. The doors and walls to the Situation Room located in the basement of the White House were soundproof. "The victim was a former Russian spy we had taken in by the name of Steven Hoag. You can look up his obit in *The New York Times*. He came out of special school in Russia; one we know a good deal about. Red Banner, under the Andropov Institute. This particular agent was taught to be an American, to come here, to blend in, then wait to be activated. He was still a sleeper who was still sleeping when the Soviet Union fell."

Campanis sat up straight. He was quite familiar with the legendary Red Banner.

"I believe he was killed because someone feared he either *could* or *was going to* provide us with an important bit of information."

"Oh?" the national security advisor commented, now vastly more interested.

"The identity of another sleeper?" Secretary Langone concluded.

"Maybe more than one," was the DCI's reply. "Who?" the vice president and the national security advisor asked in unison.

Roarke took over again. "I said I was coming to the good part. But before I get to it, I have to admit that we still do not have the proof in our hands to make any of this stick. Not Bob at the FBI. Not Jack at the CIA. And we're not at the point where the attorney general can follow up. But we think we know where we can find it."

"Anyone need a break?" the president asked.

No one did. *Good*, Roarke thought. He didn't want to waste a second. "Now for the audio-visual part of my briefing," he said as he placed his chart on one of two easels in front of a statue of Dwight Eisenhower. "Just take in the connections we've established for a moment." He gave them time to absorb the information in black and white.

"I want to play a DVD with footage that you've all seen. The moments leading up to and including the death of Mrs. Lodge.

"The footage was shot by a local cameraman up in the Hudson Valley named Chuck Wheaton. I met him, and in my mind he's not a crackpot." He spoke about Wheaton's credibility; his full time teaching job, his interest in law enforcement, and his sincerity. "Wheaton's studied this like it was the Zapruder film," Roarke added. "He's lived with it for months. Frame by frame. And while there's some debate even in this room over Wheaton's theory, I want you to see what the cameraman believes he discovered."

Roarke reached for the remote. The TV set was built into a massive bookshelf containing other monitors usually tuned to the all-news channels. "I'm going to roll this and talk you through. Look closely. Eventually, I think you'll see why we're all here today."

Roarke ran the raw footage at normal speed, then slowed it, pointing to the same clues that Chuck Wheaton had shown him. "His deliberate speech…watch his fingers…as if he's counting. His head. Moving forward. Now! Just as the bullet is fired…It's as if he knew."

After sixteen straight minutes without comment and numerous passes at the footage, Roarke turned to his audience.

"Anybody?" Roarke asked. "Nobody?" He held up his hands inviting reaction.

The FBI director didn't hesitate. "You know I have a problem with this, Roarke. We can't take this out. We'll sound like conspiracy nuts."

"I agree," Bernstein added.

Roarke focused on Evans. The CIA director gave him a very visible endorsement with a tip of his glasses, but nothing else. Secretary Langone made another notation on his pad. The national security advisor said nothing, but Vice President Poole surprised Roarke when he quietly asked, "Would you mind playing that again?"

While the footage ran, Mulligan joined Morgan Taylor across the room. "I'm extremely uncomfortable with this, Mr. President," he said softly.

"Say what you mean, Bob."

"For the record, it's bullshit. I thought that when Bessolo and Roarke went up to Hudson. And I think the same thing now. You have a lot of faith in your boy here, and he's done a great job of drawing lines on a board. But he doesn't have diddlyshit to back it up. Not a damned thing. And quite honestly, if you pursue this course of action *without* proof, I have to tell you that I can't be your man. You'll need to find someone else. Even at this point."

The president put his arm on Mulligan's shoulder and bore down. The FBI chief felt the pressure of Taylor's fingers.

"Bob, why don't you put a pin in that until Roarke is finished… before you say something you'll really regret."

"Mister…"

Morgan Taylor cut him off. "No, Bob," he said raising his voice. "I don't want to hear you're not *my* man."

"But Mr. President."

"We're not finished, Bob. Don't you want to know what one of your *own* men has come up with? Thanks, in fact, to you."

"What are you talking about?" the FBI chief asked in amazement.

"Scott," the president said raising his voice, "I think we've seen enough. Why don't you turn off the TV and bring out those photos of yours."

Roarke nodded and went to his locked attaché case.

He thumbed through the tumblers until the right digits came up. Roarke took a few moments to make sure he had the proper sequence for the photographs and computer renderings. Then he placed them on another easel, beside the first.

"The human face is remarkable," he said segueing to his lecture on age progression photography. "It shows where we're going and where we've been. We can change our expression, but we can't hide who we are. I'm going to tell you a story about somebody who tried." Roarke finished quoting Touch Parsons. "According to the FBI's own age progression expert, Duane Parsons, this Boy Scout," he pointed to the picture of eleven-year-old Teddy Lodge, "and this man," the recent campaign photo, "are not the same person."

"One more time?" National Security Advisor Campanis requested.

"Right to the point, then. Gentlemen, the man running for president under the name Teddy Lodge is a fake." Roarke's stinging declaration seemed to suck the air out of the room. Poole and Campanis gasped. Even Jack Evans caught his breath at the power of the accusation.

"What's more, I believe the real Teddy Lodge died three decades ago. The same for the real Geoff Newman."

Roarke recapped the history of Lodge's traffic accident, the disappearance of Newman at Heathrow, the lack of family pictures, even the death of his high school sweetheart.

"My god!" Bernsie concluded.

"He murdered his own wife," Morgan Taylor said, officially validating everything that Roarke had outlined. "I'll be damned if he's going to step one foot into this office!"

No one spoke for a long moment. Finally the FBI director stood, cleared his throat and faced his the president. "Morgan, I just want you to know, I'm not going anywhere."

"Thank you, Bob."

The vice president followed Robert Mulligan's cue and rose. "I'm with you, too."

Next it was John Bernstein, who nervously smacked his lips and stood. "What the hell are we going to do? I mean the constitutional ramifications alone are astounding." His mind raced. "The attorney general has to get up to speed." Bernsie turned to the president. "Does Eve know anything yet?"

"Almost nothing. Just that we're still investigating and we're making some assumptions. She doesn't know what they are. You're right, though, Bernsie. We will have to brief her soon."

The president now addressed his secretary for homeland security. "Nathan, we haven't heard from you yet."

Nathan Langone stood up, looking grave.

"Mr. President, every day I review a staggering number of reports from the department and whatever Jack and Bob have for me. As my predecessor said, 'They're not for the faint-hearted or timid.' So if you're asking *do I believe this*?"

"That's the question," Taylor stated.

"I believe that the ways, means, and manner that individuals around the world have devised to disrupt or destroy our economy, our government, or our lives is beyond our wildest imagination. But we must recognize the possibilities when they are presented. Mr. Roarke has done that most effectively. So do I believe?" The head of homeland security put the cap on his green and gold Waterman rollerball, returned it to his jacket pocket and declared, "You're damned straight!"

The president gave an appreciative and satisfied nod. "Thank you, Nathan. Now what are you thinking, Arthur?" Morgan Taylor asked the only man who still had not announced his position.

The national security advisor studied the chart once more. Arthur Campanis then slowly spoke in a monotone voice, with each phrase measured equally.

"Mr. President, in my opinion we're sitting on a ticking bomb. I don't like bombs unless we've dropped them. Let's find out how the hell to defuse this one...and fast."

Roarke smiled and took a full, massaging breath of air in. He'd done it. He went straight to Arthur Campanis and shook his hand.

"Now that we're on the same page," the president interjected, "I need everyone's thoughts on what we can do to beat Lodge *before* the election. We don't go public. And absolutely no leaks. Do I make myself clear?"

"Yes, sir," was the resounding response.

"Bernsie, you need to shore up the campaign. Work with the party. Maximum exposure. Maximum effort. And fill in Joyce."

"Got it," the chief of staff replied.

"Bob, get anything that looks like evidence. Eve won't be able to move without it."

"Yes, Mr. President."

Roarke suddenly let out an "Oh shit!"

"Yes, Scott?" the president asked. "Something else?"

"Forget about any DNA matchup with Lodge's parents. I just remembered another thing. They were both buried at sea. And guess what they died of?"

"Just tell us," Bernsie stated.

"Heart attacks."

"Two more for your chart, Scott," Jack Evans said pointing to the easel.

"And one more likely dead end for you Bob," Roarke added. "Parsons recommended I try a dental match. Who wants to bet Teddy Lodge's early records are gone, too?"

"We'll check anyway," Director Mulligan said, now fully committed.

"Okay," continued the president. "I'll want to finish the assignments. Jack, I know you're working the field. You tell me if there are any additional resources I can give you. Ships. Planes. Satellites. Anything."

The CIA Chief tipped his glasses again.

"And George, Stanley, Arthur, and Bernsie, clear your schedules. We'll spend some time together right after this meeting. I want ideas. What can we do if all our attempts fail prior to the immediate deadline."

"Meaning the election?" the vice president asked.

"The election."

The room fell silent again.

"Finally, thank you Scott. You've followed this from the beginning. You'll be involved through the end. Whatever that is."

"Thank you, boss. But I do have one thought."

"Yes?"

"Why don't we tickle the tiger."

"I beg your pardon?" the chief of staff interrupted.

"Tickle the tiger, Bernsie," Roarke repeated, not taking his eyes off the president. "Let's see what happens if we start playing a little mind game with *them*."

Roarke saw Morgan Taylor's face light up.

"If you mean fucking with their heads? I'm already ahead of you."

CHAPTER 44

THE WHITE HOUSE
THE OVAL OFFICE
TUESDAY, OCTOBER 28

"Thank you, Louise." The president took the call from Wendell Neill. He was not surprised. There really was no reason Lodge should have accepted his invitation. But it was the president's opening volley, strategically designed to unnerve his opponent. The rejection finally came through the Democratic Party Chairman. He was businesslike and direct, but Taylor heard something else in his voice. He recognized it instantly. Distrust.

He hung up the phone and called in the chief of staff.

"Bernsie, go with me on this for a bit. You're Lodge. What are you thinking?"

"Good question. I'm confident. Damned confident. I'm way ahead and there's nothing that can stop me. So there's no reason to see you in private. But I've just turned down an invitation from the president and I didn't even ask why he wanted to see me. That would make me a little worried."

"Fair assessment. I want him to worry. And he'll see me all right. I'll make the opportunity."

WASHINGTON, D.C.
SUNDAY, NOVEMBER 2

"Wednesday's headlines? How are they going to read?" snapped the host in the first round of his weekly TV program. "I predict it'll be *Taylor Dis-Lodged*. To you Victor Monihan—columnist for *The Philadelphia Inquirer*, your take?"

"Lodge has it wrapped. America loves him. He's developing a formidable presence in the world as well. Quite honestly, it's over. Those papers can go to press today."

"So noted," interrupted the host of the long running *McLaughlin Group*.

"Moderate through and through. Acceptable across party lines. And yet he's a Democrat. I haven't seen anyone quite like him. He can't lose."

"Morton Blowen, what will National Public Radio report on Wednesday's 'Morning Edition'?" the host said, pivoting to the opposite side of his panel.

"Hail to the *new* chief. Teddy Lodge," Blowen said, peering at the revered moderator through his designer glasses. "It's not that Taylor is bad. He isn't. We could have lived with him another four years. But once Teddy took New York, he owned the nomination. And now he's going to win the election."

That's the way the conversation went. Lodge watched at the Bel Age Hotel in Los Angeles. Taylor ignored it at his Presidential Suite in the Century Plaza Hotel.

LOS ANGELES, CALIFORNIA

This was Ben Bowker's first time directing a presidential debate. He had seven cameras to call, though he could have gotten away with five. The blocking went well earlier in the day with stand-ins. But of course, the run-through wasn't with the opponents who would soon take the stage.

Bowker, a network television director for three decades, planned his shots with precision. His cameras would cover the debate like zones in a football game. The audience hoped for real excitement. It was, after all, the last debate, coming only two nights before the election.

In half an hour the President of the United States and the

Democratic Party candidate would face one another. Reality TV didn't get any more exciting than this.

The drama, however, was beginning to unfold out of view of Bowker's cameras.

President Morgan Taylor knocked on Teddy Lodge's door. This was highly irregular. The Secret Service agents assigned to both men were bumping into each other.

"Who is it?" Lodge asked.

"Teddy, it's Morgan. Just a quick word with you."

Inside Newman flashed a surprised look at the congressman. "What the fuck does he want? You can't see him."

"Teddy…" the president said again.

"I'll handle it," Lodge said to Newman under the knocks on the door.

From the other side they heard the president again, even more insistent. "It'll only take a moment. We're both made up, with time on our hands."

"Don't," Newman warned. But Lodge ignored him. "Coming, coming." He turned the handle. "Hello, Mr. President," he said, offering his hand. "You know Geoff?"

"Yes," Taylor said acknowledging the congressman's number two. "And would you excuse us for a few minutes? I'd just like to have a little chat with your boss."

Newman was shocked. He uncharacteristically looked to Lodge for instructions.

"It's okay, Geoff. He won't bite."

"Quite correct," the president said with a laugh.

"Now if you'll close the door behind you. We won't be terribly long." The campaign manager left. The two candidates were finally alone.

"Sit down, Congressman."

Lodge wavered.

"Sit down," the president said with authority. Lodge obliged, aghast at the command that Morgan Taylor exhibited. The congressman relied on his own well-honed charisma. But what he had just experienced was sheer presidential power. He knew he should have remained standing, but he had lost the moment and the advantage.

"Teddy, you've done pretty well for yourself over the past few months. I should congratulate you." Taylor picked up the photograph of Jennifer Lodge that sat framed on his dressing table. "Nice touch. Did you bring it yourself or is it something Newman took care of?" He paused, but only for a fraction of a second. "...Like everything else."

"I beg your pardon," Lodge finally managed. He got up and grabbed the photograph. "Look, if you're trying to rattle me tonight it's not going to work. Not in here and not out there!"

"You misunderstand me. I really came in to wish you the best." Now the president sat down in a chair, his mood lightened. "Come on, you don't look comfortable. Relax."

Lodge hated that Taylor controlled a room that wasn't his. "No, I think I'll stand for awhile." Now out of his seat, he towered over his opponent. *My advantage*, Lodge thought.

Taylor helped himself to a bottle of Evian from the spread prepared by the caterer. "Do you mind?"

"Not at all," the Democrat said. "But I think I'd like a little quiet before we go on the air." He nodded to the door.

"Not quite yet."

"I can ask the Secret Service to have you removed."

"Oh Teddy. You have to remember. They still work for me. Let's just talk like old Capitol Hill chums. An old-fashioned boiler room chat."

What was on the old man's mind?

"Please," the president said calmly. "Have a seat."

Lodge returned to the couch.

"You really have come a long way. And God knows what's going to happen in the next few months. I just want to get a sense of where you want to take the country. That's all. Hell, everyone's saying the election is yours to lose. You're leading by a yard."

Lodge corrected him. "More like a mile. But you've put up a good fight."

The old flier didn't hesitate. "That's what I'm trained to do." His eyes took on a fierceness that Lodge had never seen before. He was facing a man who could fire a missile without hesitating; a man who knew how to play the game.

"But we're getting much too serious, Teddy," the president said unexpectedly. His face warmed up again.

"Do tell me, though. And not the bullshit we'll both be spewing in a couple of minutes. What do you have in mind?"

"With what?"

"Everything," Taylor continued. "The world. What will it look like when you're through with it? There are so many delicate relationships to consider. Pakistan and India. The factions in North Africa. North and South Korea. Israel and its Arab neighbors."

"Don't patronize me."

"Come now Teddy. You have a great challenge ahead of you. Those of us who have been in the hot seat know it."

"It's not a happy world, Mr. President. We've been living some lies for a long time."

"Not all of us, Congressman." The president grew deadly serious again.

"What's your point, Taylor," Lodge said, sharpening his reply.

"Nothing. Everything."

"Well, under *my* leadership we'll reassess our relationships. I'm sure you've had to do the same."

The president laughed. "Oh most definitely. I've learned to publicly eat some pretty disgusting humble pie. Then on the other hand, I've taken care of a few things very quietly."

The congressman thought he saw an opening. "Anything the Judiciary Committee should hear about?"

"Oh, heavens no. That would spoil all the fun."

Even Lodge laughed now. "I understand, Mr. President. I see there's a lot I can learn from you."

"Yes. I guess that's why I wanted to come by. To give you a *hint* of what I already know." *And I know a lot.* Taylor took a prolonged sip of the water, never taking his eyes off Lodge. He was beginning to tickle that tiger.

"Teddy, you're probably going to be elected next week. I'll be out of a job. Former presidents have a hard time. We're like the country's ex-wife. Nobody knows what to say to us, whether to invite us to the party. Well, I'm not ready to disappear."

"Am I to take this as an early concession speech?"

The president laughed and stood up. "Oh heavens no. We have a few days to play out our drama. Then who knows."

Lodge also got to his feet. "Then let's make it a good one."

"My sentiments exactly. The honorable thing." Taylor smiled as if to consider the comment. He put his hand on the doorknob, ready to turn it, then casually glanced back.

"That reminds me," the president asked in the tone of a passing thought.

"Yes?"

"You were a Boy Scout…"

"What?" Lodge asked.

"A Boy Scout. An Eagle Scout if your biography serves you right." Lodge stared ahead.

"Well, considering you may be taking the most important oath in your life," the president said sharply. "How's that one go? You learned it when you were a kid?"

"How's what go?" Lodge asked with complete annoyance.

"You know. The Boy Scout Oath. An Eagle Scout never forgets it."

Lodge froze. He utterly froze. His mouth dropped open in a gasp but he was completely speechless.

"Teddy, Teddy, Teddy. Come now. '*On my honor I will do my best, to do my duty, to God and my country…*' Well, it goes on. Perhaps it'll come to you." His eyes never left Lodge's. He had made himself perfectly clear. "Goodbye, Mr. Lodge. See you on TV."

Geoff Newman barged past the president with a disingenuous smile.

"Fucking asshole. I'll be glad when he's out of the way," Newman said when he re-entered Lodge's dressing room. He slammed the door and didn't care who heard it. Then he saw Lodge on the couch, ashen and nervously rubbing his hands. "Now what the hell is the matter with you?"

"Standby, in five…four…three…" Bowker called out. The last two seconds went unspoken on the floor, but counted down by everyone in the TV control room. "Roll music, graphics, up on one with key, cue announce."

"From the Campus of the University of California Los Angeles, welcome to the third and final Presidential Debate between President Morgan Taylor and Congressman Theodore Wilson Lodge."

The stage was stark. The host, the latest in a long line of NBC News anchors, stood behind a clear glass podium at stage left. Opposite him, the two candidates. They each stood at dark solid oak podiums that provided them stability and a place to hold their notes.

For Teddy Lodge, this was important. He gripped the surface with both hands to steady himself and to hide a nervous twitch in his right leg.

The president, noting his opponent's discomfort and the placement of the cameras, moved to the side of his podium and appeared relaxed and in total control. His twin lapel microphones would cover him wherever he walked. Columnists immediately noted the difference and Ben Bowker called to his cross shot on camera three to adjust for the president's repositioning.

There were four journalists to the host's right. Two from television, two from print.

Following the announcer's introduction, the NBC anchorman offered his welcome.

"Good evening. Tonight the world sees what America is all about. Freedom of speech. It exists for us, members of the press, the candidates who will soon engage in debate, and for you the voters. With your own free will, you will decide which of these two men will be sworn in as President of the United States. Traveling the world, I've learned to value how awesome this fundamental constitutional right truly is. Tonight we see it in practice; a model of freedom; a measure of the goodness and greatness of America."

Geoff Newman hung close to the wings, off camera, to the left of Lodge. Alone. Newman allowed no others, with the exception of Lodge's Secret Service detail.

On the other side, was the president's wife Lucy, then John Bernstein, the leader of the party, followed by his retinue of guards. Roarke, who ordinarily would have stayed with the president's camp, slipped closer to Newman. He was authorized to go anywhere.

The host introduced the panel and then invited the candidates to begin.

"This evening, it's been agreed that we'll start with the challenger, Congressman Lodge, then go to President Taylor. Final summations will be in the reverse order." The cameras picked up pictures of both men as they were identified. "Each candidate will be permitted two minutes now. Then our format calls for questions from our panel to be directed in an alternating fashion to Mr. Taylor and then to Mr. Lodge. The candidate who originally takes the question will have up to two-and-a-half minutes for his answer. Then we move onto a ninety-second rebuttal. Gentlemen, that's the way we will proceed until the final summations. First, Congressman Lodge."

Teddy Lodge was wearing a blue double-breasted sports coat, gray slacks, and a blue print tie that complemented his light blue shirt. He looked strikingly handsome, but totally outside the traditional debate uniform.

"Good evening," he began. The words came out, but they weren't delivered in the dynamic, convincing manner the country had come to expect in recent months.

In the wings, Roarke leaned in to Newman's ear.

The president had cued him up a bit on his private conversation.

"Seems like the congressman's off his game a bit." Newman swiveled around. Who even dared to talk to him now? Newman recoiled when he saw that it was a mere Secret Service grunt acting completely out of line.

"Excuse me. I'm trying to listen." He faced the stage again.

"Oh, no problem," Roarke said softly. "But you have to admit he's looking a little shaky out there." Roarke was picking at a scab. He'd never met Newman before and he instantly loathed the man. He'd push him all the more.

"The public likes a man who can be in control." Newman half turned. "Look I don't know who you are. But get the hell away from me right now."

The president could see that Roarke had sidled up to Newman offstage. He smiled to himself. *Just a little more agitating. We'll see where it goes.* Then he re-focused on Congressman Lodge. He was wrapping up his opening remarks.

"And so, as we all heard a moment ago, we're here exercising one of the most important freedoms of all. The process of freely deciding who should be president. I hope I'll be your choice."

Lodge finished by nodding to the camera, then to the crowd, not to President Taylor. There was polite applause. Not the resounding cheers he was used to.

"President Taylor. We're ready for your opening remarks," the moderator said,

The president wore his favorite black, pinstriped three-piece suit with a solid red tie gleaming out from his white shirt. An American flag pin was affixed to his lapel. He smiled and again stepped from behind the podium, in contrast to the stiff way Lodge had presented himself.

"Thank you, and thank you Congressman Lodge. And now to the esteemed journalists comprising our panel, the students and faculty of UCLA, and my fellow Americans watching at home—of course, you're all looking for answers from us, for the means to distinguish our points of view, and for clear understanding of our position on the important issues. I promise there will be no automatic stock responses from me. I encourage you to require the same from my opponent. So in the interest of time, I'll forgo any real opening statement. Let's get to business and make this time count."

Morgan Taylor was in control. He was concise, establishing the tone and the pace. The rest of his comments throughout the ninety-minute debate flowed the same way.

Ibrahim Haddad screamed unrelenting obscenities at his 50-inch plasma television screen in his Fisher Island home. *What happened? He can ruin everything.*

Haddad was ready to turn the set off altogether, but he stayed with it. Hopefully, Lodge would recover, or at the very least not suffer any more self-inflicted harm. He had a substantial lead, so Haddad reasoned that Lodge could probably afford one bad night and a few percentage points. Still, he gave a quick prayer in thanks that the election was only two days away.

The same speech was carried in Tripoli, downlinked to a television set in Fadi Kharrazi's TV station. However, Fadi lacked the sophistication to recognize that Lodge was faltering in front of the world. It wouldn't matter to the Libyans anyway. He would help manipulate the news as needed. For all the younger Kharrazi son knew Lodge was proving himself a strong, articulate leader.

Michael O'Connell watched the debate and raced his fingers across his keys. He wrote an article explaining how the rigors of the campaign and the emotional turmoil of the past six months took its toll on Congressman Lodge. He explained that the usually self-assured congressman faltered from the start. In contrast, the president exuded uncharacteristic conviction. It would mean votes on Tuesday.

Taking a cue from the president's first words, the reporters fired off their questions expecting straight-forward responses. They covered the uneasy peace between Pakistan and India, the downward spiral of public education, urban violence, and airline bailouts. Taylor had specific solutions involving corporate sponsorships. Lodge called for more government spending. Only when it came to the Middle East did the congressman speak with any authority, but the president had already scored his points.

Morgan Taylor never took his eyes off Teddy Lodge during his rival's answers. This served to further unnerve him. Lodge, in turn, drank too much water to quench his parched lips, which he soon regretted.

Why aren't there any fucking commercials, Geoff Newman wondered? He'd go out there and talk to Lodge. But there were none tonight.

Twenty minutes into the debate Newman finally got his candidate's attention while Taylor took the rebuttal to a question. He motioned for Lodge to puff out his chest, straighten his body and shake off the negativity. Lodge got the message, aware of the dubious image he had been projecting. Newman pointed to his eyes and then to the audience and mouthed the words, "To them. To them." Lodge understood.

Roarke leaned closer to Newman again to comment. "Coaching from the sidelines?" he said barely over a whisper. "I bet you can't wait to get into the White House where you won't have to be so quiet."

Newman swung around so fast he bumped into the agent. They stood eye to eye.

"The one thing I can promise," Newman gloated, "is that you'll be out of a job one minute after the congressman is sworn in. That's a promise. Now get out of here."

At that same moment the president wrapped up his latest parry to the most enthusiastic applause of the evening.

CHAPTER 45

TRIPOLI, LIBYA
MONDAY, NOVEMBER 3

Omar Za'eem understood the consequences. If caught spying he would suffer indescribable horrors in some basement chamber, then sell out his boss just before a bullet released him from his pain. So Za'eem prayed for strength and for courage and for a hint to what he was supposed to find for Abahar.

"Za'eem, come here!" Lakhdar al-Nassar shouted a moment after hanging up his phone. There was none of the camaraderie that they shared over drinks. His supervisor was in a foul mood.

"Yes, sir."

"I am far too busy to do all this shit. You take it. Clear my desk and put all of these away." He pointed to a foot high pile of newspaper clippings, folders, sports magazines, and books.

"They belong in there," he referred to Fadi's inner sanctum.

"I can't go into his office," Za'eem protested.

"You idiot. I'm telling you to put these away. That means you can go in there!"

Za'eem stood in place, uncertain. He knew the rules, "But I've been told…"

"And now you're being told something new. Put these back!"

Al-Nassar enjoyed intimidating people, especially when it meant he'd have less work to do and could go out and have a smoke or visit his mistress. Za'eem didn't know which it would be today or how long he would be away, but with such urgency he was sure Lakhdar was out to get laid.

"Yes, sir. But where? I've hardly been in…"

Al-Nassar grew furious. "You know the alphabet, don't you?"

Za'eem nodded.

"Then figure out which fucking file goes in which fucking drawer and how to put clippings away properly!"

With that al-Nassar removed a pack of cigarettes from his shirt pocket and lit up. After taking a long, satisfying drag he yelled to Omar who was gathering the materials. "Get it done right, otherwise

Fadi will have my ass. And I don't need to tell you what that will mean for you!"

Al-Nassar bolted out of the office, into the hall and down the elevator.

Omar Za'eem smiled. *It would be my pleasure.*

Fadi Kharrazi had left his office hours earlier extremely pleased that his plants in *Al-Fatah* had again successfully distorted the news for his countrymen. And now Lakhdar al-Nassar was also gone.

Omar Za'eem assessed his window of opportunity. His over-sexed supervisor wouldn't be back for a good ninety minutes. With luck, Fadi probably wouldn't return until later. To be sure, Omar checked Fadi's daily appointment calendar and smiled. He finally had the chance he had been waiting for.

Omar entered Fadi's office, a shrine to his own achievements. Kharrazi surrounded himself with framed photographs showing him at receptions with famous Arab leaders and parties at Cannes with prominent international movie stars.

He was an organized man; anal compulsive. There wasn't a paper out of place, not one book sticking out further than another on his bookshelf. Omar recognized he needed to take special care. Such a fastidious man would notice even the slightest change in his immediate environment.

He surveyed everything, getting his bearings and figuring out Fadi's filing system. He decided to begin the assigned work, then leave it while he looked for the details Abahar sought. His one limited communiqué had set off alarms. He'd been hounded for more information ever since.

Al-Nassar was in such a rush that he didn't even point Omar to the correct file cabinets. There were three different banks. One labeled *Political*, another for *News/Sports*, and five stacked cabinets grouped nearest his desk. These were marked *Personal*.

At first Omar dismissed the *Personal* ones. He assumed they probably dealt with his affairs: women's names, addresses, phone numbers. But he didn't doubt there were also details about his family, with possible notes about his father and the abusive things he had done. Everyone in power or close to power in closed societies always held some "get out of jail free" card. For Fadi, it might be something the

French, English, or Americans might want in exchange for granting him safe harbor. No, the *Personal* files were not his business today.

He also decided to skip the bank of file cabinets that contained news and sports stories. One of his jobs was to constantly clip articles about his boss. He figured that Fadi had been collecting them for years.

It was the set of cabinets marked *Political* that called out to Za'eem the most. Considering the level of interest from Abahar Kharrazi, the material must be political in nature. He'd return to them shortly.

First, he dispensed with some press clippings, speeches, photographs, and some hand written thank you notes from people obviously trying to remain in the good graces of the tyrant. The photographs and articles were easy. He found where they went in the *News* cabinets. After ten minutes he was ready to start working for Abahar.

Omar crossed the room to the *Political* cabinets. He tried a logical alphabetical approach. *Andropov*. Nothing. *Ashab al-Kahf.* Nothing again. He leafed through the folders but didn't find what he was looking for. If his memory served him right, one of the pages had a coffee-smudged right edge. He'd look for that, too.

The noise of the traffic rose up to the open windows. Though the temperature was comfortable for this time of year, Omar was sweating under the pressure.

Nothing in the first drawer, or the second. He checked his watch. He'd been in Kharrazi's office for six minutes now. He continued file by file, ready to pull anything else that looked interesting. Omar was trained to memorize what he read, which is why he didn't carry a miniature camera. Besides, if one were found on him, Fadi would probably shoot him in the balls himself.

After a half an hour he had gone through all of the *Political* filing cabinets without finding *Ashab al-Kahf* or any of the other key words. He bitterly swore to himself. Thirty minutes and nothing. Omar would have to go through the same files again, possibly even slower. At least this time he'd get some of al-Nassar's work done, too. As he crossed the room to pick up the work, the cabinets closest to Fadi's desk caught his eye. He suddenly realized his mistake. It wasn't *political* after all, or at least solely political. This was Fadi's *personal* business. That's why his brother wanted it. Family business. And he'd wasted thirty minutes to come to that conclusion.

He started the routine all over again going through the files looking for *Andropov* or *Ashab al-Kahf*. He prayed to Allah for guidance, but after examining the first file cabinet he still had nothing. There were two left, each with three filled drawers.

Omar had to sit down for a moment. He'd been bending over for too long and his fingers were numb from rifling through the folders. He'd already gotten a paper cut and sworn at himself for dripping blood on a page. He had heard that in the United States DNA evidence could convict him. Fortunately, Libya's police weren't so sophisticated.

Omar was now fully seventy minutes into his search. He tried not to panic, but this was dangerous and he was scared to death.

He began to wonder if he could even trust his senses. Was he actually reading the names of files or simply thumbing through them blindly? He couldn't remember. Now two of the three *Personal* cabinets were done. *What if I don't find anything here?* He forced the thought away. *I have to.*

The noise of cars honking and people yelling from outside increased as the late afternoon traffic started clogging the street below. A traffic jam would be good. He prayed for a major tie up as he began on the lowest file drawer.

Nine minutes later he feared he was truly on borrowed time. There was no telling how long before al-Nassar would come back from his quickie, or worse, when Fadi Kharrazi would return. Suddenly he stopped and discovered why it had taken him so long. Al-Nassar had stupidly misfiled the damned folders. He had read it wrong. Omar had to laugh. *Lakhdar is brainless.*

So simple and so stupid a mistake in the reading of *Ashab al-Kahf.* Al Nassar mistakenly took the first letter, an "Alif" for a "Waaw." *What a fool,* Za'eem thought. *He stuck it in at the end of the alphabet, instead of where it belonged.*

The master folder was at least five inches thick and full of other files, one labeled *Red Banner*. Omar cocked his ear toward the door to hear if anyone was coming. He was still alone.

He looked at the principal tab again. He whispered the words.

"Ashab al-Kahf." Now they sounded familiar. *Why? A story?* He said them again. "Ashab al-Kahf."

A story? Yes, a story. But about what?

He started to read and then he remembered. *The Legend of Ashab al-Kahf.*

CHAPTER 46

Ashab al-Kahf. A passage in the Qur'an. Translated to English it meant *"People or Companions of the Cave."* While Omar wasn't a dutiful Libyan servant, he was a devout Muslim. He had studied the Qur'an and the fascinating details of the passage returned to him.

The actual text was contained in Sura 18:9-27, but the folklore was often better conveyed in the spoken word. *Ashab al-Kahf* tells of a number of men, several centuries prior to the arrival of Mohammed, who roamed the desert and the highlands, seeking *the truth* about the revelation of the Prophet. They were accompanied by their faithful dog. Wherever they went, they befriended people, asking them if the words of the yet unseen, unknown Prophet might have come to them. Eventually they arrived at a cave, presumed to be in Iraq or Jordan, although most believers argued it was in Syria. Exhausted from their journey, they rested inside, away from the scorching desert sun. They soon fell asleep. Their dog curled up outside, guarding the entrance and also slipped into a fitful sleep.

Allah, recognizing their goodness and the righteousness of their quest, put them all in a deeper, magic sleep, to awaken only when the Messenger received the revelation. The men and their pet slept undisturbed for 600 years. At a time appointed by Allah, Gabriel was dispatched with the Message for Mohammed.

In time, Mohammed learned of the sleepers. Touched by their devotion, he sent four *Companions* to them to proclaim the coming of the ultimate truth. Allah awakened them after their six-century sleep.

One of them visited a nearby souk for food. They had, after all, woken up with a strong hunger, matched only by their thirst for knowledge.

When the one Sleeper tried to pay a merchant for the food, he was told his money was old and no longer in use. The Sleeper soon realized he and his friends had not slept one night, but through thousands of nights.

When the Companions arrived, they explained the mission Allah had sent them on. They invited the Sleepers to return with them to Arabistan. But the Sleepers felt unworthy to accept such an offer. Allah, they believed, had given them—as faithful disciples—many lifetimes just so they would be able to hear the true Message.

After the revelation, the Sleepers decided there was no earthly reason to go to Arabistan. They believed the only path ahead for them was to Paradise.

The Sleepers and their dog returned to the cave. Allah smiled upon them and granted their sole wish. He invited their spirits aloft.

The Companions returned to Mohammed and shared the mystery of what they had seen. The Prophet Mohammed asked how many Sleepers they had seen.

One said four. Another five. The others remembered six and seven.

The Prophet observed their difference of opinion and noted, "The ways of Allah are wondrous and only He knows how many Sleepers there are. Only He knows when one will awaken. The world is full of Sleepers and only Allah knows their number and when they will awaken."

Ashab al-Kahf. A tale of sleepers in a *Personal* file.

Omar Za'eem read as quickly as he could. *The People of the Cave* was a code name for some contemporary operation. He scanned quickly; nervously reviewing what he had seen before.

The Syrians. Hafez al-Assad. His son. Saddam Hussein's son, Uday, and now Fadi Kharrazi. They were all noted, and so was something called Red Banner.

So much to absorb. The more new material he read, the more he lost himself in the content and the less aware he became of time. Forty-five minutes. One hour. Ninety minutes. Too many names, places, and dates to memorize.

Almost two hours.

Pictures of children. Articles on the American political system.

Suddenly, a noise in the hall. *An elevator door opening?* It was hard to hear.

A moment later the sound of heavy footsteps in a staccato rhythm. *Damn.* There was more to read. But he couldn't ignore the danger.

Fadi had a distinctive gait, a bit of a shuffle, but fast and heavy. Za'eem pushed the drawer closed. He realized that despite the orders of his direct superior he couldn't be caught in Fadi's private office. The sound of steps grew louder. He was nearly at the outer office door and Za'eem could never make it back to his desk in time.

He started to the door, then remembered he left the files he had been holding. *Where were they? On top of the third Personal cabinet.* "Shit!" he said aloud. He'd left them there when he got engrossed in the Hafez al-Assad to Uday Hussein connection that pre-dated Fadi's fingerprints on the plan. He doubled back, retrieved them and dashed to the door, which he now knew he'd never make.

Someplace to hide? He quickly perused the room. *Nowhere.* Besides, he should be at his desk. He imagined he had less than a minute to live.

The shuffling was closer. Then a voice. The steps stopped. *Al-Nassar calling to Fadi?* It sounded like both men were coming back, but al-Nassar had to explain why he wasn't at his desk.

Omar Za'eem used the time to rush back to the inner office, put the unfinished work back on al-Nassar's desk, reach for his scissors and start a cut in the first newspaper page he found. Al-Nassar's own excuses to Fadi bought Za'eem twenty seconds.

For Omar Za'eem it was nothing short of a lifetime.

Omar had never heard such a string of obscenities from Fadi. He launched into al-Nassar, calling up every disgusting phrase imaginable. It made Omar laugh to himself, partly out of relief that he was safely back in his seat. But when the younger Kharrazi son walked by Za'eem's desk without even acknowledging his presence, he knew that al-Nassar would soon take his own anger out on the closest target. Him.

Fadi slammed his door shut. The entire room shook.

"What was that all about?" Omar asked quietly.

"Who the fuck knows. Maybe he couldn't get it up."

Za'eem wouldn't be baited into the dialogue. But as al-Nassar's hateful eyes wandered, he could feel what was coming.

He didn't have to wait long. Al-Nassar slid into his chair, rubbed his own sore crotch, indicating that he probably didn't have the best of times either, then saw the unfinished work lying on his desk.

"And you? You can't complete a simple task?" He grabbed the files and clippings. It was time for his anger to trickle down. "What were you doing? Jerking off in some comer?"

Za'eem lowered his eyes.

"I'm asking you a fucking question? Do you want it to be the last one you ever hear?"

"No sir," he answered tentatively.

"Then why isn't this done?"

"I've never spent much time in Mr. Kharrazi's office before. I was," he paused for effect, "I was confused by the system."

"You are a complete moron." Al-Nassar picked up one file. "Pictures of the United States Congressman? That's political! Or haven't you heard." He threw the folder directly at Za'eem. It flew open, sending papers in every direction.

"Pictures of Fadi with the General? News!" A second folder came at him even faster. And then another and another. Omar dropped to the floor to try to pick up the pages and put them back in as fast as he could.

"One simple task a six-year-old could accomplish, but I get the village imbecile. Some reject from the army. I can't leave the office for an hour without you screwing up." Omar thanked God it was longer than an hour.

"Well, I've carried you long enough. You're an ass-kissing little nobody. Get out of here!"

"But sir," Za'eem offered apologetically, "I tried."

"And you're incompetent! Go, get out of my sight for good!" His voice rose, probably intentionally so Fadi could overhear. Fadi would now reward al-Nassar for striking his inferior down, just as he had done. The food chain at work.

"Now!"

"But I need this job. My mother and sister." He was falling back on a well-rehearsed lie about his family in the old town of Germa. "I have to…"

"You have to get out of here before I count to ten."

Al-Nassar removed a pistol from his desk.

Za'eem was gone before he got to five. He couldn't have planned the day better himself.

CHAPTER 47

WASHINGTON

Scott Roarke had no idea what news tomorrow would bring. Where the votes would fall. Immediately following Sunday night's debate, Lodge took a definite hit. One instant phone poll conducted by Fox News showed the congressman trailing two to four points. MSNBC's own survey had him drop by four to eight.

The conservative talk shows, more partial to the president, revved up on Monday afternoon, taking predictable shots at Teddy Lodge, claiming he was on the run. But no amount of polling or talk show hyperbole could truly tell where the country would go on Tuesday. In truth, it was becoming too close to call.

So Roarke did what he always did to calm himself.

He exercised. His workout, long overdue, included the best of his Army Special Forces training and everything the gym could offer. Deep down inside a voice told him to be ready. That voice never failed him.

Another voice called to him as well. Katie's.

He dialed her as he jogged home with the hands free earphone in his ear.

"Hi, Katie." he said barely revealing he was running. "How are you, sweetheart?"

"I would be better if you were somewhere else."

"Where?"

"Someplace warm and cozy."

His mind went exactly where she intended. Roarke unknowingly stopped and leaned against a tree, feeling himself get excited. On a call of this nature, he didn't even worry about the extended time they talked. No government secrets here, only his own.

"Right now," she continued.

"Right now?" he asked.

"Right now. Wanna come?"

"Hmmm. Oh, I wish I could. But I have to see what's going to go down tomorrow. And I suppose I have to do my civic duty."

"The shuttle can get you here by dinner," she cooed.

"Soon. I just can't now."

The mood passed and he continued his run toward Georgetown.

"Tell me. You're in Lodge country. What's everyone talking about up there?"

"A *Globe* editorial claimed that people shouldn't place too much emphasis on the debate. That the whole campaign just caught up with Teddy. The *Herald*'s front page was 'Hodge Podge Lodge.' And they tore into him."

"And on the street?"

"Still all Lodge, I'd say. Local boy. He's got the Kennedy magic. Massachusetts will go for him. All New England. Maybe New Hampshire will be close. Otherwise, no change up here."

"What do you hear?" she asked.

"Florida's definitely still Lodge. Georgia, the Carolinas, Virginia. I just don't know. It's shifting to the Prez. I think Pennsylvania and New York are solidly Lodge's, though. It's gonna be the Midwest and west coast that decide this thing."

"And when it's over?"

"Hey, maybe you'll come down and visit me. But better hurry. There may not be much opportunity to score you an insider's tour of the White House."

"But you'll still be there."

"Not after my talk with Newman Sunday night."

"You didn't make nice with the potential new landlords?"

"No. I can't say I did."

"Very bad boy. Well, don't forget my law firm represented Teddy. So maybe I'll be the one who arranges the next tour."

Roarke stopped again. For a moment he had forgotten how they had met. The circumstances. The tête-à-tête. And the attraction.

What if she were right? What if Teddy Lodge really became president?

Katie continued to flirt with him, but Roarke had tuned out.

TRIPOLI, LIBYA
TUESDAY, NOVEMBER 4

Omar Za'eem did all of Sami Ben Ali's heavy lifting. Pity he'd never be able to thank him personally for all his help.

Abahar's spy dutifully reported his findings to Walid Abdul-Latif. Abdul-Latif, in turn, typed up the details of the conversation for his boss, Major Bayon Karim Kitan, who presented them to Abahar Kharrazi. Sami Ben Ali would read them first.

He got his opportunity earlier than expected. Walid received a phone call that he needed to respond to immediately.

"I have to go out. I'll be back in a few hours," Walid said. He grabbed his gun and his billy club.

"Where are you going?" Sami asked nonchalantly.

"None of your business." But Walid would tell him anyway. He had to brag.

"If you have to know, it's time to *explain* some things again to a group of whining students at Nasser University," he said swinging his weapon.

A few years ago, thirty-two students from Nasser were reportedly arrested for converting to Christianity. They were blindfolded, tied together, and taken to prison. Challenges to General Kharrazi's beliefs. Most people learned. Some didn't. People like Walid were quite ready to correct their behavior in the name of the Great Socialist People's Libyan Arab Jamahiriya. Undoubtedly, a few students would land in Abu Salim Prison for a time. Others might not even see graduation, ever.

Once alone, Sami got to work. He knew that Za'eem had made progress. Now to download the report and clean his tracks afterwards.

This time he did it faster, quickly catching a key word: *Ashab al-Kahf*, and then saving the file.

When Walid didn't return by 1830 hrs, Sami assumed he was raping one of his female captives or taking delight in clubbing a man. So he left. Amazing that after all of his years undercover in Tripoli, it all came down to one computer disc.

The last directive Sami Ben Ali received from Langley was simple and to the point. "Call home. Want to hear from you. Maybe we'll visit as soon as we know where."

It was the "as soon as we know where" that had kept him up at nights these last few weeks. The words had long ago flamed into nothingness; burned and gone when he ignited the flash pad they'd been written on. But they were burned into his consciousness. *"Soon"* actually meant "urgent." And *"know where"* was all about identifying precise details about a hard target. Apparently this was tremendously important information for Evans. Very important. Sami would trade it for a ticket out of Libya.

First things first. He had to get word that he had something. And he had to be careful. Then, when it was safe, he'd hand over the entire report.

As he walked through the maze of Tripoli's shops and restaurants in the souk, he thought of Detroit and football season. He'd like to take in a game again at Ford Field and have a cold beer. The Lions didn't have to win. He'd be happy simply being there.

But to get there, he'd have to be careful. There was always the possibility of being watched.

Tonight it looked clear. No one seemed to be following him as he made his way to a favorite bookstore in the bazaar.

A bell attached to the door clanged when he entered. No one bothered looking at him and Sami Ben Ali didn't make eye contact with anyone else. The shelves were lined with decades-old dog-eared editions of "approved" historical books, Islamic religious texts, and Arabic folklore. He meandered around for ten minutes, then approached the front desk.

Like many booksellers in the area, Hamid Salim Sahhaf bought, sold, traded, and bartered his stock. He claimed to have read every volume. Whether or not it was true, he certainly knew their location on the shelves.

"Do you have a 1920s edition of *Gilgamesh*?" Sami asked politely.

"Why, yes I do," the old man answered. "Three copies. But I'm afraid that you won't be happy. Many of the etchings are missing in the oldest one. Fine ones, too. A big book on the third shelf down that aisle." He pointed to a row at the far end of the room, away from the door. "All the way on the left."

"Thank you," Ben Ali said, bowing politely. He casually walked through the store, between dusty shelves, which smelled of the mildew eating away at many of the books. At the back was one row that dead-ended against the wall. That was where he was told to go.

In relative short order he found what he was looking for. Not the copy of *Gilgamesh* with the etchings missing, but one directly to the right.

He removed it, began leafing through the pages and stopped at page 134. He turned his back to aisle and quietly read. The story, one of the oldest in the world, always fascinated him.

According to the epic legend, Gilgamesh, born one-third mortal and two-thirds god, was a Sumerian king around 3500 B.C. The story was passed down for generations by word of mouth, then, possibly in the 7th century B.C., recorded in Akkadian cuneiform symbols onto twelve clay tablets. Sami loved the story and its characters, finding personal meaning in Gilgamesh's quest to understand his true purpose and sense of self.

Without anyone noticing, he casually folded up a quarter inch of the lower right hand corner of page 134 and folded down the upper left corner of page 179. Sami Ben Ali had just left two numerical messages. "Found what I was looking for. And I want out."

After a few minutes he picked up the larger tattered edition he had been directed to, skimmed through it, then looked at the third book. Five minutes later he nodded in a manner that would make any observer think he was finally satisfied. He tucked the last book under his arm and returned to the front to pay.

Now for the customary haggling over the price. This took a good three minutes. Hamid Salim Sahhaf and Ben Ali settled on the middle ground. Sami left as pleased as the old man; each convinced that he had out-tricked the other for the best price.

Ben Ali settled into a restaurant a few doors down from the bookstore. He ordered a green apple tea, lit up a cigarette, and opened his book as if to read it. In actuality he was back to work; taking everyone in to see who might be lingering or watching. A sixth sense told him someone was out there.

CHAPTER 48

ELECTION DAY
TUESDAY, NOVEMBER 4

Jack Evans arrived at Langley at his usual 0545. It took him an hour to digest the overnight reports. One message in particular caught his eye. Sandman had reported in. It took only 15 seconds to gather the importance of the message. He called to his driver to bring his car around. They'd be heading to the White House early today.

"Want to stop and vote on the way back, sir?" the driver, a fifty-eight-year-old CIA officer named Si Marvin asked. "They say the race is closer than predicted. I think the Chief can use your vote."

The morning polls reported a virtual dead heat.

"You get me there as often as you can, Simon. The way I feel right now, I think it's only fair I vote a hundred times."

Marvin had no idea what Evans was talking about. But he laughed and put the pedal to the metal.

Ibrahim Haddad pulled the lever on his district's voting machine. The old punch cards with the chads that decided the Bush-Gore election were retired following a primary in March 2002. Now Miami-Dade County, Florida, used computers.

Haddad, an American citizen for more than thirty years, actually liked to vote. But this election was special. He cast his ballot for a man who would, as he'd promised in his campaign speeches, "Change the world." He voted for Congressman Teddy Lodge and walked out of the voting booth happier than he'd ever been.

Michael O'Connell correctly figured he'd be on the road election day. He voted for Lodge ten days earlier using an absentee ballot.

Detective Harry Coates cast his vote for the congressman, as did St. Charles Hotel employees Carolyn Hill and Anne Fornado.

With what Police Chief Carl Marelli and Chuck Wheaton knew, they went row "A" for President Morgan Taylor.

The Idaho State Policeman, Duke Hormel, said he liked the president, but he and his wife voted for Teddy Lodge.

Touch Parsons was the first in line at his polling station. He was on the president's side, especially now. So were the rest of Taylor's key advisors and Bureau heads.

Katie Kessler had always voted Democrat until today. And Scott Roarke who tended to make up his mind in the voting booth didn't abandon his boss.

In Burlington, Vermont, Geoff Newman voted just ahead of Teddy Lodge. The news cameras followed them as far as they could up the walkway to Ward 6's booths located at Edmunds Middle School.

The same was true in Washington when Morgan and Lucy Taylor cast their ballots.

And, in the complete privacy of a makeshift voting booth in Precinct 48, the so-called "tree" and "poet streets" district of Billings, Montana, Governor Lamden did precisely what his heart told him to do.

One man heavily involved in the election process didn't vote. For that matter, he wasn't on any registration rolls. Not as Roger C. Waterman or Frank Dolan or Dr. George Powder. The man was anonymous again, driving leisurely across the country, ignoring the early election reports on his radio in favor of a satellite station playing authentic bluegrass.

The CIA director had to wait for the president to return from a scheduled breakfast after voting. Evans sat in the West Wing, sipping some freshly brewed coffee, not once letting his briefcase out of his hand.

When the president charged into the White House, he said, "Jack, you're in a bit early this morning."

"Something to share with you, sir." He offered no hint of small talk. Morgan Taylor read the signs.

"Come right in."

Once the door was closed Evans didn't wait for an invitation to begin.

"A message from Sandman. He found what he was looking for."

Neither man had sat down. They stood eye to eye, barely two feet from one another.

"What is it?"

"We don't know yet. He gave us the sign that he had located exactly what we needed. Hard copies."

"Any hint?"

"Our instructions to him were explicit. He contacted us in the manner prescribed if and when he located information. But with the chance he could be watched we have to be careful."

"So when?" The president asked. *And why the hell didn't this happen earlier?*

"It'll take a drop. An e-mail is too risky. He doesn't have a satellite phone. So I've got to think about this. But he knows *where* it is and presumably *what* it is. Oh, and there's one more thing he communicated."

"Let's hear it."

"Sandman wants out. But if he suddenly disappears people will notice. It could raise suspicions. Tip the Kharrazis."

"Meaning…?"

"We're very close and he's far away. That puts us slam bam in the middle of a shit sandwich," Evans explained. "It's hard to pass the information and we can't get Sandman out."

CHAPTER 49

The Constitution of the United States provides for a popular vote for president. But the overall national numbers are secondary to a candidate taking a majority of the important states. Winning a state means you're awarded the Electoral College votes. Add enough of those votes up and a candidate becomes president.

On the Monday following the second Wednesday of December, each State's Electors convene in their state capitals to cast their electoral votes for president and vice president. Larger states hold more electoral votes; smaller states fewer. The system is flawed. A candidate can win the plurality of national votes, but not earn enough state Electoral College votes to move into 1600 Pennsylvania Avenue. Al Gore could still bend an ear on that topic. He won the national vote in 2000, but George W. Bush came out ahead in the electoral numbers.

The same scenario threatened to keep the Taylor-Lodge election in limbo for hours. It was definitely going to be a close call today. One state could make a difference.

Voting picked up in the late afternoon. People went to the polls on their way home after work, following school carpools, and before the late shift began. Instant polls shed no new light on where it would end up. The final hour of votes from commuters would decide it.

All of the networks, independent stations, and news organizations continued the policy of not reporting precinct, city, or state results until the polls were closed in each time zone. By 7:00 P.M., as initial tallies began coming in, graphic boards behind the anchors lit up. Blue for states going to President Taylor. Red for Congressman Lodge. Some of them switched back and forth since the earliest numbers didn't necessarily reflect the ultimate direction of the entire state.

New England was assuredly Lodge country, as predicted. Even conservative New Hampshire. So was New York. But Pennsylvania, first given to Lodge, went to Taylor. The same for Delaware and Maryland. The president also took the District of Columbia and the Southern states in the Eastern time zone, with the exception of Virginia and North Carolina.

As the polls closed in the Midwest, the same flipping occurred. Consequently, no one could accurately predict the outcome. Fox got caught twice trying to make a reliable prediction only to see the numbers swing. NBC and its affiliated news channels decided not to call a state until 50 percent or more of the vote was in. CBS said it for everyone: "We might as well settle in. It's going to be a long, nerve-racking night."

Two hundred seventy out of a possible 538 Electoral College votes are required to win. At 11:30 Eastern Time, Morgan Taylor had 237 to Teddy Lodge's 196. A half hour later, the close results from Colorado, Montana, New Mexico, Arizona, and Utah. And still no winner. 249 Taylor. 216 Lodge. Both within striking distance. Alaska would go to Taylor, and Lodge would take Hawaii.

The West Coast states would decide the election. Together, Washington and Oregon carried 18 Electoral votes. The president was projected to capture those, which would leave him just three electoral votes short. California's 55 were a toss-up. The state posted a record turnout, but early precinct results failed to show a decisive trend. San Francisco and Los Angeles went to Lodge. Orange County and San Diego belonged to the president. The critical votes would be in Central and Northern California, but due to downed phone lines and computer issues, they were slow to be reported.

And this is how it went. Up and down for the next two hours.

"Wine country to the Oregon border will go to Congressman Lodge," offered CNBC. The anchor circled the massive land area south of San Francisco, north of L.A. on his telestrator. "Now this is where it'll come down to. California's Central Valley. The region is composed of eight counties: Fresno, Kern, Kings, Madera, Merced, San Joaquin, Stanislaus, and Tulare, amounting to ten percent of California's population. To put it another way, the Central Valley outranks 20 states in population.

"One portion of one state. Roughly three million voters will decide for the entire country who will serve as president."

Of course, Fadi Kharrazi didn't understand any of the process. He watched the numbers rise and fall over a satellite feed of CNN International. He believed that many commentators were merely Taylor's paid mouthpieces; that they'd only report what they were told. *How things would soon change.* In his naïve view of American free speech, he wondered which members of the press the new president would fire first.

At 1104 hrs Tripoli time, well after midnight in the United States,

CNN analysts felt they could finally declare a winner. Fadi Kharrazi turned up the sound.

So did Morgan Taylor in Washington, Teddy Lodge in Burlington, and millions of other viewers who were still up at 4:04 A.M. in Washington—1:04 in the morning on the West Coast.

CHAPTER 50

TRIPOLI, LIBYA
WEDNESDAY, NOVEMBER 5

The bookseller's eyes didn't give him away. But for a brief moment the old man peered over a stack of magazines piled on his desk and noted the familiar customer who was interested in *Gilgamesh*. He shifted his eyes downward and lost himself in the lies of the day's newspapers. For Hamid Salim Sahhaf, reading was required for his cover. He had quietly served as a CIA information officer for twenty-nine years, surviving two regimes to become the longest living mole in all of Libya.

Sahhaf's only duty was to fold down pre-determined pages of books as instructed and, in turn, let his contact know what pages he discovered were folded down. He never knew what it meant and he didn't care. In fact, he regularly complained to customers to be good to the books. "You illiterate fools," he would complain. "How am I supposed to make a living selling books when people turn them into shit?"

At one point, the grumbling worked its way to Abahar Kharrazi's Office of Internal Security. But Sahhaf was easily dismissed as senile and harmless. The paperwork never even reached Abahar.

Even Sami Ben Ali failed to peg Sahhaf as a spook. He simply knew that the bookstore was his primary drop. It worked this way. He browsed the shelves again. Replies were always on a shelf below where the questions were left. It was the third day of the week. So he counted in three books from the left. This is where he'd find the answer, if one was there for the day. To any other browsers, it looked as if he was searching for a text. Sometimes there would be nothing. Like yesterday. He hoped his people would have something for him today.

He found it in a novel titled *Sirat Bani Hilal*, a story of a fictitious black tribal prince named Abu Zayd. Sami didn't know the tale. Perhaps one day he'd read it—hopefully back in Detroit. Quite a few pages were flagged. His coded flash pad for the day would help him turn the numbers on the pages into meaningful content.

After three rounds of haggling with the shopkeeper who barely gave any ground this time, Sami finally paid.

He casually walked back to his office at Abahar's OIS, trying not to draw any attention to himself. Sami kept thinking about the Lions and how well he heard they were doing this season. He was oblivious to the real news that was breaking on the radio.

The ABC anchor looked straight into the camera. The alphabet network was ready to make the call exactly the same time CNN committed. NBC was 30 seconds behind. CBS and Fox, which had gotten it wrong before, made the announcement barely a minute later.

The full frame picture of the veteran anchor effected to a three-way split screen allowing room for live shots from both the Taylor and Lodge headquarters.

"We now feel confident to tell you," he stated, "that we have a clear winner."

The anchor noted the time. "Exactly 4:04 A.M." He explained again that the California results were later than expected because phone lines were blown down during a blast of Santa Ana winds across Southern California resulting in late computer tallies. That's where Fox had made their projection errors.

As he continued, worn-out volunteers and staffers waited patiently, holding on to every word. The reaction wasn't immediate. It took time for it to sink in. Then viewers saw the contrasting shots. One campaign headquarters erupted into chaos. The other fell totally silent.

The anchor repeated the announcement. "The most closely contested presidential election in American political history now has a victor. Closer than Kennedy-Nixon. Closer than Bush-Gore. With a total of 271 Electoral College votes, just one more than required, the winner of California will be sworn in as President of the United States on January 20th—Theodore Wilson Lodge."

Fadi leaned back in his chair, quite satisfied with the report on CNN International. It was a good day; the second critical date he had circled on his desk calendar. One more remained.

PART III

CHAPTER 51

TRIPOLI, LIBYA

At the end of the day, Sami was back in the confines of his pitiful apartment closet. He sealed the cracks between the door and the door frame with duct tape. His radio was turned up to cover the sound of his work should any eavesdropping devices be in place. If only the communiqué would guarantee his ticket out. Twenty minutes into the deciphering he learned he wasn't going anywhere. Not yet.

Sami had to get his disk to Langley. The company needed the whole thing.

He wished he could simply walk up to one of Tripoli's many Internet cafés, like Al Dalil at 15 Gargach or Sendibadat at Hai Demashq, and e-mail the data to a safe address. But that was not wise. Tripoli was fairly open to Internet use, however loading an incriminating disk would be plainly stupid. So would typing a coded message out in the open. It could be easily observed by another patron or stored in backup hard drives that were likely hidden somewhere in the cafés.

He certainly couldn't take the chance of sending it out through his apartment phone and a cell phone was completely out of the question. Kharrazi had outlawed cell phones for all but high level government use.

Sami Ben Ali had to rely on the old fashioned methods. This would require more thought. But not tonight. He was sweaty and exhausted sitting so long in the closet. And having heard the election results on the street, he wondered what the news back home would mean.

THE WHITE HOUSE

At 10 A.M. Washington time, the President of the United States spoke to an audience of housewives and executives, the people generally watching daytime TV. It was an intentional low impact appearance for a concession speech.

"Hello, everyone. Early this morning, it was reported that there will be a new president." He didn't mention Lodge by name. "He's going to have a great deal on his plate. The vote, as you know, was extremely close, the circumstances of the election were quite unexpected. But for now, as true Americans, we must prepare for the transition and let the unique and wondrous constitutional process unfold.

"To my supporters, I offer my heartfelt gratitude. To my successor, I ask only one thing." He stared directly at the camera lens, his expression deadly serious. "Be true to the United States of America." His face then warmed up again. "And to all citizens, I continue to pledge *my* allegiance to our great country. Thank you. God Bless America." He left the podium bearing the symbol of the president, passing on the opportunity to talk to reporters.

The president had done the expected, but with words that asked more questions than they answered. Morgan Taylor conceded the election without acknowledgement of defeat. Some commentators looked for meaning and intent. Others considered it merely tired ramblings from the loser. Teddy Lodge heard exactly what he was supposed to.

BURLINGTON, VERMONT

"He didn't even fucking congratulate me."

"It doesn't matter. He's out," Newman said to the infuriated Lodge.

"Out? He was giving me the finger on national television. '...*be true to the United States.*' What kind of bullshit was that?"

Lodge brushed his hair back off his forehead, but not in the sexy manner he did for the cameras. He felt pure rage. "He's setting me up."

"Forget him. He's nobody. Now it's your turn to talk to the country. Tuck your shirt in and get ready. I've had the makeup girl waiting all night for you."

"But he's…"

"History. Just another ex-president."

Newman was exerting his decades-old control over his puppet. And Lodge, as always, listened. "Pull yourself together. You're the new President of the United States. Put him out to pasture with style. The press won't give a damn about Taylor after you say thank you for honoring your wife's memory by the way they voted."

Lodge nodded as he straightened himself out and fastened a bright yellow print tie.

"That's a new one," noted Newman. "Where'd you get it?"

"Christine gave it to me. Oh, and I want you to keep her around."

"Well, hi there," proclaimed Teddy Lodge over the cheering of his campaign staff. "Did you have a good night?" he joked. "I sure did."

The screams were ear shattering. The glass in the Sheraton Burlington Hotel ballroom windows, site of the Lodge victory party, actually shook.

"I guess we did it!"

The chants of "Ted-dy…Ted-dy…Ted-dy…" took over for a good two minutes, until the Congressman lowered his arms from over his head. The network cameras all had the same handsome three-buttoned shot.

"It wasn't me," he continued. "It was all of you!" And with another burst of enthusiasm, the crowd showed exactly how they loved him.

Newman watched on TV. His man was doing what he did best: rewarding his followers and seducing new devotees. He'd been doing it ever since college. Even the people who abandoned him because of his performance in the last days of the campaign would come back. The polls would bear that out after this speech.

A question nagged at him, though. *Did Taylor really know anything?* He bit his lip. *No. He's nothing but a powerless lame duck.* Newman turned his attention back to the television screen.

"I want to thank President Taylor for his clean and spirited fight.

I think I speak for the nation when I say, thank you for your service, Mr. President. You have distinguished yourself honorably throughout your term. The country owes you a great debt of gratitude."

The crowd politely applauded, which allowed the congressman to move on. That door was now shut. With the accolade, Teddy Lodge had ever so nicely willed Morgan Taylor to the corn field.

"Now to the future, which is hard for me to separate from the past. I am here because you are ready for a change and you've made it happen. I am here because I wanted to be your president and you've granted me that privilege. And I am here because of your love and the love of my wife. Thank you on behalf of Jenny. Thank you."

The crowd, hypnotized by a run of Lodge's triplets, began its chanting again.

"Governor Lamden and I will begin talking later today about our transition team. We will assemble a vital group of men and women who will help plot a course for greater prosperity, a stronger nation, and a better world. I thank you for all of your support. And now, if you'll excuse me, I'll head home. I suddenly have a bit of packing to do."

Teddy Lodge waved goodbye and left, making sure he shook as many hands as the cameras were willing to cover.

Morgan Taylor turned off the TV set. He'd run out of time and ways to stop Teddy Lodge before the election.

Now he wondered if he'd even have the means to prevent him from assuming office.

Proof. I need some goddamned proof.

CHAPTER 52

TRIPOLI, LIBYA
FRIDAY, NOVEMBER 21

He was being watched. But he didn't know if the eyes belonged to Abahar Kharrazi's men. And he couldn't figure out which would be worse: the Secret Police personally torturing him with electrical devices or Walid cruelly clubbing him into submission. Sami desperately wanted out of Tripoli, but he couldn't act hastily. Instead, he took the path of least resistance. He casually sauntered around, spending his evening reading the books he bought and drinking the spiced teas that he had come to enjoy.

After three days he clearly identified the principal spooks; six of them playing a tag team game of hide and seek. They weren't particularly good at what they were doing, which was to Sami's benefit. So he decided to point that out.

"Why am I being followed?"

"What?" Walid Abdul-Latif answered. For the first time in memory, an underling actually dared to challenge him.

"I said, why am I being followed?"

"I don't know what you're talking about. Go back to work."

Sami stood his ground.

"I demand to be told."

"You demand? Is that what you said?" Walid put down the German photo magazine he'd been reading. He pushed his chair away from his desk and stretched his legs out on the desktop.

"Yes, because I haven't done anything wrong."

Walid laughed. "So, you're being followed. Everybody's watched at one time or another."

"I don't need to be watched. I work for you. You work for Abahar, son of our Great Brother Leader. We're on the 'inside.'" Sami defiantly declared.

Walid laughed. "Quite right. But it was your turn. I've had mine. But since you've smoked out your tails, probably more out of their ineptitude than your brilliance, perhaps you're owed a break."

"Get them off me. There is no reason."

"Oh, there is always a reason. But you won't see them again," Walid said. "And like I said, get back to work."

Sami nodded once and returned to his desk aware that he'd have to be even more careful next time. He couldn't risk a contact today. And none tomorrow. Or the day after. *You won't see them again,* is what Walid said. That didn't mean they wouldn't be out there.

"*Al salaam a'alaykum*," the stranger said in greeting, "Is this seat taken, my friend?"

Sami looked around. There were other empty seats at the café, but the man was already pulling out the chair, expecting certain hospitality. He looked to be forty years old, but maybe younger, definitely tired, weather-beaten and haggard under his loosely fitting dirty sand-colored robe. The only thing odd was his beard. It seemed only recently grown where his overall impression suggested he should have been covered in a knotty growth.

"No. Help yourself."

"Thank you. I am visiting from Ghadames and I am looking for work. Soon it will be too hard to find. Ramadan begins only two days from now."

The man seemed to be telling him like he didn't know.

"Yes," said Sami. "We won't be drinking like this in the daytime."

Ramadan, the holiest of all Muslim holidays, lasted a month. The devout fast from dawn to sunset for an entire month, eat only small meals, and visit with friends at night. The observance falls on the ninth month of the Muslim calendar and much of the day-to-day life comes to a halt, replaced by a time of deep worship and personal contemplation.

"Much to pray for this year," the man commented. "Praise be to Allah. Perhaps this new American president may be our hope for peace."

"If he can be trusted," Sami proposed.

"Ah, quite right. There is a saying, 'Trust in Allah, but tie your camel.'"

Sami laughed. "The Great Satan would have us believe that all is well, then send our camels galloping away. Only to cause us further despair."

The man signaled to a waiter for the same drink that Sami was sipping. A red tea. "But what if the Great Satan needed to hear something we said." The man leaned into Sami. "How would such a message be communicated? A whisper may not be heard."

Sami suddenly felt he was being lured in by an expert. *A false flag? One of Kharrazi's men trying to trap me? Maybe.*

"But we must always rely on our Leader, my friend," Sami said cautiously.

"A great leader indeed, with rival sons."

Why would he say that? wondered Sami. *I am being baited.*

"Perhaps we may one day choose between them. A difficult decision."

"Allah has a saying about choosing leaders of peoples," Sami responded, straightening his body. "'And your Lord creates and chooses whom He pleases, to choose is not theirs.'"

"Your knowledge of the Holy Qur'an is impressive, my friend. But what does Allah see for you? A trip perhaps?"

Sami Ben Ali froze. The question was much too pointed for a rhetorical aside.

"Who are you?"

The waiter arrived with the tea. The unknown man smiled. Sami noticed he had perfectly capped teeth and silver fillings; definitely not the work of an inadequately equipped Libyan dentist's office.

"I am someone who seeks to learn from you."

Sami asked his question again. "Who are you?"

"Someone who brings you news of lions that dare strike this year. They may fulfill their destiny."

If Sami knew one thing, it was that the Detroit Lions were indeed vying for a playoff berth. The team that dominated football in the early 1950s had failed in all the years since. CNN International reported that it looked extremely possible this season.

The man speaking to him now in perfect Arabic probably could put him into a great 50-yard line seat at the Super Bowl. *He's American.*

"There is a story from the desert," Sami offered more confidently. "It is a story of Imam Ali, who at the gate to the City of Knowledge, used to tell the Shiites who gathered, 'Ask me about anything, for the Messenger of Allah taught me about one thousand doors of knowledge, each one of which opens one thousand more doors.'"

"It is enough that we meet one another now. We shall fast and worship. Join me in two days. Then the doors of knowledge will open for both of us."

Sami smiled and thought about going home. He found a friend in his midst, hiding in plain sight.

The mountain had just come to Mohammed.

Jack Evans was used to moving mountains to get what he needed. He literally dropped his man back into Libya three days earlier, forty-eight kilometers west of Tripoli along a secluded beachhead. An Army Apache attack helicopter off the USS *Carl Vinson*, seemed to hug the ocean before depositing Vinnie D'Angelo on the sand. The insertion took less than fifteen seconds and the copter never touched the ground. D'Angelo proceeded on foot to various check points and found Sami Ben Ali with relative ease. He also discovered the people following him, and he had to wait for a safe time to step out of the shadows. The extra days it took also allowed him to steal into an open apartment and shower away the sand which had weighed him down after his trek.

D'Angelo slept in the streets of the medina, as many did. He brought no particular attention to himself. He was sure of that. He looked completely different than his last visit, when, as Tomás Morales, he didn't speak a word of Arabic. Now his mastery of the language, something he even kept from Roarke, served him on this visit.

At one point the day before, he saw his inquisitor from his previous mission. Colonel Yassar Hevit. He considered a swift act of revenge, but his sense of duty kept him focused. *Another day*, he promised himself. And so he lurked, watching and waiting for the chance to talk with Sami.

After the encounter, D'Angelo returned to a secluded park on the outskirts of Tripoli. He hadn't been there before, but he had memorized the exact location where a hand-held PDA with e-mail had been stuffed arm's length up a hollow tree trunk in a grove. He spent four hours in the park, resting, walking, praying on the rug he carried, and talking to himself before he made his way to his destination.

It was 2145 when he found the tree he sought. D'Angelo was certain he was alone, but to be safe he decided to take a long, refreshing pee. Should anyone be watching, a beggar was just relieving himself. Simultaneously, he reached inside a hole in the tree at shoulder level and began groping for the device left for him.

D'Angelo felt a creepy tingling sensation. *Oh Christ, ants!* At first only a few, then dozens, then hundreds, crawling on his arm, up his sleeve and into his armpit. He closed his eyes, which helped him resist yanking his arm out. He had experienced worse. Far worse. But the sensation was unnerving.

Just then his fingertips touched a plastic bag. The CIA operative forced his arm in further, ignoring the bites of the ants. In one quick motion, he jerked the bag out.

D'Angelo shook the ants off and hoped that any eyes that might be trained on him would simply think he was shaking off his dick. He matter-of-factly tucked the bag under his garment, put himself back together and started away from the tree, flailing his arms every few seconds to get rid of the remaining ants. *There's got to be a better way to earn a living.*

LANGLEY, VIRGINIA
CIA HEADQUARTERS
MONDAY, NOVEMBER 23

An alert chimed from Jack Evans' Cambridge Soundworks computer speakers. It signaled the delivery of a high priority encoded e-mail.

For the fourth straight night Jack Evans slept on the brown leather DeCoro couch opposite his desk. At least after the third night he had ordered up sheets and blankets to make himself more comfortable. He figured over the next few weeks he'd be spending a lot more time at work than at home. While the subject of Sandman's discovery remained unknown, Evans' experience left him with an ever-nagging concern of its importance.

The CIA director wiped his eyes, got his bearings, and typed his password into his computer.

Most messages were deciphered by his staff under the strictest secrecy. But the president had told him to keep this close to the vest. Very close. He never took exception with Morgan Taylor's requests. And at this point he knew full well how explosive any information from Sandman would be.

The DCI copied the e-mail to a special program protected by multiple firewalls, and entered a number and letter sequence that would translate D'Angelo's message. The process took two minutes, enough time for Evans to start a latte dripping on his coveted Barista coffee maker.

By trade he was not a nervous man. He couldn't be. But today he felt his heart pounding quicker as he waited to read the report.

Contact. Shrt. Watchrs. Xpct 2 days.

Evans had hoped for more, but the communiqué from the field reinforced what the CIA chief had seen over the live real-time satellite pictures. A tiny GPS radio transponder implanted in D'Angelo's shoulder constantly signaled his location to the eyes and ears orbiting high above him. A satellite camera tracked him, down-linking the pictures without sound to a dish at Langley.

Evans had followed D'Angelo for days. The pictures clearly showed the operative's insertion by the Apache, then his movements from the beach to Tripoli. He watched him sleep on the streets, and finally sitting down with his contact. Evans even saw him shake off the ants, though he didn't know what he was doing until an aide explained.

"*Watchers.*" The word disturbed him. But two days was encouraging…*if it were true.*

LANGLEY, VIRGINIA
CIA HDQTS, METEOROLOGY STATION
TUESDAY, NOVEMBER 24

"It's not good news."

"Go." Evans said gruffly.

"It's rare, but it happens."

"What happens?"

"Well, we don't normally talk about the Mediterranean Sea in terms of hurricane force storms, but…"

"You've got to be kidding."

"Well, there's an event I'm tracking. A band with potential cyclonic activity," the man said pointing to his charts. "And it looks like they're in for a bad spell."

Jack Evans was getting a primer on weather patterns in the Mediterranean Sea from Dutch Tetreault, the Company's resident meteorologist. The fifty-nine-year-old metropolitan DC forecaster had worked for more than two decades in local television. However, when forty-eight was getting too old for TV, he took his skills to a place where age didn't matter. Now, eleven years later, Tetreault was an invaluable resource. Director Evans only wished he had a sunnier forecast.

"Most of the year, the Med is warm and comfortable. Of course, during the summer the Sahara is hotter than blazes. And winters get a little wet, particularly along the shore. Tripoli's annual precipitation averages 380 millimeters. That's a hair under fifteen inches."

"And this winter?"

"Like I said. I think they're on a massive storm track, Mr. Director. I've asked for the Marine Meteorology Division at the Naval Research Laboratory in Monterrey to get me regional history and current analysis. They're working it up."

"It's the fucking desert, for Christ's sake, Dutch."

"You're right, but North Africa is prone to some real weather. It can get pretty blustery in the winter and spring. The Hamson or Scirocco winds originate when the hot, dry, desert air flows northward into the southern Med. They often reach cyclone strength." Tetreault pointed to a map on his computer screen. "Strong southwesterly winds at the surface start driving toward the sea. Desert sand and dust kicks up below. It's rare, but those winds have lasted for weeks without abating. Visibility can be poor to nonexistent. Flying? Not a good idea."

Tetreault inputted another computer depiction. "Then at other times there are even more wind regimes. The *bora* flows from the Adriatic, the *estesian* channels through the Rhodope Mountains, the *levante* cuts southeast across the Strait of Gibraltar, the *mistral* pushes south from the coast of France. There's real weather there."

"Stay with what we're dealing with," Evans requested.

"Well, here's the latest computer model showing the development of a powerful extratropical cyclone that's dug far south in the storm track. It's got a leading squall line with heavy dust behind it. It looks like the kind of storm that brought down a passenger aircraft in Tunisia a number of years ago. Behind it, another…"

"There's more?" the DCI exclaimed.

"Well, yes." He called up the image. "This first one is marked by a line of clouds that extends from the coasts of Libya and Tunisia north-east, across the Mediterranean over Italy, Greece, Albania and onto the Adriatic Sea. The model calls for this second one to develop right behind it. I can't say for sure, but I think this is building to something similar to episodes last seen in January '82 and again in January '95."

"And your prediction for the next few weeks?"

"Heavy rain where it rains, snow in higher elevations. A lot more than usual. For a lot longer."

As Tetreault expanded his explanation, Evans watched a step frame projection of the weather system play out on the meteorologist's computer. Light shades of blue, representing fair weather clouds in the lower atmosphere, thickened to the hallmark ominous dark green shades of cold convective towers. Evans had enough background in satellite imagery interpretation to know that these areas corresponded to rapidly intensifying thunderstorms.

"And what about here?" Evans demanded. He stuck his finger on the screen right on top of Tripoli. "What's going to happen right here?"

"It's not a place I'd pick to vacation."

"Mr. President, I have to talk to you," Evans said on the secure line. "You better call J3, too. And the Secretary of Defense."

TRIPOLI, LIBYA
THURSDAY, DECEMBER 2

The meeting between D'Angelo and Sami Ben Ali did not take place on the second day, or the third or the fourth. Ramadan observance should have given the two men opportunity to meet and speak. However, D'Angelo saw that the men following Sami took extra precautions. He'd be surprised if Ben Ali noticed the two new men. They were better than the first team of clowns. So D'Angelo couldn't chance contact. As a result, he had nothing to report home.

More than a week after they first met, the fifth day of Ramadan, the CIA man took a seat at an empty chess board under an awning and out of the rain. Sami would walk by. D'Angelo would catch his attention. He had to. Time was running out.

D'Angelo figured that there was nothing more boring than watching people play chess for two hours. He expected the men following Ben Ali to lose interest and go for a drink.

"Checkmate," Sami said laying down his opponent's king. It was the second game he'd won since they started hours earlier.

"Another?" Sami added. "Maybe your men will learn the moves they need to take."

"I'm ready, my friend," D'Angelo said, understanding the meaning.

They set up the pieces and D'Angelo was ready to get the information he came for.

Indeed, he played a better game, putting Sami on the defensive early. He looked nervous and began tapping the only pawn he'd taken upside down on the chessboard.

After ten more minutes his tapping stopped. However, he slowly passed his right foot closer to the stranger's right leg. The computer disk was under his shoe. He had casually put it there while scratching his ankle during the second game. After a few more moves, which had not gone his way, he took his pawn and tapped out a simple message in Morse code.

-.. .- .-- -. / .-. -. -.. .-. / .-. -.-. - / .-.. -

To anyone paying attention, and nobody was, it would have seemed like Sami was just another chess player under stress. It was crude and low tech, but by the third pass D'Angelo got the message.

dwn undr rgt ft

Very lightly D'Angelo rested his left foot on top of Ben Ali's. Sami stopped tapping, never once looking directly at the man opposite him. Sami gently slid his foot away and brought it back under his chair. D'Angelo put his foot directly on top of the floppy disc. They took forty minutes to complete the entire transfer. D'Angelo waited another entire game before he reached down to palm the disk. He smiled and lost the final game.

BOSTON, MASSACHUSETTS
WEDNESDAY, DECEMBER 3

Louise Swingle placed the call for the president. She knew Scott was in Boston visiting Katie.

"Hello, Scott," she said when he answered.

Roarke was in the middle of steaming the clams for his surprise dish of linguine vongole. He cradled the phone between his neck and his ear as he dumped the pasta into the colander.

"Hello, sweetheart."

Katie looked at him and frowned. Roarke hadn't explained how he flirted with the president's secretary. He pointed to the phone and saluted with his left hand. It didn't help. When he mouthed the word "work," she got the message.

"The boss needs you," Louise said.

"How soon?"

"Very soon."

"Dinner's cooking."

"There'll be a Navy driver waiting outside in thirty minutes."

"Aw, come on, Louise."

"Sorry, Scott. He's scheduled you for a briefing at 23-hundred."

"Subject?"

"You'll have to ask him."

Roarke knew that D'Angelo had returned to Libya. He could only assume, based on the urgency of the call, that his summons home was related. A deeper, inner voice told him even more. *D'Angelo got what he went in for. The events in the U. S. and Libya are connected and the common denominator is Lodge!*

"What flight?"

"Your very own, courtesy of your special uncle."

Roarke said goodbye to Louise and faced Katie. He pulled her close.

"Do you have to?" was all she said.

Roarke sighed deeply and looked into his lover's eyes, seeing so much more than he'd ever seen before.

"Why?" she appealed to him. "Why? I still don't understand."

For the first time in his life his heart spoke to him louder than his devotion to duty. He whispered in her ear, "I'll tell you."

CHAPTER 53

WHITE HOUSE BRIEFING ROOM
THURSDAY, DECEMBER 4

A message in bold red letters on the 50" plasma screen caught everyone's attention.

TOP SECRET

Ten people—all key players in the Taylor White House—were assembled around the conference table when the president burst into the 24-hour watch and alert center known as the Briefing Room, downstairs from the Oval Office.

"Good morning. Let's get started." He reached forward and tapped a pad at the desk. The overhead lights lowered, but individual lamps at each seat lit up. "You all have a folder in front of you." Everyone had already seen it, but noted that in addition to the *Top Secret* designation there was a specific instruction that they knew to follow:

Do Not Open
without permission of
the President of the United States

The president politely reinforced the point. "Hold off looking at it until I talk you through things first. Some of you are more up to speed than others." He gave Roarke an appreciative acknowledgement. "I apologize for that inequity. But in a few minutes you'll all know everything."

Taylor looked to everyone for the affirmation he sought. Vice President Stanley Poole flanked him on the left, different from his usual position across the table in the Cabinet Room. Directly to his right was Chief of Staff John Bernstein. Going around the table from Bernsie's right were General Johnson, or J3, then FBI Director Robert Mulligan. Beside him, Eve Goldman, the nation's attorney general. Next to her National Security Advisor Arthur Campanis. Coming around the table, CIA Chief Jack Evans was opposite the president. Then Scott Roarke, Secretary of State Joyce Drysdale and Defense Secretary Norman Gregoryan.

The president intentionally discarded established White House seating protocol. He placed people in the know next to members of his administration who were about to be shocked out of their wits. The inner circle would widen in the next few minutes, and the debate couldn't feel like it was *us against them.*

"This briefing is protected by the National Security Act of 1947, as amended in 1996." Taylor announced the ground rules in such a way that no one would misunderstand his meaning. "You will soon see and hear details of an operation. Only a handful of people will be privy to the exact purpose *until* we have successfully accomplished our mission. You are those people. There *will be* no leaks.

"Should anyone even harbor the notion that what you are about to learn is an attempt by this president to maintain personal power, dismiss it now. I assure you this concerns the very security of the United States of America and the integrity of its Constitution."

The attorney general surveyed the room. This sounded like more than she ever expected when she was called to the briefing.

The silence told Taylor that he had everyone's undivided attention.

"Now, allow me to tell you what we've discovered. And then what we're going to do about it," the president stated with authority. "You will have to get past the fact that I've kept some of you out of the loop on all or parts of this investigation. Suffice it to say, it simply had to be."

Goldman looked around the room again. *What's going on?* She noticed that some of the others were shifting uncomfortably in their chairs.

"Ladies, gentlemen," the president continued, "there has been an attempt by a foreign government to insert a deep cover inside our government."

Goldman caught Arthur Campanis tightly pressing his lips together. He was nodding ever so slightly. *He knows.* She looked around. *So does Bernsie, J3, Evans, Mulligan, Gregoryan and that agent Roarke.*

"How deep?" Secretary of State Drysdale asked first.

"Very deep."

"How deep, Morgan?" she asked again, but calling out the president's first name.

"Inside the White House, Joyce."

"Impossible!"

"Impossible?" the DCI said taking over for the president. "The CIA has had spies. Bob Mulligan knows all too well that the FBI's not immune to infiltration. So why not the White House itself?"

Drysdale pointedly asked, "Where in the White House?"

"I think all of your questions will be answered shortly." The president, still standing, finally took his seat.

"A member of the Kharrazi family, in a plan that was acquired through Syria by way of Iraq, has been controlling a number of sleepers—deep cover spies on a slow, sure, and deliberate track.

"Great patience went into making this scheme succeed. Over many years. It was conceived following the Yom Kippur War in '73. According to our intelligence, this plan was originally the work of Syrian President Hafez al-Assad. He controlled it for the next twenty-seven years."

Solid intelligence, thought Goldman. She blurted out a question to the CIA Director. "Twenty-seven years, Jack? How long have *we* known about this? Or in my case, not known about it," she coldly added for the rest of the room.

Evans looked to the president for permission to answer. He got what he expected.

"I'll come to that, Eve," Taylor stated. She wrote a notation on the file in front of her. *Indictments.*

"After al-Assad died, his son passed the plan, no, I should say, sold the plan to Uday Hussein; you remember, one of Saddam's boys. We have no idea how much was paid. But the goal remained the same.

"Just days before the fall of Saddam and his family, Uday contacted a friend in Libya with his own political aspirations—Fadi Kharrazi. He wanted to unload the plan, perhaps in an attempt to negotiate a safe haven for himself or for hard currency. Why Fadi? We're not sure, but it does suggest that Saddam and his sons were aware of plans for a coup in Libya even if they weren't around to see it through. In fact, Hussein could have helped fund the revolution which brought General Kharrazi and his family to power. Jack has the CIA gathering further intelligence on that matter. But as I said, Fadi bought the plan from Uday, lock, stock, and ultimately *barrel*. His purpose was threefold. On a basic level, to give him political clout at home.

Second, to move up in the favored line of succession. Third, and most importantly, to upset the balance of power in the Middle East by affecting or maybe better, *infecting* the American political process. That relates to a fourth point which I'll get to shortly."

The president reached for the glass of water in front of him.

"Please, Mr. President?" It was Eve Goldman. "Again. How long have we known? I need to see all of the evidence immediately."

"And what about the impact on our allies?" Secretary of State Drysdale added. "Since I also seem to have been kept out of the loop, when can I expect to see *if* or *how* we've been compromised?" She was obviously annoyed. It appeared to her that once again the boys ruled this club. She assumed Eve was equally pissed.

Morgan Taylor slowly sipped his water. He wanted to press on, but decided to answer her in the briefest of terms.

"First of all, Joyce, I said there has been an *attempt*. It has not fully succeeded. Not yet. To your question, Eve, we've only known for a very short amount of time. And no, we're not prepared for you to go further right now. Let me continue."

Goldman slowly nodded, knowing that Morgan Taylor would play this out on his own time table.

The president cleared his throat and proceeded. "Once Kharrazi's father came to power the plan became more realistic to Fadi. And now, with the General dying, Fadi is in the catbird seat thanks to his long-term investment."

"It's still not clear to me," Drysdale added. "For what purpose?"

"Oh, that's the easiest part. Fadi bought a very well managed and comprehensive operation, some thirty years in the making, that placed agents in the U.S., trained at a very special Soviet school called Red Banner."

"Trained to be what?"

"To be Americans," the president snapped. "Sleepers. Long-term assets. Likely from Syria originally, but we're not certain.

"I'll explain how they were inserted into life here and what happened to them over the course of three decades. How they grew up, entered college, and launched successful careers. How people were killed to assure their secrecy and how they advanced to the critical point we're at today. Make no mistake, this has been an extremely well-financed operation. We believe the ultimate goal, still operational, is to destabilize Israel by illegally influencing the government of the United States and changing public opinion here."

"Influencing?" Drysdale wondered aloud. "How? How would they get someone in the White House?"

"Right through the front door," Taylor solemnly concluded. "They've plotted to take over the Executive Branch, with the unknowing help of the American people. And if we don't stop them, come January 20th we'll have a Russian-trained, Arab-national spy serving as the elected President of the United States."

"Now for the bad news. At this point, *nothing* can be positively proven," the president said. "This meeting is about getting that proof."

Eight men and two woman declared in unison, "Yes, sir."

"J3, it's all yours." The president turned over the briefing to General Johnson, the head of US Special Operations Command, or USASOC. The general had been meeting with his senior command and Jack Evans since 0500 that morning.

The fifty-six-year-old black man slowly rose from his chair. He spoke with authority; his voice as big as his huge frame. General Jonas Jackson Johnson, or J3 as he had been called since West Point, expanded—the best possible way to describe his build—to 6'4". He was the proud descendant of a decorated Allentown, Pennsylvania soldier who bravely fought for the Union against the South some 150 years earlier. He commanded attention in any group, this one being no exception.

Morgan Taylor clearly viewed J3 as presidential material should he ever decide to hang up his uniform. But the General represented the fourth generation of his family to earn stars on his shoulders—in his case, four of them. He had no desire to wear anything but Army green for the rest of his career. Now he proudly served as Taylor's senior officer in the Army Special Forces.

A slight drawl accent added some gentility to his otherwise tough demeanor. He used it now.

"Gentlemen. Ladies. Thanks to information provided by Mr. Evans' own asset, code name Sandman, the objective is this building." J3 pointed to the monitor. A freeze frame of Fadi's complex now filled the screen. The picture was not from the roll taken by

Vinnie D'Angelo. His film and memory chips had been seized by Abahar Kharrazi's men. This was a satellite image captured from 250 miles away at roughly 35 degrees off axis. It showed the building with amazing clarity.

"With the help of the Pentagon," he acknowledged Secretary of Defense Gregoryan with a nod, "we're going in very secretly. We may be exiting with a little more noise. The top floor is our hard target." The pictures were being fed from a laptop computer. The general pressed a key and the picture zoomed in tighter. "Specifically the southwest corner office.

"Rear Admiral Boulder Devoucoux is readying the USS *Carl Vinson* for staging. He reports we will be operational in twelve days. In the meantime, we've been training at a site we constructed in Kentucky. We're aiming for the night of a new moon. Total darkness. December 18th. In two weeks we'll take the building without signing in at the front desk."

"Rock and roll," Roarke said under his breath. He knew that subtlety was not one of the rear admiral's traits, hence the nickname "Boulder."

"Boulder Johnson's flying shit cans," J3's terms for the Black Hawks, "will be dropping the team in. Air support will close down the nearby streets. Our intel reports that what we're looking for is contained in Fadi's file cabinets. We're going to extract not just one, but a whole bank of them. In and out in under four minutes. A little faster than Atlas Van Lines." He paused and took a breath. "And then *everyone's* coming home.

"In front of you are our plans. Please open them now."

J3 waited until everyone had ripped open their materials and the paper shuffling had subsided.

"Going forward, this is 'Operation Quarterback Sneak.' Swift. Daring. And dangerous."

The participants read along as J3 reviewed the strategy. Twelve minutes later, the general asked the obvious. "Questions?"

"What if the files have been destroyed?" the attorney general proposed.

Jonas Johnson looked to the president and read his eyes very clearly. "Madam, I'd say we have one helluva problem to deal with back home. They're our proof."

"And if the files are there *and* you get them back?" Secretary of State Drysdale asked.

"Then, Joyce, we have one helluva problem to deal with back home."

With that they began discussing the operation and the biographies of the principals who would comprise the assault team.

They'd been training as a unit for weeks.

Lethal firepower would come from two men: The Army's Special Forces' best sharp shooters, Sgt. Andrew Aplen and Lt. Lee Gardner.

The communications officer, Lt. Shawn Recht, would keep USASOC focused on the maneuver every step of the way, while also providing the eyes and ears for the internal communications on the ground. Recht was backed up by Sgt. Wil Jones, who was a good second with a camera, but first with a knife.

And at the command was Colonel Samuel Langeman. Langeman grew up in Tulsa, and by all accounts, should have died on the streets long ago. But he was always bigger than everybody else. And that kept gang members away. He hated being called Samuel or Sam. Nobody dared. So for as long as he could remember, his name merged into simply *Slange*.

As a member of the Special Forces, Slange had no equals. He was a 6' combination of pure muscle and intellect. That's why he had the command.

Aplen liked him the most. He shared the Special Forces spirit and, like Slange, had a survivor's instinct. Aplen was a Missouri boy, age twenty-nine, an avid hunter and the son of an Olympic rifler. He excelled at everything. Aplen was the best marksman in the Special Forces, the strongest swimmer, and the quietest commando. He hardly spoke. Most people never knew he was around even when he was at work.

Gardner was the brain in the group and yet the one most easily bored. That's why Harvard didn't offer enough challenges. He sought more excitement and turned to the military. When he found the basics too mundane he discovered Special Forces school in Florida. Finally Gardner had a place to express himself physically and mentally. At age thirty-one, he was on his first real mission. He'd already memorized everything about the plan and was eager to go.

Recht, age 30, always chewed gum. Ordinarily a superior wouldn't allow it. But for Recht, there were special allowances. He could make a radio out of wrappers and used his ABC gum like solder. Recht was a ham radio operator by nine. He had an internet TV station at fourteen and a patent for a collapsible parabolic reflector when he was fifteen. It was the only one ever registered with two key components found in a pack of Juicy Fruit.

At age twenty-six, Sgt. Wil Jones was the "kid" of the group. But experience made up for age. Jones could double everyone's job and kill without prejudice. Slange knew his skills and was alive today because of them.

General Johnson had one additional point to make, but the president cut him off.

"If you'll excuse me for a moment, J3," he said.

"Certainly, Mr. President."

"I should explain to everyone what we have in mind for Lt. Recht and Sgt. Jones," Morgan Taylor began. "They're the cameramen. They'll be shooting the entire time. I want them protected as if they were what we were goddamned looking for. This entire mission must be on camera. Every second of it. It'll come back simultaneously to command and also archived on DVD. I want to see live pictures, focused on the operation and then on the man carrying the files, once they are in our control. No camera cuts. From the time they leave the deck of the *Vinson* right through their return.

"That camera isn't going to stop down for anything. The entire operation, for better or worse, will be documented."

Everyone understood. The president could not be accused of creating a diversion merely to hold onto his office. Not by Democrats, not by Kharrazi. The evidence had to be totally verifiable. Morgan Taylor's place in history, let alone the very foundation of the president-elect, would rise and fall on what the cameras revealed.

"The floor is yours again, General."

"Thank you, sir. My men will be coming back with more than just one set of files."

He had everyone's undivided attention.

"We're going to load up every fucking thing we can put our hands on." J3 smiled at the attorney general. "Pardon my French, Ms. Goldman, but we want everything there is. Everything."

There was no disagreement at this table today.

ONE HOUR LATER

"Scott. Stay for a moment, please," the president asked as Roarke was preparing to leave.

"Yes, boss."

After everyone cleared the room, leaving their folders for shredding, only Morgan Taylor and Scott Roarke remained.

"Wondering why you're here?"

"No question in my mind. My guess is that you want one person holding the goods." He smiled at his friend. "I'd say that was me, sir."

"You got that one hundred percent."

"And I'll hand deliver it to you right here."

"You won't have to go that far, my boy." Now Roarke was confused.

"You'll give them to me in the Med."

"What!" Roarke exclaimed. "You're completely craz—" Taylor held up one hand to stop him in mid-sentence.

"Aboard the USS *Carl Vinson*," the president finished stating.

"You can't."

"Oh, I think I can. And I will."

"You're the President of the United States of America. Not a fucking Top Gun anymore."

"Unless you've forgotten, Scott, I am *the* Top Gun Commander in Chief of the Armed Forces. And there's a coup going on. I want to be the first to see the evidence. The very first. And then I'm going to hunt down the entire ring of conspirators if it's the last thing I do—in office or out."

Roarke settled into his chair in the briefing room and laughed.

"You're really going to do it."

"You bet your sweet ass," the president said.

CHAPTER 54

SATURDAY, DECEMBER 6

By no means did Jack Evans consider the insertion routine. "But surprise will be on our side. It's the exfiltration where we could have problems. Hopefully the little diversion we have planned will help," he told the president.

"And the damned weather?" the president asked. "The latest?"

"Not good and not getting any better."

"What's the worst conditions we can accept as operational?"

"Something better than what they're getting. I'll get the risk assessment and then we can make the decision."

The morning briefing then went on to India and Pakistan and a suicide bombing outside of the U.N.

Four dead in terrorist suicide bombing.

Ibrahim Haddad put the paper down. *The whole idea was to stay alive and see change through. Not die by blowing yourselves up,* he thought. *These people. What was the benefit in that? Such a stupid way of trying to accomplish the goal.*

Haddad considered himself smarter than the martyrs who disintegrated in an instant of misplaced glory. He had plotted for decades, strategizing for the day at hand; a day that would begin to reshape the allegiances of the world. Yet, he would have to be patient. *A few more weeks, that's all.* The new president would need time to redraw the map.

Roarke joined up with the team at the staging area in Kentucky. He was weeks behind in training, but he only needed to master the basics: Where to go once he jumped off the chopper. What to do when he got inside. How to get out safely with his package in hand.

For any typical civilian, it would have been impossible to assimilate into a tight unit on a critical mission. But Roarke was not a typical civilian. He was in excellent physical shape. While the rigors didn't bother him, the weather did. He knew the reputation of the Black Hawks in less than ideal conditions. It was the unspoken worry among the team.

Roarke had one more concern: what could he tell Katie. The answer was—very little.

"Hi, hon," he started in a call from a telephone booth.

He hadn't seen Katie in weeks, although they spoke regularly.

"Hey, you. Where are you now?"

"Visiting." That was their shorthand for him not being able to talk. "Then I've got an errand to run." Which meant he'd be busy for a while.

She didn't speak up, mostly out of fear. Roarke read the sign.

"I'll be okay."

"I understand," she said. Then Katie corrected herself. "No. No. That's completely wrong. I don't understand. I don't understand any of it. I haven't seen you. When you call, you can't…" She hesitated knowing she should be careful.

"I can't. I wish I could." Roarke didn't like hiding things from Katie.

He heard a deep sigh. "I wish you could, too." Her voice trailed off. "And I can't do anything to help."

They were both silent.

"Katie?"

"Yes."

"There may be something."

"Yes?"

"Something you can do."

"Okay?"

"Well…" He had to be careful. They were on an open line. "Let's just call it Civics 101."

"I don't understand."

"Well, you must have a copy of the U.S. Constitution at home, right?"

"Sure. Only in about twenty of my law books. Why?"

"Read it and think about our discussion a few weeks ago. I'll get back to you later."

"But…"

"That's all. Just read it. And think of me. I'll call you later. Bye bye, sweetheart."

Katie hung up and peered out her Beacon Hill apartment window. The late afternoon sun was beginning to silhouette the buildings across the Charles and cast a warm glow on the water. She took a deep breath and replayed the exchange she'd just concluded. After flashing on how nice *sweetheart* sounded, Katie thought about what he'd said. "*The U. S. Constitution. Read it and think of our discussion.*" After a few minutes she racked her focus from the river onto her own reflection in the glass and smiled broadly. *That son of a bitch. He's just enlisted me.*

"*Read it.*" That's exactly what she did. Over a cup of coffee. Over many cups, and into the evening. She read the Constitution of the United States like she had never read it before.

Katie dove into the words, losing herself in their magnificence, their poetry, their brilliance and simple eloquence.

"We the People of the United States, in Order to form a more perfect Union, establish Justice, insure domestic Tranquility, provide for the common defence, promote the general Welfare, and secure the Blessings of Liberty to ourselves and our Posterity, do ordain and establish this Constitution for the United States of America."

It was a document for all time; living, breathing, full of the American character, so hard for much of the world to comprehend.

Katie immersed herself in the rhythm, the texture, and the meaning. She thought she knew what she was looking for, but she didn't know if it existed.

It was as if James Madison was speaking directly to her, affirming the basic goodness of the republic and the foundation of laws. She moved through the context to subtext, what the words said and what they implied, from the primary laws of the land enumerated in the Bill of Rights through the subsequent amendments.

The first ten amendments were proposed to legislators of the existing states by the First Congress on September 25, 1789. A three-fourths majority of the original states ratified the amendments between 1789 and 1791. Amazingly it wasn't until 1939 that the legislatures of the three remaining states, Massachusetts, Georgia, and Connecticut, ratified the Bill of Rights.

Katie continued reading. The 11th Amendment on Judicial powers, the 12th enumerating how electors shall meet in their respective states and vote by ballot for president and vice president. The

13th established in 1865, abolishing slavery. She stopped on Section 3 of the 14th Amendment.

"No person shall be a Senator or Representative in Congress, or elector of President and Vice-President, or hold any office, civil or military, under the United States, or under any State, who, having previously taken an oath, as a member of Congress, or as an officer of the United States, or as a member of any State legislature, or as an executive or judicial officer of any State, to support the Constitution of the United States, shall have engaged in insurrection or rebellion against the same, or given aid or comfort to the enemies thereof."

Unconsciously Katie underlined the last phrase, "*shall have engaged in insurrection or rebellion against the same, or given aid or comfort to the enemies thereof.*" Was it something Scott had said or her own uneasy feeling?

She read on for hours. Sleep was beginning to overtake her when she came to the 25th Amendment. It was one of the last Amendments, "*proposed by the Eighty-ninth Congress by Senate Joint Resolution No. 1, approved by the Senate on Feb. 19, 1965, and by the House of Representatives, in amended form, on Apr. 13, 1965, and finally ratified by the states in 1967.*"

At first she read it casually, then she read it again. And once more. By the time the phone rang, Katie already had filled eleven pages of a yellow pad with notes. It was Scott and she was grateful for the break. She checked her desk clock, a simple art deco repro from Restoration Hardware. 12:15 A.M. She'd been working for more than nine hours.

"Katie, honey, I'm sorry I'm getting back to you so late."

"It's okay. I've been just doing some light reading. That thing you *mentioned*."

"Oh, and are you enjoying it?"

"Like never before," she explained. "It's beautifully written. Really. Amazing what you'll find in it." She suddenly realized she was excited. Very excited. "Look, I better go, I've got a lot to think about."

Roarke smiled. Special Forces now had another team member.

CHAPTER 55

SATURDAY, DECEMBER 20

For the sixth straight week, Teddy Lodge met with prospective cabinet appointees. He was partial to liberal Democrats, Ivy Leaguers, and think tank brains. A few newspaper reporters and some of the more conservative Sunday morning political quarterbacks observed that he was shaping a remarkable team of eggheads who could bore America's enemies to death; a potent left wing rubber stamp and not a leader among them.

Women. Blacks. Latinos. They were just what the president-elect wanted. And none of them were Jewish.

Ibrahim Haddad fell asleep with the day's *New York Times* on his lap. He slept peacefully, dreaming of the changes that would come one month to the day when the new president would take the oath of office.

The cheering crowd. The band playing "America the Beautiful"…

Haddad watched it high and above, as if on a cat-walk over a giant stage. It was all a wide shot. A blur of faces. Full of grandeur and excitement. This was Haddad's dream every night for decades; automatic, programmed, controlled, and willed into his subconscious, complete in every detail.

Speeches ushering in a new era. Troops marching past the grandstand … He zoomed closer in his mind's eye. From wide shot to medium. Faces still unrecognizable, but images he so desired to come true that he began to become aroused in his sleep.

Jets soaring overhead. A man slowly coming to his feet…

Now closer. Faces almost discernible. *A man now stood before tens of thousands of people at the Capitol steps. His right hand raised, his left hand on a book. The Bible.* Haddad smiled in his sleep. *The Bible.*

The masses quieting. The words echoing.

Closer. The man who would be president. "*I do solemnly swear that I will faithfully execute…*" Closer. "*…the office of President of the United States…*"

Closer, his face almost recognizable. "*…and will to the best of my ability, preserve, protect and defend…*"

Haddad was throbbing with anticipation. "*…the Constitution of the United States.*"

He often climaxed with the excitement as the man before the crowd proudly proclaimed, "*I do.*"

But tonight his sexual arousal snapped short of completion, replaced by an aching in his chest, the pain of an asthma attack. *The face. The face!* His dream, suddenly transformed into an unrecognizable nightmare.

Haddad lurched forward in his bed, violently awakening. He reached for an inhaler in the drawer of his marble-topped nightstand. He filled his lungs with two blasts of Ventolin. Then two more. The attack subsided, but he still couldn't shake the image of *that face.*

WHITE HOUSE SITUATION ROOM
TUESDAY, JANUARY 6

"We're just sitting on our asses. When the hell are we going to go?" Bernsie demanded.

"Not yet!" J3 bellowed.

General Jonas Jackson Johnson didn't ordinarily argue with civilians. Especially Morgan Taylor's trusted right hand man, John Bernstein. But then J3 was not about to lose any advantage in this operation.

"Mr. President, I'm sorry, but the weather is still a fucking mess. We can't get a decent look-see from our birds and the high winds—they're running 80-85 miles an hour—put the Black Hawks in jeopardy."

"Mr. President," the chief of staff sounded exasperated. He turned to General Jackson. "If this doesn't work, then what's Plan B?"

"Plan B? We use our fuckin' Friends and Family calling card and ask Mr. Fadi Kharrazi to please send us the fuckin' files via fuckin' Federal Express. Jesus, there is no fuckin' Plan B, Bernsie. And pardon my fuckin' French."

The tension had been building for weeks. An argument was probably inevitable.

"Gentlemen," the president spoke softly. His delivery carried very easily across the near empty Situation Room. "J3, your colorful language notwithstanding, Bernsie has a good point."

"Respectfully, Mr. President," the general solemnly and now politely offered, "we have run alternate scenarios. Nothing is acceptable short of our primary objective: vertical insertion by helo, strategic distractions"—J3's term for pinpoint bombing of neighboring intersections—"and an assault on the target. And for that I need those fucking winds to die down!"

Bernstein thought quickly. "There's got to be some way. We had a man inside before, can't we get others back in? They hang around the building after it closes. They break in."

"'*Mission Impossible*' style, Bernsie?" the president quipped. "They rip off their latex Arab masks and rappel down the walls to waiting motorcycles?"

"Mr. President. I'm only trying to be helpful."

"Your concern is noted and appreciated," J3 said. "We have fourteen days. I'll consider every option available to us."

"Thirteen. If you want to stop Lodge *before* he's sworn in," Bernstein reminded everyone. "Just thirteen days."

"Bob, a question for you," the president said shifting the conversation to the FBI chief.

"Yes, Mr. President."

"One word. Abraham."

Mulligan had the information in front of him. "Some 12,000 possibles. We're trying to narrow it down, sir."

"Find this guy and we're a step closer to finding the assassin."

The FBI chief swallowed hard. "I don't think anyone here disagrees, but…"

Morgan Taylor abruptly stood. The act stopped the FBI Director in mid-sentence. "Thirteen days, Bob. As the chief of staff reminded us, you also have just 13 days."

WASHINGTON, D.C.
FBI BUILDING
THURSDAY, JANUARY 8

Mulligan added another sixty-five field officers to the search. No one was told why they were only questioning men named Abraham. They were merely informed that they had only eleven days to narrow the list and zero in on someone who was apparently important enough to be brought in before the outgoing president left. "We're looking for someone presumably rich, at least 60 years old. With a current passport. Middle Eastern."

The FBI chief misled his own people as a cover, explaining it was a top priority investigation into an Al-Qaeda arms smuggling operation.

With an elaborate but cryptic nationwide manhunt on, it wasn't surprising that a source inside the Bureau tipped off *The New York Times*. No one took special interest except Michael O'Connell. *What's the old man up to now?*

"Hello, Director Mulligan," he said after being put through.

"Hello, Mr. O'Connell."

"Thank you for taking my phone call, sir." He set a friendly tone.

"You're welcome, Mr. O'Connell," the FBI chief answered coolly.

"A few questions, if you don't mind?"

"If you don't mind not hearing any answers," Mulligan offered in response.

"Fair enough." The reporter noticeably toughened. "There's a major investigation going on. Nationwide."

Robert Mulligan did not answer.

"Sources tell me it may involve a search for a Middle Eastern man."

"I do not respond to questions based on unnamed sources, Mr. O'Connell."

"You investigate crimes based on tips, Director?"

"Yes."

"Well, I investigate stories based on tips."

Again no response.

"I also understand that this search was possibly ordered at a very senior level." Morgan Taylor's name was not mentioned.

More silence.

"The reason for locating this man is unknown by even the people looking for him."

O'Connell could hear Mulligan's breathing, the only indication that he was still on the line.

"Can you comment?" the reporter finally asked.

"Mr. O'Connell," the FBI Director said, measuring his words very carefully. "I'm sorry. I can't help you. The Bureau is involved in a myriad of investigations. I couldn't even begin to comment. I'm certain you understand."

"Can you deny the report?"

"Is there a specific crime you're talking about, Mr. O'Connell?"

"I don't know. Is there?"

O'Connell ignored the redirect. "Do you deny that such an order for the investigation came from you?"

"I can categorically deny that such an order came from me." *Whoops.*

O'Connell seized on the slip. "Then there is a manhunt?"

"I didn't say that."

"You did say that the order didn't come from you, it came from someone else. Higher up?"

"Mr. O'Connell," Mulligan said trying to regain ground, "this is not a police state. We do not round up people at the whim of the FBI Director."

"Or *anyone* else, Mr. Director?"

It was O'Connell's most pointed comment. "I hope I've answered your questions."

"Well, I…"

"Perhaps another time, Mr. O'Connell. Goodbye, now."

Mulligan rested the phone on the cradle no more than two seconds before dialing the White House.

"Louise, it's Mulligan. I need the president," he somberly said.

"Yes, Mr. Director. I'll see if he can speak with you." A minute later she was back. "Connecting you now, sir."

"Mr. President," Mulligan began.

"Still am," Taylor joked with a degree of gallows humor. "What's on your mind, Bob."

"I'd like to meet with you and the attorney general. Immediately."

Ibrahim Haddad was also getting a call from a phone booth in Arlington.

"You might be interested," the caller explained, "that friends are looking for a Middle Eastern man with means. Approximate age, mid-sixties. California, Arizona, Texas, Louisiana, New York, maybe to Florida."

"Oh," was all that Haddad offered in response.

"Someone with the name Abraham."

"Spell that, please."

"Abraham, with an 'A.'"

"I think you have the wrong number," Haddad said hanging up the phone.

FADI! he swore to himself.

Mulligan made it to the Oval Office in under twelve minutes. The president postponed signing a proclamation honoring a Michigan 4-H Club. Bernsie was present, having gotten the call from Morgan Taylor to join him, "Pronto!" So was the AG, Eve Goldman.

"Well Bob, you wanted an audience. You've got it."

"Thank you, Mr. President. I got a call from *The New York Times* regarding the net we cast."

"Is that unexpected?"

"Not entirely. And the cover seems to be working."

"Seems to be working?" The president didn't fail to catch the exact meaning of the words.

"The call was from O'Connell, the reporter following Lodge." Mulligan took a deep, telling sigh. "I don't think he buys the story completely. I stopped him one question short of you."

The president glanced at Attorney General Goldman. She was in the Oval Office to make certain every move the president made was on sound legal ground.

"Go on," the president requested.

"You've brought the AG up to date?"

"I have," Taylor answered. "What did you give him?"

"Nothing." He paused. "Which was everything...unstated."

The attorney general made notes, then asked, "Will he go with the story?"

"Of course he will."

"When?" she asked.

"Soon," Mulligan replied. "He'll talk to his source one more time. Probably miss today's deadline for tomorrow's paper. I suspect the day after tomorrow. Front page."

"Mr. President, I don't need to tell you how dangerous this is for you," John Bernstein offered. "We have to shut him down!"

"Be careful, Mr. Bernstein," the attorney general warned. "It's you who are on dangerous ground with talk like that."

"I can just see the way he'll write the story. You'll be dead, Mr. President."

"You made your point, Bernsie. Bob," the president calmly asked. "What kind of reporter is this O'Connell?"

"Arrogant. Egocentric. And smart. He's a rising star in the press. Sees himself as a modern-day Woodward or Bernstein. He's already been booked on the Sunday talkers."

"And what kind of *person* is he?"

The question caught Mulligan unprepared. He looked to the others in the room, totally uncertain how to answer it. "I don't really know, sir."

"Then we shall see." Taylor walked to his desk and handed the telephone to the FBI director.

"Get him on the phone."

"Call him?"

"That's the general idea."

"Now?"

"Now, Bob."

Mulligan complied, dialing a number from his notes.

"Put it on the speaker, Bob."

The FBI chief pressed the button marked *Spkr* and everyone heard, "You've reached Michael O'Connell's desk. Leave your number, the time you called, and a message."

The president gave him a cut sign. Mulligan hung up and Morgan Taylor gave another order. "Try Louise. She finds everyone."

At the president's request, the FBI Director called on the services of the ever-reliable Louise Swingle.

Minutes later, after going through the news desk, she called "a friend" in Virginia whose job it was to track everyone's cell phone numbers. The president's phone beeped twice. Morgan Taylor pressed his speaker button. "Yes, Louise."

"I have Mr. O'Connell for the director."

"Thank you. Put him through."

The president nodded approval to Bob Mulligan who engaged line one.

Without indicating he was in the White House, he said, "Hello, this is Bob Mulligan." Everyone listened over a speaker phone. They were certain it would be *interesting*.

"Director Mulligan, I didn't think I'd be hearing from you. Or at least so soon. I take it you've re-thought our conversation and you have something you'd like to really say?"

"Well, not exactly, Mr. O'Connell," Mulligan replied.

"What do you mean? And are we on a speaker phone? I'd prefer if…"

The president pointed at himself and nodded.

"You are on a speaker and there's someone who'd like to talk with you."

O'Connell was quiet. "He's right here. Hold on."

"Okay. But…"

"Mr. O'Connell," Taylor said.

"Yes. Who is this?" he answered sharply.

The people in the Oval Office lowered their eyes. They could only imagine the expression that was about to come over the reporter's face.

"Mr. O'Connell, this is Morgan Taylor."

The president smiled at the silence that usually came after the pronouncement. "Mister O'Connell, are you there?"

"Ah, yes, Mr. President." He obviously recognized the voice.

"Mr. O'Connell, are you all right?"

"Yes. I just didn't expect to be talking with you," he said awkwardly.

"I understand. I'm used to that."

"I guess you would be, Mr. President."

"Well, Mr. O'Connell, Bob Mulligan's been filling me in and I have a little proposition for you."

"Yes, sir?" he paused. "This really is Morgan Taylor?"

"No doubt in my mind," the president joked. "You can call me back if you'd like."

"Ah, this is fine, sir."

Talking to the president was a humbling experience, no matter who you were.

"Good then. As for my proposition. How would you like the story of a lifetime?"

John Bernstein gasped audibly. Bob Mulligan was equally surprised. But Attorney General Eve Goldman grinned. She knew exactly where the president was going. He was about to erase any and all suggestion of impropriety. Forever.

"Well, you have my undivided attention. What is it?"

"Not on the telephone, Mr. O'Connell."

"Oh?"

"You'll have to come down to my place."

"Your place?"

"The White House, Mr. O'Connell. And I have two non-negotiable stipulations."

"Which are?"

"Number one. No one knows."

"I have to tell my editors."

"Positively no one."

"But I've got to say something."

"Tell them…" the president thought for a moment. "Tell them you're meeting an *inside* source. They don't get much more inside than me."

O'Connell let out a nervous laugh. "No, I don't suspect they do, sir. And the second?"

"You hold the article you were working on. The one you spoke with Director Mulligan about."

"Now wait, I'm too deep into it and I know…"

"I said non-negotiable, Mr. O'Connell." The president raised his voice above a friendly level. "And the truth is that you know nothing. Believe me, if you want to be the one who breaks a story far bigger than you can ever imagine, you will do *precisely* as I say."

When O'Connell failed to answer, the president prompted him. "I need to know now."

O'Connell spoke very quietly. "You know, in other countries, this is how people like me end up disappearing."

"Quite right, Mr. O'Connell. But this is the United States of America and I am offering you alone the opportunity to be on the inside of a tremendous story, no matter what happens. So your answer is?"

"I agree to your terms."

"A wise career decision," Taylor said with a laugh. "Now get yourself down here by breakfast.

"And again, you tell no one; positively no one knows."

"You have my word, Mr. President."

"Oh, one more thing."

O'Connell was quite slow on the comeback only offering a faltering, "Yes?"

"Pack for all sorts of weather. You'll be away for a while."

CHAPTER 56

THE WHITE HOUSE
FRIDAY, JANUARY 9

"Welcome, Mr. O'Connell," the president said with a calculating grin and a fiercely strong handshake. "Welcome to the *Taylor* White House."

The reporter smiled nervously, half believing he was being drawn into the web of a black widow spider. "Thank you, I think." This was their first official meeting, although O'Connell had been at a number of White House press conferences, fairly well back in the pack.

"You can put your things down near the bureau. I hope the Secret Service didn't give you too much problem with your bags." Of course everything had been checked by scanner and then by hand.

"It's a different world, sir. They've got to consider all of the possibilities."

The reporter slung his backpack down and took off his olive green winter parka. He wore a light gray turtleneck sweater, black dress pants, and a gray wool sports jacket with black leather elbow pads.

"You're a good reporter. Have you figured out why you're here?" the president asked.

"I've run a few possibilities."

"Oh, Mr. O'Connell, I don't think you have a clue. Take out your pad. I've cancelled my next two appointments. And you've got a lot of writing to do."

The president loosened his red and blue striped tie, took a seat in the John Adams chair, which held no meaning for the reporter, rested his feet on the coffee table and proceeded to light up a cigar.

"The first thing you'll learn about me is that I don't give a flying fuck about the smoking laws inside this office." He took a puff.

"Why do I sense there's more coming, sir," the thirty-four-year-old reporter managed, suddenly taking a liking to the man.

"More? Oh there's lots more." Morgan Taylor laughed through a cloud of smoke. "Is it bothering you?" he asked.

"No. Thank you for your concern."

"You'll find me concerned about a lot of things. Like the most fundamental laws of this country." He took a satisfying puff.

"The laws, sir?"

"Well, one in particular."

Another long drag of his cigar.

"According to the Constitution, the president is supposed to be a natural born citizen of the United States."

He let the concept hang in the air just like his smoke.

"That's correct. But you didn't call me here for a discussion in civics."

"Oh, quite the contrary, Mr. O'Connell. The constitution is the very foundation of our opening discussion."

And with that blunt of an introduction, Morgan Taylor began telling Michael O'Connell everything he knew and even some of the things he believed. It was a soliloquy that broadsided the *Times* reporter. Yet, for the first time in his professional career, O'Connell didn't have to ask a single question. He just listened and wrote faster than he ever had in his life.

While Michael O'Connell was trying to keep up with the president's litany, Scott Roarke boarded an Air Force C-32A Executive Transport from McGill. The modified Boeing 757-200, generally reserved by the Air Force 89th Airlift Wing to ferry the U.S. Vice President, members of the Cabinet and Congress, and other government officials, offered a level of luxury that Special Forces never received. The passenger manifest logged a group of congressional aides en route to Germany for a tour of Ramstein Air Base. But not a single staff member was on that plane.

Ramstein, home of the 86th Airlift Wing (AW), would be an intermediate stop. Roarke and the other members of the Special Forces team would rest at the base, waiting for a break in the weather. It was expected that they'd deploy to the *Vinson* in three days.

Their plane lifted off at 0830, escorted by three fully armed Air Force versions of the Super Hornets, equipped with long-range APG-70 radar. The planes' targeting pods also contained a laser designator and tracking system that directed the onboard AIM-7F Sparrow missiles, AIM-9L Sidewinder missiles, and AIM 120 AMRAAM missiles. The F/A-18F's two-man crew were extra insurance that General Johnson had ordered.

They flew south down the Gulf of Mexico, then banked left and crossed over Miami air space, seven miles above the exclusive residential community of Fisher Island.

Ibrahim Haddad hadn't been sleeping well recently. He was sipping a second cup of morning coffee to keep himself awake, smoking his third cigarette, and watching the contrails of four planes streaking high overhead out across the Atlantic. They looked like little dots with long white tails. "Military," he reasoned before opening up his newspaper.

The front page of *The Miami Herald* carried a story about Teddy Lodge's likely liberal cabinet choices. They had enthusiastically supported his candidacy and hardly missed a day without another Lodge report. Today's pleased him, but Haddad couldn't finish reading. He knew why. His attention span was diminished due to lack of sleep.

All of his planning and strategizing was coming to fruition. With his life's principal work nearly complete, what role was there for him in the years ahead? An even harder question, would his benefactors no longer view him as an asset, but consider him a liability? *That would be unfortunate*, he thought as he crushed out his last cigarette. He would need to reaffirm his value, maybe even awaken another sleeper he had acquired and prepare for a new ascension. Ibrahim Haddad had many at his fingertips. One for each branch of the American government.

Yes, he would start a new game with a new identity. After all, Haddad was, by his own estimation, smarter than any of his adversaries and each of his three successive employers over the years.

Katie Kessler had never been more determined to research the law. She linked into Internet sites at Harvard Law Library, Georgetown University and even the Library of Congress. Now she had two notebooks with case histories in the right columns and her questions and suppositions on the left.

Katie took a leave of absence from Freelander, Collins, Wrather & Marcus. It was just short of a resignation. She'd probably never return. The question she pondered now was, *Where will all of this lead me?*

One person she didn't bother saying goodbye to was Witherspoon. That very act kept her departure from being reported to Ibrahim Haddad. Witherspoon was on Haddad's payroll, but the Miami man was clearly overpaying for his services.

"Mr. Lodge, we hear that you haven't talked to the president since the debates."

CNN scored the president-elect 11 days prior to the inauguration and the host got right to the point.

"Well, I'm sure Morgan Taylor is a busy man with things to do."

A few blocks away Taylor watched alone in the Oval Office. "You better believe I do," he said to the TV.

"Undoubtedly he'll have last minute pardons to grant and some goodbye speeches; the usual. We'll get together on January 20. That's soon enough?"

"And when you do see him, what will you say?"

"What anyone in my position would say—'Thank you for all that you've done for America. Now may I please have the keys to the House?'"

The host laughed. "And the fact that President Taylor hasn't made overtures to you? What does that say?"

"It means I want you to worry, you sonofabitch!" the president declared to the screen. "Worry about everything."

"To be perfectly honest, I don't know what he's thinking. You'll have to ask him," Lodge told the anchor.

"We have. The formal word from the administration is, 'No comment.' To me, that suggests he has some real issues with you. Do you have any idea what they are, Congressman?"

Lodge politely offered, "No. I don't," and then he stopped and wondered. *What was going on? It was too quiet.* He missed the newsman's next question, which made him look awkward.

"Congressman?" the moderator had to ask.

Morgan Taylor walked right up to his television monitor and stood face to face with his opponent. "I'm getting to you, aren't I? Just wait."

"Congressman?"

"Yes, sorry. You had me thinking for a moment."

When the stage manager announced, "Clear," a few minutes later, Teddy Lodge quickly shook the host's hand, thanked everyone on the crew, and hurried out of the CNN Washington studios onto First Street, N.E.

"Nice job," Newman whispered to Lodge.

"Oh, cut the crap." They brushed past three TV reporters waiting for a quick sound bite and into the raw January air. The temperature hadn't gone above 20 degrees in days and neither Lodge nor Newman had overcoats. Once in the warmth of their limo, Lodge pressed the button to raise the glass between the driver and passenger compartment.

"We go on the offensive," Lodge began, obviously pissed at his performance. "Set up interviews with Mulligan at the Bureau. Evans at CIA. If they meet and it's cordial we leak that we're actively asking them to stay on—for now. If they brush us off, then word gets out that we're looking for replacements. And we call Taylor. He won't respond, so we get indignant and embarrass the motherfucker. Let the lame duck shoot himself in the foot."

"Good," was all Newman managed before Lodge started again.

"Make the calls today. I sucked out there and I want to turn this around. Get me on *The Today Show* Monday morning. 7:35. There are a lot of women watching home alone after sending the kids off the school."

Newman beamed. Lodge certainly knew his constituency.

"Mulligan," the FBI director said to Louise Swingle.

"I need the man again."

The fifty-four-year-old White House secretary put him right through with her usual efficiency.

"Yes, Mr. Director."

"Mr. President, I just received a phone call from Newman."

"Oh?"

"Said he wants to chat. I suspect that means he's interested in sounding out my intentions to stay or Lodge's intentions to keep me. What do you want me to do?"

The president let out a single, short laugh. "Well, it appears that Lodge is trying to reclaim some political high ground after stumbling this morning."

"Yah, looked that way to me, too."

"You're a policeman, Bob. Spook him out a little. This could be interesting."

"I thought you'd want me to do that. I have just the guy to do it, too."

"Who's that?" Taylor was intrigued.

"Someone he'd be surprised to see in the room. Roy Bessolo, the agent in charge of the investigation in upstate New York. I'll have him ask a few pointed questions. We'll see what happens."

"You know, pissing him off will cost you a job in the new administration."

Mulligan's voice deepened. "What new administration, Mr. President?"

Most of Ramstein Air Force Base's mission history is classified. It's headquarters of the Department of Defense's European Command, America's muscle in the North Atlantic Treaty Organization. That means the U.S. Air Force gets to park its hardware there.

During certain "operations" the planes are a lot lighter on their return than when they took off.

Bragging rights have included official and unofficial missions in support of Operations Desert Shield, Desert Storm, air protection over Bosnia-Herzegovina, the NATO-led air war over Kosovo, air strikes against the Taliban, and Operation Iraqi Freedom.

Security begins with the Ramstein website. Nobody gets further than the home page without permission. It continues right to the front gate and the airspace overhead. Roarke had been there before, but nobody would find the paperwork to support the stopovers.

The twin-engine jet touched down softly at 2135 local time, having traveled close to the edge of its 5,500 mile range. The C-32A taxied directly into a hangar, which was then locked tight. Only then did the door open and the members of the Special Forces disembark. For now, this was a black op, although the president had explained the mission to one reporter.

The hangar would be their home until they received their orders to move on. No one was allowed outside. No one inside. Specially prepared food had been brought in via a catering truck. There would be no alcohol during the stay. They'd be living on low carbs, fruits, vegetables, and high protein until they completed their assignment.

The six-member team talked to no one other than Colonel Sam Langeman. And Slange, as he was always called, only talked to J3 at McGill's super secretive Integrated Battle Command Center (IBCC), located in a sub-basement of a nondescript five story communications building. So far Slange was the only member of the Special Forces squad who'd ever seen the 10,200 square foot room, enclosed in forty-five inches of concrete wall and ceilings. The others were about to learn a little bit about it.

"Okay. Grab some java and sit down." It was just short of an order, but Slange made sure it sounded like one. He had assembled his squad—Aplen, Gardner, Recht, and Jones, along with the president's man, Roarke. When they were all seated, he began.

"We've trained to be self sufficient. But there will be extra eyes and ears watching out for us," he said. Slange began describing the complex Command Center in general terms. Enough to give them some added confidence. Not enough to cause harm if the enemy ever found out. Even though these men were the elite, they didn't need to know what they didn't need to know. There was always the threat of capture and torture.

"This ain't a place you'll be able to go trick or treat," he quipped. "First there's a set of security doors." There were three. "Then a steep hike down a 200-yard ramp pitched at a 20-degree angle. That'll lead you to a pair of fifteen-inch steel blast doors at either end. And I'm afraid it wouldn't qualify as handicapped accessible. One person enters at a time and the doors close two-seconds after you enter whether or not you're all the way in."

"Hey Aplen, you can count to two, right?" Recht joked.

"Shut the fuck up!" Aplen countered. The men simultaneously broke into a chorus of "woos" at Recht's expense.

"Okay, okay, settle down," Slange barked, bringing order back to his briefing. "The room was developed by the whiz kids in Anaheim. And I'm not talking Disneyland. It's all Boeing. You don't penetrate this place without passing through a combination of retinal scans, fingerprint, and voice identification. And you don't get to try unless you've got the highest clearance." Slange left out a few extra particulars. There were even more *he* hadn't been told.

"At the center of the far side wall is a fifteen-foot-high television screen. It's got multiple images, including incredibly clear down-looking satellite views; moving geometric shapes of triangles representing the four Apaches equipped with air-to-surface Longbow Hellfire missiles and air-to-air Stinger missiles that'll give us support en route to the arena; squares for the Black Hawks carrying us; and circles with wings for the F-18C's overhead. There's a big fat Capital 'X' in a circle, too. That's for the AWACS recon at 39,000 feet."

Roarke had been through enough situation rooms to get the picture. Computer terminals everywhere. Command that could, with a basic key stroke, change disparate weapon systems, satellite views, and other real-time data on the large screen. But IBCC was clearly leaps beyond what he'd ever seen.

Slange continued. "They've got eighteen engineers out of MIT and Stanford overseeing everything. Three are there to track the audio communications between us and our taxis and escorts." He was intentionally sarcastic. "Another four are glued to screens programmed to follow personal infrared cameras mounted on our helmets. Two doctors have consoles where they'll monitor real time blood pressure and vital sign readings and even tell if you peed in your pants. And another four techs are assigned to reading personal-space radar. So ladies, smile a lot. You're gonna be stars of the show back home."

"Personal space radar, sir?" Jones asked.

"It's laser tag to the max," Colonel Langeman explained. "Each of us will instantly know if an *unfriendly*, not identified by the computer program as a team member, is approaching."

"And we can count on it?" This was Roarke's first question.

"Do you get the right number when you call information?" Roarke laughed.

"Use your instincts first, boy. Then go for the toys."

The toys included C41SR processors which create 2-D and 3-D views of the battlespace. These pictures are routed to the large screen television at command and transmitted to the USS *Carl Vinson* where the president would be.

The result was an array of real time eyes and ears that put American forces at quite an advantage. In truth, Slange never placed undue confidence in the technology. Training and teamwork meant everything to him. They had run the plan in the dark, in driving rain and heavy winds, surrounded by explosions and smoke, and under real fire. If the "toys" worked, so much the better. But they were ready if all of the electronic eyes went blind on them.

"We'll get our ATO through McGill." The ATO was their Air Tasking Order. "Then tomorrow, the next day, the day after that, or whenever it is, we'll have more people watching us with their tongues hanging out than Trixie gets at a fuckin' peep show."

Not so many years earlier, Norman Schwarzkopf had to move an entire command and control center to Saudi Arabia to direct fighting in the Gulf War. But in more recent years, command supervised the battlefield via telecommuting. The Bush White House even watched live television feeds of strikes against the Taliban in Afghanistan, transmitted by unmanned spy drones, satellite relayed to the Florida command center, then fiber-optic linked to Washington.

This was the digital battlefield, fostered by George W. Bush's Defense Secretary Donald H. Rumsfeld. "And today," explained Slange, "it's the pride and joy of our boss. And we're connected right through handheld PDA's. Pretty fucking amazing."

Roarke aptly added a hyphen into the description. "Gives new meaning to the word *super*-vision."

"Here, play with this tonight." Slange reached into a knapsack and tossed each of his men a handheld PDA. "Your very own connection to IBCC. We'll run a full systems check at eleven-hundred. You could even send dirty e-mails to your girlfriends in the middle of the maneuver through these things. But don't."

The "don't" put it all in perspective. Slange had given them a flyover of the technology. Silicon Valley had indeed come to Valley Forge. But there was no substitution for teamwork, training, and the human component.

"The point of all this is you've got help you'll never see. But help yourself and the guy next to you. If you do that, we'll all get out alive."

Roarke let his mind drift to Katie for a moment. Her eyes, her lips, her body. Moving with her. Kissing and loving her.

"Here, Junior G-man!" Slange said. "Catch." He tossed a PDA to Roarke. The Secret Service agent snatched it in the air and Katie was instantly gone. He had his Special Forces face on now. He needed it to survive. Roarke was back in the game.

CHAPTER 57

MONDAY, JANUARY 12

"Are you counting the days, Congressman?" the host quipped over the fiber-optic link between New York and Washington.

Teddy Lodge was determined to look completely in charge during this *Today Show* appearance. "I think I've got fifty days of work to fit into just eight. I've got a cabinet to finalize and decisions to make. So I'm counting the days and adding the nights. I need every second."

"You're a Democrat, and you'll have a Democratic majority in Congress. It's been years since a chief executive from your party has enjoyed that luxury. How will your administration use that kind of power?"

"It's not a function of power, it's the American political system at work. Sometimes the president has the benefit of a supportive Congress. Sometimes not. The job doesn't change, just the number of votes across the street and the number of laws that get passed. And the legacy you leave behind."

"And your legacy, Congressman?"

"Oh, heck, I haven't even been sworn in yet. And aren't legacies for you guys to assess? But if you're asking about what I'd like to accomplish?"

"All right," the host agreed.

"I'd like America to be viewed with understanding around the world. And America needs to see the rest of the world as the rest of the world sees itself."

The anchor, long the nation's favorite morning host, asked the natural follow up. "And that would be?"

"A world where we understand and respect the differences among people and nations. A world not bound by old treaties."

"Are you declaring a shift in American foreign policy?"

"American foreign policy is always shifting."

"Anything more specific, Congressman?"

"That's a question for a president," he said with a smile. "Ask me again in a few days."

By now Michael O'Connell knew the heavy knock. It was his very own Secret Service agent at the door of his well-appointed room at the Hay Adams.

"Coming, coming."

He turned off his TV set. He'd been watching the *Today Show* interview with Teddy Lodge. *Funny what a difference a few days makes,* he thought. He made a mental note of the moment. He'd write about it later.

"Wheels up, Mr. O'Connell," the man on the other side of the door said with a deep, no nonsense voice.

O'Connell stopped short. *Oh my God! It's really time.*

"There's a car waiting. You're already checked out," said the voice from the hallway.

The reporter tried to walk, but he was suddenly immobile. It was as if the weight of the past few days had finally settled right into his feet. He literally couldn't move. Now his heart raced and his breathing accelerated. He ordered himself to calm down, if only in recognition that the worst was yet to come.

"Exactly where are we going?" was the best he could manage. *And what was it that the president said?* He remembered. "*Bring clothes for all sorts of weather.*"

"I don't have that information, sir. Do you need any help?"

"No, no. Just give me a few more moments." O'Connell managed.

When the agent didn't hear anything after two minutes he knocked again.

"I have specific orders, Mr. O'Connell."

With five deep breaths he filled himself with enough confidence to get through the door. "Look. Just tell me what I need to take."

There was a long pause. Finally, a cryptic answer. "I think you could use your raincoat."

"Mr. Newman, it's nice to meet you," Bob Mulligan said, leading Lodge's chief of staff into his office. "I'm sure we both have a great many questions for one another."

"That's why I thought we should get together," Newman said, acting as aloof as possible.

"Have a seat then, and say hello to Special Agent Bessolo. He's been heading up the investigation into the…" he chose his words carefully, "…the assassination attempt on Congressman Lodge."

"Yes, we've met. But it's the death of Mrs. Lodge that I'd like to talk about." He nodded, but didn't extend his hand.

"Yes, Mr. Newman, I'm sure you do," Bessolo said matching Newman's iciness.

"Well I damn well hope you've finally got some news for me! It's been almost eight months and you don't have anyone in custody."

"Oh not yet, Mr. Newman," Mulligan said closing the door. "But soon, I believe very soon."

Mulligan was convinced he saw Newman's eye twitch.

O'Connell expected to see the president's 747-200B waiting at the tarmac. Instead there were five Navy jets with a range of missiles under their wings. The engines on four were idling.

The car was hardly stopped when the trunk flew open, an agent reached in for his backpack and ran it over to one of the jets at the rear.

A pilot wearing a flight helmet climbed down the ladder of the nearest jet. Over the rising roar of the lead jets which were rolling forward, the man's voice bellowed. "I suggest you take a good long piss right now. The next chance you'll have will be in nine hours."

The flier removed his head gear.

"Oh my God!" O'Connell managed. He was completely shocked to see it was Morgan Taylor.

"Christ Almighty! *You're* flying *me* in this thing? You can't do that, you're the president."

"Oh, Mr. O'Connell. Rest assured. Your plane is over there." He pointed to an identical two-seater. "I'm in this one. Officially, it is Air Force One, but for security reasons, you might say we're flying under the political radar. However, if you'd rather come with me..."

"No thanks."

"Thought that'd be the case. While I prefer the fact not be for public consumption, I do get to fly these things when nobody's looking. And a tad better than George Dubya, I'll have you know," he added the reference to President Bush's celebrated landing on the *Abraham Lincoln* off the coast of Southern California in 2003.

O'Connell forced a smile, however his rattled nerves couldn't hold it in place.

"Like I said, Mr. O'Connell..." The president pointed to the writer's crotch. "Now's the time."

After pushing out every last drop of pee and getting into a flight suit, O'Connell stood in for the basic pre-flight instructions—a lecture on what *not* to touch in the cockpit and how to eject.

His pilot, Lieutenant Commander Rico M. Rupp, explained the flight plan over the comm, "We'll be up to 44,000 feet real fast."

"Will my stomach be far behind?" O'Connell managed.

"It'll be along anytime, sir," Rupp laughed over the headset. "And once we level off, I'll give you a smooth ride. Sorry about the lack of in-flight services. There's not much available up here except the gas station."

"Gas station?"

"We'll get topped off in a bit for the long haul and again about two hours out from the deck."

"Good. Some stops."

"I didn't say that, sir. The Air Force is sending KC-10 tankers to rendezvous inflight. The first is already over the Atlantic. It goes on the company card."

Oh shit! O'Connell swore under his breath.

"Any questions sir?"

"Yeah. What do they call this thing?"

"This baby's a Super Hornet. The F/A-18F. The most advanced high-performance strike fighter in the world. The single-seater version is the E. Both of 'em pack a wallop." Rupp got his clearance on the radio. "Here we go."

At first the F/A-18F moved forward slowly. Then Rupp fired the after-burners and O'Connell felt like he was strapped to a rocket. The Hornet accelerated at an enormous rate, pressing the reporter into the back of his seat.

After two minutes of bone-crushing acceleration the pilot asked O'Connell if he was all right.

"Yes," O'Connell forced out, feeling like a ton of bricks was still lying across his chest.

"You said the plane packs a wallop. Did you mean this or weapons?"

The pilot laughed again. "I meant our stores. Part of the Navy's portable arsenal. We've got an alphabet soup full of goodies. AIM-7 Sparrow and AIM-120 AMRAAM air-to-air missiles, and a few other little surprises. Not a full load cuz of the distance we're covering tonight, but I guarantee you, it's enough."

"Enough?" The reporter didn't need to add *for what*. He looked out at the wings, first one side, then the other, and saw the twin drop tanks loaded with extra fuel. But O'Connell couldn't see any of the armaments. "Where?"

"Just a fingertip away," Rupp, a combat veteran, coldly explained.

"That's comforting."

"It doesn't get much better than this, Mr. O'Connell. The Super Hornet is built for the future. We've got seventeen cubic feet of 'growth space' for advanced avionics. As newer technology becomes available, we'll be ready with room to spare."

"Tell them to put in a First Class compartment," O'Connell joked.

"Yes, sir."

O'Connell was mesmerized by the cockpit. A touch-sensitive control display responded to Rupp's simple commands. Tactical information, none of which the reporter could comprehend, came to life on a larger multi-purpose liquid-crystal color screen. The cockpit also contained two additional monochromatic displays, an engine fuel readout, and color digital map night vision goggles. O'Connell had the wits to keep his notepad on his lap and commit this undeniably exhilarating experience to paper.

Five minutes later, he turned his attention to the planes in formation around him. One flew ahead in lead position. Two planes were behind. He was flanked by another. Just off his starboard wing he could clearly see the president, no more than 175 feet away. *Was he actually piloting the thing?*

Morgan Taylor intuitively looked out, as casually as a driver on the Interstate. But it was his flying instinct that told him O'Connell was watching. He tipped his right hand to his forehead in a salute. His Super Hornet, slicing through the morning sky at 458 mph, was fully in his control, even if the events that lay ahead were not.

The realization actually calmed the reporter. For the next few days, he would probably be one of only a handful of people in the entire world who knew the whereabouts of Morgan Taylor. It made him smile.

Michael O'Connell relaxed in his seat and decided to enjoy the ride.

CHAPTER 58

Nothing could have prepared O'Connell for what came next. A nighttime landing. He doubted if that was even the right term. *How can you land on something floating?*

"It'll be fast and hard," warned Rupp. "Just like the hired girl likes."

The writer tried to laugh, but couldn't. He tightened his body, bracing himself for the shock ahead. He felt strong gusts buffet the plane and watched as the great ship in front of him heaved up, then down in the ocean's swell.

"Just like the hired girl likes," he whispered over and over trying to give his mind a way to relax. "Any more words of wisdom?" he managed louder.

But Rupp had no more jokes. Not right now. He had to concentrate on the signal lights ahead.

Directly in the center of the shortest runway O'Connell ever saw—no more than 200 feet—were amber and red lights. The writer looked at the gauges and heads up display in front of him and was amazed that the Super Hornet was still flying at 150 knots. And with every slight pitch, one of the lights seemed to glow. When the lights appeared above a green horizontal bar in the cockpit, O'Connell noted that Rupp nosed the plane down. When it was red, he arced it up.

A Super Hornet equipped for carrier-based operation has a hook bolted to an 8-foot bar extending from the after part of the plane. This tailhook drops with the landing gear. It must catch one of four heavy steel cables across the deck, each forty feet from the next. Miss one, the plane has to hook the next. Miss them all and the pilot has barely a blink of an eye to add enough power to stay aloft.

They were seconds away from touching down on one of the most dangerous places on the earth and O'Connell wished he'd never learned to diagram a sentence.

If O'Connell was concerned about his stomach on take-off, he was in for an even greater surprise as the plane's tailhook caught. At that precise moment, gigantic hydraulic pistons below the deck absorbed the forward energy of the speeding aircraft, letting out just enough cable to stop the Hornet safely on deck. All of this as Rupp had his plane at full throttle, just in case they missed a wire. The F/A-18F jerked to a stop, O'Connell's restraints pulled his chest with such force that he thought he would black out and his eyes would shoot right through the cockpit window like a cartoon character. O'Connell saw a ballet of lights, like a field of lightning bugs wavering around the aircraft. Only a moment later he felt another sensation. He seemed to be floating in a vast darkness. Before he even realized it, his plane was going down on an elevator, one of four lifts.

Hardly a minute more, enlisted men and women in various colored vests were all over his plane. These were the deck crew of the nuclear powered Nimitz class aircraft carrier, USS *Carl Vinson*.

"Welcome to my second home," a voice shouted across the noise. It was Taylor, lively and dynamic. In sharp contrast, O'Connell felt wobbly and dazed. He stood up in the cockpit and put one leg over to the ladder. After getting down, he removed his helmet and shook his head to recover his senses. It didn't help much. "How was it, son?" he asked. "Not many civilians come in the way you did."

"I can't imagine many would want to," O'Connell said laughing. "The service sucked."

"Well, it's better onboard. You're on a great city."

On a city? mused the writer. What an odd expression, but it was true. He'd been told that the *Vinson* had everything a city of 4,500 could possibly need.

Next, Morgan Taylor saluted the ranking officer, Rear Admiral Boulder Devoucoux.

"Permission to come aboard, sir?"

"Permission granted, Mr. President. The command is yours."

It was a formality, and even though Morgan Taylor had left the service as a Commander, he now commanded all of America's armed forces.

"Thank you, sir, but I think I'll leave that in your able hands, if you don't mind."

"Not at all, sir. It's an honor to have you aboard."

"It's good to be back."

"Rear Admiral, I'd like you to meet Michael O'Connell. He's our historian for this little adventure."

Devoucoux had been advised that the reporter was accompanying the president.

"You'll extend him every courtesy and answer his questions *by the book*."

"Yes sir." Devoucoux offered his hand.

"Good to meet you, Mr. O'Connell." The career officer was pleased that Morgan Taylor had added the caveat "by the book." He picked up on the cue immediately. It allowed him to explain ship's operation in strictly *Popular Science* terms and nothing beyond. The reporter smiled thinking he would get more. Everyone was happy.

"Nice to meet you, sir. And about the only question I have right now is 'where's the nearest bathroom.'"

The president smiled to his former commanding officer. "Boulder, our guest actually has a good idea. We'll hit the head and get on with things." Morgan Taylor raised his hand in the air and Secret Service, which had arrived earlier, seemed to come out of nowhere. They fell into place around him.

"You're in good hands, Mr. O'Connell. I'll catch up with you soon." With that Morgan Taylor moved in double time and passed the five planes that had made the trip across the Atlantic. Their wings were now folded up, like bats ready to sleep.

"Mr. O'Connell," a young enlisted man called out. "This way. I'll get you where you need to go."

"Thanks. And you're?"

"Seaman Pearlman, sir. At your service. We'll let you get freshened up."

O'Connell followed slowly; he didn't have his balance yet. Pearlman noticed. "Don't worry, sir. You'll have your sea legs soon." He thought better of telling him the truth.

While O'Connell was in the head, another plane landed on the deck. He heard the rumble but didn't think to ask about it. Had he inquired, he would have been politely told it was a heavy lift CH-53 transport from the mainland. No one would have said who was onboard.

The men who did de-plane talked to no one along the way. There were only salutes. They had other things on their mind. First and foremost, the weather. Like President Taylor, O'Connell, and the escorts, they'd used a short break in the storm system to land on the *Vinson*. That window was closing again.

THE WHITE HOUSE BRIEFING ROOM
TUESDAY, JANUARY 13

"Where's the president?" asked the CBS reporter at the daily White House news briefing. The city lived on rumors. A number were circulating; quietly leaked by high level staffers under instructions from Morgan Taylor's Press Secretary, Bill Bagley; instructions he didn't even understand.

"I have a report that the president is at Camp David with severe depression and is under medical supervision."

That was a new one to Bagley.

"I can assure you that the president is in complete control of his faculties. He could probably hop back into a fighter and take the stick if he wanted to," said the press secretary. "He is right where he belongs. At work."

A young CNN reporter took up the charge. "My sources have him in secret meetings in India."

"Not true."

"Talking to Boeing about joining the board?" asked another.

"No."

"Vacationing?"

"Look, a man who's scheduled to be out of work in eight days doesn't need a vacation now." Bagley went on to explain what he knew to be the truth, which was very little. John Bernstein said to handle the questions directly. The president was busy and unavailable. Everything on the street was rumor, or more to the Beltway parlance, "disinformation," partly to give the press something to write about, partly to suggest to Teddy Lodge that Morgan Taylor was isolated in his final days.

"Look, he's not scheduled for any public appearances until the Inauguration. He's got a great deal to do in a very short time. Next question?"

Newman's speechwriter and Lodge's plaything was busy at all of her jobs. All three.

Christine Slocum had an impressive grasp of words and a natural feel for the way Lodge could deliver her lines. That made her invaluable to both men. But she also provided the eyes and ears for another.

Though she only cryptically communicated via sex chat rooms, her correspondent knew exactly what to read into the messages. She conveyed mood, manner, strengths and weaknesses to her benefactor; a rich man who had provided college scholarship money when little else was available. A thoughtful businessman who flung open doors of opportunity to her that would have otherwise remained closed. In return, she wrote a little, she spied a little, and she fucked a lot. She liked all three and prided herself for her talent in each area.

For Slocum, it was a game where she advanced with the winner. Slocum was already getting noticed by some members of the press corps. The twenty-five-year-old *wunderkind* from Miami was likely to head the White House speechwriting staff. Lodge even hinted it himself. Newman said it directly.

And once again Ibrahim Haddad's patience had paid off handsomely. He had groomed the talented writer for years, always manipulating things her way. Of course, if she eloped with some undergraduate love interest, there were others with the same ability. Haddad *always* had others. But she remained a faithful prodigy and a willing associate.

As a result, Haddad now had two people to watch over Lodge. Newman controlled the politics. Slocum played with his emotions. There was no question in Haddad's mind that Lodge had become tense over the last few months. That's why he sent her in; that, and her ability to write for him.

Haddad thanked Christine Slocum for the words she wrote in Lodge's speeches and the words he assumed she whispered in his ears. He thanked her with a bonus in a Cayman Island bank account; money that could never be traced back to him. And he thanked her each time the press wrote another glowing article or heralded the new chief executive.

"Move over Taylor. Lodge is moving in," trumpeted the host. *The Bennington Banner* editorialized that their favorite son would "breathe life into a government-gone-stale." "Lodge to reinvent the role of America," touted *The Los Angeles Times*.

Reporters everywhere were tripping over one another to score a personal interview with the president-elect, now even Fox News. And then Haddad thought for a moment. *The* New York Times *reporter? O'Connell. Where's he been?* He'd get word to Slocum. Maybe it was time for her to cultivate another "friendship" on the side.

WEDNESDAY, JANUARY 14

"More unseasonably bad weather's in store for the south-central Mediterranean. With gale force winds blowing onshore, continuing inland with downpours through Northern Libya and Tunisia."

The CNN International weatherman didn't delve into specifics. It meant nothing to most of the audience. But some very important people were interested in more information. Fortunately, they had their own private meteorologist.

Onboard the USS *Carl Vinson*, the CIA's Dutch Tetreault explained why the system had stalled out. Rear Admiral Boulder Devoucoux listened. He knew the winds all too well and the dangers they brought. But he only needed a short window to open up.

Devoucoux instantly flashed on D-Day and the uncertainty Dwight Eisenhower must have felt before proceeding with the invasion of Normandy. The one thing Ike couldn't control was the weather. Now with his own operation to launch, Devoucoux drew the parallel. General Eisenhower only waited a day. *How long will I have to?*

"Come on, Tetreault, there's got to be a break coming."

The meteorologist handed a sheet of paper to the rear admiral that answered his question.

ALERT 01500 CHARLIE JAN 14.

SUBJ/JAN 14 MEDITERRANEAN SEA HIGH WIND AND SEAS WARNING//

1. THIS WARNING SUPERSEDES AND CANCELS ALL PRV.

2. WARNINGS ARE FOR OVER WATER AREAS BUT ARE DESCRIBED FOR BREVITY AND OVERLAP LAND MASSES OR AREAS OF LESSER WINDS/SEAS.

3. WAVE HEIGHTS REPRESENT THE AVERAGE HIGHEST ONE-THIRD (1/3) OF COMBINED SEA AND SWELL. INDIVIDUAL WAVES MAY BE SIGNIFICANTLY HIGHER.

4. WIND WARNINGS. A GALE WARNING VALID FOR THE 48-HOUR PERIOD BEGINNING AT 01500 CHARLIE JAN 14. MAX SUSTAINED WINDS EAST AT 73-76 KTS WITH GUSTS TO 88 KTS.

5. SEAS 22 FT OR GREATER FORECAST FOR THE 36-HOUR PERIOD.

6. NEXT MEDITERRANEAN SEA HIGH WIND AND SEAS WARNING WILL BE 1800 CHARLIE.

Devoucoux read it and passed it down the line to Colonel Langeman. "Here Slange. Get out your Dramamine."

"Fuck me!" he shouted as he read the report. No one in the chain of command took exception with his comment. They all were feeling that they'd run out of time. Most of all the president.

"Dutch, I want the bottom line," Taylor said.

"Mr. President, we've got very cold upper air and steep temperature lapse rates. In turn, high atmospheric instability supports thunderstorms overshooting the tropopause. In addition, rotating storms embedded within the squall line are throwing off tornados and waterspouts."

"In English," insisted the president.

"Mesocyclones."

"English!"

Tetreault had to go back to his TV weatherman days. "Ah, the squall line's stalled and we're right under it."

Morgan Taylor turned away from the others. He put his hand to his forehead and stroked his hair grabbing and holding the nape at the back of his neck. He kept his expression and immediate anger out of sight.

"Worst of it is," continued the meteorologist, "this thing's still intensifying. I'm waiting for the latest high resolution images from our satellite sounders. But right now I don't see how anybody's going anywhere."

The president circled the room and faced everyone again. There was no sign of hopelessness on his face; only determination. "The very second," he paused to correct himself. "No, make that the very *nanosecond* we have achieved even minimal acceptable conditions between 2200 and 0330 hours, we launch. I will not put our team in jeopardy, but we *will* go."

There wasn't a man on the bridge who didn't read President Morgan Taylor loud and clear.

However, the weather was not under Taylor's command, and the USS *Carl Vinson* rocked in the waves for four more nauseating days. When the seas finally calmed where the *Vinson* sailed, a new squall, with heavy winds and rain, stalled over Tripoli.

FISHER ISLAND, FLORIDA
SATURDAY, JANUARY 17

Ibrahim Haddad used his influence to learn that Michael O'Connell hadn't been at his desk in ten days. He had missed invitations to *This Week* and *Meet the Press*. Nobody passed up that kind of exposure, especially twice. One of his editors was heard to say in the men's room that O'Connell was on the network's shit list. "And he's gonna be covering the New York State Assembly instead of the White House if he doesn't check in." However, a friendly call to a *Times* editor indicated that he was working with an "inside source" on an important story.

Haddad ran the possibilities. *O'Connell was onto something. He covered the campaign. They wouldn't take him off it now. He wasn't with Lodge. That left only one other person.*

He left a message that was picked up by his source at the FBI. Soon he learned that a DC cab driver remembered dropping off a man at the White House who fit the description of O'Connell. *And now Taylor was AWOL. Why?* Haddad wondered if Taylor took him to the Pakistani-Indian border to get him away from Lodge.

At the end of his mental exercise, Haddad concluded that he needed more information. He decided to do two things in the morning: Press his contact at the FBI for something concrete and send another encoded message in a picture to a business associate waiting in Washington. It was time to implement a contingency plan.

As his bedroom digital clock clicked over from 11:59 P.M. to midnight, Haddad turned off his night light and willed away his anxiety. *Two days and it would be over. Two more days and the country will have a new president. It took the conservative Republican Nixon to open up relations with the Chinese communists. It will be the liberal Democratic Lodge who will undo the United States' allegiance to Israel and eventually install a new generation of Kharrazi leadership in Libya. Yes, just two more days*, he thought.

One hour later, Haddad slipped into a fitful sleep. His dream returned. This time more vividly. The speeches. The bands. The jets overhead. The swearing-in ceremony. The face. The face laughing now. Laughing loudly. The sound reverberating in his head, echoing as his body bolted upright again. Cold sweat drenched him. Haddad

groped for his inhaler and stared across the darkness of his room. The
room was pitch black, but for the first time he could see the face.

Morgan Taylor!

CHAPTER 59

MEDITERRANEAN SEA
ABOARD THE USS *CARL VINSON*
MONDAY, JANUARY 19
2347 HRS LOCAL

The ceiling was low, almost on the deck. But it wasn't pouring and the
winds had died down. The only illumination for miles emanated from
the glow of the *Vinson* in the temporarily calm seas. The pulsing tracer
lights on the flight deck dotted the active runway. The massive vessel
headed into the cold 15 knot winds, now just 150 nautical miles off
the coast of Libya.

High overhead, a USAF AWACS, with its saucer disc mounted on
the fuselage, scanned the skies and the ground below. It flew parallel
to and 60 miles north of the Libyan coast at 36,150 feet.

Boulder Devoucoux gave the order. "We commit in 38 minutes.
This is it. Stations."

First to takeoff from the USS *Carl Vinson* were a pair of UH-60
Special Forces Black Hawks, each carrying three members of the
Special Forces team. They flew inside an envelope created by four
fully armed Apache AH-64D copters 500 hundred feet away.

At 0040, four single seat F/A-18E's, known for their night attack
precision, shot into the skies over the Med, accelerating from 0 to 160
mph in just three seconds.

Operation Quarterback Sneak was officially and finally underway.

TRIPOLI, LIBYA
TUESDAY, JANUARY 20
0057 HRS

Many tea rooms and cafés were still open, though most of the customers had left or were just completing their nightly rounds of backgammon.

In the corner of one small establishment near the Hotel El Kabir sat a tired traveler in ragged African garb. He was listening to an old, cracked, portable radio through worn earphones. He tuned to a specific station, adjusted the volume to minimize static from the fluorescent lights, and heard what sounded like the play-by-play of an English language football game. It was unusual to listen to football, but not illegal. If anyone heard it they wouldn't understand the coded plays that were being called to an audience of one—Vinnie D'Angelo.

D'Angelo could change the station just by tilting the radio 45 degrees. He'd immediately do that if someone of authority approached.

The announcer punched through the recorded crowd noise to describe the 1st quarter—the flight to Tripoli. The second quarter would be a "fake." There would be no halftime in this game. The big action would come in the 3rd quarter. The 4th quarter—the return flight to the *Vinson*. And if the game went well, there'd be one spectacular celebration in the locker room, which he'd miss.

Five blocks away, a man took a seat under a park bench lamp. He wore casual slacks and a turtleneck covered by a heavily worn windbreaker to keep him warm. Once comfortable, he lit up a cigarette, then removed a paperback book and a flashlight from his jacket pocket.

There was nothing immediately suspicious about the man or his actions. But in fact he was on what he hoped would be his final Libyan assignment.

Like D'Angelo, the man had a special piece of equipment. For him, his flashlight. When the bottom battery compartment of the flashlight was given a quarter turn to the right, the on and off button was pressed in a 3-2-4 sequence, and the back returned to its locked position, the flashlight could "paint" a four story office corner building hundreds of feet away with a powerful, narrow laser beam.

"Painting" had a specific purpose. The building was a target. The computers in the cockpit of the lead F/A-18E Super Hornet would lock onto the reflected laser. The laser's reflection would then be "ridden" by a pair of the plane's missiles all the way to the target.

This was Sami Ben Ali's job. The 2nd quarter *fake*. He had to help the fliers create a diversion, clearing the way for the actual assault. Ben Ali had exactly five minutes before aiming his light down the street. He prayed that the Mavericks would be accurate. He was only 1500 feet from the building. Close enough to die if a missile was off its mark.

The two men, D'Angelo and Ben Ali, took special care tonight. Surprise was on their side now. But that would change. Hopefully, after *the game* they'd still have a window of opportunity to slip through the Libyan infrastructure to freedom.

Sami lit his fifth cigarette and turned another page he hadn't read. Three minutes to go.

The young agent knew that the sound would follow the flash. He wouldn't hear the incoming Mavericks' rocket engines. But their presence would be unmistakable.

He truly hoped no one was in the building. It was of no real military value. Targeting it was strategic only because of its position. The missiles would come in from the northwest. They'd hit the corner a few feet above the ground, forcing the building to crumble onto the narrow intersection below. Within seconds, the rubble would slow or block the route of any armed personnel carriers, tanks, or light artillery called in to combat the Special Ops forces due down the street.

Two minutes.

Three delivery trucks approached the intersection, followed by what looked like an old man slowly peddling a rusty bicycle.

He forced himself to turn away from the faces of the people who might die. They were working late, despising their jobs, wanting a better life that General Kharrazi or his sons could ever provide. Who would live and who would die? It all depended on whether they'd clear the intersection in 90 seconds.

Sami hadn't been briefed on the full playbook. However, he did assume that Special Ops men would come from the air, hit the roof of Fadi's building and somehow get inside.

Helicopters? Did he hear the sound of helicopter blades approaching? *They'd be moving slower than the Super Hornets or the missiles. That would be about right.*

He checked his watch. Barely one minute.

Sami put his book on his lap at precisely minus-sixty from the 2nd quarter. He turned the flashlight off and deftly twisted the bottom of the tube and entered the code. He aimed it at the building and gave the battery compartment the quarter turn back to the left. At minus 45 seconds to his play he aimed the thin laser beam across the sky to a support pillar at the first floor of the building.

Definitely helicopters. It sounded like two.

His hand shook and the light bounced off the building into the darkness. He steadied his whole arm on the park bench, found the precise targeting point. The missiles had to be on their way, adjusting to his arm movements, receiving computer instructions on their destination. He held his breath and focused every sense on staying perfectly still. It took all of his will.

Helicopters passed to his right but he resisted the urge to look at them. He lost track of the time. *Any second.*

The flash transformed night into day. A hot, blinding force blew debris up the street toward Sami at an ungodly rate.

He dove for the tree to his left and pressed his back up against it. He remembered to open his mouth. It helped prevent a concussion. Then the sound. The awful sound. And the faces of the last truck drivers and the bicyclist came to mind. *Did they even know?*

When the noise abated he peered out from behind the tree. The corner building was obliterated. The Mavericks had done their job. So had he.

TRIPOLI, LIBYA
TUESDAY, JANUARY 20
0105 HRS

D'Angelo heard the explosion. *A perfect fake,* he hoped. Less than twenty seconds after the two missiles hit, he saw the Black Hawks hover 10 feet over the eight story high sports complex, home to Fadi's growing empire. Four Apaches covered them from another 500 feet above. Each had their fuselage-mounted 30mm automatic Boeing M230 chain guns tilted downward, ready to let loose with 625 rounds per minute of ground-suppressing fire.

D'Angelo was on the move, listening to the play-by-play and waiting for the next quarter to begin. If all went well, they'd be out on their own. If it didn't, he was on hand with an alternate escape route for the Special Ops.

As he approached the building, he couldn't see what was happening eight floors above him. However, the president aboard the USS *Carl Vinson* could, though approximately two seconds behind real time. The signals were being individually uplinked by satellites to the IBCC command at McGill, then relayed to the *Vinson*. The lag time was normal, but it still made everyone nervous.

"Going for first and ten," squawked Slange over the comm line. "Hitting the field now."

Morgan Taylor sucked in a deep breath as he watched Slange's men rappel the ten feet to the roof. The wind from the rotor blades kicked up only a little bit of dust. Most had been washed away in the torrential rain, so the video was very clear.

One after another they leaped to the roof. Slange, Gardner, Recht from Black Hawk One. Jones, Aplen, and finally Roarke from Two. A technician at the *Vinson* control panel switched from a Black Hawk down-looking camera to Recht's helmet cam. He carried another on his shoulder covering his back. Aplen was similarly wired, but with wider angle lenses. They kept ten feet between each other, giving ample four camera coverage of the playing field.

"Setting for Hail Mary," Slange commanded over the radio. The team moved in a swift coordinated effort, anchoring their aluminum alloy, 4 1/12" locking D carabiners to the roof with fast drill bolts. Next, they fastened the end of their 11mm rappelling ropes to the anchor, pulled against the carabiners which would stand a 5500 pound test, and laid out fourteen feet of slack in parallel lines to avoid getting tangled with one another. Four members of team— Slange, Recht, Aplen and Roarke—stepped to the end of the ledge and awaited the colonel's call.

"On five."

The president could see the nods. They looked like cyborg troopers ready to take on an alien force; each with their night vision optics in place over their helmets. Only the American flag patches on their arms told the viewers what this was all about.

"Hut one. Hut two. Ready. Three. Four…Five."

In one motion the Special Forces team leaped off the roof. Four men in simultaneous descent pushed out to about ten feet from the building. Their slack tightened and they arced back toward the windows to Fadi's offices. With feet first, they each hit a double pane. Four windows in all.

Gardner and Jones remained on the roof for cover. Once Jones had confirmation of the team's entry, he signaled for Black Hawks One and Two to move up and out until exfiltration. Hopefully in a matter of minutes.

0107 HRS

Roarke felt the glass shattering around him. Fortunately, none of the shards penetrated his clothes or helmet. Still, the moment played out very differently than any scene from a martial arts movie. Even his old Master, Jun Chong, crashed through treated Hollywood glass in his films. The real thing could kill. And this was the real thing. One long piece on the floor could puncture a vital organ.

Like the other members of the team, Roarke had been taught to push beyond the impact point and land solidly on two feet.

Two feet, he told himself in a moment of suspended animation. Training paid off. Roarke nailed his landing. Everyone quickly disconnected their cords from their belts by depressing a hook lock.

An alarm blared. The team didn't have intelligence on the actual security system. But they weren't surprised. After all, they were breaking into the inner sanctum of General Kharrazi's son.

Recht panned the room with his camera. Aplen did the same. Both were fitted with infrared optics and the room, though dark, was clearly visible in their viewfinders.

The men stepped forward in pairs, each with their back to a partner. This way every unit was able to survey the room with a 360-degree sweep.

"Second and ten," shouted Colonel Langeman. Only fifteen seconds had elapsed since they jumped from the roof. "Proceeding to goal." The filing cabinet was in sight.

Aplen and Slange then broke to the outer offices and into the darkened hallways, scanning for the enemy through their infrared. Their immediate targets were the elevator shafts and the stairwells.

One of the two elevators was already on the move. Aplen took a nod from Slange, pried open the metal doors with an adjustable utility tool from his belt and lobbed a grenade into the shaft. The blast immediately sent the cage plunging down to the basement. No one would survive. While he did the same to the second shaft, Slange concentrated on the stairway. Two guards rounded a corner, firing as they came into his sights. Slange popped off eight rounds from his Heckler & Koch MP5 submachine gun with its HK 100 laser aimer; four into the chest of the first poor Libyan security guard, four into the other. Then he added a grenade for good measure. All of this bought them needed escape time and cost only forty seconds.

The wail of ambulances and fire trucks pierced through the night air. They were on the way to the collapsed building a short distance away. The cacophony easily masked the fanning of the helicopter rotors above Fadi's building. This was a residual benefit. The emergency vehicles were tying up traffic. No armored personnel vehicles could possibly get through the mess the Mavericks had created a few blocks away. They were forced to seek an alternate route. That would take three or four more critical minutes.

Slange returned to the office and went for *the goal*—Fadi's filing cabinet. Once there, he called into his microphone. "Next play, hand-off to fullback." That was Roarke. Recht positioned himself to get complete game coverage for the fans in the bleachers.

The cabinet stood some four feet high. There were no locks to blow or booby traps to disable. Fadi obviously never considered theft likely.

Aplen aimed a light at the old metal cabinet and Roarke stepped forward. Thanks to the intelligence report he knew exactly where to look. Thirty seconds later he had it in his hands.

He pulled out fifteen inches of files and held it up to the cameras. Recht moved in. The president told J3 to get even closer. The word was relayed. "'Top Gun' wants to be able to be close enough to read the fine print." Recht obliged.

Roarke imagined his audience 285 miles away, watching the multiple television screens. It was also being recorded on hard drives and burned onto DVDs. Every effort had been taken to insure proper authentication. The Western press would need it. So would the Muslim world.

Roarke removed his backpack within view of Recht and Aplen's field of view. He took out a roll of gaffer's tape and wrapped it around the entire thick file. He checked his watch. 0110. Using a Sharpie tucked in his sleeve, he wrote across the tape. *011 0/20 Jan/Fullback. Open at locker.*

Roarke carefully placed the package in his backpack and stepped aside. Now the rest of the team unloaded the other files from the cabinets and split up the cache in their own knapsacks. No one knew what secrets they held. But they weren't about to leave without them. In under two minute's time they carried the sum total of Fadi's *Personal* files on their backs.

"Reverse action play," Slange squawked. They returned in formation, back to back, covering each other as they stepped to the window sills.

Almost immediately two harnesses dropped directly in front of the window. Roarke grabbed one, Recht the other. His camera never strayed from the fullback. "Hike" was Slange's next command and the power winches aboard the lead Black Hawk immediately jerked both men up to the waiting helicopter.

Suddenly shots rang out from below. An armored personnel carrier had gotten through earlier than expected. Recht took a bullet in the leg. "Shit!" he yelled as Gardner pulled him to the roof.

Twenty seconds later, the harnesses were down again. Slange and Aplen's turn. But now they needed a play from the sidelines. They didn't have to wait long. An Apache gunner answered the attack from the ground, taking out the enemy with a volley from an M230. The lead Apache hovered looking for another target to pop up. There were none.

"Reverse complete. Let's go for touchdown."

At that moment, Black Hawk One sharply descended. Captain Dale Coons put its wheels lightly on the roof while still hovering. He knew that the weight of his armored helicopter—some 20,000 pounds at this point in the mission—could collapse what assuredly was a sub-standard top floor ceiling. Quickly, all six men leaped through the open door and belted themselves. The Black Hawk immediately lifted up and flew off, joining the twin Black Hawk another 800 feet above the building. At 3500 feet they scrambled for the goal line. The fourth quarter had begun.

It was at that point that their Lockheed Martin AN/AAR47 mis-sile approach warning system detected a threat.

Michael O'Connell sat in the back tier of the CommCenter located on the upper deck of the USS *Carl Vinson*. He had asked for and been granted five requests: Desk space to type notes on his Sony ultra-light Vaio. His own video feed with a running clock to track the real time images closely. A separate video camera focused on him and his immediate work area establishing a non-stop audio/video record of O'Connell's "in the moment" presence. An intelligence officer to remain at his side to translate any techno speak. And finally, contin-ued access to the president.

O'Connell typed for speed, not accuracy. Initially he was full of questions, but from the moment the team crashed through the win-dows he never uttered a word. He touch typed, watching the screens, totally caught up in the events which were unfolding at a dizzying speed. The writer was astonished at the clarity of the pictures from Fadi's offices. He could read the lettering on the files that Roarke held up to Recht's camera and he automatically ducked when bullets passed by Recht as he was hoisted onboard.

Michael O'Connell was so caught up in the images that he missed the shrill deedle-deedle-deedle alarm that pulsed out of the helicop-ter's threat detectors.

"Targeting SAM's," the pilot of the command Black Hawk announced.

From another speaker, "Confirmed." The overflying AWACS reported in. Nothing passed unseen or unheard from its powerful elec-tronic eyes and ears. And everything was automatic. Seconds earlier, the location and range of the threat had been diagnosed by computer, fed to the circling F/A-18's, and an attack plan had been plotted.

The *Vinson* command center heard a faster deedle-deedle-deedle now.

"Oh shit." The president knew that sound first-hand.

"Missiles away," was the report from the AWAC's cool radar officer, Lt. Linda Rodriguez. She plotted four missiles targeted for the Black Hawks. "Probably old Volga SA-2 SAM's." Old, but still deadly Soviet-built surface-to-air missiles with a range of thirty-one miles.

"Down range 17 miles," Rodriguez called out. "On course to intercept." She ran some fast calculations and keyed a command to the Eagles. The Black Hawk pilots knew what to do.

The SAM's maximum velocity was Mach 3.5, or approximately 2640 miles per hour. It was deadly enough to bring down Francis Gary Powers' U-2 over Russia in 1960, and reason enough for the United States to prepare for war when they were shipped to Cuba in 1962.

"Thirty seconds."

A technician onboard the *Vinson* superimposed a digital clock on screen.

"Countermeasures," was the only word from Coons in Black Hawk One. He dropped his chaff and flares in hopes of drawing the incoming missiles away from his two T700-GE-701C turboshaft engines. Captain Spencer Dayton, piloting Black Hawk Two, did the same.

Even Michael O'Connell knew what was happening now. He stopped typing and watched the monitors.

Army captain Dale Coons might have had fewer than 30 seconds to play with, but he certainly didn't act as if they'd be his last. He was calm and focused in the cockpit of his lead Black Hawk. His tactical display showed the threats, but also his assets—the Super Hornets.

They were all computer linked to the AWACS for targeting. Thirty seconds was like the two minute drill in football. Ample time for a solid offensive play; time for Quarterback Sneak to get pass protection.

The computer fed the coordinates to his missiles' onboard guidance systems. The chief weapons in Coons' stores were Hellfire missiles. These miniature aircraft carried copper-lined-charge warheads, powerful enough to burn through the thickest tank armor in the world.

His Black Hawk employed eight of them—a pair mounted to each of four pylons split between the wings. They would target the mobile SAM launch sites that sent the missiles aloft, as well as their radar guidance centers.

Coons triggered the release sequence, igniting the propellant. In an instant and with 500 pounds of force, the first two missiles broke free of the firing rail, accelerated and locked on their aiming coordinates, which read a laser light reflecting off the target. Another two fired, followed by two more, then the final two.

Coons banked his helicopter away. His work was done. The rest was up to the F-18's.

High above them, Commander Rico Rupp was earning his day's pay as pilot of the command F/A-18E. Within eight seconds of the SAM launches, he had called up two AIM-7 Sparrows, attached to his nacelle fuselage stations. Not waiting for a launch order, for they had been authorized in his briefing before takeoff, he released the two 500 pound super-sonic missiles. The air-to-air heat-seeking missiles had earned their stripes in the Persian Gulf War. Testament to their capabilities were the twenty-two Iraqi fixed-wing aircraft and the three helicopters that were downed by the radar-guided AIM-7 Sparrow missiles during that brief war. Most of them were killed within ten miles of launch. Rupp's missiles, and those of the other three Navy pilots in the skies, had just under nine miles to work with now.

Rupp's second wave came from his AIM-120 AMRAAM, or Advanced Medium Range Air-to-Air Missile. This killer had even greater speed and range than the enemy's SAM's. At supersonic speeds, the distance quickly closed between the incoming and returning fire.

"Six to impact," Rodriguez radioed.

Exactly twenty-six seconds after the first SAM launch, and barely four seconds from intercepting the Black Hawks, Rupp's missiles scored.

Seconds later the SAM sites were obliterated by the Hellfires. The same for their radar installations.

"Opposition sidelined," squawked Rupp.

Coons cut in, "Four blocked field goals."

"Heading back to the showers. Fullback has the ball for coach," chimed in Capt. Coons from his Black Hawk.

Ground radar painted them three more times on the return leg.

The installations were quickly turned to smoldering cinder blocks when their radar was answered by the deadly force of the aptly named Hellfires. No more Libyan SAM's gave them trouble after that.

CHAPTER 60

TRIPOLI, LIBYA
0216 HRS

"What do you mean?" screamed Fadi Kharrazi. "Who came? From where? How?"

The self-appointed heir apparent expected better from his aid, Lakhdar al-Nassar. Al-Nassar was lucky for now that he was on the telephone and not facing Fadi in person.

"They came in on helicopters and went through the windows."

"Who came?"

"It had to be Americans."

"And the building guards. Exactly where were they?"

"Downstairs." He decided to add, "Like always. But they were cut off. Four were killed, more on the street in an armored vehicle. By the time the rest made it to the top floor it was all over."

"What was over?"

"The break-in." Al-Nassar smiled. "But good news. All they took were some files."

"What files? Tell me in the name of the Prophet what they took!"

"I don't know. The guards who got there just said the file cabinets were ransacked."

"Which ones?" But Fadi knew the answer even if al-Nassar was too stupid to figure it out.

The chaos on the Tripoli streets successfully stalled General Kharrazi's troops. The single armored vehicle that did get through had been taken out. No others made it across the debris field in time. It had all been too quick.

Vinnie D'Angelo slipped into the busy street scene and disappeared. But he had one more bit of business. Purely personal. He knew exactly where Secret Police Major Yassar Hevit lived and where he would die.

Sami Ben Ali followed his pre-arranged escape route, not waiting another moment. He was finally going home, vowing never to return.

One hour later the Black Hawks carrying the Special Ops team touched down on the USS *Carl Vinson*. The Apaches landed three minutes later, followed by the four F/A-18C's.

The cameras kept rolling. A Secret Service officer took over Aplen and Recht's video cameras, assuring uninterrupted coverage to the CommCenter. Smiles, handshakes, and high-fives greeted the Special Ops team.

A Navy detail led Roarke through a maze of corridors. No one offered to take the files from him. They didn't know what he was holding, but rumors had spread that it was explosive.

Roarke and the accompanying vid ops entered a heavily-guarded conference room at a running clip. It was brightly lit for optimum video coverage and completely mic'd for sound.

Three six-foot-long folding tables draped with white tablecloths formed a U-shape in the room. Men and women were at each with piles of books Roarke presumed to be foreign dictionaries. Two copy machines were humming against the back wall. Two scanners and a pair of printers were also online. A grease board marked *Assumptions/ Strategies* hung at the head of the room. A fourth table with food was in the far corner.

"Scott! So good to see you." The first words were from President Taylor, who greeted him with a sincere and gratifying bear hug.

Roarke let out a sigh, and allowed his body to relax. "I felt like an old man out there."

"Well, you don't look too worse for wear," the president said to Roarke. "Then again…"

"Someone had to do the heavy lifting," Roarke joked.

"And while we're on the subject, let's take that package off your hands."

"Be my guest." Roarke handed over the backpack. At the same

time, four Secret Service agents brought in backpacks carrying the rest of the material snatched from Fadi's offices.

"Thank you, Scott. Let's give it to some people who can make more out of it."

The president passed the signed and sealed parcel to Jack Evans, who in turn opened it in view of an overhead camera.

"Now, Scott, while they're getting started, how about some coffee. There's also cold cuts from the mess. What's your pleasure?"

"I'll just go for the java, sir."

The president nodded and walked Roarke over to the food table.

"What's the situation? Are we gonna make it in time, boss?" It was already very early in the morning of January 20th in the Mediterranean. But the time difference was on their side. Washington was seven hours behind. It was still evening on the 19th.

"We have sixty-eight minutes to wheels up," the president explained. He didn't tell them that the weather wasn't going to hold much longer. They *had* to get back to Washington. "First to Ramstein, then we'll high tail it to Andrews on Air Force One. We'll be home by oh-eight-hundred local time. It'll be tight and we've got a helluva lot to pore through before we go."

By poring through, Taylor meant translating. He had Arabic and Russian experts from the NSA waiting at two of the tables. Everyone wore a microphone, feeding discreet audio channels to multi-track DAT machines. Every word they said or read would be part of the record.

"Any idea what's really there?" Roarke asked.

"Probably more than we counted on. We'll know soon enough."

"And then?"

"Then we do everything we can to stop this. I have the attorney general working up legal precedent."

Roarke swallowed hard. "Sir…"

Roarke's unusual use of "sir" immediately put the president on alert.

"You should know I also have someone on it." He had to tell the president what he had done; which was a direct violation of his security clearance.

"Mr. President," he continued.

Taylor thought that something was way out of line. *Sir* and now *Mr. President?*

"My lawyer friend may be further along in that research than the AG."

"What? What are you talking about?"

"Sir, my decision. The woman in Boston…"

"Who?"

"Kessler. The woman at Marcus' law firm. The one I'm seeing…"

"You did what?"

"I told her…confidentially."

"You risked the entire security of the operation?" the president shouted right into Roarke's face.

People couldn't avoid overhearing the president.

"I trust her. And I ask you to trust her, too."

"I could have you arrested on the spot."

Other members of the president's Secret Service team stepped closer. Morgan Taylor nodded for them to stay away.

"Mr. President, I believe she can help us. Give her the chance. Let her present what she has to the AG."

Morgan Taylor, still inches from Roarke, studied his eyes; the eyes of a man he also trusted with his life. "Roarke, you realize you've broken the law?"

"Yes, sir."

"And willfully?"

"Yes, sir."

Morgan Taylor continued to look deeply into Roarke's eyes. Finally, he relaxed his stance.

"And you think she's that good?"

"Yes, sir."

"Stay right here. Don't move a muscle."

Morgan Taylor went directly to a secure phone across the room. Roarke, watching him, now prayed that he was right about Katie. The president talked for two minutes then hung up.

Taylor then motioned to O'Connell to join him across the room. He mouthed the words, *"Come meet someone."* It was Roarke.

Without explaining anything about the last few minutes, the president launched into a casual introduction. "Mr. O'Connell, this is

Scott Roarke, Secret Service. He's going to fill you in on what went down." Roarke nearly choked on his sandwich.

"But sir," he complained without going further.

"We're going to release the videotapes, Scott. He might as well have the details first hand."

Then the president told O'Connell, "But no names, O'Connell. He's simply a member of the Special Forces team. Is that okay?"

"Is that all?"

"Yes," Taylor answered.

"I can live with that."

"Thank you. Now if you'll excuse me, gentlemen. I've got some reading to do. The translations are going to be coming fast."

"But Mr. President," Roarke said trying to get him to stay.

"Yes?"

"What we were talking about a moment ago. Then the call you made."

"We'll discuss it later, Scott. Right now, do as you're told." It was an obvious slam.

Taylor left Roarke and O'Connell together. They took two seats in a corner near the door. Roarke, visibly on guard, kept his distance.

"I saw you on the tape."

"Yeah."

This one's gonna be like pulling teeth, the reporter thought. He had no idea they'd talked before.

"Did you expect opposition?"

"Yes."

"How many Libyans did your team engage?"

Roarke took immediate exception to the question. "I believe that's classified," he said without expression.

"I can find out later," O'Connell responded.

"Your prerogative."

"On the way back? What did you encounter?"

Roarke had the same answer, only shorter. "Classified."

"Look, as you heard, you have permission to speak with me. I'd appreciate some cooperation." O'Connell added a sincere, "Please."

Roarke caught the president's eye who recognized he'd left his man squirming. "Okay, Mr. O'Connell. The basic facts. Four SAM's were up our ass. Four SAM's scratched."

"On whose authority?"

"The Authorization for Use of Military Force Joint Resolution. Senate Joint Resolution 23. Signed by President George W. Bush, 18 September 2001." He paused. "If I remember correctly."

"Which means?"

"Which means, Mr. O'Connell, that the president can take necessary and appropriate actions to ensure that the United States can exercise its rights to self- defense and to protect its citizens against unusual and extraordinary threats to the national security and foreign policy of the United States. In plain English it means the president has the authority under the Constitution to take action to deter and prevent acts of international terrorism against the United States."

"Come on," he said, playing devil's advocate. "Do you believe there was enough proof to invoke such extreme means?"

"Enough proof to put us *in country*?"

"That's my question."

"Yes."

"And you had this proof?"

"I did."

"And where did you get it?"

Roarke's antagonism now dissolved. He suddenly realized why Taylor allowed him to speak with the reporter directly. *Payback time.* He grinned through his response. "As a matter of fact, Mr. O'Connell, I got it from you."

O'Connell's pen slid across the paper right off the page. "From me?"

"From you."

"How? I never gave you anything."

"Yes you did. A photograph."

"I don't understand…"

"From a barbershop," Roarke explained. "In Marblehead, Massachusetts. You found it for me."

O'Connell's mouth opened wide in utter shock.

"You?" the *Times* writer finally managed.

"Yes. Perhaps I called you under somewhat false pretenses. I said I was with the convention."

"You?" O'Connell asked incredulously again.

"Me."

"You're a sonofabitch."

"That's me. And you should have checked your sources."

"You used me. You fucking used me!"

"So did Lodge. But I used you to undo the damage he had you doing. And I gave you something in return. Information on Newman, remember?"

"Yes, but…"

"And now you're here because you're going to tell the truth, Mr. O'Connell."

The reporter closed his eyes. It seemed everyone used him. When he opened his eyes he nodded, finally understanding why he'd gotten the call from the president.

"It's Roarke?" he asked without any edge in his voice.

"Yes. Scott Roarke."

"I guess you had me at a disadvantage."

"No more than the rest of the country's been."

"Point taken. Tell me one thing."

"I'll try."

"How did that picture make the difference?"

Roarke beamed. He tested the strength of his chair, leaned back and put his feet on the table. "Well, let me explain all about a man named Touch Parsons and the particular skills he has."

This was supposed to be *his* day. The third circled date in his calendar. The inauguration of the new President of the United States—*his* president. But it had all gone wrong.

Fadi Kharrazi tore the calendar to shreds and cursed Morgan Taylor. He cursed his dying father for making him a rival with his brother. He cursed his mother for bearing Abahar. And he cursed his brother Abahar—supposedly *the brilliant one, the more magnificent one*—for living.

The best thing that could happen was for everything to remain quiet. Perhaps Taylor would have the presence of mind not to create an international crisis. However, he couldn't assume that. Depending upon how the events played out, his brother could try to assassinate him. If circumstances were reversed, that's what he would do.

Fadi needed a strategy and a scapegoat. First he would have a personal conversation with his father to explain the attack, leaving out key details, then ask him to round up some spies. That useless al-Nassar for one. The Arab world was familiar with CIA-conspired plots. This would be the Mother of them All. Then he would plant a news story expressing his outrage. Finally, he would phone his loving brother and claim how he was about to be framed.

But there was one international call he had to make first. A call to Florida.

FISHER ISLAND, FLORIDA

Ibrahim Haddad's nightmares. They had told as much as the man ranting on the phone in Arabic. He instantly gathered the gist of the outburst.

Haddad slammed his phone down without saying a word after "Hello" and went to his computer. He had one more message to send out.

CHAPTER 61

WASHINGTON, D.C.
MONDAY, JANUARY 19
11:58 P.M.

Washington belonged to Teddy Lodge. An army of Lodge supporters had descended days earlier for the pre-Inaugural dinners, parties, and fireworks. Now, all told, probably 450,000 admirers and string-alongs were in town for the revelry. Close to a half million spenders. Washington was happy.

Another two thousand reporters were on hand to cover everything from the important to the uneventful. In the past two weeks, they'd devoted an enormous amount of coverage to the president-elect's prospective cabinet appointees. Lodge himself called local talk shows to push his team and his agenda. He handled unknown callers like they were lifelong friends. They loved him.

Lodge also appeared supremely confident on the morning network news shows, laughing his way through softball questions. The customary honeymoon had begun.

A few reporters took snipes at Morgan Taylor for dropping off the radar scope. But most Americans showed almost no interest in the outgoing president.

This was exactly what President Taylor had counted on.

"Hello?" the vice president-elect said as he answered the phone in his suite at the Willard, just down the street from the White House.

"Henry, it's Morgan. I hope I'm not disturbing your celebration."

"Why no, Mr. President," he said as he put down his nightcap. "I'm just getting ready for bed. It's going to be a full day tomorrow."

"Oh, it certainly will be. May I start it a bit earlier for you?"

"Of course, but…"

"I'd like to speak to you confidentially at the White House. Oh-eight-thirty. And Henry," the president's tone changed. "I do mean confidential."

"But, Mr. President…"

"My way, Henry."

The governor was suddenly aware that the call had the distinctive echo of a mobile transmission, with a slight delay and a digital quality. He felt a rumble in his stomach. It was the kind he used to feel before battle. The governor finished his scotch with one gulp.

"Your Secret Service detail will be at your door fifteen minutes before and lead you out."

"Morgan, this sounds serious."

"Oh-eight-thirty, sharp!"

The line went dead. Lamden poured himself another scotch, taller than his first, and wondered, *What in God's name is going on?*

ABOARD AIR FORCE ONE

The president, wearing a Navy flight jacket and faded blue jeans, sat at his desk in the forward compartment of Air Force One. He and his two most trusted associates, Bernsie and Jack Evans, were reading English translations of the *Ashab al-Kahf—People of the Cave*—pages delivered to them by the CIA translators. The portions that dealt with Andropov Institute were the most intriguing.

The original of each page was copied onto the back of the typed translation. Then the English side was signed and dated by two people—the translator and J3—to confirm authenticity. Many of the pages were typed on original Andropov letterhead, the formal home of the Red Banner curriculum.

Taylor made specific notes in the columns of various pages and wrote general thoughts on a yellow legal pad. Undoubtedly, this would be his last flight in Air Force One. He was making every minute count.

After reading each page, he handed it to Evans, who in turn absorbed it, then passed it to John Bernstein.

"It's amazing Fadi even kept these," said the chief of staff.

"Ego," Morgan Taylor explained, not even looking up.

"But not even in a vault?"

"The president's right," acknowledged Evans. "Supreme arrogance. But he might not have known the detail in these papers. Remember, he acquired this well-hatched plan as a hand-me-down only a short time ago. Plus, our intelligence on Fadi shows that he's wildly impulsive and impatient. He runs his media conglomerate with an iron fist. He's impetuous and, as we've seen, very greedy. And like many megalomaniacs, he collects and archives everything he ever touches."

"Could any of this be a plant?" the chief of staff asked.

Jack Evans voice boomed, "Bernsie, the only thing that was planted was the seed of this scheme a long, long time ago."

"You have to admire the patience of the planners," the president said. "Decades of waiting."

"And millions of dollars," the CIA Director added.

"Yes, lord knows how much," the president said. Then he softened.

"I wonder, if Lodge had been the Democratic front runner all along, whether Jennifer Lodge would still be alive?"

Evans weighed the question and framed a response. "Maybe. But he wasn't. Short of waiting four more years, he needed to jump start the nomination. Which he did. And if, by some reason it wasn't this year, or this wife, then next election. Who knows, he even might have been willing to sacrifice a child. He was a deep sleeper. As deep as they get."

"Maybe not as deep as they get, Jack," the president offered quietly. He just finished reading another excerpt that had been underlined in red by one of the CIA translators.

"Someone who works for or with Fadi is tracking more graduates from Red Banner. You're not going to like the areas they're into. Here, read."

Evans took the paper. After a minute he exclaimed, "Jesus Christ!"

"This is amazing. They've earmarked state legislatures, corporations, federal bureaus. The courts."

"Currently seated judges?" John Bernstein asked horrified.

"Don't know. There's a lot of research to do. This is going to have to go to Bob for the FBI to vet."

"And it was all part of the Russian strategy from the 1970s," the president explained. "Infiltrate the very fabric of American society. Then wait for instructions."

"You knew this kind of thing went on," Bernsie inquired.

"Yes. To some extent. Not anything of this magnitude. Most of the Red Banner sleepers were never activated. When Communism tanked in the early '90s, they just curled up and got comfortable with the lives they had in the States. They made America work for them."

"Except maybe the ones that weren't Russian. Lodge and some of the others didn't swear allegiance to Mother Russia. They never had to. They went to school with Russians, but these young men…"

Bernsie interrupted, "And probably women…"

"…and women," the DCI acknowledged. "These men and women have been time bombs with very, very long fuses."

"And since they weren't Russians, they didn't give a flying fuck about the demise of the Soviet Union," Bernsie concluded. "Commuter students."

"And when another sleeper decided to come forward about one of his classmates…" Evans continued.

"Like Steven Hoag…" Bernstein added.

Evans nodded. "Yeah. We suspect he was going to finger Lodge or Newman. But somehow the command was tipped off and they decided to take him out. Maybe from good intel. Maybe from a leak." That last bit of news was particularly disturbing.

"So, gentlemen. Tell me Lodge's ultimate goal." the president asked.

The chief of staff spoke first. "He's a brilliant physicist. I'd say nuclear technology gets in the hands of more Arab countries."

"What about Israel?"

"I wouldn't want to be an Israeli citizen and count on the U.S. for help," Evans figured. "The whole balance of power would shift to the Palestinians. Open elections for a few years inside Israel and not one seat in the Knesset would be held by a Jew. They'd have their own state and Israel, too. From the inside."

"But now that we have the evidence, we stop it," the president said, noting the clock at the front of the cabin. "Fadi loses out to his brother and goes on the endangered species list, and we get Lodge." He stopped just short of adding, *If there's time.*

WASHINGTON, D.C.
INAUGURATION DAY
TUESDAY, JANUARY 20
12:01 A.M.

CNN led the midnight news with a report on the plans for the inaugural, the parade that would follow, and a review of Teddy Lodge's turbulent and successful year. A commercial break followed, then a brief reader with no video about an apparent missile attack at an undetermined number of radar facilities in Libya.

An unnamed Pentagon source indicated that F/A-18's deployed from the USS *Carl Vinson* carrier task force over-flew Tripoli. *"Four SAM's were fired at the Navy jets from Libyan launchers, but failed to bring down any planes. The Americans struck the missiles installations in self defense, destroying them. It was the first engagement between the U.S. and Libya in years,"* the report concluded.

But Ibrahim Haddad knew this was not just a fly-over that turned sour. This was a surgical strike. *The call from Tripoli. Now the news report. Taylor was behind this.* He'd have to leave. *Tonight. Now!*

Haddad ignored the clothes. He had a full wardrobe where he was going. However, he did take $100,000 in cash from his bedroom safe and remove his computer hard drive. Although he had a complex Silicon Valley program that automatically rewrote over any deleted files, Haddad didn't want to risk leaving even broken remnants in the hands of some young CIA hotshot nerd. *No, this will go to the bottom of the ocean.*

He closed the door to his apartment for the last time. Two of his bodyguards were already watching the entrance. Together, they rode across the opulent Fisher Island grounds on a golf cart, reaching his dock in five minutes. Four of his men always slept on his yacht in shifts. They were all awake when he stepped on board.

"Cast off," he ordered. Before Haddad settled in his cabin, they had the moorings unlashed and were quietly slipping out of the harbor. *Patience* was well out to sea within fifteen minutes of the first report on CNN. Any of his neighbors still awake were too busy watching television to notice his departure.

Another CNN viewer up at that hour also believed that there was more to the story than initially reported. Henry Lamden, a decorated Navy veteran himself, now suspected that Morgan Taylor had been there for the action. He was a shrewd politician. But he was an even better commander. And now Lamden couldn't wait for his meeting with the president. He was more excited about that possibility than being sworn in as vice president in less than twelve hours.

CHAPTER 62

BOSTON, MASSACHUSETTS
1:15 A.M.

The phone rang four times.

"Hello?" Katie Kessler said, stirring from her sleep.

"Ms. Kessler? Kate Kessler?" an unrecognizable voice asked.

"Yes." she said forcing herself to some semblance of consciousness.

"I'm calling for the employer of your *friend*."

Katie bolted upright. "My friend?" She resisted asking the obvious.

"He's fine." The news woke her up fully. "But his *employer* has requested that you bring everything you've been working on to a meeting that he's set up in the morning. Take down this flight information."

"Flight?" Katie asked.

"You're going to Washington," the monotone voice told her.

"Wa—wait." She flicked on her light and found a paper and pencil. The lead broke; she carried the phone over to her desk, and pulled a pen from the middle drawer. She had expected a call from Roarke days ago, but none had come. "Okay, ready."

"Yes," was all she got back.

"Where am I going? Who will I…"

"You'll see when you get there," the man interrupted. "You're booked on American out of Logan at 7:00 A.M. You have a meeting in Georgetown at 9:30. You're expected."

"But…"

"A car will be waiting outside your apartment at 5:45 to pick you up. Another will be in DC when you arrive. 9:30," he repeated. "You'll have fifteen minutes to make your argument. Do you understand?" The man on the phone stated.

"Well, I—"

The line went dead.

Katie composed herself. *Make your argument? What the hell's that supposed to mean, "Make your argument."*

And then it came to her, along with the realization that she'd get no more sleep tonight.

Headwinds slowed Air Force One considerably. A winter storm over the Atlantic set the 747 on a circuitous route; Morgan Taylor would be late for his meeting with the vice president-elect.

0530 HRS

Air Force One buffeted the turbulent headwinds that were costing precious time. Hours they'd never get back. Given the delays, Morgan Taylor would need to helicopter straight to the Capitol. Louise had the good sense to send a business suit on the out-bound flight. *At least he'll look good for whatever happens.*

During the night, the president's staff had been busy communicating over secure satellite phones, faxes, and e-mails to the vice president, Cabinet members, and the intelligence community.

Taylor still intended to see Governor Lamden. As the next in the line of succession, Lamden needed to understand what was about to go down. It would be complicated and disruptive, appearing much like the insurrection they were seeking to abort. The nation would look for fast answers, often in the wrong places. The people needed a calm voice to explain things. But before that, the Supreme Court had to consider the basic constitutional issues. That's where Morgan Taylor decided the Kessler woman would come in. Roarke said she was up for the job. The whole country would soon find out.

Katie gave great thought about the correct outfit for the day. She tried on four different choices from her closet, finally settling on a conservative black skirt that landed just below knee length, a slate gray silk blouse accented by the set of pearls her mother had given her when she graduated Harvard. The black heels and full length black overcoat completed the ensemble.

She looked in the mirror one last time. *Not bad. Now if I only knew how the attorney general will react.*

The driver was downstairs to meet her as promised. 5:45 A.M. She didn't know he'd been there all night; as much an FBI bodyguard as a chauffeur.

"This even beats picking up a Zipcar on Phillips Street to get across town," she nervously joked. But the man said nothing beyond the most serious *"Good morning"* she'd ever heard.

Maybe he's right, she thought on the way to Logan. *It is going to be a very serious morning.*

Katie's plane touched down twelve minutes ahead of schedule at Reagan Washington National. As planned, she was met at the gate by a driver she took this time to be Secret Service. He was all business; totally different than Roarke.

"Ms. Kessler?"

"Yes."

"Identification please."

"You first." she said.

The man reached inside his jacket pocket and produced a government ID.

She examined it and saw his revolver as he returned the wallet.

"Now you."

Once satisfied, he escorted her to a Town Car with darkened windows. A second agent, equally ice cold, sat in the driver's seat. "Breakfast?" he said, looking at her in the rear view mirror.

"No thanks. But we have a few minutes. I sure could use a computer with Internet access before we get where we're going."

Seven minutes later she was escorted into the Pentagon and cleared through security. An officer led her to an office with a sign in simple block letters: General Jonas Jackson Johnson.

What did they call him? She remembered. *J3.* Katie wondered if he was here or with Scott. *And where was Scott?* She pushed her personal thoughts away and set her mind to the screen in front of her. Her fingers attacked the keyboard, going straight to a U.S. Constitution website that detailed the U.S. Codes. She worked for forty minutes until her escort told her in no uncertain terms they had to leave.

WASHINGTON, D.C.
0928 HRS

Her driver stopped directly in front of an immaculate 18th-century three-story brownstone with muted red wood trim. He unlocked her door with the push of a button, but remained at the wheel. "Right in there, Ms. Kessler. Number 304." Katie stepped out clutching her black leather Coach attaché case.

She glanced across the street and noticed two other Lincolns pulling into an illegal parking space reserved for a fire hydrant.

Compose yourself, she said to herself. *You can do this. She's just the Attorney General of the whole United States.*

Katie looked at her watch. It was 9:30 exactly. *Here goes.* She walked up the five brick steps as confidently as possible and rang the bell.

She heard footsteps, then "Yes, yes," from inside.

A well-tailored older man opened the ornate, hand-carved oak door.

"Hello," he said.

She didn't recognize him.

"Hello. I'm Kate Kessler, an attorney. I was," she swallowed hard, "asked to come here for a meeting. And you are?"

"This way please."

She bit her lip and said to herself, *Stupid. He's the valet. Or the butler.* Katie vowed to do better with the next introduction.

The man led Katie into a stately study lined with rich cherry wood paneling. The room looked and felt austere. There were portraits of men whose reputations were as old as the wood. Famous men. Jefferson. Madison. Monroe. Lincoln. But also on the walls were classic movie posters in matching wood frames. Beautiful original prints celebrating films that dealt with the law—*Anatomy of a Murder, To Kill a Mockingbird,* and *The Verdict.*

Katie examined the artwork, feeling the room was surprisingly more masculine than feminine. *Presidents and movie posters? An odd combination.* A voice broke her concentration.

"I live between two worlds, counselor."

She turned to the sound of a man's voice and gasped. "On one hand, the historic and irrefutable. On the other, the imagined and dubious. Fact and fiction, Ms. Kessler. Two completely different worlds, yet in law inextricably related. Facts can be debated and refuted. And fiction can be made to look like the truth. So where is the truth? I presume you're here to present some."

"Yes, sir, I am," she answered respectfully. Katie shifted her attaché case from her right hand to her left and extended her palm. "Katie Kessler. Thank you for seeing me."

"You've picked an inopportune time," the man said, taking her hand.

"It wasn't my choice. I was told to meet with…" She stopped. Nobody had actually said who she'd be meeting. She had *assumed* it would be the attorney general. A false assumption was not a good way for a lawyer to begin.

"As was I," the man affirmed. He studied her the way he studied everyone who came into his chambers. It was said that he had an uncanny sixth sense about people. He could read them instantly, see through their lies and slice through their defenses. That's why Leopold Browning was Chief Justice of the United States Supreme Court.

At age sixty-seven, Justice Browning projected a vital and commanding image for the court; younger than most of his colleagues, wiser than his seniors. He was a Democratic appointee, but respected on both sides of the aisle for his constitutional wisdom. He wore a sharply tailored black suit, no pinstripes; all straight lines. He offered the inviting face of a college professor, but he had the eyes of an astute investigator. And the eyes scared her. They told Katie she needed to be succinct; completely and unequivocally. He was a precise man, not given to small talk, and especially mindful of his time and duties ahead.

"I really do have a busy day, young lady," he said as he motioned for her to sit down opposite his desk. "You've come here at the president's request, and yet you do not work for him or the White House. So I am at a loss. If you know anything about me, I do not like entering a session, any session, unprepared. So you have me at a disadvantage and that, Ms. Kessler, makes you someone I already do not like."

Katie sat down uncomfortably.

"Chief Justice, it is not important that you like me. It is important that you listen to me."

"Begin, counselor," he commanded. "You now have twelve minutes left of my precious time. It better be important."

"I can assure you, Chief Justice, that this is of the utmost importance." She chose her words carefully now. *No opinion. Just state it.* "A number of areas to cite, sir. Amendment 14, Section 3, also Article II, Section 1."

The nation's Chief Justice sat motionless, tempting her to continue, but with an unsettling gaze that warned her to beware.

"Do you want it paraphrased or the precise words, Chief Justice?"

As an Illinois prosecutor, Browning gutted opponents who blindsided him. As a District Court Judge, he would slam the gavel down at the first hint of legal theatrics. When he became a Federal Judge, he'd find ways to rule attorneys in contempt if they colored anywhere outside the lines. Now he presided over the highest court in the land and Katie realized that no matter how hard she tried to frame her opening remarks, she had led off with the wrong line. She knew it by the way his nostrils flared and his body stiffened. She saw it in the eyes boring into her.

"Direct and accurate, counselor."

"Chief Justice, 'no person except a natural born citizen, or a citizen of the United States, at the time of the adoption of this Constitution, shall be eligible to the office of President.' There is more to the Article, but that is the applicable portion."

She waited for the inevitable reaction. It wasn't going to be pretty.

To his credit, the chief justice didn't raise his voice; he simply pronounced, "Ms. Kessler, this conversation is over." Browning abruptly stood.

Katie did not.

"I said this conversation is over."

"Sir, according to my watch," she checked, "I have eleven and a half minutes remaining. If you would be so kind."

"You have come to my house on the day of the Inauguration, within hours of the time I am to administer the Oath of Office. And you supposedly bring into question Article II, Section 1 of the United States Constitution. I don't like jokes."

They stared at each other for a good fifteen seconds. Katie struggled to keep focused on the angry eyes that were drilling into her.

He's testing me, she hoped. *He stopped telling me to leave.* Katie believed this would be either the moment she would win a personal reprieve to continue or she would lose her chance. *I have to keep talking.*

"Chief Justice, you and I both received a phone call from a very high level." She was on shaky ground here, but she continued. "That request deserves utmost respect and I deserve the courtesy for you to listen to me, *not* evaluate me."

Browning didn't smile, his face never changed. But he did slowly sit down again. "Courtesy granted, I believe you have ten and a half minutes left, counselor."

THE WILLARD HOTEL
0933 HRS

For the second time this morning, the knock at the door had the tell-tale feel of the Secret Service. A heavy hand.

"Governor."

The voice confirmed it.

"Coming." he answered. Henry Lamden was dressed to be sworn in, but he was headed elsewhere. He grabbed his topcoat, kissed his wife goodbye. They'd meet at the Capitol.

"The White House?" the governor quietly asked once he was in the hallway. By now it was almost an hour later than the time Morgan Taylor had set for their meeting. He showed his concern asking again, "The White House?"

The agent ignored the question and indicated they should proceed to the stairwell.

"Not the elevator?"

"No, this way, sir."

Another Secret Service officer stood at the exit with the door open.

"Are we going to the White House?" he asked again.

"We'll find out in the car, sir."

The answer indicated the Secret Service didn't know themselves.

Lamden recognized that was the best he'd get, so he stopped asking.

Three minutes later they were on the way to Pennsylvania Avenue heading toward the White House. But once they cleared the guard house, Lamden was met with another surprise. The agents opened the door to the car and swiftly walked him to the South Lawn and a waiting Sikorsky helicopter with Marine markings.

Lamden stopped in his tracks when he saw that no one was getting off, but he was required to go on.

"Sir," the Secret Service agent ordered.

"Hold on a second. I'm not boarding that thing until somebody tells me exactly what's happening." Most of Lamden's tirade was covered by the slow whomping of the rotor blades. The massive copter was ready to lift off.

"Governor, please get on board," the agent said above the din.

"No fucking way. In two hours I'm supposed to be sworn in as vice president. And right now it looks like I'm being kidnapped."

"Governor, we have our instructions. You are to get on board." He added another word for emphasis. "Now."

Another two agents came forward to move him along. But the governor stood his ground.

"No, not until I know where you're taking me."

"Governor," the agent commanded, "This is a presidential order. Now board!"

Lamden nodded his head. "Okay. Okay."

The governor climbed in and consoled himself with that thought that Morgan Taylor did call him the night before. Obviously he wasn't in the White House and ground transportation wouldn't do.

"*Andrews?* We're going to Andrews!" he yelled just before sitting down. *The president wasn't here after all. He hasn't been here in weeks!*

"Sir, sit down. We need to take off."

Lamden consented. Seconds later they were rising above the lawn and heading east. Andrews it is, the governor told himself. *That old sonofabitch is coming into Andrews.*

THE JEFFERSON HOTEL
0935 HRS

Geoff Newman looked over Teddy Lodge's shoulder and into the mirror. As always, the congressman was torn over which tie to wear.

"Go with the red. It's distinctive."

"I don't know. The blue looks more stately," Lodge responded.

"The red will stand out in the history books."

That was that. Like most things in Teddy Lodge's career, it was decided by Newman.

Lodge fastened the knot and turned to Newman. "Christine's written one helluva speech. The finest thing I've seen since Kennedy's *Ask not what your country can do for you.*"

"The country's going to be behind you. You'll have the strongest approval rating of any new president. They're all yours."

"I'm not so sure about these Middle East pronouncements," he said referring to the inaugural speech. "Maybe we should wait a month."

"No. It'll be completely unexpected. And bold. Besides, the country is ready for a leader to finally lead. It's all in the text. *The time is now.*"

"*The time is now.*" That was the theme of Christine Slocum's speech. Lodge realized how her writing style was so similar to Jenny's. Newman had picked a good substitute. Just for a moment he wondered if he really had loved his wife. Christine more than aptly replaced the sex, but did he love her?

He searched for the feelings. They weren't there. So Theodore Wilson Lodge, President-elect of the United States, puffed out his chest and reached for his new black pin-striped Armani wool jacket that Newman held. "The time *IS* now," Lodge said aloud. "Let's get going."

THE CAPITOL
0937 HRS

No one would freeze waiting for the parade. Unseasonably warm weather had rolled into the District the day before. Forecasts called for 47-degree temperatures at the appointed hour. With the exception of some light gusts, it was turning out to be a perfect April day in late January.

Among the happiest people were the members of the Secret Service who wouldn't have to stand around shivering. They rarely wore over-coats when they were protecting the president and vice president. Today, they also had the president-elect, the vice president-elect, and the chief justice among many others. Their favored Sig Sauer P229, .357 caliber pistols, Uzi submachine guns or MP5 automatics were easily accessible and their fingers weren't cold.

It was less of an issue for the U.S. Capitol Police who were on guard inside and throughout the grounds. They wore their Glock 22 .40 S&W's in the open.

The reputation and the duties of Capitol Police, described in the 1860s as a force of "thirty-three bored, yawning, inexpressibly idle men about the Capitol," have changed considerably. Now they number some 2,000 and are quite literally charged with protecting the lives of America's 535 lawmakers and 200 very important square blocks of Washington, D.C. real estate.

Today's Inauguration called for increased security. Everyone available clocked in. So many officers covered the grounds that not everyone knew everyone else.

Officer Leon Chandler patrolled the hallways and the Rotunda. He acknowledged his colleagues, but never stopped to chat. This was not just any day at the U.S. Capitol.

The thirty-five-year-old officer, in his newly pressed uniform, looked like a tough cop, intent on his job. He had an expression that didn't invite conversation. Not today. His fingers, never more than an inch from his service revolver, signaled that he was very much on duty. Chandler looked like the kind of man you hoped would be around if there was trouble.

As he made his rounds he opened every unlocked door, checked the bathroom stalls, and demanded from anyone with or without visible ID to state their purpose for being in the Capitol. When he was through with one pass, he reversed his route. By 9:40 he knew everyone in sight. The procedure took him through the Rotunda every twenty minutes where other officers stood, seemingly bored like the thirty-three idle men of the 1860s. *They should take their jobs more seriously,* Chandler thought. *After all, the Capitol isn't impregnable.*

0941 HRS

"Your honor. A candidate who seeks the office of president must be a citizen of the United States."

"Yes Ms. Kessler. That is a fundamental basic."

"And if he is not?"

"Then fundamentally he cannot be President of the United States," the chief justice declared sarcastically.

"But what if he was elected?"

"Irrelevant. He wouldn't qualify. Therefore, he could not be elected."

"But what if it *appeared* that he met the qualifications, that he did run, and *he did get elected?*"

"Get to your point, Ms. Kessler."

The chief justice exhaled a loud, purposeful breath. She could feel it across the desk. It was filled with aggravation. She also smelled the coffee. Katie could use a cup herself. She'd passed up breakfast and wished he had offered her some. But this wasn't a social call. And Browning wasn't a social man. She could see that he was thinking. *Just keep talking*, she told herself.

"I've examined the law for any precedent by which you could delay administering the Oath."

"Precedent?"

Determined, she continued. "Something that you could consider. There were contingencies enacted by the founding fathers—the 1792 Act," she said referring to her notes. "It expressly allowed the president pro tempore of the Senate, and then, if necessary, the speaker of the House to *act* as president while retaining their congressional offices pending a special presidential election."

"Ms. Kessler!"

"But the 1792 Act was revoked by passage of the Presidential Succession Act of 1947, Section 19, Title 3 of the United States Code. It remains the applicable law of the land today, imposed by the passage of the 25th Amendment in 1967. So, you can neither delay the Oath nor invoke Constitutional powers for a special presidential election. And…"

"Ms. Kessler, stop. The essence? Just the essence or your argument. Now!"

Katie Kessler looked directly into the eyes that no longer frightened her and said, "Chief Justice, what if you did swear in a foreign national as president?"

"Is this a hypothetical question, Ms. Kessler?"

"No sir, it is not. It will happen today if you administer the Oath to Congressman Lodge."

0942 HRS

The crowds were already lining up along Constitution Avenue. It was like parade day in Hudson, New York seven months earlier, only on a far grander scale. Bands comprised of excited students from Montpelier, Bennington, and Burlington, Vermont high schools turned up for the state's hero. In a few hours, they'd be marching with other bands from across the country in the nation's most celebrated pageant.

The side streets were filled with baton twirlers, cheerleaders, horses, cars, and floats decked out with red, white, and blue bunting. Spectators crowded behind concrete barriers. Small white tents, strategically located along the route, housed temporary security checkpoints with armed officers manning metal detectors. Every bag and backpack was checked.

Inside buildings lining the avenue, residents of law firms and other non-government businesses were holding parties for clients, friends, and families.

According to the schedule put out by the Senate Radio-TV Gallery, the Pre-Inaugural Music would begin in less than an hour, at 10:30 A.M. Sixty minutes later, cameras would focus on a large platform constructed on the west steps of the U.S. Capitol. There, at precisely 11:50 A.M., the vice president would be sworn in first, followed at noon by the president.

The U.S. Marine Band was assembling, and key Lodge supporters holding tickets for the coveted assigned seats had settled in early. The Blue Angels flew in formation overhead. Television news anchors from all of the broadcast networks and cable news channels were on the air describing the scene and recounting the career of the president-elect and the history of the transition process.

The day was laid out by President-elect Lodge's Inaugural Committee. According to tradition, they worked with the Joint Congressional Committee on Inaugural Ceremonies and the Armed Forces Inaugural Committee. America's version of a royal coronation was underway, right down to the Marine guards who carried replicas of the Mameluke sword presented to an American lieutenant in 1805 by a prince of Tripoli.

0947 HRS

Lodge placed a courtesy "Good morning" call to Henry Lamden, only to discover that he wasn't in his room. Newman, buttoning his own handmade Savile Row suit jacket in front of a full-length mirror, asked him what happened. He had overheard Lodge's side of the conversation. "His wife just said some Secret Service agents took him out and he'd meet her at the Capitol."

"Oh?" Newman frowned. "Why?"

"Who knows. The man's a cowboy. As far as I'm concerned, after today he can spend as much time as he'd like back in Montana," Lodge whispered.

Newman continued to wonder *why?* while Lodge dismissed the point as meaningless.

"Come on. History's waiting," Lodge said at the door of his suite. Newman joined him, still troubled by Lamden's absence.

They walked briskly with their entourage out of the Jefferson Hotel, on 16th Street, NW, just four blocks from the White House. Their caravan of limos, Secret Service agents, and military escorts waited in front of the historic hotel.

Newman dropped back to talk to their Secret Service agent in charge. "The president-elect wants to know if Governor Lamden has arrived at the Capitol yet."

The man cued his microphone. "Unity wants to check on transit of Big Sky, over." The code words were the Secret Service designations for the president-elect and the vice president-elect, based on their respective states. "Freedom and Unity" is the state motto of Vermont and "Big Sky" is Montana's.

He listened to his earpiece for a reply and nodded. "Roger. Big Sky in transit," he repeated to Lodge's annoying man.

"Where?" Newman demanded.

"I'm sorry, sir," the Secret Service agent answered. "But we don't communicate that kind of information over open lines."

"Then he's on the way to the Capitol now?"

"He's in transit, sir. That's all I can tell you."

The information was true. Governor Lamden had left his hotel, but on a government arranged detour.

0949 HRS

"State your evidence," demanded Chief Justice Leopold Browning. "Your time and my patience are quickly running out."

"I don't have any. I *suppose* it's on the way," Katie stated.

"Suppose? That's from an attorney?"

"I haven't exactly been told, sir."

"Then young lady, *who* do you *suppose* does have this defining evidence?"

"The president…"

"The president?" he offered incredulously. "The president who will only remain president for another two hours and," he checked his watch, "fourteen minutes. That president?"

"Yes. President Morgan Taylor."

"So President Taylor will provide proof?"

"I believe he will."

The chief justice shook his head, ready to end the dialogue once and for all. Katie read his growing anger.

"Please, let me continue. I'm certain that you will be presented with credible, verifiable evidence." Katie prayed that she was right.

She paused to read him. *He didn't disagree.* "That's why he put us together," she said more confidently.

"You bring up another point that I've been curious about. Why you, Ms. Kessler? Why not the president's own highly trained legal staff. Why isn't the attorney general here? Intending no disrespect, the country does have experienced legal minds. Particularly in this city."

"I became involved after I met one of the president's own Secret Service agents." She decided not to go into personal detail. "He began investigating Congressman Lodge's background following the death of Mrs. Lodge. His investigation led him to the law firm where I work. The law firm that represented the Lodge family estate."

"Have you violated any lawyer-client privilege?"

"No sir. I properly limited the material I shared to the public record. But that record, under close scrutiny, begins to beg many questions. Questions with answers I cannot provide."

"Return to *my* question, Ms. Kessler. Why you?"

"This agent very recently asked me to review constitutional law as it applied to succession." She exaggerated the instructions. "He couldn't tell me why."

She caught her breath. Was she actually lying to the chief justice?

He immediately read her hesitation, "Ms. Kessler. Am I to believe you've gone off on your own whim to defend the Constitution of the United States?"

Katie realized she had to trust the chief justice. She answered the question again properly.

"He took me into his confidence."

"Thereby violating the nation's secrecy laws?" Browning thundered.

"Chief Justice, please. There's no time to interrogate me. I don't know how much the president has told you. I know very little."

He looked at his watch. "Go on."

"As I said before, I was asked to research case law in anticipation of…" She stopped.

"In anticipation of what, counselor?"

"First, a definitive question answered by the chief justice."

"How you dare to question me?"

"To obtain your legal knowledge, sir. Does the Court have any constitutional authority that prevents the chief justice from administering the Oath of Office..."

"None!" Browning shot back.

Katie had come to the same realization as well.

"In your learned opinion, is there any way to forestall 'the process'?"

Katie saw that her second question actually shook his composure. Without a word he went to his bookcase and pulled a well-worn edition of the U.S. Constitution off the shelf. She prayed that the chief justice could come up with what she couldn't.

After three silent minutes, Katie had her answer.

"No."

"Then, sir, we need to discuss the basis for the House to take the appropriate steps toward the removal of the new president."

"And when do you propose that?" he added sarcastically.

"Immediately after he is inaugurated, in a special session of Congress."

"Indulge me once more. You have no proof for your allegation. Now you propose House Impeachment hearings? What would the charges be? Besides lying, I suppose."

Katie turned to her research which she'd added to online at the Pentagon.

"I have a shopping cart full," she said smiling. She read from her notes. "14th Amendment, Section 3. *No person shall be a Senator or Representative in Congress or elector of President or Vice President,*' skipping sir, '*shall have engaged in insurrection or rebellion...*'"

"Proof to come?" he added.

"Proof to come," she reiterated, "And now U.S. Code Title 18, Sections 2381 and 2384. High crimes, sir. Treason and Sedition."

The chief justice sat back down in his leather chair taking in everything he'd just heard.

He's not yelling, she told herself.

"Ms. Kessler, for the sake of argument," his voice was amazingly calm, "detail the sections for me."

"Section 2381, U.S. Code. Title 18. Treason. I quote, '*Whoever, owing allegiance to the United States, levies war against them or adheres to their enemies, giving them aid and comfort within the United States or elsewhere, is guilty of treason,*' and skipping ahead again, '*shall be incapable of holding any office under the United States.'* And Section 2384, Seditious conspiracy, *'If two or more persons in any State or Territory, or in any place subject to the jurisdiction of the United States, conspire to overthrow, put down, or destroy by force the Government of the United States...'"*

"Two persons?" he asked.

"Yes, sir. I can go on."

"Ms. Kessler, are you prepared to explain how?"

"To the best of my ability."

"And you believe your recital will be supported by this still unseen, all encompassing evidence?"

She closed her eyes and nodded hopefully and affirmatively, "Yes I do." But he was right. *I'm arguing theory with no fact.*

The chief justice let out another huge, coffee flavored breath. "Any other surprises for me?"

She thought for a moment, then bravely continued. "Well, yes, one more. And well within the definition of High Crimes. A heinous act, Chief Justice."

He didn't challenge her this time.

"Conspiracy to commit murder. Teddy Lodge was directly involved in the murder of his wife."

The nation's chief justice fully settled into his chair. His body, tense throughout most of the conversation, now gave way to the weight of her extraordinary allegations. He stretched his neck in a circle and pulled down the collars of his shirt. Then he looked at each of the portraits and posters in the room. Katie recognized it was a device he used to think. Thirty seconds of her valuable time slipped away before he finally asked, "You are serious, young woman?"

"Completely. I've never argued anything more seriously."

"And refresh my memory. The courts you've argued before, Ms. Kessler?"

"Actually," she said shyly, "You would be my first."

Chief Justice Leopold Browning finally smiled. "Nothing like starting at the top."

ABOARD THE SIKORSKY
0951 HRS

Governor Lamden watched the hills across Maryland rise and fall below him. The Sikorsky VH-3d Sky King flew about 1500 feet above the houses and bare maples and oaks, banking occasionally, but keeping a steady course toward Andrews.

What's old Top Gun got in mind? Whatever it was, Lamden figured, it was going to be good.

CHAPTER 63

0954 HRS

"Let's have the law one more time, Ms. Kessler," Chief Justice Browning said.

"There is nothing that can prevent Congressman Lodge from being sworn in as scheduled."

"Quite right."

"Even a motion before the full court."

"Not even a motion. The lawful process of removing a president is reserved for Congress through Impeachment *after* the Inauguration. The House did consider an alternative to the current Succession Laws established by the 25th Amendment. But that is not applicable."

Katie amplified the point. "Yes, I know. H.J. 67, introduced after 9/11; proposing a constitutional amendment that would have authorized governors to appoint interim House members whenever 25 percent of the seats in the House became vacant due to death or incapacity. But it didn't stipulate presidential succession."

"Very astute, counselor. As you implied, even if the bill had been ratified as an Amendment, it wouldn't controvert the swearing in of the president-elect."

"Your honor, you are familiar with the work in the *Stanford*

Law Review, November, 1995, 'Is the Presidential Succession Law Constitutional?'"

"I am," he answered.

"And the argument put forth on the usage of the word 'Officers' in the Constitution?"

"You will find no sympathy to your cause by engaging in polemics over the definition of 'Officer' and who in government qualifies for that title. Quite simply, the 25th Amendment provides, among many other things, the only constitutional means of filling a presidential vacancy. But the vacancy must exist first. We have a man who has won the vote of the Electoral College, let alone the popular vote. He must take the Oath of Office. Should it subsequently be proved he was not a qualified candidate, and therefore not legally eligible to serve as a president, then, as you rightly stated, the Constitution provides for his removal and for the order of succession. All of which brings us back to the evidence."

Just then the private telephone line rang in the chief justice's study. He ignored it, not being able to disengage himself from the severity of Katie's argument. On the fourth ring he finally answered it.

"Browning," he stated sharply. "What?" He listened for a few moments. "Yes, yes. She has." The chief justice turned his back to Katie and continued in hushed tones.

She stood and pulled herself together. Katie still didn't know if she had convinced the chief justice.

"Ms. Kessler," Judge Browning said.

"Yes, sir."

"There's someone who wants to speak with you."

"Me?"

"And it appears as if you've won your first round in the Supreme Court."

"Hello?"

"Hello, Ms. Kessler." The voice was familiar, but she couldn't completely place it.

"Who is this?"

"This is Eve Goldman. I understand that you've been honing your debate skills."

"Ah," she stammered. "Yes, Ma'am." She looked directly at the chief justice who had pulled a heavy text from his bookcase. "I've been trying to do my best," she admitted to the attorney general.

"Indeed. I can't expect you've been having an easy time. He's a tough old bugger. But I just gave him a hint of the material he'll have for review. As much as I was prepared to reveal on the telephone. Constitutionally we're—how shall I put this delicately?—screwed, unless you've found anything substantive. I certainly haven't."

"No. Only if we could turn back the clock. Section 19a of the 1947 Presidential Succession Act undid the 1792 law," Katie added. "But now…" She couldn't finish the sentence.

"I know. Just ask Browning if there's anything he can think of. Anything. After what little I just told him I guarantee he'll listen."

Katie saw that the chief justice was engrossed in a law book. "You've got that right."

THE CAPITOL
1007 HRS

Lieutenant Chandler could hear the Marine Band outside. They were well into their patriotic medley, playing to a crowd that already swelled to 220,000 people on the Capitol steps and down the Mall. More were still on their way.

Chandler hadn't voted for the man, but that didn't matter. Like everyone else there in uniform, he had his job today.

Teddy Lodge would arrive soon. Chandler retraced his steps again. Diligence counted. That would make him sharper than the rest of the Capitol Police if he needed to act.

ANDREWS AIR FORCE BASE
1058 HRS

Two things happened simultaneously.

The wheels of Air Force One hit the ground a fifth of the way down the primary Andrews AFB runway and a Sikorsky Sea King helicopter swooped in from the west, landing exactly inside a large red circle at the other end of the base. The only passengers aboard the Sikorsky were Governor Lamden and four Secret Service agents.

Three minutes later, the president's plane taxied directly to a portable ramp next to the helicopter.

When Morgan Taylor stepped out, Lamden was already at the bottom of the stairs.

"Mr. President!" Lamden called up.

"Henry." The president bounded down the stairs. "Thank you for coming."

The two old friends shook hands on the tarmac, then the governor asked, "Now what's this all about?"

"We'll talk on the way." He led Lamden and a number of other men, only some whom Lamden recognized, back to the Sikorsky. The helicopter now had the designation of Marine One, the official call sign whenever the commander in chief is aboard. "There should be just about enough time to fill you in. It has a great deal to do with your immediate future."

The Marine One pilot shaved every possible second off the normal flight time to the Hill. He played catch up to another Sikorsky which had taken off a few moments earlier—the one ferrying Secret Service Agent Scott Roarke.

Roarke watched as the commanding presence of the Capitol dome finally came into view. He tightened his stomach muscles and exhaled slowly. Everything had to be handled properly. No mistakes. Of course, this was made particularly difficult since the Capitol Police had not been briefed. Even the Secret Service wireless communication remained discreet. The only heads up would be a two-word alert from the FBI at 1130 hours. "Red Light." With that signal, agents would secure the exits to the Capitol.

Roarke realized that President Morgan Taylor's idea to allow Michael O'Connell full access had been wise. He'd have the story of a lifetime, but the writer would also help settle down the country. They'd need that very soon.

Roarke had one immediate responsibility: isolate his targets until the president arrived.

All of this played out in Roarke's mind as his helicopter approached the parking lot on the East Side of the Capitol, away from the Mall.

"Sir," crackled a voice over Roarke's headset. "We have a problem. Satellite TV trucks all over the lawn." the pilot said. "I don't have enough room to set down safely. Too many, sir. Marine One is going to have the same problem. Stand by while I radio them."

The uplinks from the various global news networks encroached on the landing space. Roarke looked at his watch. 1134.

"Can't they move them out of the way quickly?" Roarke demanded. He had to repeat the question. The pilot of the Sikorsky was on with Marine One.

"Sorry, sir. What was that?"

"Can't they get those fucking TV trucks out of there?"

"Not quickly." the pilot answered. "Hold on, sir."

The helicopter hovered 500 feet above the Capitol as the pilot continued to get instructions on his radio. Roarke peered around for a landing zone. Besides the satellite trucks he saw hundreds of thousands of people.

He felt the sudden surge of the two General Electric T-58-Ge-402 turboshaft engines, each capable of delivering fifteen-hundred horsepower. The helicopter broke left sharply and climbed. "We're going to the top of the FBI Building. The elevator will be up and waiting. You'll have an escort from there back to the Capitol."

The combination of the turn, the acceleration, and the steep climb brought on a wave of nausea. Roarke fought to contain it. He reminded himself that it didn't take a Super Hornet catapult launch off a carrier to experience serious g-forces.

The pilot knew the effects of the maneuver. "Sorry, sir," he offered. "But I was told you're in a bit of a hurry. Another forty seconds and we'll be down."

Forty seconds was about right. Forty bone-crushing and stomach-churning seconds. Roarke never wanted to relive any of them.

The Sikorsky landed hard on the roof. A Marine swung open the door and extended the stairs. Roarke used both hands to slide down and sucked in the fresh air. He felt renewed and strong enough to dash to the waiting elevator.

"Haven't we been busy," an FBI agent said. Roarke had to laugh. Shannon Davis was on the roof to meet him.

"Busy doesn't begin to explain it." They hugged, but only for an instant. Roarke was mindful of the time. 1137.

They ran toward the rooftop elevator, covering the distance in fifteen seconds. The agent gave a key in the lock a quarter turn. "Express to the first floor." The doors closed and a little more than a minute later Roarke tore through the lobby, vaulting the security station and out the door, ignoring the alarms.

An agent flung open a Navigator door for Roarke and Davis. The SUV started moving before they were even seated. The siren blared.

"We'll be there in about three minutes." The voice belonged to the driver, Roy Bessolo.

"Look who the cat dragged in," Roarke said.

Bessolo laughed. "Yeah, and we've got one helluva rat to catch." Then he added, "I owe you an apology."

"Can it. It's just good to have your help."

Roarke blocked out the wailing and concentrated on checking his Sig Sauer P229. His double action/single action semi-automatic housed twelve rounds in the magazine, one in the chamber. He examined the three control levers, all on the left side, all in order. Roarke was ready.

Marine One altered its route and increased speed. Taylor noted the time on his watch as they headed for the FBI headquarters. 1141.

CHAPTER 64

THE CAPITOL
1143 HRS

Teddy Lodge pulled the sleeve of his suit back to glimpse his watch. Seventeen minutes before noon. Seventeen minutes until he walked out to the podium; the first president to be sworn in without a first lady at his side since James Buchanan in 1857. The president-elect smiled with extreme satisfaction. It had been a long road, requiring exceptional preparation, perhaps the most any man had ever undertaken to get to the White House.

He made a final check of his appearance at an anteroom mirror off the Rotunda. He brushed his famous locks back, replicating the figure in his campaign posters. Rugged, athletic, handsome. Once more he straightened the tie that Newman had selected and stared at his reflection. *Seventeen minutes*, he gloated.

Outside, piercing sirens. But nothing distracted Lodge. It was noisy, active, and wonderful; a day better than he ever imagined.

Lodge turned to a knock at the door. "Mr. President." It was Geoff Newman. He opened the door and continued.

"Mr. President. I like the way that sounds," Lodge answered.

"Get used to it. It's your name from now on." He looked at Lodge. "You're ready."

Lieutenant Chandler remained in the Rotunda, scanning the faces, keeping an eye on everyone who had access to the area. He counted seven Secret Service agents, three other members of the Capitol Police, fifteen congressmen, eight Supreme Court Justices, and an official White House photographer. The first lady and Mrs. Lamden were also present, talking to each other. A number of Lodge's principal campaign staff hung together, including Francine Carver, his personal secretary, who had prayed for this day to come.

The Capitol Police usually recommended against having too many key political figures in one place. But they felt prepared. No one, except perhaps Officer Chandler, showed any concern today.

It was the wailing sirens that drew his attention. Sirens usually meant trouble somewhere. Chandler stiffened. He scanned the room, but everyone was in good spirits, waiting for President-elect Lodge, his chief of staff, the vice president-elect, and the chief justice.

The chief justice isn't here yet, Chandler noted. *And where is Governor Lamden?* He approached a Secret Service agent.

"Are we running late?"

"I don't think so." The agent read his name tag and added, "... Lieutenant Chandler."

"But we're missing some of the stars of the show. The president. Governor Lamden."

The Capitol Policeman was absolutely right. "Hold on. I'll see what I can find out," he said. He made a quick inquiry via his radio and repeated the words he heard on his earpiece. "Roger that," he said, getting an answer. "On the way with Top Gun." Then to Chandler he said, "They're on the way."

But Lt. Chandler had actually heard more. "On the way *with* the president."

Chandler tipped a salute in thanks and inched back toward the corridor that led to the Senate side. He had a clear view of all the entrances. A sixth sense told him something wasn't right.

Across the Rotunda a door opened. Chandler turned to see what was happening. Congressman, soon to be President, Lodge strode in with Newman behind him. The White House photographer began snapping digital pictures of the president-elect. The legislators and justices applauded. Lodge smiled to them all, but motioned for Francine to step forward. He hugged her.

"I knew you'd get here, Mr. President," she said. "Jenny would have been proud."

Lodge acknowledged the comment with a simple "Yes, yes." He released her and walked to the center of the Rotunda, relishing the applause.

Chandler cocked his ears. The sirens had stopped. Seconds later he heard footsteps on the stone floor. They were heavy, full of authority, and bearing down fast.

The lieutenant's fingers inched toward his pistol. A man entered the area and flashed a Secret Service ID. He was recognized, but Chandler observed that he wasn't dressed for the occasion. It looked as though he'd been in the field. Behind him, two others in the more typical FBI business suits.

Chandler relaxed his fingers, but kept them close to his holster. He split his attention between the incoming trio and the president-elect. Lodge was now politely shaking his friends' hands. The agent who arrived in such a rush now planted himself at the West Entrance. He kept his back to the door, assuming an offensive posture.

Roarke scanned the room as he was trained to do. Only a Capitol

Police Officer seemed to take any interest in him. That was good. Soon the president would arrive with a Marine detail.

He checked his watch. 11:49 A.M. Roarke knew that Morgan Taylor, only minutes behind him, also had to take a detour. Three questions went through his mind. *What would he do if the president didn't arrive in time? What authority did he have to prevent the swearing in? Was it even possible?* And then he worried about Katie. *Where the hell is she?* The president told him what he had done and now Roarke was worried.

He saw that the Supreme Court justices were in a spirited exchange, intentionally standing away from Lodge. Roarke side-stepped closer. Justice Ronald Coffey, a tall, distinguished man, spoke. He was one of two black members of the Supreme Court and clearly the most commanding personality of the group.

"We're already behind. The vice president should have been sworn in by now. But we'll wait until noon for the chief justice. If he has not arrived, we will proceed according to schedule."

There was no dissent, only nods. After all, it was proscribed law; Article XX of the U.S. Constitution. *"The terms of the President and the Vice President shall end at noon on the 20th day of January…and the terms of their successors shall then begin."*

"But," Coffey added, "I might walk very, very slowly," to which his colleagues laughed.

In Roarke's mind, Justice Browning and Katie should have arrived. He motioned to another Secret Service agent to come over. It was the same man who'd spoken to Newman. He recognized Roarke and was keenly aware that Roarke had rather special access to Top Gun.

"Littlefield," Roarke whispered.

"Yeah?"

"Where's Gavel?" Roarke asked using the agency code for the chief justice.

"En route, but late. Hell, everyone's late today."

"He's supposed to have someone with him. A woman. Check for me."

"Stand by." The agent called on his transceiver. "Status on Gavel? Does he have a companion?"

Roarke saw the agent shake his head no.

"No?" Roarke's blood pressure rose. "A woman? Ask about a woman named Kessler."

"Say again. Is Gavel with a woman named Kessler?"

He waited for an answer and then shook his head again as he heard the reply. The agent repeated it for Roarke. "No, sir, there's no woman."

"What? I never should have gotten her into this."

"What was that?" the other agent asked.

"Nothing. It's just that…"

"Wait," the agent said. He held his finger to Roarke as he listened to muffled communication in his ear. It sounded urgent. Roarke, as a special agent, never used the transceivers. Now he wished the damned thing was plugged directly into his brain.

"Roger," Littlefield said. He pointed to the East Entrance. The other Secret Service agents heard the same message and they all turned to the commotion that followed the report—people running down the corridor toward the Rotunda.

CHAPTER 65

Two men, looking like well-dressed linebackers, led the way. Behind them were two others in suits. They were followed by five Marines and a civilian in a leather jacket and jeans.

"Congressman Lodge!" a voice called out.

Lodge turned to the direction of the greeting. It had come from the pack bearing down on him. He automatically smiled, still not knowing whose voice he heard.

Newman saw him first. "Taylor," he whispered to Lodge. "Well, he's finally out of his cocoon. Let him come to you."

"Teddy, I'd like to have a few words with you before you step out," the president announced.

Lodge stood his ground as Newman recommended. He saw Governor Lamden a few steps behind Taylor. "What's Lamden doing with him?" Lodge asked his chief of staff. Newman didn't know. He drifted back as the two approached, allowing Lodge center stage.

Morgan Taylor separated from the pack, zeroing in on his opponent. The two Secret Service agents raced to keep up. The Marines remained behind.

"Teddy..."

"Ah, Mr. President!" Lodge raised his voice. "You made it."

While Lodge engaged the president, Newman became acutely aware that the Marines had their automatic weapons in their hands and Secret Service agents had virtually encircled Lodge, Taylor, and Lamden.

Newman wasn't familiar enough with protocol, but there was *something* about the way they held their ground. And then he saw another man who at first had been blocked by the Marines. *O'Connell!* He was wearing a Navy flight jacket and he had a video camera at eye level.

Newman instinctively moved further away.

"Teddy," the president said to Lodge as he approached. Lodge held out his hand. The president, dressed in the Brooks Brothers suit that Louise Swingle had provided, did not return the gesture.

"Mr. President. Governor. Good to see you."

"Perhaps not, Congressman."

"Oh?" Lodge frowned then assumed he understood Taylor's meaning. "Morgan, I know this is a hard day for you. You staged a solid campaign. But it's over. You can help make this transition much easier."

"There won't be a transition," the president said coldly.

"Well then," he said sarcastically, "Let's just go out and smile for the cameras." Lodge dropped any pretense of being friendly. "Quite honestly Mr. President, I thought we'd have to get you out of the White House with an eviction notice. The way you sequestered yourself these last weeks."

"I wasn't in the White House, Teddy."

"No?"

"I was out of town and not checking all my messages."

"Where? Back in Tibet, or looking into retirement villages in Florida," he joked.

Taylor ignored the snide comment. "Out of the country. Haven't you been following the news?"

Suddenly Lodge became flustered. He peered over his shoulder to Newman for help. Newman could hear the exchange, but had not come forward. He shook his head slightly. Lodge read the signal.

"The news?"

"Tripoli. Earlier today."

Lodge had not heard the reports. But the word "Tripoli" suddenly sent a shiver through him.

"I'm sure it will all be in *my* afternoon briefing," Lodge proclaimed, showing nervous disinterest. "Now if you'll excuse me," he said looking at his watch "We're overdue for Governor Lamden to be sworn in." He indicated to the ranking Supreme Court judge to come forward. "Justice Coffey, I think you have the honor in Chief Justice Browning's absence."

From across the Rotunda came a booming voice. "That won't be necessary!"

Chief Justice Leopold Browning moved toward Lodge like a man half his age.

"Gentlemen, I'm sorry I'm late." He addressed Morgan Taylor and the president-elect. "Mr. President. Congressman Lodge." When he saw the vice president-elect he extended the greeting to him as well. "Governor Lamden. I see we're all assembled."

"Mr. Chief Justice," Lodge cut in. "I'm so glad you're finally here."

"Thank you, but I do believe I've interrupted an important discussion."

"No, not at all," Lodge answered.

The president disagreed. "Well, as a matter of fact it is important, *Mister* Lodge. It's about your future..." He played the moment out. "...And your past."

Lodge's eyes narrowed. He stared at Governor Lamden, who stood next to the president. Then the chief justice. Neither man gave him any of the answers he sought.

"Mr. Lodge. You surprise me," the president said. "You're usually so eloquent. What, no comment now?"

"What are you talking about, Taylor?" Lodge didn't hide any of his contempt for the man.

"First things first, Congressman." He motioned for Newman. "Perhaps Mr. Newman would like to join our chat. Please, this is for you, too."

Newman inched forward, taking a position behind and to the right of Agent Littlefield.

The lively acoustics in the Rotunda actually amplified the conversation so that every word was audible around the room. Scott Roarke heard them. So did everyone else, including Michael O'Connell, who raised his camcorder higher.

"We have a document in this country known as the Constitution, Teddy. I'm sure you've read it."

Lodge rolled his eyes.

"You've read it?" he declared so loudly everyone felt the urgency of an answer. "All of it?"

"The debates are over, Taylor. What's your point?"

The president addressed Chief Justice Browning. "Chief Justice, where do we stand?"

"Right on the edge, Mr. President. I will need to confer with the other Justices momentarily. I'm waiting for a volume to be brought to me by a bright young Boston lawyer; a recent acquaintance of mine. I must say, she's quite tenacious."

Roarke breathed a sigh of relief. *Katie!* He glanced at the president and caught a fatherly smile.

"She stopped by my office just this morning," Browning continued. "She'll be along shortly."

"Will someone please get this ceremony going?" Lodge demanded.

The president ignored him and addressed the chief justice. "Would you like to proceed?"

"No, Mr. President, I think this moment belongs to you. But I presume you have some footing where you're about to venture?"

"I do." He called to a Marine sergeant. "Sergeant Stonie."

The biggest Marine that even Teddy Lodge had ever seen walked forward, carrying a duffle bag marked 'Top Secret.'

"Proceed, Mr. President. I'm very interested in seeing where this will all lead," Browning admitted.

"And I'm not!" Lodge said angrily. "Governor Lamden has to take the Oath of Office. Now! Henry, let's go!" he arrogantly ordered his running mate. Lodge pivoted toward the Capitol steps and began to leave, but he was met by a wall of immovable Secret Service agents, plus Davis and Bessolo.

"Out of my way!" he demanded.

They wouldn't.

Lodge spun around furiously. "This is unbelievable! I have been elected President of the United States. You have no right to block me!"

"You may have been elected president, Teddy, and according to the Constitution I fear you will be sworn in. Unless I'm told otherwise."

Taylor saw Justice Browning close his eyes and shake a declarative *No*.

"Then you will become the first President of the United States to do so who's also already under arrest."

"What on God's earth for?"

"As it's been pointed out to me, a charge of treason," offered the chief justice.

"What? You can't be serious!" Lodge said obstinately.

The chief justice explained. "Treason, Mr. Lodge. The offense of attempting to overthrow the government of the state to which the offender owes allegiance, or of betraying the state into the hands of a foreign power," he said so seriously it chilled the air. "High Crimes." He didn't need to explain the punishment it carried.

"In your case, it's betraying the state into the hands of a foreign power, since you have no allegiance to the United States," proclaimed the president.

"I don't know what—"

"Oh, I understand there's more," Chief Justice Browning interrupted. "Sedition. Unlawfully conspiring with the intent to oppose the government of the United States or impede the operation of any law of the United States, or to intimidate or prevent any person holding office in the government of the United States."

"Well, as you can see, there's a lot for us to work with," Morgan Taylor offered quite calmly.

"This is bullshit!" Lodge screamed.

"No it's not. It's the law," Taylor said. "United States law. The shame of it all? It seems you will become president. But I guarantee your face will never show up on any postage stamp."

"And the evidence you've returned with, Mr. President," Chief Justice Browning asked.

"Irrefutable. Enough to make your head spin and warrant impeachment of Theodore Lodge."

If Taylor felt disappointed, he didn't show it. Instead, he glared at his opponent.

Lodge looked back toward Newman. His eyes darted around. He saw and heard everything in slow motion now. O'Connell reaching closer with his video recorder. Francine Carver with her hand to her face in shock. The Capitol Police stepping forward. An officer at the opposite wall holding a gun.

"Oh, and one more thing," the president added. "We'll nail you on the death of your wife, too."

"Newman! Tell them we have to go now!" Lodge shouted, not knowing what else to say. When his chief of staff didn't obey, Lodge stammered, "I have been elected President of the United States. You are interfering with the constitutional process."

"No, we are ensuring that the process is upheld," the chief justice stated. "Article II of the Constitution. Clause 5 and Clause 6 to be specific." The chief justice spoke from memory. *"No person except a natural born citizen, or a citizen of the United States, at the time of the adoption of this Constitution, shall be eligible to the office of President."*

"And *you* are neither!" the president proclaimed.

Lodge became totally enraged. "This is insurrection!"

"That's how we see it, too."

"You have no idea what you're saying."

"We know full well. We just returned from the Med. We raided an office in Tripoli. Fadi Kharrazi's offices to be exact," the president continued. "Want to know what we found?"

Lodge's posture tightened. His eyes glared with utter hatred but he said nothing.

"I'll tell you anyway. It's long and involved. It starts with a boy from Massachusetts who had the potential to become President of the United States. Whatever happened to that boy, Teddy? The real Teddy Lodge. The boy who's identity you assumed decades ago?"

The declaration hung in the air and everyone watched Lodge and the president, which was a mistake. No one was on Newman, who used the opportunity to shove Littlefield, the agent closest to him. The Secret Service man's coat opened as he stumbled on his left foot. Newman reached in and grabbed his service revolver. Littlefield wrestled to get it back, but Newman had control. He aimed point blank at his chest. The agent died instantly.

Then he swung the gun around to the president.

Roarke shouted, "Get Top Gun down now!" His Sig P229 was already in his right hand.

Two agents converged on the president as Newman's gun came up. Lodge slammed into another one of the agents, throwing him off balance, leaving the president wide open.

Roarke took a leap forward and dove onto the president, knocking him to his knees. He then rolled to his right, scrambling to his feet and raised his gun.

Lodge sprinted to the opposite end of the Rotunda. A Marine tried to tackle him, but missed.

Newman fired another shot. It was off the mark, but took down a Capitol Police officer who was covering the Supreme Court judges.

So far his two bullets went unanswered. Now Bessolo had his gun out. Roarke, once again up, had the best angle on Newman, but Justice Browning was in the way, preventing him from making the kill. He was also vaguely aware of Lodge picking up the downed Capitol Policeman's Glock further away.

Too many distractions. He had to focus. He fired at the same time Newman let off another round directly at the president. He put a bullet in Newman's left shoulder. Out of the corner of his eye he saw Morgan Taylor go completely down. Another agent fell on top of him.

Michael O'Connell was too stunned to move, too scared to even hit the floor. His DV camera offered a record of the entire event.

Another shot rang out. This time from a third gun. Roarke didn't see where it came from. Maybe from the side where the Capitol police officer had been posted.

Roarke tracked Newman's steps. *One, two, clear.* He held his breath and fired a better placed, but still not deadly, shot. Newman had turned sideways and the bullet only grazed his arm. *Damn.*

Newman saw the president on the ground. Blood flowed onto the floor under him. He searched for a new victim. *Lamden!* Twenty feet away and unguarded. He uttered a sick laugh. Roarke sidestepped to the right. He ran and vaulted over the Speaker of the House, who was prone on the floor, as Newman squeezed the trigger. But Roarke was just that much quicker. He put a bullet into his target's chest. It joined two others discharged by Bessolo and Shannon Davis. Newman was dead by the time his head cracked open on the floor.

"Lodge!" Roarke exclaimed. His eyes swept the area. He quickly found him leaning against a wall at the Rotunda. Lodge had the gun in his hand, but he would never get off a shot. Blood trickled out of a tiny hole directly between his eyes. The man purporting to be Theodore Lodge was dead.

CHAPTER 66

Secret Service scrambled to protect the president.

Lodge, Newman, Agent Littlefield, and one Capitol Police officer were dead. Blood flowed from where President Taylor went down. Officers shouted instructions. The president's detail surrounded Taylor, who stirred and rolled out from under a Secret Service agent.

"I need medical attention now!" Davis shouted. But the president waved him off and patted the agent on the ground next to him who had taken the bullet.

"I'm okay. But this man needs help. He saved my life." The Secret Service agent who had fallen over the president had been hit in the stomach and was bleeding badly.

"Hang on son." The agent fought the pain and nodded. The president took his hand and squeezed hard.

Orders drowned out the rest of the commotion in the Capitol. The president's wife and Mrs. Lamden automatically offered to help the downed agent and the Capitol Police secured all of the exits. Five more plainclothes officers flashed their ID's and ran past the guards at the East entrance. Behind them a woman carrying heavy books and an attaché case struggled to keep up.

"Oh my god!" exclaimed Katie Kessler. She had never seen a battle zone or smelled the sickly mixture of explosives and blood.

Some of the most recognizable faces in the country were all around her. Judges, elected officials, cabinet members. Many were pulling themselves up onto their hands and knees; others would never rise again. Katie searched the room.

"Scott!" she yelled out.

Roarke was helping Governor Lamden to his feet when he heard her voice. "Over here."

She drew a deep breath. The Rotunda was a grisly spectacle, but seeing Roarke was life affirming. Her eyes said it all. Relief. His gun was still out. She'd not seen him kill, but she was certain he had. Katie left him to his job and found the chief justice in the crowd.

"Chief Justice."

Leopold Browning acknowledged her with a nod. "The situation has changed a bit since we talked, Ms. Kessler. Do you have any miracles for us?"

"No, Chief Justice. No miracles." She realized she was clutching her materials tightly. Katie released her grip and rested her leather case on the floor but opened one book. "There's no allowance for a revote. December 12, 2000, Bush v. Gore underscored the Court's complete determination to insure that a president, elected by the Electoral College, take office at the appointed time whether or not the election itself was called into question."

Michael O'Connell moved closer. A Secret Service agent tried to muscle him out, but the president, now on his feet, allowed him to remain.

Katie surveyed the bloody scene. Teddy Lodge was slumped against the Rotunda wall where he had been killed. She quietly added, "We're looking at the rules of succession."

"But the election was a fraud!" O'Connell blurted out from behind his portable digital camera.

"That's not the issue. Governor Lamden must be sworn in. It's the law."

"What if he's involved?" O'Connell argued.

"That is for Congress to decide. The Constitution grants the House the authority to impeach."

More running footsteps echoed across the marble. A Secret Service agent and a woman in high heels.

"Just in time, Attorney General Goldman," Chief Justice Browning called out. "We have an unexpected turn of events here. Join us."

Goldman dispensed with any greeting. She acknowledged everyone with a quick, polite nod and took Katie, the only person she didn't know, as the Boston attorney. "The Secret Service briefed me on the way in. Let's get to it."

"For the record," Governor Lamden said, "I had no knowledge of this plot until I was informed by the president this morning. I assure you, I will be prepared to testify to that fact."

"Thank you, governor. That will be necessary. Now, Ms. Kessler, if you would kindly continue," Chief Justice Browning ordered. "Time is a factor."

Katie swallowed hard and shut out everything around her. People were dead at her feet, but she had to concentrate on the life of the country. And indeed, time was critical.

"Yes sir. Your honor, members of the court, Mr. President, Mr. Vice President, Article XX, Section 1 of the United States Constitution firmly stipulates that the term of the president begin at noon on the 20th day of January following the general election. Furthermore, and noting the circumstances of today," she said scanning down a text she had marked, "Section 3 states that—and I quote—'*at the time fixed for the beginning of the term of the President, the President elect shall have died, the Vice President elect shall become President.*'"

She lifted her eyes above the paper and took a tentative step forward to Governor Lamden.

"Mr. President."

Roarke made his way to Katie's side. He had hoped that she would have found some way for Morgan Taylor to stay in power; maybe even declaring a State of Emergency. But apparently that was not possible.

"Confidence in the government must come from the faithful execution of the laws," she continued. "And the law is clear. There is no legal justification for delaying the Inauguration. The constitution firmly asserts, and I believe the public demands it, that in two minutes, somebody must be in charge."

Now it was Morgan Taylor's turn. "Henry's clean. And he's going to make a damned good president. You can investigate him all you want."

"The House will examine the evidence, then make a decision," the chief justice added without prejudice.

"And he'll pass every test you throw at him," the president concluded.

There was a long silence, finally broken by the chief justice. "Thank you, Ms. Kessler. You've had quite an eventful morning. Now it's my turn." He nodded for his fellow Supreme Court justices to join him for a quick conversation.

Katie felt a warm breath over her shoulder and then a whisper in her ear. "You were great."

"I was terrified."

"Well, it was your first argument in front of the U.S. Supreme Court. What do you expect?"

She reached around and squeezed his hand, then turned and looked in his eyes. They were inviting and strong, loving and proud. She reached up and lightly kissed his lips.

"I expect to win."

Chief Justice Browning's voice boomed again. "Governor Lamden?"

"Yes, Chief Justice," the vice president-elect said as he approached the chief justice.

"There are going to be a great many surprised people when we walk out to the Capitol steps. How are you at making spontaneous speeches?"

"Not bad, your honor."

"Well Governor, get ready to make the speech of your life. It's time we swear you in as the next President of the United States."

A line formed, led by members of the Secret Service.

"One moment, Ms. Kessler," the chief justice said.

"Yes sir."

"I'd like to take those books off your hands. I believe I owe the country an impromptu class on the Constitution."

"Right here, sir," she said handing over the texts he requested. "The pages are tabbed as you asked."

"Thank you. And Ms. Kessler…"

"Yes, Chief Justice?"

The man with the most serious face she'd ever seen smiled broadly. "Hope to see you back in court someday."

She returned the smile, proudly. "Thank you, Chief Justice. I'll be there."

"Do me a favor, though. Next time, give me a little advance warning."

The chief justice led the dignitaries to the door. Behind him, President Taylor and the first lady, Governor Lamden and his wife, and the other witnesses to the events that had just unfolded in the Rotunda. Each and every one of them shook attorney Kate Kessler's hand as they walked by.

CHAPTER 67

"Mr. President, if you have a second?" Governor Lamden whispered to Morgan Taylor at the door. The two men slowed down.

"Yes, Henry?"

Lamden guided him away from the others. The chief justice frowned. "Just a few words, then we'll be along," the governor said.

Browning tapped his watch, indicating the hour, but then nodded an okay. He stopped shy of the door and left the two men alone, or as alone as they could be with the Secret Service around.

"So what are you going to do now, Morgan?"

"You mean after testifying on the Hill to save your sorry butt? I was planning on going fishing. Some place with no cell coverage."

"I'd give that a week. Maybe two," Lamden laughed.

"You think so?" the president stated.

"No more than three. And then?"

"Then?" Taylor hadn't really taken any time to think about what he'd do.

"You know, Morgan, they say there's no job for an ex-president except being an ex-president. But I disagree."

He leaned over and whispered something that even the Secret Service agents couldn't hear.

The president let out a gasp. "What?"

Chief Justice Browning turned and loudly cleared his throat to get their attention.

"Gentlemen, it is time."

"One more minute, Mr. Chief Justice," Lamden said. "We're just working something out."

"Who the hell got Lodge?" Roarke asked. He remained behind in the Rotunda.

No one knew.

The fact that Lodge was now dead didn't really bother him. But who fired the shot did. Roarke examined the body. Shannon Davis joined him. He worked out the scenario in his mind. *Lodge had picked up a gun. He ran. But he hadn't fired. Any number of agents could have stopped him without lethal force before he escaped.*

He asked the question again. "Who shot Lodge?" A dozen men and two women shrugged their shoulders. "Come on. We have a dead man here."

"Scott, there's marble all over the place," Davis offered. "He must've been hit by a ricochet."

Roarke examined the bullet hole, squarely between the eyes. *No,* he judged. *Lodge was killed with an expertly aimed shot.*

"No one leaves," Roarke told the Secret Service agent in charge who peered over his shoulder. "I want to talk to the Cap Police, the Marines, and all of your men. And tag all the guns."

The Rotunda was now an officially designated crime scene.

The NBC anchor described the unfolding scene.

"There's President Taylor and the first lady, Governor and Mrs. Lamden, Chief Justice Leopold Browning, Speaker of the House Barney, and the rest of the members of the Supreme Court taking their seats. We're still awaiting the arrival of the president-elect. It should be any moment now."

The newsman observed that the inauguration of the vice president had not occurred on schedule at 11:50, but apparently would now. "Congressman Lodge's seat remains empty, but the chief justice is now standing, ready to swear in Governor Lamden as Vice President of the United States."

The crowd quieted.

"Governor Henry Lamden, will you please rise," Chief Justice Browning said.

Lamden stood and joined the nation's Supreme Court Chief Justice at the podium. Browning was about to give the country a lesson in the law. He held open a large book, with his finger on the page citing Article XX of the United States Constitution.

"This is America," he began, departing from the established protocol. "A republic whose foundation rests on a remarkable set of principles expounded in the Constitution of the United States. Though written well over two centuries ago, this document lives and breathes today, providing a firm foundation for our freedoms and all that we hold dear.

"As citizens we rely on the Constitution in peace and war, through the calm and through crises. It is what's constant in the life of every American. It offers the resolute answer for what we must now do.

"Soon you will hear much about the laws of the land. The amendments and the articles. The intentions of the architects of the Constitution and how we uphold its doctrines. But presently, and according to the requirement of the Constitution, it is my duty to administer Article II, Section 1, Clause 8, the Executive Oath of Office."

The chief justice stated, "Governor, please raise your right hand and repeat after me, I…"

"I, Henry Winchester Lamden…"

"Do solemnly swear…that I will faithfully…"

"Do solemnly swear that I will faithfully…"

"…execute the Office of President of the United States…"

"*What?*" the NBC anchor exclaimed over the Oath.

Another anchor uttered, "My God! Did he say…"

Lamden continued, "…execute the Office of President of the United States…"

"…and will to the best of my ability, preserve, protect and defend the Constitution of the United States."

"Congratulations, Mr. President."

The crowd, stunned as much as the reporters, remained silent and entirely confused. The chief justice raised his hand.

"Now let me explain."

Ibrahim Haddad was anchored off the Bahamas listening to the Inauguration over a radio. He was no longer aboard his Aleutian. He and his men scuttled the multi-million dollar craft during the night, taking with it the computer's hard drive. Then they transferred to a pre-arranged deep sea sport fishing boat capable of making San Juan in two days. Haddad also abandoned the identity of the Florida businessman. He'd clear customs in Puerto Rico as Luis Gonzales, a prosperous Argentinian art dealer heading out for a vacation, fishing for blue marlin.

The chief justice concluded his speech which outlined the law and the rules of succession. President Lamden would explain the rest. The audience at the Capitol as well as the television viewers at home were still trying to figure out what happened.

"It appears that Governor Henry Lamden was just sworn in as *president*," said the startled NBC anchor. "We're now getting reports of gunshots inside the Capitol a few minutes before the ceremonies began." Like the others providing commentary, he struggled for words that weren't there. Almost gratefully he noticed that Lamden approached the microphone. "Governor, I should say, President Lamden is about to speak."

Henry Lamden adjusted the microphones higher, then turned his back to the crowd and shook hands with the chief justice and the Speaker of the House. He kissed his wife who had stood by his side during the Oath of Office and executed a sharply dramatic salute to Morgan Taylor.

Teddy Lodge's speech was actually in the teleprompter ready to roll until the operator, realizing what was happening, killed the feed.

"Ladies and Gentlemen, my fellow Americans, and friends around the world, let me tell you how good this country of ours is."

With those words Henry Lamden began to win the hearts and minds of the people. He spoke of the intent of Washington, Jefferson,

Lincoln, Roosevelt, and Kennedy; the character of the American people; the lengths to which good people had gone to protect the legitimacy of the country. And he told the story of Teddy Lodge as best he could.

As he delivered his remarks, none of the network anchors, White House correspondents, commentators, or political pundits interrupted with commentary. President Lamden spoke. The world listened.

Lamden lowered his brow and recounted the events which had led up to this moment. For the first time, Americans saw what the Navy had long known and the people of Montana had since discovered. Here was a man who could take charge without difficulty.

"We have witnessed the work of a deadly, deep-seeded cabal, the extent of which we are only beginning to grasp. To the degree that they ever want to be identified, you may also hear about a high school teacher, a barber, and a young attorney." He intentionally left out reference to Scott Roarke. "These are people who found themselves involved, unwittingly. They helped prevent a catastrophe today. There were others, lesser known, who died because of this conspiracy. We will mourn them.

"Nothing short of insurrection was prevented today. The laws of this Republic were usurped and that cannot, that will not be allowed. Blood was shed under the Capitol Rotunda. A member of the president's Secret Service is dead. And so is a career officer from the Capitol Police. Another officer was seriously wounded. And the conspirators, two of them, died when they chose guns instead of facing our Congressional and Judicial process. We will all learn of their plan in the coming hours, days, and months. And there will be hell to pay.

"But for all the visible players in this scheme, there remain the invisible puppet masters, the leaders, and the assassins.

"We will find them." The determination in the new president's voice was startling. They saw the deep, dark side of Henry Lamden as he spoke directly into the camera without the aid of a teleprompter. "We will find *you*. You failed in achieving your primary objective. Now it's our turn."

While President Lamden delivered his inaugural address, General Kharrazi oversaw an interrogation in the dank basement of Abu Salim Prison. Audio crackled from a short wave radio. Lakhdar al-Nassar didn't recognize the voice and couldn't understand the English. But the ailing Kharrazi did. And with every hated word from the newly installed infidel, he beat his son's aide mercilessly. In all his pain, al-Nassar really had nothing to admit except that one spied on the other. And that was nothing new.

The crowd followed every word spoken by the new president. He was becoming *their* man.

Lamden stepped away from the microphone to clear his throat and compose himself. When he returned he was even more intent.

"The nation must move on. It was the wish of the founding fathers and it is demanded of me. In a few minutes I will formally submit my nominee for vice president to the Senate. I ask for unprecedented bipartisan approval, without delay," President Lamden continued. "Of course, I will be held to great scrutiny for my association with the man the nation elected as president; the man I ran with. That is as it must be. And should I not be considered worthy of holding this office, my nominee is.

"The nation requires a fully functional government. For the people and by the people. We shall have that with the confirmation of a man who has proven his allegiance to our country time and again. That man is Morgan Taylor."

EPILOGUE

SUPER BOWL SUNDAY
SUNDAY, JANUARY 25

The Lions didn't make it to the Super Bowl. They were eliminated in the playoffs. But Farouk Azzarouq was still extremely happy with the tickets he and his father had for the game at New Orleans' Superdome. A friend *in high places* had scored him great 50-yard-line seats along with tickets for next season's home games at Ford Field. As he jumped to his feet and threw his hands straight up as the first wave circled the stadium, Farouk actually hoped that Abahar Kharrazi was watching. He enjoyed imagining his reaction; how surprised he'd be to see Sami Ben Ali cheering for a team called the Patriots.

Bill Crawford listened to the game while driving along Interstate 84 toward Sun Valley, Idaho. He drove a rented SUV out of Salt Lake City with newly purchased $400 Dynastar Concept skis strapped to the roof rack. The 33-year-old man looked like any other ski bum, with five days of stubble and a recently shaved head.

The Patriots completed a 65-yard drive and led in the first quarter. Crawford found it ironic that he rooted for the Saints. He was far from one himself.

In his own way, he tried to put the events of the past year into perspective. He'd been busy being so many people, most recently a member of the Capitol Police. Now he was grateful for the time just to be himself. But that wasn't entirely true. Bill Crawford wasn't his real name either. He'd given that up long ago.

Ahead, a week of skiing fresh powder at Sun Valley. Powder. He laughed at the word. He remembered the last time he'd visited the area was for business. This time it was going to be for pleasure.

A contingent of ten Marines lowered the second body into an unmarked grave on Hart Island, just off Manhattan.

President Lamden decided that since the identities of these men were unknown, they would remain as unrecognized in death as they truly were in life. With permission of the Mayor of New York, they were brought to Potter's Field, named for a passage in the Gospel of St. Matthew (27:3-8). Here they were laid to rest, unceremoniously and far from the nation's capital and the job they sought.

MARBLEHEAD, MASSACHUSETTS
THURSDAY, FEBRUARY 12

A heavy snow had fallen most of the night. By morning, five inches covered the old Waterside Cemetery on West Shore Drive. The weight pushed many of the branches of the weeping willows down to the ground, casting an added sadness over the landscape. The snow continued lightly and began drifting, blown by the cold wind off the ocean.

Three cars slowly drove through the main gate, cutting parallel tracks in the unplowed narrow road. Two Lincoln Town Cars flanked a limousine. The cortege moved deliberately, winding for a quarter mile until they stopped at a lonely gravesite.

Eight men stepped out of the Lincolns and scanned the cemetery. They communicated through radios to a helicopter overhead. When they were certain that the terrain was clear, one man tapped twice on the car roof. The Vice President of the United States opened the door and stepped out.

He stretched his arms and took in a heavy, invigorating breath of the frigid air.

The Secret Service agents had stationed themselves twenty yards apart, marking the way through the blanketed path.

After a three-minute walk, made difficult because of the heavy snow, the vice president stood before a headstone. He sighed, took the remaining two steps forward, kneeled and wiped the snow from the letters. The monument was showing some aging from the harsh New England elements. But the words could still be seen. He stepped back.

In memory of
Oliver and Katharine
Proud Parents

Morgan Taylor rested his hand on the granite and quietly wept. His tears trickled down his cheeks, freezing halfway.

The newly confirmed vice president removed a brass picture frame from a manila folder he carried. He crouched down and placed it at the base of the memorial. It showed a little boy getting his first haircut with a man standing behind him. Teddy and his father.

Taylor heard the sound of snow crunching as someone approached. He didn't need to turn to know it was Scott Roarke.

"The Lodges could have raised a real president, Scott. Who knows, I might have even run against him."

"From what I learned about the boy, you would have had a helluva time," Roarke said as he studied the photograph for the last time. An utter sense of sadness came over him. The Lodges were memorialized here, but not one of them was buried below.

"Someone destroyed an entire family," he said. "And nearly the country, too." Morgan Taylor whispered as he slowly straightened.

Roarke offered his arm for support. The Secret Service agent gazed across the landscape. His thoughts went to Katie; the most important woman ever to come into his life. In a way, he had to thank Teddy Lodge for that. Not the man posing as him, but the boy they came to honor today.

"It's not over is it, sir?"

The vice president looked at his friend; his eyes revealing the simplest answer. *No.*

The two friends now silently wondered what tomorrow would bring, as the drifting snow began to build up on the photograph already frozen in time.

ACKNOWLEDGMENTS

Ronald Weich, partner in the law firm of Zuckerman Spaeder, LLP, for his assistance with U.S. Constitutional law; U.S. Navy Lt. Commander Greg Hicks for a clear window into the U.S. Navy; Peter Loge for sharpening my understanding of Capitol Hill; Antonio J. Mendez for his insight on secret Soviet cities; Boston University Law School Professor T. Barton Carter; Steve Miller Ph.D., Jeff Hawkins, Rich Bankert and Arunus Kuciauskas at the Naval Research Laboratory: Marine Meteorology Division; Gaylan Warren, Forensic Microscopist, Columbia International Forensics Lab; Roger J. Bolhouse, Speckin Forensic Laboratories; Dr. Yasin Alkhalesi; Nancy Barney; Ken Browning; Jacob Arback; The New York Statewide Police Information Network (NYSPIN).

New York State law enforcement colleagues of my father, Stanley Grossman; my mother, Evelyn Grossman whose experience as a campaign manager gave me early firsthand knowledge of politics; and Sandi Goldfarb for her dynamic and creative sensibilities, tremendous marketing help and personal caring.

Additional heartfelt thanks Byron Preiss, Roger Cooper, Dwight Zimmerman, Nancy Cushing-Jones, and Robb Weller.

I also have so many friends and fans to thank for encouraging me to move into the exciting world of e-books. Your e-mails and letters have meant so much to me. You put me in the company of truly incredible mystery and international thriller writers who have influenced and entertained all of us for years. I'm honored to be considered part of such remarkable and talented group. I am also incredibly grateful to be working with Scott Waxman, Mary Cummings and the terrific team at Diversion Books on the e-book launch of *Executive Actions*.

I have to extend special thanks and encouragement to Michael Palmer, Dale Brown, and Larry Bond for the wonderful things they have written about my novels. Also, my sincerest thanks to Mark Mollenkamp and David and Annie Mollenkamp for the time, effort and true attention they put into editing this edition.

Finally, it is astounding how fact can follow fiction. Readers have pointed out that lead stories about Russian sleeper spies, presidential qualifications and even the headline grabbing accomplishments of America's Special Forces seem to spring right from some of the plot lines and descriptions in *Executive Actions*. Believe me, I am as amazed as anyone. I guarantee you, I am not clairvoyant. But perhaps this does reinforce the debt of gratitude we owe the members of the intelligence community and armed services for their dedicated work in the *real* world. Thank you for keeping us safer.

GARY GROSSMAN's first novel, *Executive Actions*, propelled him into the world of political thrillers. *Executive Treason*, the sequel, further tapped Grossman's experience as a journalist, newspaper columnist, documentary television producer, reporter and playwright. The third book in the series, *Executive Command*, nearly brought his trilogy to a conclusion. But there was more—and *Executive Force* covers new ground. Grossman has written for the *New York Times*, *Boston Globe*, and *Boston Herald American*. He covered presidential campaigns for WBZ-TV in Boston, and has produced television series for NBC News, CNN, NBC, ABC, CBS, FOX and 40 cable networks. He is a multiple Emmy Award winning producer, served as chair of the Government Affairs Committee for the Caucus for Television, Producers, Writers and Directors, and is a member of the International Thriller Writers Association. Grossman has taught at Emerson College (where he is a member of the Board of Trustees), Boston University, USC, and Loyola Marymount University, and is a contributing editor to *Media Ethics Magazine*.

For more information visit
www.garygrossman.com

Follow Gary Grossman on Twitter
@garygrossman1